Boom Boom Bang

Also by Sam Evans

Love & Lawlessness Trilogy
(written with Travis Walter)

Boom Boom Bang: Love & Lawlessness 1

Standalone Novels

Kill the Puckers: A Dark Hockey Romance

Stevie Diaz Mysteries

In the Woods Somewhere: Stevie Diaz 1

Down by the Water: Stevie Diaz 2

Boom Boom Bang

Sam Evans

Travis Walter

Super
Gravity
Press

Published by Super Gravity Press

BOOM BOOM BANG

ISBN-13: 979-8-9985201-7-4

To all the Judys who are allergic to vitamin C.
- Sam

To Sam, for always making me better. Of course a lawless adventure romance is what we would create together.
- Travis

Content Warning

This book will self-destruct in 5... 4... 3... 2...

Kidding. Just kidding.

However, this book does contain bombs and explosions.

There are brief mentions of domestic terrorists and ecoterrorism.

There's a decent bit of on-the-page sex. (And voyeurism! Ooh la la.) Both the booms and the bangs are literal, figurative, and euphemistic.

Our main characters may like to... play with their food. Yes. That kind of play.

This book is one big morally grey cloud. Read it at your own discretion and don't say you weren't warned.

Boom Boom Bang Playlist

Because every book should have a soundtrack

Apple Music

Spotify

Each song corresponds to a chapter on a 1:1 basis in accordance with its number on the playlist and the associated chapter number in the book. Enjoy!

1. *Bad Reputation* by Joan Jett & the Blackhearts
2. *Rise Above* by Black Flag
3. *Sick Ride* by Karen Dió
4. *Where Do ya Draw the Line* by Dead Kennedys
5. *Fireplace* by Sincere Engineer
6. *Damage Control* by The Dirty Nil
7. *My World* by Karen Dió
8. *Badge of Pride* by Pennywise
9. *Wet Dream* by Wet Leg
10. *No Fun* by The Stooges
11. *Mind Your Own Business* by Delta 5
12. *The Cause* by NOFX
13. *Born to Kill* by Social Distortion

14. *DON'T WALLOW* by Winona Fighter
15. *Blame* by Girl Tones
16. *Ruby Soho* by Rancid
17. *Pedestrian at Best* by Courtney Barnett
18. *Spiral City* by CARR
19. *Oh!* by The Linda Lindas
20. *Bad Mouth* by Fugazi
21. *Should I Stay or Should I Go* by The Clash
22. *The Wars End* by Rancid
23. *Chaise Longue* by Wet Leg
24. *Gimme A Second* by Gully Boys
25. *I Think We're Alone Now* by Billie Joe Armstrong
26. *Fuck Authority* by Pennywise
27. *Basket Case* by Green Day
28. *Short Skirt/Long Jacket* by CAKE
29. *Have You Ever Seen the Rain* by Ramones
30. *Sinking* by Black Flag
31. *Future Starts Slow* by The Kills
32. *Fall Back Down* by Rancid
33. *Let's Make Out* by Dream Wife
34. *Something Wrong With Me* by Pennywise
35. *Nervous Energy* by Fresh
36. *California King* by Sincere Engineer
37. *Here Comes Your Man* by Pixies

Boom Boom Bang

Chapter 1
Small Town Hall

FIONA

"The current proposal would have Henley and Montank breaking ground on the new resort site during the third quarter of this year and—"

"This is in addition to their projects on Bridal Mountain and Hay Creek?" a voice from the back of the room shouts angrily.

I spin in my seat to find the speaker and see Richard Alan White the Third, AKA Tre White, AKA *That Asshole*. I turn back to the front where Councilman Nammier is scowling at Tre and raise my hand.

"Yes, Dr. Carson?" the councilman asks, and I resist the urge to wince. I hate being called doctor outside of work. I'm not even a big fan of people using it *while* I'm at work.

"*I* think it sounds like a great idea. It'll bring so many new jobs to the community," I say. In reality, I don't think it sounds like a great idea at all. I actually agree with Tre, not that I would ever tell him that —he can eat a flaming bag of dicks. It's a terrible fucking idea. But I don't bother saying so because it doesn't matter. Standing up and telling the city council that their plan to 'revitalize' the town should go kick rocks because it'll destroy pristine local habitat and contaminate the watershed will achieve absolutely nothing. This is a done deal. This is the city informing us they've greenlit Henley and Montank's third project. As if the previous—but still ongoing—projects haven't been disastrous enough. I'm only here to hear firsthand how bad this is going to be, and it sounds like the answer is pretty damn bad. The words 'ecological disaster' spring to mind.

"Yes. Thank you, Dr. Carson. As I was saying, Henley and Montank will be breaking ground in the third quarter, with construction anticipated to last for the next two and a half years. At the end—"

"They've already contaminated Hay Creek!" Tre shouts, interrupting once more. "Last year the salmon didn't even spawn in the creek, and you're giving them permission to ruin the rest of Kalomish? The runoff from the dig site alone has the potential to fuck up the entire watershed! That's not just the fish. That's the birds, the beavers, the foxes, the bears. It's us! Our drinking water comes from the same watershed!"

"Mr. White. I will ask you to hold your comments until the end for the question-and-answer session—"

"The question-and-answer session that will last all of ten minutes? The one where you'll politely brush aside everyone's concerns by saying that 'Henley and Montank will take the utmost care to minimize any environmental impact'?" Tre yells.

He's an asshole, but he may have nailed their lip service quote verbatim.

Councilman Nammier sighs as if he finds the entire exchange distasteful, but his dark eyes light up gleefully when he says, "Deputies, if you wouldn't mind escorting Mr. White out?"

The deputies leave their positions flanking the dais and head down the aisle toward the back of the room, where Tre is leaning against the wall with his tanned arms folded across his chest, appearing completely unbothered. And maybe he is. He's been escorted from all five of the last town halls. It's practically an old game for him by now.

"You'd think he'd give it a rest at some point," Ewan whispers from my right.

"Mmm."

"Although you didn't need to egg him on."

"Whatever. He's an asshole. I hope he takes a swing at one of the deputies and lands his ass in jail for the night," I say as they finally reach out to grab Tre, and he shrugs them off.

"Sis," Ewan chides.

"What? He's an asshole!" I reiterate quietly.

The entire hall is watching as the deputies reach for Tre again, dragging him toward the door this time. Unfortunately, he goes with them without a fight, denying me my one real desire to see them throw him face down on the floor and slap some handcuffs on him.

"He's right though," Ewan says. "And you know it."

"So? It's not like it matters. They're going to do what they're going to do. Same as always. This is just a dog and pony show." I turn back to face the front of the room, where Councilman Nammier looks undeniably smug as he adjusts his tie. I think he enjoys throwing Tre out of these meetings as much as Tre enjoys being thrown out of them. It's simply a leftover pissing contest from high school for both of them—small-town guys with big-time egos. Tre's dad is—was?—the richest man in town, and Jacob Nammier always resented the fact that no matter how good he was at whatever varsity sport he was playing that month, Tre had more money, a nicer car, nicer clothes, and at least as much interest from every girl in school.

"It seems like now may be an appropriate time to open the floor for questions," Councilman Nammier states with a smirk.

I plaster a pleasant smile on my face to match his smirk as I nod in agreement. Because fuck him. Fuck them all.

HALF AN HOUR LATER, EWAN AND I WALK INTO THE BAR across the street. It's just after eight-thirty. Normally, Malcolm's wouldn't be so busy on a Wednesday night, but it looks like everyone had the same idea. The town hall meetings have been a shitshow during the five months I've been back, and it sounds like they've more or less been this way for the past couple of years. I'm guessing that Malcolm is well-accustomed to the post-town-hall-meeting rush by this point.

"Hey Carson," someone calls out as we shove our way toward the bar. "I always knew you never gave a fuck about this town, but I can't believe you're stupid enough to think this is a good idea!"

I don't even bother looking. Having heard the voice so recently, it's burned into my memory. Hell. It's been burned into my memory since I was sixteen. And I know he's talking to me and not Ewan. Mostly because I've heard the insinuations that I don't care about Kalomish again and again. Turns out leaving for fifteen years will do that. Doesn't matter that I came back and took over for Dr. Restin when he decided to retire and sell his practice. It only matters that I left.

"Hey Dickie," I reply over the din of conversation and clinking glasses, not caring who hears me. I'm the only doctor in town. I don't have to be nice to anyone. "Does shouting about your problems make you feel like more of a man?"

"Sis, you know he hates being called that."

I spot Tess and veer toward her. She managed to save us two stools.

"Why do you think I do it? Besides, if he has a problem with it, he should take it up with daddy. Hey Tess," I say as I slide onto the stool next to her. I lift two fingers when I catch Malcolm's eye and receive a small nod in response.

"Hey Fiona. Hey Ewan. Took you long enough. I practically had to fight off half the bar to keep these seats free," she says, her dark hair shining in the light.

Tess and I have been best friends since her family moved to Kalomish the summer before eighth grade, when her dad took a job with White Construction. Our dads ended up working together doing demolition, and my mom invited her family to a barbecue. I'm pretty sure she was hoping that the three of us would become friends, and Tess would know people before the school year started.

"Hey Tess," Ewan says, before resuming our conversation. "If you'd give him half a chance, you'd see he's not the same person he was back in high school."

"He doesn't deserve half a chance, Ewan," I mutter.

"Tre?" Tess asks.

"Yeah," I answer before returning my attention to Ewan. "I don't know why you're defending him, anyway."

Ewan shrugs. "People can change."

I side-eye him as I ask, "You and he aren't…?"

Ewan laughs, his green eyes full of amusement. "No. I'm pretty sure you're more his type than I am."

"Gross."

Tess grins. "He's okay, Fiona."

I shoot her a glare. "You're supposed to be on my side."

She shrugs and takes a sip of her beer.

"Seriously though," Ewan continues, running a hand through his russet hair, "if you stopped antagonizing him long enough to actually *talk* to him, you'd probably get along."

"I don't want to get along with him, Ewan. You know what he said about mom!"

"I know, but he was a dumbass sixteen-year-old."

"Whatever, Mr. Live-and-Let-Live. It was like three weeks after she died. I'll keep holding my grudges, thank you very much," I say over Tess's snicker as Malcolm sets two pints in front of us. "Hey Mal."

"Hey Fiona. Hey Ewan. Want me to add them to your tab, Fi?"

"Yeah, thanks," I reply before he nods and moves away. "Anyway," I continue, focusing on Ewan again as he lifts his beer to his lips. "I don't want to make peace with that asshole. I fully intend to outlive him and then spit on his grave."

Ewan nearly sprays beer across the bar as he smothers a laugh. "Okay. Fine. Do I need to hate him, too?"

"No. You can do whatever you want," I tell my twin.

"Changing the subject," Tess says, her brown eyes still dancing with amusement, "I was talking to Cath and Kelly earlier. We were thinking about doing a climbing trip in the Gorge over the Fourth of July. Want to come? We can camp out all weekend. I'll bring fireworks—"

"Those are bad for the environment," I interject. "The animals don't like them."

"It's one night, Fi. And *people* like them. It'll be fine. Are you in?"

"Yeah. Fine. I'll come," I agree, already planning to see if I can change her mind about the fireworks.

"Ewan?" she asks.

He stares off into the middle distance for a few seconds. "Sure. Sounds like fun."

I PARK IN THE DRIVEWAY BEHIND MY DAD'S BEATER AT nine-fifty. The main floor of the house is dark, but I can see light leaking from the basement windows as I get out of my truck.

I left Ewan at the bar about fifteen minutes ago because, unlike him, I'm not a river rat, and I have to wake up before ten in the morning.

My keys jingle as I unlock the door and step inside. I flip the deadbolt and drop my keys on the table next to the entryway before sliding my shoes off and making my way through the living room toward the basement.

"Hey dad," I call out as I open the door and start down the bare wooden steps.

"Hey Fi. How was the town hall?"

"Exactly how you'd expect," I say when I reach the bottom. My dad is seated at his workbench, headlamp on his head, fiddling with a soldering iron.

"They greenlit the whole project, then?"

"Yup. Jacob was very pleased with himself, and Tre got thrown out on his ass again. So, par for the course."

My dad makes a small sound that might be a repressed laugh.

"What?" I ask.

"Just imagining Rich's reaction to hearing Tre was booted from another town hall."

I shrug, not really caring about Tre or his dad. "Ewan says hi, by the way. And he'll be here for dinner on Friday."

"Alright."

"So? Did you think about it?" I ask, shifting my weight.

"Did I think about what?" My dad turns off the soldering iron and sets it down.

I sigh. "Building me a bomb."

"Didn't figure you were serious." He shuts off the headlamp too, then rotates to face me.

"Bullshit."

He holds my gaze, his blue eyes boring into mine, as he says, "You're a doctor, Fi. You have your whole life ahead of you."

"Yeah. And *this* is what I want to do with it, dad. If you don't help me, I'll do it myself and probably lose a few fingers or an arm in the process," I threaten. I'm sure I *can* figure out the basics of bomb-making. But I'm a whole lot less sure I can figure out how to make a shaped charge, which is what I want. Though if the bomb is big enough, chances are I don't need to figure it out. It's not like McVeigh's bomb-making skills were all that sophisticated. Just a truck full of fertilizer, and I don't want to take down a building. Only a support column. Still, I'd prefer finesse to brute force if it's an option.

"You didn't spend years going through medical school to start blowing things up, Fiona."

"Yeah, well. Plans change."

"Fine." He pulls off the headlamp, setting it on the table next to the soldering iron before folding his arms across his chest and leaning back. "Convince me. You want me to build you a bomb? Convince me that I should. And not just because you'll lose a few fingers if I don't, because if you want to fuck around and find out, that's on you. Convince me that building you a bomb is the right thing to do. Convince me that you can get away with it. Convince me that I'm not helping you throw your life away."

This is familiar ground, and though I want to tell him that it's my life to throw away, I know that won't get me anywhere. My dad has enough regrets about having thrown his own life away. After my mom died the winter Ewan and I turned sixteen, my dad checked out for a while. Ewan and I were lucky that we had each other. And we were old enough—and had been raised to be independent enough—that we managed alright during the two years following my mom's death that my dad spent at the bottom of a bottle. But he lost his job, nearly lost the house, and definitely lost his self-respect by the time he climbed out of it.

"Fine," I agree. "You know why I left the hospital and bought out Dr. Restin?"

"No. You told me some nonsense about missing home, but we both know that was a lie."

I don't deny it because he's right. It was a lie. "About four months before I quit, a woman came into the emergency department. No one knew it when she came in, but she had a brain aneurysm that had ruptured. I was the hospitalist assigned to her case when she was transferred to the ICU, but by then, she was already on a ventilator. It was too late for us to do anything."

I take a breath, remembering her husband's sobs when life support was disconnected two days later, and push the memory away. "It happens. Anyway, this time it shouldn't have happened. She'd been complaining about headaches and numbness, and her primary care physician referred her for an MRI, but her insurance company wouldn't pre-authorize the claim. Some shit about her symptoms not being severe enough, or whatever. And because the insurance company wouldn't pre-authorize the claim, the hospital wouldn't do the MRI without her and her husband agreeing to pay the full amount out of pocket, which they couldn't afford. So the aneurysm ruptured, and she came to the hospital and died before we could help her. All because she couldn't get an MRI.

"And when the CEO of UnitedHealthcare was murdered, and my only thought was 'good,' I decided I needed to get out. I was already considering coming back here and heard Restin was looking to retire, so I bought him out, figuring at least this way I could treat people regardless of whether or not some corporation thinks they need it."

"Okay, and what does that have to do with blowing up Henley and Montank's aerial gondolas?"

"It's all the same thing, dad! They're just another corporation who thinks they can come in and fling enough money around to flout the rules! So what if it's critically endangered habitat if they have enough cash? Who cares if they fuck up the ecosystem and the water supply if they can afford the lawyers to say they didn't? Who cares if the community doesn't want it, as long as the council members are getting whatever kickbacks they demand?"

My dad snorts, the lines around his eyes tightening. "You sound like Tre."

"Tre's a dumbass."

"If you set off a bomb on Henley and Montank's site, this won't stay local. That'll automatically bring in the ATF, Fiona," he says in a way that implies *I* might also be a dumbass.

"I can get away with it. Everyone thinks I'm pro-development because I've made sure of it! What do you think I've been doing for the past five months? I'm a mild-mannered lady-doctor who doesn't know how to build bombs, dad. I'm the least likely suspect in the entire town. You build me a bomb, and then you go make yourself seen while I detonate it. You can't have done it, and no one—including the ATF—would ever *believe* I did."

He sighs and runs a hand through his silver hair before spinning on his seat and picking up the soldering iron. "I'll think about it."

It's the same thing he said last time, but this time there's a hint of resignation and maybe acceptance that makes me believe he'll actually think about it.

Chapter 2
Throw a Monkey Wrench in the Works
Out for the Best

TRE

"HEY, HOW WAS THAT SHOW LAST NIGHT?" I NEARLY HAVE to shout to be heard above the noise.

"Oh man, she kicks ass. You should've come with us," Ewan calls over the counter to where I'm working the grill.

"Dude, look around." The diner's packed, and I'm nearly done with the last tickets from the dinner rush, but I'm glad for the distraction. Ewan doesn't have the same perspective on work-life balance that I do, which is part of why we're friends. He helps make sure I take some time away once in a while. Plus, when you spend all summer working as a rafting guide, a lot of your work hours are still pretty fun. "I can't just take off to go to a concert in Portland on Friday night. Especially for someone I don't even know."

"Tre, I've told you to listen to Bishop Briggs like five times. Come on, man."

"Yeah, alright. I'll check her out. You couldn't have had that much fun, though, if you all made it back here for work in the morning." I smirk, even though he can't see my face.

"It's a good thing, too. Beautiful day. River's running high. It's perfect."

"Awesome. I've been looking forward to getting out there."

"Hey, uh… Bad news, man."

"What's that?" I ask over my shoulder.

"I won't be able to go on the rafting trip."

"What?" I turn from the flattop to face Ewan. "Say that again."

"Yeah, sorry man. I can't go."

"Ewan, you're our guide. You *have* to go." I am no longer glad for the distraction.

"I know, I'm sorry. Kyle'll go with you."

"Great. Kyle," I mutter as I turn back to the grill, trying to make sure nothing burned while I looked away.

"He's fine. He knows the river."

"Yeah, and I'm sure both words he says all weekend will be a lot of fun."

I take a minute plating the meals and set them out for Sandy. "Order up!" With no more tickets right now, I step over to the counter where Ewan is sitting. He's sipping a mug of coffee, watching me over its rim.

"We do this every year, and we planned this year's trip weeks ago. Why can't you go all of a sudden?"

Ewan winces as he sets his mug down. "I'm, uh, going climbing with Fiona now."

"Are you kidding me?" I don't bother hiding my irritation.

"Look, it's her first summer back. It's finally warm and dry enough to climb, and that's the one outdoor sport she actually likes. She asked if I'd join them, so I had to say yes."

"*Them?* She's already going with people and she still had to get you? It's not enough to support ruining Kalomish with these developments? She has to ruin our rafting trip, too?"

"Hey, enough man. I swear, you two are exactly the same. If you'd shut up and talk to each other for five minutes, you'd probably be friends."

"Fine, whatever. But you're paying for your burgers now," I grumble, returning to the grill as Sandy walks over with a new ticket.

"THERE'S ALWAYS SOMEONE WHO WANTS TO SIT AROUND until closing," Sandy complains from halfway down the counter where she's completing the last of her side work, having already bussed all the dishes.

"Well, I'm here all the time, so some of the guys like to hang out." The only occupied booth erupts with laughter, as if to punctuate my point. "I'll stay. You can clock out."

"I know, but it's not just them. Even if they don't have anywhere to go, don't they realize the rest of us would rather spend Saturday night doing something a little more fun?" Sandy asks in mock-indignation.

"Oh, you've got a hot date planned. I see. Let me guess, you're finally giving Eddie that chance he's been literally begging for since high school? You know that eye is perfectly functional, it just looks like that," I tease with a grin as I walk back to the kitchen to run the final load through the dishwasher.

"Ugh, please. I wouldn't date that little creep if he looked like Henry Cavill. I bet he got that job at the gym so he can stare at all the girls while they work out. Anyway, I do have a date tonight, and no, it's none of your business who it's with. I've finished up here. I'm ready to head out."

"Okay, I'll walk you to your car." I hold open the back door for her.

"Tre, nobody is going to attack me in the parking lot. This is Kalomish." She dismisses me with a shake of her blond head. "You know, you should work on getting yourself a hot date sometime. You're here too much."

"Thank you for the life advice," I reply dryly, "but the diner doesn't run itself. Have fun, Sandy."

"Later Tre."

I stand in the doorway until she gets into her car, then go back inside.

I walk to the front door, flip the sign around so it says that we're *'Closed. Come back tomorrow'*, then switch off the neon *'Open'* light in the window.

"What happened to Sandy?" Jordan asks.

"It's already after closing. Unlike you losers, she has a life to get to."

"At least we're not working after hours," Cade fires back.

I grab the coffeepot from the machine and carry it plus my mug to the booth, sliding in next to Lucas.

"Thanks," his low voice rumbles as he refills his cup.

"I know these two lovebirds have nothing going on," I say, gesturing to Cade and Jordan, "but what are you doing here on a Saturday night? Shouldn't you be on a date with that girl Emma, or Emmy, or whatever her name is?"

"Mmm. Last night I found out she was… keeping her options open." Lucas scowls into his coffee cup.

"I'm sorry, dude. That sucks. Speaking of things that suck, did Ewan tell you guys about our trip?"

Everyone shakes their heads, and I sigh. "He's not going rafting with us," I say, and everyone demands to know why at the same time. "Apparently he's ditching us to go climbing with his sister and her friends."

"Ah, okay." Jordan nods, his mop of red hair bouncing, while Lucas sits back, the tension leaving the muscles under his dark skin.

"Well, who the hell's going to be our guide? We can't run the river ourselves!" Cade says with an appropriate amount of outrage.

"Kyle."

"Oh great, Kyle." Cade rolls his eyes.

"Thank you! That's what I said."

Eventually, I kick them out with the not-untrue excuse of working early tomorrow morning. I spend the following thirty minutes cleaning and finishing closing duties. After the regular tasks are done, I haul a fifty-pound bag of sugar from the storage room out to my car, which is the only vehicle left in the parking lot. I put the bag in my trunk, then return to the diner to lock up.

Beginning my long commute home, I walk along the sidewalk halfway down the building and then unlock the street-level entry door to my apartment's shared vestibule. I stop long enough to check my mailbox, but find nothing and climb the two flights of stairs to my top-floor apartment, which occupies half of the building above the diner. It's late enough that I don't encounter my neighbors as I head inside and lock the door behind me.

I check my watch. It's already eleven-forty-five. I walk back to my bedroom and change out of my grease-spattered clothes, replacing them with loose-fitting dark jeans and a black turtleneck. I finish getting ready by putting on my old hiking boots and taking a pair of black leather gloves from the small coat closet near the door. Even though I gathered my gear before work today, I double check my tool bag has everything I'll need: ratchet set, screwdrivers, hammer, rubber mallet, pry bar, electric reciprocating saw, spare battery, and, of course, the monkey wrench.

THE HEADLIGHTS CUT A LONELY PATH THROUGH THE darkness as I wend my way up the steep mountain road. The main Henley and Montank construction site is near the summit of Bridal Mountain, where they're building the terminal for the aerial gondola system. This small, two-lane road is the only way up or down the mountain, and for decades, that's all we've needed. Hell, building this road was a major controversy back in the eighties when my granddad pushed it through the town council to aid his ski resort development over on Brooks Mountain. People are only using it for recreational hiking and hunting trips these days, but that's not making money for any greedy assholes, so of course it can't be allowed.

We've been trying to stop the Henley and Montank developers in court for the last two years, but even with active cases and a temporary injunction, they're still contaminating Hay Creek and wrecking the ecosystem on Bridal Mountain. The legal system doesn't take action against corporations when they basically wave money in the faces of judges, city councils, state regulators, sheriffs, whoever. Fuck them all. Especially fuck Jacob. That arrogant prick thinks he can get away with selling off our town to some evil corporation that will trash our forests, pollute our water, and kill our wildlife in the name of tourism, which will increase the overuse of the environment. He's about to learn. If they won't follow the rules, there's no reason for us to.

It's the same with those pointless town hall meetings where they never listen. We've been trying to work within the process to fight for the land, but it's clear that those meetings will never stop anything. They're nothing but propaganda to keep people feeling like they might make a difference while lying to convince them this development is a good idea.

And I can't believe it works! At last week's meeting, goddamn Fiona Carson fell for it, hook, line, and sinker. She couldn't wait to abandon this town after graduation. Now that she's back, out of the blue, she's dumber than I ever thought. She's not even getting paid off by the developers. She actually *agrees* with them. I guess that's what you get when you live in the city—you think everything should be more city. I can't wait to see the look on her face when she realizes how much people around here don't want this. That we'll resist.

I'm nearly at the construction site when I realize I'm ranting to myself. I slow to a crawl and kill the headlights, then pull off the road and park between a couple of trees so the car is barely visible.

I chose tonight because construction doesn't happen on the weekends. Saturday night is the least likely time for anyone to be around, meaning it's almost guaranteed no one will drive up here. Also, waiting more than a week after the meeting announcing the expanded development plans makes it safer, since it's just past the new moon.

I grab my tool bag from the passenger seat and debate going to the trunk for the sugar, but decide to make an entry into the worksite first. There are a few hundred yards of road and one more bend to traverse. I'd prefer not to sneak along that entire approach carrying a fifty-pound bag on my shoulder only to find somebody there.

My course of action decided, I creep along the road with only my tools until I reach the turnoff. I pause in the darkness, pressed up against a tree, and survey the area, searching for any sign of movement or a telltale light. Seeing none, I scan for my targets and consider my plan. I leave the tool bag, then jog back to the car and return carrying the bag of sugar. I grab the tools and hurry down the dirt entrance into the site, reasonably certain the coast is clear. I'll have a busy night, and I need to make sure I'm gone before dawn.

My main priority is the container cement silo. It's where I'm going to score the biggest hit against the operation. This site is where they're building both the passenger terminal and the machine facilities—which requires a strong concrete foundation anchored to the bedrock across a large footprint.

The top of a mountain with a steep curvy road isn't a great location to send concrete mixers loaded down with ten to fifteen tons, so they've set up a stainless steel silo and brought up cement, sand, and aggregate—the components of concrete—individually. That way, they can add water when they're ready and use a pump to pour it. Mixing in fifty pounds of sugar will absolutely ruin their concrete.

I make my way up the metal ladder welded to the silo's exterior, balancing the sack on my shoulder. When I reach the hatch, I pull on the crossbar and swing the door wide. Then I rip open the bag and pour in the sugar.

Beyond the standard ingredients, builders often add chemical agents to concrete to adjust the curing time and ultimate strength of the product. Two pounds of sugar in a full ton of dry cement can actually make the structure stronger, but it increases the curing time. However, adding more than that causes problems. Four pounds per ton is pretty much all it takes to ruin the entire batch so that it will never cure. The materials are stored together and simply look like a mass of white powder. Even if anyone checks the silo after they find their site wrecked, they won't be able to tell the sugar is in there.

The best part is they won't realize there's a problem until they've spent the time and effort to set up the foundation and poured tons of concrete. They'll lose weeks waiting for the foundation to cure like it's supposed to. Then they'll have to clear all that useless concrete out of the site, regrade and reset the building footprint, get new mix, then pour and cure everything again. By the time that happens, we may be into fall, forcing the crew to deal with the rainy weather. Even if they manage that, they won't get much further before the wet and cold make it too dangerous to keep working. They'll be stuck all winter, steadily burning money. Not too shabby for one night's work.

Once the bag is empty, I drop it to land near my tools and close the hatch. Then I pause and survey the area from my higher vantage point, making out the dark shapes of the construction equipment and the massive support column that will bring the gondolas into the terminal.

Suddenly, something shifts in the night below me. Shit! I press against the silo and hold my breath, watching the area near the column like an owl hunting a mouse. It can't be the shadow of a tree branch this far into the site, and it was too big to be blowing leaves. *Someone who works here wouldn't be skulking around in the dark. Was it a cougar? Am I trapped up here?*

There it is again. Holy shit, I think in amazement, *that's a person. Who the hell would be at the site now?*

Whoever it is shouldn't be here any more than me, making me confident they won't call the cops. I rush back to the ground as quietly as I can, stopping long enough to remove the pry bar from my tool bag and heft it like a club before stalking over to the giant column.

"Who the hell are you?" I shout, opting for shock and awe to gain the advantage.

"Oh fuck!" the figure screams, spinning to face me.

"I said who are you, and what are you doing here?" I demand loudly, brandishing my pry bar club.

The figure stares for a moment, then asks, "Dickie?" in astonishment. "You asshole, you nearly gave me a heart attack!" The woman's voice shifts from surprise to anger in a blink.

"Wait... Carson? Is that you?" This whole situation has tumbled out of my grasp. "What the hell are you doing here?" I ask again, much less confidently.

"I'm just out for a walk. Thought I'd enjoy the construction site in the middle of the night. Take it all in. What does it look like I'm doing, Dickie?"

I step to the side and peer beyond Fiona Carson to look at the support column. My eyes track between the objects taped to it and her shadowed face a few times before I realize what I'm seeing.

"What the fuck are you doing with a bomb?"

Chapter 3
Jack and Jill Went Up the Hill to Die On

FIONA

"You understand what you have to do?" my dad asks for the tenth time, his blue eyes pinning me in place.

I sigh and do my best to avoid fidgeting under his gaze. "Yes. We've been over it." I look at my watch. It's Saturday night, and we're sitting inside a storage unit. We've been here for the past couple of hours, going over the plan for tonight. The roll-down door is closed, the unit is lit by a single bare bulb, and the air is stifling. Sweat has been dripping down the small of my back for at least the past hour, and I want to get out of here. The space is beginning to feel claustrophobic.

The storage unit isn't in my dad's name. Apparently, it 'belongs to a neighbor.' I'm not sure how or why my dad has a key, and when I asked, he changed the subject. But this is where he's been building me a bomb over the past several days.

"Go over it again, Fiona," he grumbles.

I know he's worried, so I do. I describe positioning the charges around the column and connecting the detonating cord to the blasting caps. I reiterate that I understand how far away I need to be standing and that, regardless of how far it is, I need something covering me, just in case. I explain how I'm getting to and from the mountain. He simply nods throughout. When I finish this time, he's apparently satisfied that I'm not going to blow myself up, since he begins packing up the bomb.

"Alright. So I'll drop you back at home, and then I'll go out."

"Yup."

"Don't screw this up, Fiona," he says gruffly.

"Dad, I won't. This is a whole lot easier than spending a Saturday night in the ICU. There won't even be any blood."

"I hope not. Let's go." He grabs the package off the makeshift workbench as I lift the door to the storage unit. Metal clatters against metal as the door rolls up, then back down. My dad slaps the lock on it, and we head for his station wagon.

"WAIT... CARSON? IS THAT YOU? WHAT THE HELL ARE YOU doing here?" Tre asks. His face is in shadow, but somehow I can make out his cloudy grey eyes and the crowbar he's holding over his right shoulder.

Damn. I spend half a second trying to come up with a convincing lie. Something that will send him on his merry way. But there's nothing. Besides, he's clearly here for exactly the same reason I am. Only he brought a crowbar to a bomb fight. One part of my brain is muttering, *'Dumbass,'* at the same time another part is interjecting to say, *'Not everyone has a dad who can build them a bomb.'* Tre does, though. Rich is just as capable of whipping something up as my dad, not that he ever would. He's even more of an asshole than Tre is.

"I'm just out for a walk. Thought I'd enjoy the construction site in the middle of the night. Take it all in," I say, rolling my eyes. "What does it look like I'm doing, Dickie?"

He steps to the side without replying, looking behind me. My body tenses—stupid fight-or-flight response—as he looks back and forth between me and the support column, which now has a bomb affixed to it. Several seconds pass before realization dawns in his eyes.

"What the fuck are you doing with a bomb?" Tre is looking at me like he's never seen me before. And maybe he hasn't.

I shrug and turn back to the support column, kneeling to check my work. "You should probably—"

A hand clamps down on my shoulder. Without thinking, I twist as I stand, putting myself inside of his reach, then I place both hands on his chest and shove. "Don't touch me, Dickie!" I shout as he steps back.

His heel catches on a rock and turns the step into a stumble as he falls backward, landing on one side with his elbow beneath him. The mountain's slope changes the fall into a tumble in a series of hard grunts and flat thuds, accompanied by the hiss of pebbles and dirt shaken loose from the impact. Next thing I know, Tre is about twenty-five feet downslope—unmoving—and I'm not sure if he's breathing.

Shit, shit, shit!

I run toward him, my feet slipping, sending streams of dirt flowing ahead of me. *Please let him be alive. Please let him be alive*, I think over and over in the few seconds it takes to reach him. I slide to a stop next to him and drop to my knees. There's an owl hooting in the distance as I reach for his wrist to find a pulse. *If this asshole fell down a hill and died...* I don't finish the thought.

Tre groans and mumbles something unintelligible just as I feel the steady beat of his pulse thrumming beneath my fingertips. He mumbles something again.

"What?" I ask, worry making my voice sharp.

"Great horned."

"Great what? Tre, do you know where you are?"

"The owl. It's a great horned owl. Don't you hear it?"

I drop his wrist. "Are you okay?" He'd better be, because I didn't bring a phone with me tonight, and I can't carry him off this mountain alone. I'd have to leave to get help, and I don't want to have to explain to Ewan or my dad that Tre stumbled over me setting up a bomb, and then I pushed him down the mountain. Well. Really, he tripped and fell. This *is* all his fault.

"You called me Tre," he says as his eyes open and immediately find mine.

"Yeah. Well. It won't happen again." I turn to head to the support column, where the bomb is waiting, seeming to absorb the darkness.

"Hey, a little help?" Tre demands before I get more than a step away. His hand is extended toward me when I look back.

I huff. I'm tempted to leave him lying on his back, staring at the sky. But I don't. I return to his side, reaching down, locking my hand around his in an arm-wrestling grip. His skin is warm against mine as I pull him to his feet. He rises with a groan, and suddenly he's way too close. I try to step away, to put some distance between us, but his hand is still locked around mine, and he doesn't let me.

"Let. Go. Dickie," I grate out.

"Ah, yes. There's the Fiona Carson I know and love so well," he murmurs, his grey eyes crinkling at the corners, looking almost silver in the darkness. He releases my hand without warning, and now I'm the one stumbling backward, scrambling to keep my footing.

"God. You're such an asshole!" I wipe my hand on my jeans before stalking up the hill once I've managed to get my feet under me. I hear his footsteps behind me. "Touch me again and I'll break your fucking wrist," I snap without looking.

"I wasn't going to… Sorry," he says, sounding embarrassed. He follows me in silence but doesn't try to touch me. "I thought you were pro-development," Tre comments as we near the support column.

"Yeah. Because, unlike you, I'm not a dumbass. Speaking of, you should probably leave. Unless you want to be implicated in this. I'll give you an hour to get somewhere else if you want."

"Why would I do that?" he asks, making no move to leave.

"Because everyone is going to think you did this." I restrain myself to only implying the 'duh' at the end of the sentence.

"I don't know how to build a bomb."

"Yeah. Me neither."

"Clearly."

"If you don't go, people will assume this was you," I warn again, watching him.

He shrugs, his blond hair glinting in the starlight as the wind breezes over it. If he weren't such a prick, he'd almost be attractive.

"Whatever," I grouse. The bomb is positioned exactly how my dad told me it needed to be, with the six linear cutting charges spaced equidistant around the column. I've duct-taped the bars that house the charges to the column several inches above the ground, and there are spacers between the bars and the column to allow enough distance for the jets to form and cut through the steel upon detonation. According to my dad—and he would know, having spent years doing this—if I set it up correctly, the damage should be limited almost exclusively to the target. It won't even crater the ground.

I connect the detonating cord to the blasting caps, and then begin unwinding it as I walk backward. All that's left now is to clear the blast zone and light the cord.

"How'd you learn to do this?" Tre asks, shadowing my footsteps.

"*MacGyver.*"

"No. Seriously."

"Seriously. You should really leave," I try for the third time.

"No. I think I'll stay and watch the fireworks."

I sigh. "It's not that kind of bomb, Dickie."

Tre raises his eyebrows and gestures toward the column as if to suggest I show him what type of bomb it is.

I ignore him and unwind the cord to nearly its full length before taking shelter behind one of the bulldozers sitting on the construction site, with Tre still glued to my side. We're about five hundred feet from the support column when I pull a lighter from my pocket.

"A lighter? I thought that was only in *Looney Tunes*," Tre scoffs.

I don't bother providing an explanation. My dad and I talked it over at length. We thought it'd make the most sense to have the detonation be as manual as possible. Since he's one of a small number of people in town who could build a bomb like this, we figured it was best to leave no doubt that he couldn't have been the one to set it off.

"Cover your ears," I say as I raise the lighter.

The flame races up the cord, toward the bomb, in a way that does look surprisingly like the cartoons. A moment later, a sharp, concussive blast rips through the night, echoing off the mountain. Even in town, they're sure to have heard something. It might take them until morning to figure out what, but I don't want to wait around to find out. A few seconds later, the breeze brings acrid smoke wafting toward us, and I drop my hands from my ears at the same time Tre does. I step out from behind the bulldozer to find the support column lying on its side, a jagged line cut through it.

"Cool," I murmur as Tre looks at me in disbelief. "Well. See you around, I guess," I say, before sauntering off toward one of the old hiking trails that travel across the mountain.

"Where are you going?" Tre calls from behind me.

"Home."

"The road is that way!"

I stop and slowly turn back to him. "Did you seriously *drive* here? In your own car? God. You really are a dumbass, Dickie. Good luck with that."

"Yeah? How'd you get here?"

"Magic," I say, resuming my walk to the tree line.

AS IT TURNS OUT, 'MAGIC' IS ACTUALLY AN OLD MOUNTAIN bike that, prior to tonight, has sat unused in my dad's garage for fifteen years. Fortunately, going home is a lot easier than coming out here was. For one, the ride is mostly downhill. For another, I'm no longer carrying enough explosives to take down a support column. But twenty miles on a bike—through mountain trails at night—is nothing to scoff at. Luckily, the headlamp I snagged from my dad's workbench provides enough light to stop me from riding straight into a tree. It's slow going, though, and by the time I make it back to the house, I'm huffing and puffing and sheened in sweat.

I put the bike back in the garage before making my way into the house via the back door. My truck remains parked in the driveway, but my dad's car is gone. He must still be in town somewhere, making himself seen. It's a bit after two in the morning though, so I have no idea where he is, or if he's planning on coming home tonight. Not that it's any of my business. My dad was nice enough to let me move into my old room when I came back to town, and I'm not in any great hurry to find a place of my own. So, as much as possible, I do my best to suppress my innate nosiness. Ewan says minding other people's business is why I became a doctor, and as much as I'd like to tell him he's wrong, I'm not sure I can.

It's two-fifty by the time I step out of the shower, wet hair dripping down my back, and the house is still empty. I briefly wonder if my dad is dating again, since it doesn't seem like he's going to make it home tonight. I'll have to ask Ewan and see what he knows.

I return to worrying about whether Tre will keep his mouth shut as I climb into my cold sheets and switch off the bedside lamp. He's never struck me as the brightest crayon in the box, and I wonder how badly I fucked up by letting him catch me at the construction site tonight. Unfortunately, I'm pretty sure I know the answer, and the answer is pretty damn badly. I promised my dad I'd be able to get away with this, and I'm less and less certain I'll be able to keep that promise with each passing minute. Short of offing Tre—and as much as I hate him, he hasn't done anything to deserve *that*—I just have to cross my fingers and hope.

Falling asleep to that thought isn't pleasant.

Chapter 4
We're All Mad
Here We Go Again

CARSON TURNS TO FACE ME, TRADING MY VIEW OF HER back for a face masked by shadow, but I can imagine her green eyes flaring in anger.

"Did you seriously *drive* here? In your own car? God. You really are a dumbass, Dickie. Good luck with that," she says, scorn dripping from her words.

"Yeah? How'd you get here?"

"Magic."

And then she disappears into the forest and the night.

I stand there, staring out at the darkness, frozen in confusion. Eventually, I give my head a little shake. Curiosity overwhelms me, and I walk to the base of what used to be a support column. The steel ends in jagged edges along a roughly horizontal line. Feet away, the bottom of the toppled column looks similar, lying in the dirt.

After admiring Carson's handiwork, I decide it's time to flee the scene of the very visible, very loud crime. I stride to the silo, collect my tools and the empty sugar bag, then jog back to my car.

"Did I drive here? In my own car?" I mutter as I load everything into the trunk. "Of course I did. This is the top of a mountain. Does she think I hiked up here in the middle of the night with all my equipment?"

I settle into the driver's seat and crank the diesel engine, listening to the soft hum as I let it warm up for a moment.

"And what's wrong with my car? The eighty-five Mercedes is rock solid, and there're no electronics in it for anybody to track. Drive my car…" I grumble as I carefully pull out of the tree line and onto the road, then make my way down the mountain.

How did I not know she was playing them, playing all of us? Was she planning this the whole time? She argued with me about these projects!

I grew up around construction sites and learned all kinds of useful info, but nobody ever taught me about explosives.

Did she make the bomb, or is she working with someone else? If so, where were they? How many people around here are ready to sabotage these developments?

There's too much I don't know. If someone does this wrong, they could cause a lot of damage to the environment or get themselves killed. If they screw this up, I might not get other opportunities.

Most of all, I don't understand Fiona Carson. That needs to change.

"I HAVE TO SAY, I LOVE THE NEW HAIR."

"Aw, thank you, Tre," Carol replies, beaming. She shakes her head to make the ends of her blond hair swing, accentuating the new bob. "You're too sweet. I haven't done it like this since I was your age, but I was ready for something different. And with these summers getting hotter all the time, it'll make everything easier."

"Well, it suits you. It frames your face perfectly."

"Mr. White," a woman's voice interrupts our conversation from the doorway beside the reception desk. "You can come back now."

I flash Carol a grin, then get up slowly, cradling my left arm against my chest. After passing the nurse, a short woman with light brown skin and hair so black it shines with a reflection of the bright lighting, she directs me to exam room two. I'm lucky enough not to need to visit the doctor outside of rare injuries, like today, so I've never met her. I immediately take the opportunity to ingratiate myself, starting with my 'I can be your best friend' smile.

"Hi. I don't think we've met. I'm Tre."

She frowns slightly, looking at her clipboard. "It says 'Richard' here."

"Ah, yeah. That's true, but I go by Tre." I turn up the smile intensity.

She sets the clipboard on the edge of the small computer desk and writes a note on the top page, completely oblivious to my most potent friend-making tool.

"How do you get Tre from Richard? Don't people usually go by Rich or Rick? Even Dick, for some reason?"

My smile falters when she says Dick. "My family thought it was important to name all of their kids after themselves. I'm the third. When I was a teenager, I didn't want to just be like my dad and grand-dad, so I came up with Tre to have my own name. The third, Tre…" I trail off lamely.

"I see. Nice to meet you. I'm Nurse Machado. Please step on the scale." She delivers all of these statements with equal amounts of absolutely zero enthusiasm.

Nurse Machado perfunctorily measures and records my vitals without further discussion. When it's time for her to apply the blood pressure cuff, I seize the opportunity to try connecting again.

"Ooh," I groan with an exaggerated grimace on my face. "You'll have to use my right arm. I can't get the sleeve myself." I point at my injured left arm, pressed stiffly across my torso. I rarely need to appeal to sympathy to make friends, but it *is* an effective conversational opener.

"Of course. Your form says you came in this morning because of shoulder pain. What, exactly, seems to be wrong with your shoulder?"

"I can move it side to side or forward and back a little bit, but if I try to rotate it, it feels like I'm being stabbed."

Nurse Machado points at a small poster on the wall with cartoon faces showing differing expressions above the numbers zero through ten. "Have a look at this chart. Using this scale, what number would you rate your pain?"

It doesn't make any sense to me because how do I know if the pain hurts eight amounts of pain? What am I supposed to compare it to? Is my eight the same as her eight?

"Seven, I guess."

She's switched from writing on the clipboard to typing my info into the computer. "When did this begin?"

Obviously, I can't talk about Fiona pushing me down a mountain. I spent a while yesterday considering what story to tell. It needs to be believable, but not something anyone will care enough to follow up on. Simple is best.

"I was out hiking this weekend and slipped on some loose scree. Landed right on it. It was dumb. I should have been paying more attention." That should probably work. "Do you get out hiking much?" I'll find a way to connect. I always do.

Over the clicking of the keyboard, she says, "I haven't had the spare time since I moved here to start this job."

"Oh, did—"

There's a knock on the door, then it opens. Fiona's tall form strides into my peripheral vision. *Right when I get an opening to be friendly!* I turn toward the door, locking eyes with her for the first time in weeks, and I literally see her in a new light. Bright green eyes shine in her soft-featured face, accentuated by chestnut-brown hair pulled back in a tight ponytail ending just at the collar of her white coat. I came here to talk to Fiona, but now I'm at a loss for words.

She focuses her attention on Nurse Machado. They quietly converse for a moment before the nurse hands over the clipboard and exits the room, closing the door behind her.

"Why are you here, Dickie?"

Fiona's irritated voice pulls me back. "I, uh, thought we should talk."

"When have I ever given you the impression that I want to talk to you?"

"Yeah, I know… Look, I'm not here to chat. I want to talk about this weekend. About what we both intend to do around here."

"There's no *we*, Dickie. If I decide to do something, it has nothing to do with you. If that's all, you can go."

"Don't be like that. How's it going to look if you're here for five seconds and then leave? Aren't you supposed to examine and treat your patients? That takes a while."

"Yeah, I do have to examine and treat patients, Dick. Real ones, who actually need my help. Which you're preventing me from doing by being here, wasting my time. How did you even get an appointment for today? My schedule isn't that open."

"Are you kidding? Carol loves me. Plus, no one wants the diner closed because I can't use my arms, so she found a spot for me."

"That's great. I see you've really grown up since high school. You've gone from bullying to lying and manipulating people. Just go home."

"Lying and manipulating? Look who's talking, Ms. Pro-development! But, see? That's what we need to talk about. We can move past this and do some good."

"You have no idea what my problem with you is," Fiona snaps. "Is that it? Is that pitch why you came to harass me at work and waste my time?"

"I'm not… That isn't… I wanted to talk," I eventually mutter.

"Great, eloquent as always, Dickie. Well, we talked, I said get lost, and now you should go do that."

"What about my shoulder?"

"Right, your *injury*." Fiona rolls her eyes hard enough for me to hear it.

"Yeah. My shoulder hurts after somebody pushed me down a mountain! Ask the nurse. She put it all in my file, so it's real."

"Please. You can stop pretending. I was there. You were clumsy and fell. After I picked you up off the ground, you were perfectly fine. Your shoulder wasn't a problem when you were following me like a puppy, getting in the way while I was busy."

I open my mouth to respond, but she continues, "I have actual patients to see, and you're keeping me from them. I'll give you a sling to walk out of here with. You have until the end of my 'exam' to say whatever you have to say. Then you're going to leave and not bother me again. I don't want to be your friend. I don't want to sit around and listen to you whine about Henley and Montank. I've had more than enough of that. I want you to forget you ever saw me this weekend."

She begins moving my left arm in various directions. "Okay, I get why taking up an appointment can be a problem for people who need your help. I won't do it again. But the way you're reacting is exactly why I needed to do it now. If I tried talking to you at Mal's or when you're hanging out with Ewan, you wouldn't let me get two words in.

"Our meeting this weekend changed my perspective—on you and on what's happening around here. I'm sorry I've been such an ass. I misunderstood you, and I had no idea what you were really like. I still don't, but I'll stop being a jerk.

"Now that I know we have these shared interests—and we're both willing to act on them—I think we should figure out ways to help each other. Even if you don't like me, imagine what we can accomplish if we work together."

"I don't have to imagine. I already accomplished everything on my own. And I didn't drive my car there when I did it. You've made yourself a suspect, and you're so effective you had a whole crowbar to take out a building site. The fact that I can't stand you is just a bonus. I have no reason to work with you because you're a liability," she says as she finishes wrapping my arm across my chest in the sling without even looking up from her hands.

Shit! This is not how this was supposed to happen. "Okay, you think I can't bring anything to the table? Unlike you, I'm friends with most of the people around here, plus I run the one diner in town where everybody loves to eat. Between what people tell me and what I overhear, I learn everything worth knowing before it's ever public. Hell, I know all kinds of stuff that people aren't supposed to. How's work at the development sites progressing? When are shifts going to be heavy on people? When is construction going to be paused?"

I lower my voice, even though we're alone. "You can get bombs, but what else do you have planned? I grew up on building sites. I was supposed to take over the family business. I know how work gets done and what equipment they need, which means I know how to wreck those things. You think you're the only one who actually accomplished something that night? That just proves how effective I am. I ruined their entire supply of cement, which they won't even realize until it's too late, and you had no idea—just like them. I had multiple other targets lined up before you interrupted, but you think I was just walking around with a pry bar.

"I have plenty to offer. Clearly you do, too. Let's meet up and talk it over. If you still don't think we can help each other after that, then we go back to how it is now, no harm done." I cross my fingers and wait. If this doesn't work, I don't know what else to say. *Did I blow my only chance? Idiot!*

She's typing notes on the computer, her back to me, when she asks, "If we did meet to talk, what would your plan be? I already told you, they're going to assume you're responsible based on your stupid outbursts. You know they'll look into you. I've crafted a reputation so I *won't* be a suspect. I don't want to be associated with you, and us suddenly spending time together would be a major red flag for any cop or corporate guy investigating what happened."

"Yeah, that's fine. That makes sense. I was going to work a double tomorrow, but with this," I shrug my shoulder in its sling, "I'll get my evening shift covered and nobody will give it a second thought. My apartment is above the diner. After you're done at the clinic, you come to my place. I can whip up some food while we plan. Consider it an apology for being an ass so often."

Fiona sits at the computer for a moment in silence, then finally spins around to face me. Once again, those emerald eyes pierce right into me, and I almost forget what I was saying.

"Dinner at your place? I almost thought you were for real. I wouldn't go on a date with you if—"

"Whoa, whoa, whoa. No, not a date," I interject. "We could meet in the middle of the night, if you'd rather, but I do prefer getting *some* sleep. We both have to work in the morning, which means waiting until after the diner closes would be dumb. I figured if you came by right after you're done here, it would be easy to explain why you're downtown, if you needed to. After work is when people eat dinner. I'm just trying to be helpful. If you don't want a free meal..." I trail off, hoping to change her mind.

She's silent for several seconds. "Alright, fine. It's not the worst plan I've ever heard. Unlike driving your own car to a... hike. Tuesday night," Fiona grudgingly agrees, then picks up the clipboard and walks to the door.

As she grabs the handle, I call out, "Oh, one more thing."

Chapter 5
Dinner with Friends and Enemies

FIONA

"Oh, one more thing," Tre says as I reach the exam room door. Like he has the right to ask me for anything. Let alone *one more thing*.

I look over my shoulder, eyebrows raised in silent question.

"Put in a good word for me with your nurse? I think she has the hots for me."

I roll my eyes and walk out of the room.

God, he's such *an ass*, I fume, already regretting agreeing to have dinner with him. I don't even want to! Sure, he made a couple of good points about having wormed his way into knowing information about what's going on at the construction sites that I don't. And, sure. Half the people in town eat at his diner, but even so. I don't want to *work* with him. I simply want to make sure he won't rat me out as soon as they start looking at him for the explosion on Bridal Mountain.

When I stopped by the gas station to get a cup of coffee on my way to work this morning, I heard mention that the construction site had been vandalized. The gas station coffee is fucking horrendous—it makes me miss Seattle every damn day—but the only other place in town open early enough to grab a coffee before work is Betty's, and I refuse to patronize Tre's diner. It didn't sound like the details about what, exactly, was vandalized had leaked yet, but that won't be long. By this afternoon, I expect the entire town will know what happened, and they'll have questioned Tre by the end of the week at the latest.

Fuck.

Maybe I should've said we'd meet tonight. I could ask Tre to reschedule, but I don't have his number—it should be on his intake form, but he left half of it blank. Ewan probably has it, though. Goddamn Ewan. Making friends with everyone. A freaking Care Bear could do a better job holding a grudge than my brother.

"Mr. Igoa is ready in exam room one," Natalie says, and I jump. "Sorry, didn't mean to scare you."

"No, it's my fault. Uh, hey. You can tell me to mind my own business, but you aren't… interested in Tre, are you?"

"Tre…? The guy who was in exam room two?" Natalie asks, and I nod. "God, no. He's got a smile like a used-car salesman."

I laugh. "Thanks. I needed that."

It's six-twenty when I park in the lot behind Betty's Diner, and dread pools in my stomach. Talk of the explosion has been all over town. Coming here to speak to Tre is a big risk. But not coming is equally risky. *Why did he have to be at the construction site?*

I get out of my truck and walk to the diner's back door, then make my way through the crowded restaurant and out the front, looking for whatever door leads to Tre's apartment.

He said it was above the diner, but how the fuck do you get above the diner? I wonder. Leave it to him not to provide specifics. And leave it to me to be too annoyed by his presence to ask. I walk down the sidewalk until I find another door. It's locked, but there are four buzzers next to it. None of them are labeled, though. *He's so sloppy. Everything he does is sloppy.*

I press the first buzzer and wait. Nothing. I try the second, and a woman's voice says, "Hello?" with a staticky hum.

"Hi, I'm looking for Di— Tre."

"He's in number three," the woman says, and the intercom goes silent.

"Thanks," I mutter to myself as I press number three's buzzer, and the static reappears.

"Carson?" Tre's disembodied voice asks.

"Yeah."

The disappearance of the static is followed by a loud click, and the door is unlocked when I try the handle. I step into a small entry, shutting the door behind me. It locks automatically. I climb the first flight of stairs and see the numbers one and two on doors to either side of the landing, so I climb the next. Three and four. I sigh and lift my hand to knock on number three at the same time the heavy wooden door opens.

"Uh, hi," I say, stepping back quickly.

Tre raises his eyebrows. "Are you always so jumpy?"

"Are you always such an ass?" I snap.

His chest rises and falls, and I swear he's biting back whatever he wanted to say next. "No. I'm sorry. Please come in, Fiona." He steps aside so I can enter.

I watch Tre warily as I walk past him into his apartment. He's not even bothering to wear the sling I gave him yesterday.

His place isn't what I expected. It's actually neat and orderly, and *not* sloppy. The ceilings are high—they must be twelve or fourteen feet—and there's a big open-plan room with the living area separated from the kitchen by a large island. There's a hallway on the far side.

"Why aren't there labels on the buzzers out front?" I ask.

"Do you have your name on a label outside your house?"

"No."

He shrugs as if that's a sufficient answer, and… I guess it is.

"I came. So what do you want? Why am I here?" I have no idea how to talk to Tre. For most of my life, all I've done is trade insults with him.

"Do you want something to drink?" he asks, walking to the kitchen, which doesn't smell half bad. "I have beer and wine, sparkling water or—"

"I'm fine."

Tre sighs and pulls two wineglasses from the cabinet. He fills them both with red wine before setting one in front of me.

"I said I was fine."

He ignores me and says, "I'm making lasagna. You're not vegetarian, are you? Ewan never mentioned... I should've asked. If you are, I can make something else."

"No. That's fine. I didn't come here to eat, anyway." I'm not sure why I came, but I don't tell Tre that.

"Sit down." He gestures at the tall chairs near the island.

"I don't want to sit down, Dickie. I want—"

"Can you not?"

"Can I not what?"

"You *know* what, Fiona. Please, can you not?" he repeats, his grey eyes earnest.

"Fine. Why—"

"Can we just start over? Hi, I'm Tre White." He extends his hand toward me and waits. Like he seriously expects me to take it.

"What? No. No, Tre. We cannot just 'start over!'"

"Okay, why not? Because honestly, Fiona, I have no idea why we hate each other."

"Of course you don't! You know what, *Tre*—no. Never mind. It doesn't even matter! I don't know why I came." I spin on my heel, heading for the door.

"Fiona, wait! Please."

I stop. I should keep moving, but I don't.

"Please. Just stay and hear me out."

I turn back despite my better judgment.

"Sit down, have a glass of wine, eat dinner, and hear me out. If we get to the end of the night, and you still don't want anything to do with me, I promise I'll leave you alone. I'll forget about Saturday night, and you'll never have to talk to me again. Deal?" He's got his hand extended toward me once more.

I look at it. "You'll forget about Saturday night?" I verify.

"Yes."

"Alright. Deal." I press my hand into his momentarily. Just like on the mountain, his skin is warm against mine. This time he lets go first.

I take a seat at the island and slide the wineglass toward me, then pick it up and swirl it beneath my nose for something to do. I don't know shit about wine. On the infrequent occasions I buy it, I either let the people in the store tell me what to buy, I pick the one with the coolest name or label, or I buy whatever's cheapest.

"Oh, you know about wine?" Tre asks.

I murmur noncommittally and take a sip. It's actually not bad.

"This is a Cabernet Sauvignon from a local..." Tre continues, and I tune him out as I take another sip.

Not only do I not *know* about wine, I don't *care* about wine. Go figure Tre does.

"You're not listening at all, are you?"

"Hmm. What?"

"Nothing. Never mind," he says. And he's frowning slightly, like I've hurt his feelings.

What the fuck?

He turns away, muttering something about checking on the lasagna.

"So you and Ewan are... friends?" He mentioned my twin earlier. No, actually he mentioned my twin *not* having mentioned that I was a vegetarian. Like they talk all the time. Like they talk about *me* all the time. Like it would've come up if I were.

"Yeah. Is that a problem?"

"No." I take another sip of wine. "Ewan can be friends with whomever he likes." I'm not surprised. Not really. But still. It's Tre. My brother needs better taste in friends. "Are you guys dating?" Ewan said no when I asked, but now I'm not sure if he was lying to me, because even though I assumed they were friendly, I didn't expect they were the kind of friendly that would lead to them discussing me. And if my brother *is* interested in Tre, I should at least *try* to be less obvious about hating him.

"What?"

"You and Ewan. Are you a couple? Friends with benefits? Some secret third thing?"

"No, we're just… Your brother's not exactly my type, romantically speaking. We're really *just* friends."

"Oh. Okay."

"You seriously can't imagine your brother being friends with me?" Tre asks, sounding wounded.

I shrug and take another sip of wine to hide my confusion. "You know, people are already whispering that you were probably behind the vandalism," I say, changing the subject. "You coming into my office yesterday didn't help matters, either. People think you got injured *while* vandalizing the site. If you and Ewan are such good friends, you could have asked him to ask me to come talk to you." Okay. I guess I'm not changing the subject after all.

"You want me to involve Ewan in this? I should pass him a note and ask him to give it to his sister, like we're back in high school? *'Check yes if you'll go on a date with me.'*" Tre stops abruptly. "Like that wouldn't piss you off."

"Alright. Fine. You're right. That would've been dumb. Ewan would've asked questions. Point taken." I fall silent, with no idea what to say next. This is uncomfortable. I want to leave. Instead, I pour myself some more wine.

A minute passes, and Tre stands in his kitchen with the overhead lighting shining off his blond hair. Clearly, he has no better idea about what we're supposed to say to each other than I do. *'So, you hate evil douchebags too? Wanna be friends? We can blow some shit up together!'* isn't exactly normal dinner conversation.

"Did you really build the bomb yourself?" Tre finally asks.

"Yes, Di—Tre. I really did," I answer without hesitation. There's no way I'm going to tell Tre that it was my dad who built it.

"Because that's a thing they teach in med school?"

"Have you not heard about the internet?"

"Okay. Fine. You're smart enough that you could've figured it out. I guess," he says, sounding unconvinced. Which is great. Just great.

"You said you ruined their concrete? How does one 'ruin'

concrete?" I'll admit I'm a little curious, but mostly I want to stop him from asking more questions about the bomb I didn't build.

"Do you know how concrete works?"

"You add water, pour it, and then it dries and hardens."

"Okay. So, no."

I open my mouth to reply, but Tre continues talking.

"Concrete doesn't harden via the evaporative process. It cures because of a hydration reaction—a chemical reaction," Tre clarifies.

I roll my eyes. "I know what a hydration reaction is, Tre. I'm surprised you do, though."

"You really do think I'm an idiot, don't you?"

"I think you're more of an asshole than an idiot," I say truthfully. "But you're a Venn diagram. There's some overlap."

"You know I have an engineering degree?"

"No. In what?"

"Material sciences. From Northwestern. I'm not stupid, Fiona."

"You realize that just makes it worse, right?"

"What's that supposed to mean?" Tre demands as the oven timer begins beeping.

"Nothing," I reply quickly. "So you put something in the concrete to stop the hydration reaction?" I ask as he turns to pull the lasagna out of the oven.

"Yes. Sugar. If you add enough sugar to cement—which I did—it prevents the formation of calcium silicate hydrate, ruining the concrete."

That's actually... smart. It might be smarter than blowing up the gondola support column, though I don't tell Tre that. I don't want to admit that I'm a little impressed.

"You said you had other targets?" I ask as he sets the baking dish on top of a trivet. He would have a trivet. Leave it to him to defy my expectations in the most unfathomable way possible.

"Yes. I was going to destroy the bulldozers and the gondola cables, too. But then I saw you," he tells me as he cuts and plates the lasagna, which smells amazing. Not that I'd admit that in a million years, either.

He sets a plate in front of me and refills my wineglass, which has somehow become empty again.

This is like being in a fun house. Nothing is quite what it appears to be, and I'm unsure if I'm about to walk into a mirrored wall. I don't like it at all. I want to go back to the world where Tre is just some asshole I don't associate with.

"Well. Are you going to try it?" he asks, coming around the island with his own wineglass and plate before sitting down next to me.

I want to say no. I know I should leave. Leaving would be smart. But if I were smart, I would've never come back to Kalomish.

I pick up my fork, slice off a piece, and take a bite. It might be the best lasagna I've ever had. It's all I can do to not groan in pleasure. I could marry this fucking lasagna.

I take a sip of my wine. "It's okay," I say. "So. If we were going to work together? What would that look like?"

Chapter 6
Making Progress,
Not Perfection

TRE

THERE'S ONLY TEN MINUTES LEFT ON THE TIMER. DID I plan this wrong? If I have to take the lasagna out before she gets here, it might cool off too much, and she'll hate it. I look from the clock on the oven to my watch. It's not far from the clinic to here. Did I miscalculate how long she'd take to close up?

Maybe I shouldn't have opened the wine to let it breathe already. This entire plan was stupid. I don't really know when she'll be here. Assuming she *will* be here. Well, I can't put it back in the fridge now. It's better if it sits a little too long than not long enough, which would make her think I'm clueless.

I check my watch again. Yup, still six-twenty. I look around. I spent all afternoon tidying up the main rooms, but I took so long cleaning the bathroom that I ran out of time to vacuum the living room rugs. I should wipe down the countertops again.

Man, I hope I cleaned everything well enough. She's going to point out every flaw. I take a steadying breath. *No, this is my place. I don't have to let her dictate the conversation. I'm going to make things better between us, and we're going to work together. That's the best way to fight these bastards.*

It doesn't hurt that if I can convince her, then I can spend the night picking her brain—that clever mind that's usually focused on finding new insults to hurl at me. We can do so much good if I can find a way to defuse this feud. Assuming she shows up. She might have changed her mind. She probably wouldn't bother telling me if she did.

BZZZZZ blares from the door buzzer, and I jump. I fly to the speaker and press the button to ask, "Carson?"

"So. If we were going to work together? What would that look like?"

Yes! She's in. I can't quite keep my mouth from curling into a grin, and I take a bite of lasagna to buy myself a few seconds. Fiona lifts another forkful to her mouth as she waits for me to respond. After I swallow, I begin, "Well, I figured we'd go after the Hay Creek development this time."

Fiona frowns. "I don't need you to come up with that brilliant plan. I wouldn't go back to the scene of the crime—so Bridal Mountain is out—and construction on the new resort won't even start until later this summer. Hay Creek is the only option."

I take a deep breath and bite my tongue. Just because I resolved to make peace doesn't mean she did. "You asked a question. I'm trying to answer it. I have to start somewhere." I pause, waiting to see if she'll respond or if I can continue.

"Okay. Fine. Go on." Fiona returns her attention to the lasagna.

"Since the condos were started first, there are a lot more options at Hay Creek for us to go after. We can't do everything in one night, which is why I was hoping we would pick the best targets tonight. I'm being vague because this is why I asked you here. If we pool our knowledge and skills, we can figure out the best plan to ruin the condo development. We'll only get one shot at it, and I want it to be as catastrophic as possible."

When I pause, Fiona sighs, seeming irritated as she sets her fork down on her half-eaten plate. "I realize all of this... Tre. I'm here, aren't I? I asked what us working together looks like."

I huff a breath out through my nose and clench my jaw. "Fine. End result, I think we bring down the central condo building and take out their vehicles while we're at it. We plan the approach tonight, avoid each other as we prepare, and hit it in about a month at the end of June. That'll let things settle a bit after last week and give us enough time to get everything ready. You supply the bomb or bombs. I'll gather the info we need, bring any gear we decide on, and gain access to the vehicles," I let out in a rush.

Fiona looks me in the eye and takes a sip of wine. "At least you're aiming high. I can bomb the building without you, though."

She is infuriating.

"And I can set the building on fire by myself," I retort. "I could even blow shit up without you, but I don't have access to high explosives. How are you going to find out how far along the construction will be at that point? You have to know what's there, and at least the general layout, to know what bombs to make, right? Just like Bridal Mountain, if we're both involved, we can hit multiple targets. Let's talk it through, and then see if you like what we can accomplish together. As you said, you're here." I force myself to look away and pretend I'm focused on my food. The lasagna is suddenly tasteless in my mouth. I chew mechanically while my mind races, trying to figure out what she needs to hear to realize this is a good idea.

We continue eating in silence for a few minutes. I'm grateful for the distraction making this feel less awkward, although Fiona looks completely calm. Her plate is already nearly empty. For someone who said the lasagna was only *okay,* she seems to be enjoying it just fine.

"I'm glad you recognize we need to stay away from each other. But if you're going to gather intel, how are you going to share it so that I 'know what bombs to make'?"

"Well, I'm open to suggestions on any of this. We're supposed to plan together. But, off the top of my head, it makes sense that I have a follow-up appointment about my shoulder, right? I can learn plenty in a couple of weeks. That'll give you two weeks to do whatever you need to do."

She pauses, tapping her fork against her plate. "Alright. It's not the worst idea I've heard, but I don't half-ass anything. If the plan isn't airtight, I'm out. And just like you swore to forget Saturday night, if I walk away from this, you can't attack the site on your own. I won't get caught because you mess things up."

She wasn't just jabbing at me. She actually thinks I'm an idiot. Was she gone so long that she thinks everyone living here is beneath her, or is it just me? My plans are at least as good as hers! I've already told her what I did—and would have done—before her interruption.

"Agreed. If you don't like our plan, I'll leave Hay Creek to you. But figuring out the details is the whole point of tonight, so can we please just work on it? This constant fighting only wastes time."

Fiona's eyes widen slightly, and the hard set of her mouth softens. She nods. "Okay. Fine."

"Since this will take a while, I'll make us some coffee." She's had a few glasses of wine, so I figure she could probably use it.

I move from the island and start the electric kettle. Once I'm facing away from Fiona, I let out a long exhale. Things aren't going quite as well as I'd hoped, but she might finally be coming around.

"I'm good with your timing. I'll be gone the weekend of the Fourth," she declares.

My hands pause, and I halfway turn toward her to comment about my rafting trip that same weekend. The trip that she nearly ruined when she made her brother abandon his plans with us to join her. Last week I would have yelled at her about her selfishness almost as soon as I saw her. But I need her to think well of me. I can't blow this opportunity to convince her to help.

Saying anything right now would immediately lead to a fight, which would derail everything. I take another deep breath and return to the coffee.

Fiona continues reflecting on the timing, oblivious to my irritation. "They announced the resort development is supposed to break ground in the third quarter, so any time July or after. If we create enough damage, they may decide not to start that new construction, so June makes sense. Waiting until the last weekend means the heat from Bridal Mountain should die down, and hopefully they'll give up on watching you by then."

I want to tell her that I don't think anyone is watching me, but she'd probably assume that meant I was clueless. "Great. Will two weeks after my clinic visit be enough time for you to make whatever explosives you need to take out the central condo building? It's a lot bigger than a gondola column, and I don't know what goes into whatever you have to do."

"I'll make sure I'm ready. You said something about their construction vehicles…"

"Right. One of the things I learned at my family's construction sites is how unsecured heavy machinery truly is. Sure, they need keys for the ignition, and nobody leaves those in the vehicle, but each manufacturer basically uses the same key for all of its machines. Whatever equipment they're running—John Deere, Cat, Komatsu, Bobcat—I can get my hands on some keys before we go. If the building isn't walled up already, we could drive them inside the structure before we take it down. If it is, maybe we park them right next to the detonation points. But if you don't like that, we'll figure out something else. I couldn't drive those massive earthmovers they have up at Bridal Mountain, but I've run lots of front-end loaders, small cranes, and skid-steers."

Fiona tilts her head slightly, considering the possibilities. *She's not immediately arguing. I'll count that as a win,* I think as I carry two steaming mugs of black coffee to the island. "I don't know how you take yours. Do you want cream or sugar?"

She shakes her head without even looking at the mug. "I'm not against the idea, but how are you going to get keys to the vehicles? More importantly, can you get them without leaving an electronic or paper trail? If you buy some 'replacement' keys online, you'll be in jail the day after we do it."

"I told you, I'm friends with most people around here. Tony's a great mechanic. His shop handles more commercial equipment than cars. I'll stop by and hang out. He keeps a drawer full of spare keys—construction crews aren't super careful with those things—so I can swipe a couple for the right make while he's distracted. Not everything needs to be a mastermind plot out of the movies, Fiona."

Despite ignoring the coffee when I brought it to her, she absentmindedly takes a sip as I explain my idea. Her eyes linger on the mug for a few seconds.

"As long as you don't just ask him for them, and you make sure there are no cameras inside facing the keys, then fine. I'll leave that to you. But this highlights my problem with your approach, Tre." Fiona narrows her eyes and stares directly into mine. "If I'm involved, you don't get to be relaxed about any of this. Being sloppy means you get caught. If they catch you, they're one step closer to me, and spending twenty years in prison is not on my to-do list. Let me explain the mistakes you made this past weekend…"

Fiona tells me—in excruciating detail—all the ways I screwed up before moving on to explaining how to avoid leaving a trail as I gather info and acquire our equipment. She also lectures me about ways to spot cameras and the problems with getting multiple items from the same store at the same time. Ultimately, listening isn't enough, and she makes me repeat her instructions back to her.

Eventually, she seems satisfied that I heard what she was saying, and she stops talking.

"I'll set my appointment at the clinic in two weeks," I tell her. "Zero contact until then. I got it."

Fiona stands to leave. "Alright. If you can do everything you say you can, we'll see how it goes. Don't screw this up."

I roll my eyes once her back is turned but don't respond.

She pauses with her hand on the doorknob. "I have to know. If I didn't go along with your idea, how were you going to take out an entire building without explosives?"

"I already told you I can set a fire easily enough. Gas and a match isn't too complicated. I don't need a high-tech bomb. Even I can load a truck with fertilizer and diesel fuel."

Chapter 7
Hot Coffee Break

FIONA

I LEAVE TRE'S APARTMENT AROUND NINE-THIRTY FEELING... confused. If I didn't *already* hate him, I might not hate him, and I'm not sure what to do about that. Generally, I try not to hate people solely on principle, but Tre is a special case. Now though...

Whatever. I have things to do. Things that *don't* involve adjusting my worldview to one where he might actually be an okay guy.

Betty's is closed—though there are a few people inside cleaning—so I can't cut through the diner like I did earlier, and I have to walk around the building.

That lasagna was *really* good. And that coffee. I might marry that lasagna, but I would kill *for* that coffee. Damn.

Maybe if I... I think, trying to rationalize a reason that I could switch to getting my coffee from Betty's instead of the gas station. I sigh as I reach my truck and climb inside. The only thing standing between me and a fantastic cup of coffee is me. That is a bitter pill to swallow. I wish we never had dinner simply so that I could've remained blissfully unaware of what I was missing by refusing to patronize his restaurant.

I start my truck and begin the drive home, still trying to find a solution to my coffee dilemma.

My dad is on the couch watching some World War II documentary when I get back. *What is it with men and World War II?*

"Hey Fi. You're home late."

"Yeah, I had a... thing," I say lamely.

"A date?" he asks, giving me a once-over.

"God, no! Just a… work thing." Once again, I consider asking him if *he's* dating since he never came home on Saturday night, but it's really none of my business. Instead, I sit in silence on the couch next to him and watch a couple of minutes of discussion about the Maginot Line. I'm not sure I've ever been so bored in my life. "So," I interrupt, and my dad pauses the documentary. "Hypothetically. If I wanted to bring down the condos Henley and Montank have been building at Hay Creek, how detailed would the information about the structure need to be to make that bomb?"

My dad laughs. Half a minute goes by before he realizes I'm not joking. "You're serious," he says finally.

I shrug.

"No. There's no way. I would need blueprints."

"What if I could get them?"

"How are you going to do that?"

"I'm working on it. But if I can get them. Could you do it?"

"I'm going to pretend you didn't ask me that."

"So you can't?" I prod, going for his pride.

He rolls his eyes, dismissing my attempt at reverse psychology. "That's a lot of explosives, Fiona. You think I just have those lying around?"

"I have no clue. But I assume you can make or get them if you don't."

"*Get* them," my dad scoffs. "Yeah, let me run down to the farm supply store and load up on some fertilizer." He presses play, resuming the documentary in an attempt to shut down the conversation.

I grab the remote from his hand and pause the documentary again. "You tell me what supplies you need, and I'll get them."

"You don't have the connections, Fi."

"Fine. I'll give you the money, and you can get them."

"Destroying the aerial gondolas wasn't enough?"

"No. That was like giving Henley and Montank a black eye. It was a nice first strike. But no. I want to cut their legs off at the knees. I want them to decide the cost of being here isn't worth it."

"Mmm. Blueprints. And five thousand dollars. That's what it'll take." He plucks the remote from my hand.

"Five thousand—" I begin, but the glare he gives me stops me from saying more. "Fine. Say I get you those. How long would it take?"

"A few weeks. And the charges will be extensive. They'll require prep work to take the building down right."

"What kind of prep work?"

"Notching I-beams. Sawing through metal."

"You're talking full-on contracted demolition work, dad. I'm talking quick and dirty and so damaged *they* have to do the actual demolition work."

"You'll still have to notch some beams. And the setup will still be extensive."

"How extensive? In hours?" I tack on before he can give me some vague non-answer.

"Without a crew? At least eight hours. There's probably not enough time to pull something like that off and make a clean getaway."

"I'll worry about that part," I tell him as I stand. "I'll let you know when I've got the money and the blueprints."

As I head to my room, he grumbles something that sounds like, "Goddamned kids…" and I grin.

I'll need to figure out how to talk to Tre before he comes to my office in order to give him time to get the blueprints, because that ball is definitely in his court.

THE GAS STATION COFFEE TASTES EVEN WORSE THIS morning. How is it possible to make coffee taste this bad? It's like they're putting used motor oil in it or something. I should make my own. The problem is that I've never had to do it myself. Between living in Seattle and working in hospitals, there was no need. A good cup of coffee was never more than two blocks away.

As much as I don't want to admit it, I'm a coffee snob. If I do it myself, things will escalate quickly—they always do. It's one of the many downsides to being a perfectionist. I'd have to buy a coffee machine and filters and a grinder because if I'm going to do it, I'm going to do it right. And if I'm going to buy a coffee machine, then why not just get an espresso machine? Next thing you know, it'd be a five-thousand-dollar hobby.

And if I'm being honest, I'd rather spend five thousand dollars on bomb-making supplies than on coffee.

I choke down another sip and remind myself that hurling the practically full cup out the window of my truck while I peel out of the parking lot in a cloud of smoke would be wrong. I'm sure it would feel pretty great, though.

Against my better judgment, I find myself parked in the loading zone in front of Betty's Diner. I fish the crumpled receipt for the abysmal gas station coffee off the floor of my truck, smooth it out, and write *'I need blueprints for the condo'* on the back. I paid cash for the coffee, so the receipt doesn't have my credit or debit card number on it, but it'll have my fingerprints all over it. *'Throw this away!'* I add on for good measure. He should be smart enough to do that without being told, but it's Tre, so who knows? After last night, I have no idea what to make of him. Years of experience tell me he's an asshole and an idiot, but he didn't seem like either last night.

Hopefully he's working, I think as I get out and walk into the diner. Bells on the door jingle as I step inside. It's a bit before eight in the morning, and I need to be in the office by eight-fifteen at the latest, so I don't have much time to waste.

I stand in the entryway for a moment, surveying the space. It's been years since I've been in here, and it looks more or less exactly the way it did when Tre's grandma owned it. Obviously he's replaced the vinyl on the booths and stools—since it doesn't look worn—and repainted the place at least once, but the color scheme is still the same: cherry red vinyl, creamy white walls, and lots of chrome.

I finally spot Tre on the other side of the counter, toward the rear, near a griddle. The air smells like sausage, syrup, and freshly brewed coffee, which gets stronger the further I move into the diner. Currently, about half the seats are occupied by people eating breakfast and catching up on the latest town gossip, which—from what I can overhear in snatched bits of conversation—is entirely related to the vandalism at the construction site. I wasn't kidding when I told Tre that he's going to be a suspect. Hell. He's going to be *the* suspect. I give it a few days at most before they drag him in for questioning.

He really is an idiot. And I'm a bigger one for even entertaining the possibility of working with him.

I stalk the rest of the way across the diner with the gas station coffee cup in one hand and the crumpled receipt in the other until I'm standing opposite the counter from him. His back is toward me, and he hasn't noticed me yet. At least he's wearing the sling today, though. "Dickie!" I say sharply.

He jumps and turns toward me, wide eyes quickly narrowing. "Carson?" he asks, and I hope he's smart enough to play along and get the message.

"Do you have anything better than this swill?" I set the cup down and flatten both hands against the counter.

His grey eyes flick to the coffee cup. "Have you been drinking that shit since you got back?" He laughs.

I want to tell him not to laugh at me—I'm not sure why I suddenly care—but I don't. I just glare at him harder. "Do you have anything better or not?" I bite out.

"Yes." He throws the cup into the trash. Then he grabs a thermos, goes over to a utility sink, dumps it out, and awkwardly washes it with his one and a quarter arms before filling it with coffee. A moment later, he sets it on the counter.

"What's this?" I eye the thermos suspiciously.

"Coffee."

"Don't you have regular cups?"

"No. They're bad for the environment. And I need that back. Bring your own cup next time."

I huff, feeling like I'm being lectured. "Whatever. Do you always leave crumpled receipts littering your counter?" I ask as I lift my hands and flick the message about the blueprints toward him.

He picks it up, smooths it out, and looks at it. "This isn't..." He flips it over. "Yeah, okay," he mutters, then throws it into the trash.

"How much is the coffee?"

"Two-fifty."

I pull three dollars from my pocket and toss the money on the counter before heading to my truck.

"Bring back my thermos!" Tre calls after me.

My only response is the bells over the door jingling as I leave. I take a sip. It's so much better than the gas station coffee.

Chapter 8
Sounds About Right to Remain Silent

TRE

"Order up!" I shout.

Sandy scoops the plates onto her serving tray with practiced ease and vanishes to deliver another table's lunch.

The bell above the door rings as I check the ticket for the next order. I glance over my shoulder and see two of the sheriff's department's brown uniforms. "Hey Kev, grab a seat wherever you can find one," I call out and then slap a couple of burger patties on the grill.

I step over to the fryer and check on the fries when Kevin replies, "Actually, Tre, we need you to come with us."

I turn around to make sure I heard correctly. "Excuse me?"

"We have some questions we'd like to discuss with you back at the station."

"Questions? About what?" I demand.

"Please, just come with us. We'll give you a ride to the station and sort it all out there."

"I'm kinda busy here."

"Don't make this difficult, Tre. Sheriff just wants to ask you some questions."

"Well, unless you want to explain to half the town why they don't get to eat on their lunch break today, you can wait until I'm off work. My shift doesn't end for a few hours, so I'll stop by sometime this afternoon."

A thin man with dark brown hair and pointy features, who I've never seen before, steps out from behind the deputies. "Mr. White, this is a very serious matter that requires urgent attention." I can tell from his pale skin, white button-down shirt, and pressed black slacks that he's the sort who spends all day in office buildings and doesn't get outside enough. He's clearly not a local.

"And who the hell are you? What's the matter, Kevin? You guys are hiring contractors now, too?"

The background noise of the diner has dwindled to almost nothing. Everyone seems to realize news is happening right in front of them, and they aren't going to miss a word. I may love Kalomish, but small communities live for gossip.

"I'm a representative of Henley and Montank—"

"Get out. You're not welcome in my establishment. You need to leave."

"Sir, that's not necessary—"

"The courts have been very clear: I am within my rights to refuse service to anyone. If the bigots can do it, so can I. If you don't go now, I'll have you arrested for trespassing, harassment, loitering, soliciting, and anything else I can think of. Thankfully, the long arm of the law is here already." I stare him down, and Kevin raises his hand in front of the guy, who hesitates for a moment, then walks out the door.

"It doesn't need to go down this way, Tre," Kevin tries again.

The bell over the door jingles, announcing the arrival of three road construction workers who are momentarily oblivious to the standoff they walked into.

"I already agreed to come by this afternoon. There's nothing going down. Just let the sheriff know he has to wait a few hours. Unless you really want to shut down the diner with all these people in it—in which case you'll need a warrant—and how does that benefit anyone?"

The deputies glance around. I scan the restaurant as well and notice a couple of phones pointed our way. *Shit. Fiona is definitely going to hear about this. It's going to be one more reason for her to want to avoid having anything to do with me,* I realize. She came in for coffee this morning, but this might be enough to make her decide not to come back.

Kevin and his partner, Deputy Wassermann—according to his name tag—decide a delay is better than becoming a spectacle. "The sheriff doesn't enjoy waiting, Tre. For your own sake, don't take too long. If you aren't there this afternoon, I wouldn't expect the next visitor to ask politely," Kevin says, and they head outside.

"Welcome, grab a seat wherever you can find one," I tell the three newcomers. The smell of burnt meat hits my nostrils. "Oh crap!"

I rush to the grill and scoop the slightly charred burgers into the garbage. Then I check the fries again, but they're overcooked, too. "Jackie! Can you go grab me some new fries? These are trash." I pull the basket out of the oil to drain before dumping them in the garbage. "Hey Sandy, can you make sure those water pitchers are refilled?"

They jolt back to activity, and the rest of the diner takes the cue to resume their conversations as I work the next ticket.

The rest of my shift is uneventful until I swap out at two o'clock. I go to my apartment and change out of my greasy clothes. I consider taking a shower, maybe drawing things out as long as I can, but decide there's no point in antagonizing them. I'm not worried about their questions, though. If they actually had any evidence, they would've already arrested me. It's like Fiona said, of course they're going to suspect me. I've been one of the loudest opponents of the developments. I'll let them ask their questions and play dumb. Eventually, they'll realize they don't have any good reason to think I'm the one who did it.

I drive the few miles over to the sheriff's department, arriving around three. I take the closest space in the nearly empty visitor parking lot and walk in. In the entry vestibule, a few spartan chairs are spread along the wall facing the reception desk, where a single deputy is seated behind a computer monitor trying not to show her boredom. I beam a smile at her and say, "Hey Aimee. I'm here to see the sheriff. Do you know where I should go?"

She frowns. "Do you have an appointment, Mr. White?"

Cops always love to lean into formality, as if it gives them more authority. They tend to think a uniform and a title should impress or intimidate people, but that doesn't mean I need to play along. Especially not when I know the majority of the department. Aimee got the job because she's Sheriff Morris's niece, and she's more desperate than most to be taken seriously.

I look at her for a moment before answering, gauging whether she's messing with me or if she's been kept so out of the loop she doesn't know they want to interrogate me. Maintaining my smile, I cheerfully supply, "Oh, he's expecting me. Should I go on back?" I point at the door on the back wall next to the end of the reception desk and take a step toward it.

"Wait here," she orders, picking up the phone. After a brief conversation that's too quiet to overhear, she tells me, "A deputy will come escort you shortly."

I haven't bothered sitting, and I'm watching the interior door when the one behind me opens. "Ah, Mr. White, I'm in time."

I turn to see a tall, round man with a bald head and bushy black eyebrows entering. I make room as he extends his hand to me. "Arthur Kostas. I'm here to represent you."

I take his hand because it's the polite thing to do. "I'm sorry, but I don't know you, and I didn't call you to represent me."

"Of course. I've been retained by your father, or rather, my firm has. He called this afternoon to make certain we would be present to provide counsel. He was very insistent." Arthur passes me a business card, as though it's enough to prove what he's saying.

I guess word of the incident at the diner made it to my dad already. That means Fiona has probably heard about it by now, too.

"Mr. White, please come with me," a deep voice booms from the interior door.

I'm facing my supposed attorney but pitch my voice so that the deputies should be able to hear. "I don't need a lawyer because I didn't do anything. This is all a waste of time. But since you're costing my dad a lot of money, you may as well stay."

I turn and follow the new deputy further into the building. Normally, I'd strike up a conversation to fill the silence, but I'm too interested in looking around to chat. Despite being escorted out of every town hall in recent memory, I've never been inside the sheriff's department.

We pass through a doorway with Arthur trailing uncomfortably close behind me, saying something about letting him do the talking. There's a large room with multiple desks—each containing a very basic-looking computer workstation—and several deputies. However, we immediately turn left down a narrow hallway that blocks the room from sight.

We walk under fluorescent lights, past two closed doors before stopping at a room near the rear corner of the building where we're told to wait inside.

Arthur and I enter, and this, like everything else I've seen so far, is disappointingly boring. I was looking forward to a bare table with chairs on opposing sides and a wall that's a two-way mirror, maybe a bright lightbulb hanging overhead. Instead, it's a long room that has a rectangular table in the middle with six chairs. The walls are all old wood paneling without a single mirror. Arthur moves to a chair on the opposite side of the table, facing the doorway, and gestures for me to sit next to him.

He takes the quiet as an opportunity to explain how to talk to the cops—or rather, not talk to them—like we're cramming for a final exam. "Don't say anything unless directly asked, and then let me answer for you unless I say otherwise. You're here voluntarily, and since you haven't been detained, much less Mirandized, you're free to leave at any point. You aren't required to answer any questions. Nobody has ever talked themselves out of being a suspect, but plenty of people have talked themselves into it. They'll try to find ways of using every word you say against you."

The door opens, and Sheriff Morris walks in, trailed by two deputies. He's a slightly overweight white man in his fifties who moves through the world with the expectation that people will do whatever he says because he's the one saying it. You can't live in a small community like Kalomish as long as I have without encountering the sheriff. He's the sort who thinks being loud and cocksure are virtues. I guess you don't get elected to the position by being laid-back and easy-going.

The sheriff sits across from me, frowning when I don't react to his entrance. "You his lawyer?"

Arthur, who stood to greet him, responds, "Yes, sir." He then nods at the two deputies in the room. The man who escorted us looms in the doorway. The other deputy sets up a camera on a small tripod.

The egotistical sheriff personally questioning the suspect in the high-profile case while using deputies to outnumber and intimidate. I smirk at how stereotypical they are.

"I've seen you around, White. Always talking tough, but as soon as there's a problem, you run back to daddy's money to save you," Sheriff Morris sneers.

I open my mouth to set him straight, but Arthur is faster. "My client's familial relationships are not under criminal investigation and therefore not germane to our presence here today. If you summoned him purely to disparage his family, then we'll be leaving. If you have any actual questions about a criminal matter, then let's proceed."

We both look at Mr. Kostas for a moment. Morris then looks at his deputy with the camera, who nods, and declares, "We'll be recording this interview." He states his and his deputies' names for the record, and Mr. Kostas introduces both of us.

"Mr. White, where were you on the night of Saturday, May twenty-third?"

"I—" I begin, but Mr. Kostas puts his hand on my arm and responds. "What is this regarding?"

"It's regarding Mr. White's location last Saturday night," Morris responds curtly, scowling at Mr. Kostas.

"Mr. White has voluntarily traveled here to participate in this interview. So far, he has not been informed about the topic of the interview, nor have charges been leveled against him. I ask again, what is this interview regarding?"

Morris continues to stare at me, waiting for me to answer his question. When it becomes clear that I won't, he returns his scowl to Mr. Kostas. "There was an incident of vandalism this weekend."

"My client is not a teenage troublemaker. He is a hardworking, respected member of this community. Are you questioning everyone in town about the vandalism? Or do you have probable cause to suspect Mr. White?"

I'm glad this is being captured on video, given how frustrated Mr. Kostas is making the sheriff. I'm enjoying it, but I have enough sense to keep my face neutral.

"There was damage at a construction site on Bridal Mountain. Your client," Morris says with disdain, "has been one of the most outspoken opponents of the owners of that site. He's overtly stated his goal to make them leave Kalomish, and now he's taken action against them."

"Sheriff, nothing you've said indicates any wrongdoing by my client. You haven't stated any links between him and this supposed vandalism, and you neglected to mention a single piece of evidence you have, much less how it implicates him."

"He's rallied opposition to every measure they've put before the city council, he's supported the lawsuits challenging their developments, and my men have had to physically remove him from every town hall where Henley and Montank are brought up!"

"Good, I'm glad you agree with me. Mr. White assiduously follows the legal process in his activism, as is his right. Since you've succinctly described how he consistently utilizes peaceful efforts in the variety of legal methods available to him, you must understand that suddenly committing acts of vandalism is completely out of character. Clearly, my client should be your last suspect because he has a publicly demonstrated track record of adhering to the legal process and already has multiple avenues for expressing his opposition to these developers."

"What? No. I've informed you what this interview is about, so you tell me where you were on Saturday night."

I turn to Mr. Kostas and ask, "How much do you charge an hour?"

Mr. Kostas looks at me with a predatory grin. "Enough to ensure the sheriff's department won't *accidentally* violate your rights in a rush to pin a high-profile case on a fall guy so the sheriff can show his constituents how swiftly he delivers justice."

"That sounds dangerously like you're accusing me of—"

"I haven't accused you of anything. And since *you* haven't accused my client of anything, and you have no evidence for any suspect, never mind Mr. White, we will be concluding this interview."

"You just hold on. He hasn't answered a single question, so this interview is *not* over."

"You're correct. He hasn't answered your questions because he doesn't need to. This is a fishing expedition, and we will not be participating. Unless you're arresting him now, we're leaving. Have a good day, gentlemen," Mr. Kostas concludes as he rises to his feet.

I stand and smile at Morris. The desire to make a comment must be written on my face because Mr. Kostas presses on my back to get me moving. *Right. Don't poke the bear*, I think as we're escorted to the exit.

"Wow," I say once we're safely outside. "That was great. Thank you. I didn't plan on playing along, but I figured I'd be dealing with them for hours."

"Happy to help. You can thank your father for ensuring my firm sent me."

I won't be doing that, but I don't bother saying so. "I appreciate you making that so much easier, Mr. Kostas. Now, if you don't mind, I'm going to leave while the coast is clear."

"Of course. The sheriff isn't the type of person to drop this. He'll keep looking at you for whatever happened at the construction site. You have my card for when they contact you again. Take care, Mr. White."

Chapter 9
Let's Talk About Sex and Candy

FIONA

"Mrs. Ibarguen is in exam room one," Natalie tells me.

"What's she complaining about today?" Since I've been here, Mrs. Ibarguen has come in at least once a month. She's sixty-eight and in surprisingly good health. Despite that, she's here more often than anyone else in town. According to Carol, her husband died three years ago, and she's been like this ever since. It's not even hypochondria—not really—or I'd have referred her to a psychiatrist. She's simply lonely.

"She says she's allergic to vitamin C."

"That's not physiologically possible." I close my eyes and take a deep breath. "Tell her I'll be a few minutes, please," I say to Natalie before going to the reception area to speak to Carol. She's on the phone, though, so I stand near the desk, waiting.

Finally, she says, "Alright, Tre. I'm going to put you on hold for Dr. Carson."

I stop myself from reaching over and disconnecting the call. But only because it would be incredibly unprofessional.

"Dr. Carson," Carol begins, despite having been told she can call me Fiona at least a dozen times during the first month I was back. "Tre is on line one for you."

"Why?" I ask, trying not to sound too irritated.

"He has some concerns about his shoulder."

'His uninjured shoulder,' I want to say, but I limit myself to a simple, "Okay," once again closing my eyes and taking a deep breath. The irritations will never cease, apparently. "Is there a senior citizens' center in town or anything?"

"Not that I'm aware of."

"Can you check?"

"Absolutely, Dr. Carson."

"Okay. Thank you. Do you know what Mrs. Ibarguen used to do?"

"I believe she was a homemaker."

"She has kids?" I ask, surprised. "She hasn't mentioned them."

"Yes. Two boys. They moved away after high school. I think they live on the East Coast now."

"She never worked outside the home?"

"I don't think so," Carol says.

"Okay. Thanks. Let me know what you find out about the senior citizens' center."

"Will do. Don't forget about line one."

"Wouldn't want that," I snipe as I turn and move toward the small office. There are still boxes of patient records shoved against every wall. Dr. Restin had a horrible file-keeping system. I've been trying to get them cleaned up and digitized, but there's not enough time in the day.

I pick up the phone and press the button for line one. "Tre."

"Hi Fiona, thanks for returning my thermos this morning."

"Mhmm," I murmur noncommittally. "What do you want?"

"Do you have plans tomorrow night?"

"Why?"

"I know how we can get a copy of the blueprints."

"We? I thought *you* were going to take care of that."

"It's a two-person job," Tre says. "Plus, it'll give us a chance to see how we work together."

The universe hates me. I'm sure of it. He's not wrong, though. It won't hurt to make sure we can actually work together before going all in on destroying Henley and Montank's Hay Creek development.

"Fine," I agree begrudgingly. "I don't have time to talk to you about it now. Call back at six."

"Okay," he replies, and I hang up.

"Carol, any info about the senior citizens' center?" I ask when I walk by the reception area.

"No. Sorry. Like I thought, the closest one is half an hour away in Nakton."

"Great," I groan, heading for exam room one. I tap on the door and then open it and walk in. "Hi Mrs. Ibarguen. What brings you in today?"

Her lined face breaks into a smile, and her blue eyes brighten behind her glasses when she sees me. She launches into a story about almost choking on an orange last week—which, somehow, made her decide she was allergic to vitamin C. I ask her if she's ever heard of scurvy—she has!—and spend five minutes explaining that she couldn't possibly be allergic to vitamin C.

"Have you ever thought about getting a part-time job, Mrs. Ibarguen?" I eventually ask.

"I've never had a job," she says softly.

"Never?"

She shakes her head, and her chin-length white hair sways around her face.

I sigh. "Do you want one?"

"No one would hire me. I don't know how to do anything, Dr. Carson."

"Assuming someone will hire you, would you like a part-time job?" I ask again.

"Yes. I think so."

"Wait here." I go to the small office and grab a random file from one of Dr. Restin's many boxes, then return to Mrs. Ibarguen. I open the file and scan the top page. It's only vital statistics for an Emily Johnson. Nothing sensitive. "Can you read this?" I question, passing her the page.

She looks from me to the paper, then back to me. "Yes?" she replies, confused.

"Well." I gesture impatiently. "Go ahead."

She reads out the entire first page, pausing now and again to scrunch her face over sections that are particularly hard to make out, but as near as I can tell, she deciphers it accurately.

"Can you start Monday?"

"Start what?" Mrs. Ibarguen asks, as if she's trying to make me regret the offer.

"Working here. I need someone to help me digitize the records. The job is yours if you want it."

"Oh. I couldn't do that. I don't know anything about digitizing records."

"I'll show you. It's easy. The hardest part is figuring out what's written in the files, and you've just demonstrated you can do that. So. Can you start on Monday? I'll pay you twenty dollars an hour."

She nods.

"Can you be here at seven?" It's an hour earlier than I would normally show up, but it'll give me time to teach her to use the computer.

She nods again.

"Congratulations, Mrs. Ibarguen. You've got your first job."

THE PHONE RINGS AT EXACTLY SIX. *At least he's capable of following instructions*, I tell myself as I pick it up. "Hello?"

"Hi Fiona," Tre says.

"I heard the police came to talk to you yesterday." He's not locked up—and neither am I—so he obviously didn't tell them anything about Bridal Mountain, but I still want to know what he said.

"*How are you, Tre? Oh, I'm good, thanks for asking, Fiona,*" he says, having a conversation with himself and chiding me.

I huff loudly and wait.

"Yes, Kevin and another deputy came to the diner to tell me the sheriff wanted to talk to me. They brought one of the Henley and Montank suits with them when they did. I threw him out."

"And then?" *I know he went to the sheriff's department after that. I heard some people gossiping about it when I was at Malcolm's with Ewan and Tess last night.*

"I went down to talk to them after my shift ended. I was planning on having some fun screwing with them, but apparently my dad heard what was happening and sent some expensive attorney down to handle things. Can't have me sullying the White legacy by being charged with vandalism, or whatever," Tre says, sounding bitter. *I know he doesn't get along with his family. I just don't know why. I've never cared enough to bother finding out, and that hasn't changed.* "The attorney was a nice guy, though. Arthur Kostas. He managed to piss the sheriff off at least as much as I could've."

"And...? What happened, Tre?" *How does it take him so long to get to the point? I wonder. I've seen mazes that were more direct.*

"Oh. Nothing. They asked where I was on the twenty-third. The lawyer shut them down. I left." He pauses, seeming to wait to see if I'm going to say anything, but I don't, so he continues, "So, tomorrow night..." and I close my eyes.

"YOU'RE SURE ABOUT THE SECURITY GUARD TIMING?" I ASK, swatting away a mosquito buzzing near my head.

"Again, Fiona? Seriously? For the third time, I'm sure. A guard comes by every hour—on the hour. They spend about five minutes driving around and making sure everything looks fine. Then they leave," Tre says, standing next to me just inside the tree line as we look out at the site. "We've got fifty minutes if you'll stop wasting time."

"Fine," I agree, readjusting the ski mask I'm wearing before stepping out of the tree line and jogging toward the job site office trailer, where Tre said they have a copy of the condo blueprints. We hiked the five miles up here through the old trails that crisscross the area in silence. Maybe we can work together. I don't know. But we definitely have no idea how to carry on a conversation with one another.

When I reach the trailer, I cautiously circle around to the front, listening as I go, but everything is dark and silent. The moon overhead is the only source of light, and the crickets and frogs chorusing in the distance are the only sound. I turn toward the stairs that lead to the door and stop in my tracks when I find the door barred with a metal shaft, which is locked in place to prevent it from opening.

"I thought you said they had a standard door lock that we'd be able to get past with a credit card," I snap when Tre stops next to me, wearing a ski mask of his own. I insisted on them, despite his assurances that there are no cameras. I'm glad I did.

"Damn. This is new. They didn't have these last week."

I let out a long exhale but say nothing.

"Go ahead. Say it," he states dejectedly. "I know you want to."

I do. I really, really do. Instead, I look at the windows. They're about eight feet off the ground, but big enough that I could fit through. I bet they didn't put extra locks on them. "Can you boost me up there?"

Tre looks from me to the window, then returns his gaze to me. "Yeah. But they're probably locked."

"Just lift me up."

He puts his back to the trailer, bends his legs, and clasps his hands together in front of his chest. I grab his shoulder for balance, step one foot onto his thigh, and then step my other into his clasped hands. He starts to straighten his legs, and I wobble before quickly placing my other hand onto his head and wrapping my fingers into his hair to keep from falling—all while trying not to notice how soft it is.

"Ow," he hisses, and I let go.

"Sorry," I mumble as he continues straightening his legs, raising me up. "Okay, hold me here," I tell him, one hand gripping the edge of the window frame as I pull my keys from my pocket with the other. There's a pocketknife on my keychain that I should be able to use to pry out the screen. It takes a minute, but I drop it to land beside Tre.

"Hey, a little warning!" he gripes.

"Whatever. Hold me still," I order, beginning to bounce the window in its frame. These sliding windows have a locking mechanism that's very similar to sliding glass doors, and typically if you bounce them enough, you can flip the lock out of place. Sometimes it takes a minute or two, but it's never not worked.

"What the hell are you doing?"

"Unlocking the window!"

"By jumping on me?"

"Just shut up! I've almost got it." A few seconds later, the lock snaps up, and I slide the window open. "Hah!" I place both hands on the frame and wriggle my way through, landing on the floor in a graceless roll that's sure to leave some bruises.

Another handful of seconds later, Tre hoists himself through as well.

"What are you doing? You're supposed to be keeping watch," I tell him, and he shrugs.

"I'll keep watch from in here."

I roll my eyes but keep my mouth shut. I've got to find the blueprints, take pictures of them, and then we've got to put the screen back in place and get out of here before the security guard returns. Unfortunately, that means I don't have time to argue with Tre, as much as I might want to.

I search the closest desk, checking the top, opening drawers, and inspecting each rolled document. There are papers everywhere, but after five minutes, I've found the blueprints rolled up and propped against the side of a nearby desk along with other building plans.

I'm in the process of weighing down the corners so I can take a picture when I hear… something. "What's that noise?" I whisper.

"Shh," Tre says, holding a finger to his lips and tilting his head. "Shit," he breathes a second later as the glow of headlights illuminates the road leading to the job site.

"We should—" I start, but I have no idea what we should do. I haven't gotten the pictures yet, and I don't want to take the blueprints and make a run for it, because the entire point is that no one should ever know we were here.

Tre slides the window shut and lowers the blinds, pulling his ski mask off as he peers between the slats.

"What are you doing?" I hiss. "I thought you said they wouldn't be here again until one? That's half an hour away!"

"Fiona, shh. No one *is* supposed to be here until one. I don't know why they're early, but as long as we're quiet, they'll leave and never know we were here."

I move to his side and join him, pulling my mask off too—it's hot and there's not much reason to keep it on now that the blinds are closed. I look out the window as the security truck comes to a stop about thirty feet in front of the trailer.

I want to ask what they're doing, but clearly Tre doesn't know any more than I do. I stand next to him, my shoulder almost brushing his as we watch through the slats. "What did you do with the screen?"

"I put it behind the trailer," he murmurs.

"Okay."

A minute goes by, then the truck shuts off and two people get out.

"Is that Eddie?" I ask as one of the figures moves toward the trailer.

Tre nods. "Yeah, he's the one doing the overnight security checks on the weekends."

"Who's the other person?"

"I don't know. It's only supposed to be him."

Eddie unfurls a blanket on the ground, and the other person—who I can tell is a woman, but not one I recognize—comes around the truck to the blanket, carrying a picnic basket.

"Are they… on a date? At a construction site?" I ask incredulously.

"Looks like it."

I continue watching as the woman sets down the picnic basket and presses herself against Eddie, sliding her hands under his shirt. They spend a few minutes feeling each other up, then she undoes the fly on his pants, pulling them down, and dropping to her knees in front of him, wrapping her mouth around his very erect penis.

"Well. Alright then," I say, turning away from the window, avoiding Tre's eyes. I make a show of looking through the documents strewn about the trailer. I'm sure there's other stuff here that would be useful to know about, but I'm finding it difficult to focus on their contents as opposed to the throbbing between my thighs and my suddenly very hard, very sensitive nipples.

Tre softly clears his throat and takes a seat on the floor with his back against the wall. I sneak an unobtrusive glance at him. He looks like he might be as hot and bothered as I am. *I could just…* my traitorous brain starts, and I try to shut the thought down before it can go any further. It's just that it's been months and… *he's not a bad-looking guy*, my brain supplies. *He probably wouldn't say no.*

I bite my lip and return my attention to Henley and Montank's plans. These ones are for the third site. The one they want to turn into a *five hundred*—I read it again to make sure I've got the number right, and I do—room resort site. Jesus Christ. I put it in a pile with the blueprints. I'll take a picture of it, too. Eventually. After Eddie and his friend conclude their activities and leave. Whenever it's actually safe to use the flash on my camera.

I check my watch. It's been twenty minutes. I return to the window, where Tre is still sitting with his back to the wall, and peek out again.

"Are they still…?" Tre asks.

I nod. "Wow," I whisper, tilting my head as she pulls a leg behind her neck. "Wow," I repeat. "She is *really* flexible." I stand at the window, documents forgotten until Tre sends a foot out and nudges my leg. "What?"

"You shouldn't—"

"Oh."

"What?"

"They brought whipped cream. He's licking it off her face."

Tre rises to stand next to me, and my body has a visceral reaction to how near he is. I want to jump his bones. *I want to…* my mind goes in a thousand directions, each dirtier than the last.

"You're staring."

I flinch. "What?"

"You're staring. At me."

"No. No, I'm not. I'm staring at the boner tenting your pants." I tear my eyes away from him.

"Please," Tre scoffs, but I swear I can see the blush creeping up his neck and cheeks. "Like you're not just as turned on. You've been standing there, slack-jawed, watching them for the past five minutes."

I shrug but make no move to turn away. They've got a bottle of Hershey's Syrup now. He's decorating her tits. *How in the hell is Creepy Eddie's sex life better than mine?*

"You know, we could… If you wanted to," Tre says, and I ignore him in favor of the show taking place outside the window.

She's on top now, and chocolate sauce is running down her boobs in fat rivulets, dripping onto Eddie as she rides him. I'm not sure I could look away if I wanted to, and I don't want to. But the clenching of my cunt in time to the beat of my heart is driving me insane. Maybe that's why I don't pull away when Tre places his hand on the small of my back and trails his fingertips across the exposed skin between the hem of my shirt and the waistband of my pants.

But I'm the one who turns toward Tre. I'm the one who kisses him. As soon as I do, he spins us toward the wall beside the window, pressing my back against it and his hips against mine. His dick is pressing into me, and I grind my hips against him, a small moan escaping my lips at how good it feels. And I know it would feel even better if I tore off our clothes, wrapped my fist around him, and slid him inside me.

Tre matches my intensity, pinning me in place. He groans when I move my hands under his shirt and run them over his abs. It's like I'm on fire, despite simultaneously being wetter than a Slip 'N Slide. My heart is thundering in my chest.

I want to pull him to the floor of this trailer and ride him like—

Suddenly, I hear the words from seventeen years past: *'I heard her mom...'* It's like having a bucket of ice water thrown on me.

I shove Tre back at the same time I say, "No. I can't do this with you."

"What?" he asks, looking confused as I step around him and go back to the documents. "Fiona, what happened? What's wrong?"

I ignore him as I resume digging through Henley and Montank's plans.

Chapter 10
Cry Me a River
Runs Through It

TRE

"Fiona, what happened? What's wrong?"

She doesn't answer. Her back stays turned to me while she's bent over the desk, flipping between drawings and papers. I don't understand what the hell just happened. I couldn't believe it when she actually kissed me, and then it was so hot every thought left my head except to have more of her. *Did she not want me to touch her? She kissed me, though! Did I escalate too soon?*

Goddamn, that was intense. My dick throbs with the sting of being this hard but having no release. I reach down and tug my pants to get a little relief. I can't stop staring at her bent-over ass, and it throbs again.

I turn around to avoid making things worse, but that means I see Eddie finishing as his date screams his name. *Shit!* I grimace and writhe my hips in frustration.

I decide it's safest to keep watch out the window because at least that won't cause more problems with Fiona.

"They're, uh, done. They're kind of hanging out now."

"I don't care what they're doing. Just tell me when they're gone," Fiona responds curtly.

A few awkward minutes pass as they lie on the picnic blanket together. Finally, they pack everything up, get in the truck, and pull away. I duck below the window when the headlights shine over the trailer as the truck leaves.

"Okay, we're clear. Let's scan those blueprints and get the hell out of here." By the time I turn around, she's already lining up her phone over the desk. I wince as a flash illuminates the trailer. Before my vision adjusts, her phone flashes again.

I look back out the window until Fiona's done. At least one of us should have some night vision. The walls around me reflect light a few more times, then she says, "I'm done. Time to go."

I raise the blinds and slide the window open. "When you come out, do it feet first. I'll grab you."

"When I come out, you'll move out of my way. You won't be grabbing anything."

Her words sting, but I remind her, "The screen is down there. You'll need to replace it."

"Fine. Hurry up."

It only takes a moment to lower myself down from the windowsill and collect the screen. "Ready!" I say.

Fiona's feet swing over the side of the trailer, and I catch them, bracing her against my chest as I lean sideways to grab the screen, then lift it up to her. She clicks it back in place.

"That's it, set me down."

I release her, and she drops the last few feet. She wobbles, and I grab her by the shoulders. We both freeze. Fiona recovers first, half turning to shove her shoulder into my chest, forcing me back a couple of steps.

"Don't touch me," she snaps. "Let's get out of here before something else goes wrong." She turns and strides directly to the tree line.

I follow, wondering how her hair can still smell nice after hiking five miles.

"I'm heading upstream. I can feel them on the other bank," Jordan calls, pointing toward a tree overhanging the river about fifty yards away.

"Alright man. It's not gonna help 'til you learn how to cast, but good luck."

"Screw you, Tre. I'm winning today!" he fires back, then wades to his new spot.

Ewan and I slowly make our way downstream, sticking to the shallows on the west bank.

I begin casting across the water, but I'm not really expecting to catch much this morning. After a minute, I notice Ewan isn't near me anymore. When I turn, he's struggling to make sense of his rod and reel.

"What are you doing?"

"Something's wrong with this pole. It's not working right."

I close the distance between us as I say, "Let me see." Before he even hands it over, I spot the issue. "Ewan, why did you bring a spinning rig?"

"I don't know. I just grabbed the first one I saw lying around at camp. I assumed people had gear that worked. Why, what's the problem?"

I burst out laughing so hard I can't answer. After a few moments, where Ewan's face gets progressively redder, I explain. "Nothing's wrong with the equipment. It's built for a different type of fishing, genius. You can't cast a spinning rod like you're fly fishing. You work the river every year. How do you not know this?"

"Whatever, man. I don't come out here for the fish, anyway. It's a peaceful way to meditate on the water."

"Mmm, very wise. Also, a very convenient way to justify why you won't draw first blood."

"What are you using, if you're such an expert?" Ewan questions.

"The same fly rod as always. Jerry gave me a few lures that haven't been selling for him."

"Failed hand-me-downs? Sounds like neither of us is going to win today," he quips, and I shrug. "So how the hell do I do this one, then?"

"You picked it, you've gotta figure it out. Just try not to hook me while you do." I grin.

"Ha, ha. Thanks for nothing."

We space ourselves out again and spend the next few minutes silently fishing. Or at least our facsimile of it.

My hands go through the motions on autopilot while my mind wanders. Just like every other free moment over the past three days, my thoughts return to the trailer. To Fiona as she enjoyed watching Eddie with his date. To the soft, smooth skin under my fingers as I ran them over her back. To the shock of her actually kissing me. To the press of her body against mine. To the throbbing ache of desire.

Damn it. I glance down, suddenly grateful to be standing in hip-deep water with bulky waders on. *Well, no sense waiting any longer,* I think, looking around for Ewan.

He's resorted to simply throwing his hook forward weakly and tugging at it. He appears unconcerned with his ineffectiveness.

I wade over to his side. "So, look. I tried. What you said, you know. Talking to your sister."

"Really? How'd that go?"

"I don't know. Not great. She's incredibly confusing. I tried making peace, right? I realize you can't exactly flip a switch on something like that, but it's a lot harder than I expected, and I'm not sure why. We got to where she'd start being civil, but then she'd randomly go back to being mean. We almost started acting like normal people, and then suddenly she's fighting with me again. I don't get it." I lapse into silence, hoping he'll know what Fiona's deal is.

Neither of us is even pretending to cast anymore.

Ewan sighs. "It's our mom."

"What? What about your mom?"

"Fiona holds a grudge, apparently for life, for what you said back in high school when our mom died."

I stare at him slack-jawed for a moment. "What the hell are you talking about? When did I say anything about your mom?"

"Do you remember when she died?"

"Sophomore year, right?"

Ewan nods. "It was the week before Christmas when her car crashed. Basically, right after winter break started. Obviously, we were still messed up for a while, so we didn't come back to school right away in January. About a week into the next semester, our dad finally made us. It was a rough day. People were trying to be nice, but in reality they kept reminding us she was dead. Even when they weren't actively talking about it, they were giving us pitying looks. At least, that's what it felt like."

Ice runs down my spine, despite not knowing where this is going.

"Fi and I ended up leaving the lunchroom because it was way too much. We were sitting in an alcove down the hall by ourselves most of that hour, but before everyone started going back to class, you and a few of your preppy friends walked by. You were telling them how you heard our mom's death wasn't an accident. That she was depressed and hated being stuck with her family so much, she drove off the mountain to kill herself. To get away from us." Ewan finally turns his face from the water to look me in the eyes.

Fuck. I try to hold his gaze, but I have to look away from the raw emotion on his face. I want to ask him if he's sure it was me or if he heard it right, but I don't waste the breath. There's no doubt in his eyes.

"Shit, man. I don't remember that at all." I pause. I'm at a loss. There's nothing I can say that will matter at all. Nothing is sufficient to make up for that kind of cruelty. "I'm so sorry. I understand that doesn't make anything better, especially after all this time. I know I was a dick when we were younger, but I didn't think I was that terrible. That casually mean for no reason."

Ewan turns his attention back to his rod and reel, pointlessly tossing his hook for something to do.

"I hope you know that I know that's not true. I'd never even think something like that now. I bet I heard it from my mom. She's vicious, pretty much for fun most of the time. I didn't understand that then, and I was an idiot. I've been distancing myself from that family for the last decade, Ewan. You know me," I say, but it still doesn't feel like enough of an apology.

"Yeah, I do, Tre. That's why we're friends now. And why I've tried to get Fi to get to know you."

"Damn. This explains so much. Well, crap…" I trail off as I recall my interactions with Fiona, not only from the last five months but during school too.

How can I explain things to her? We're not supposed to talk until my appointment at the clinic next Wednesday. I could try to apologize then. But should I dredge up that kind of hurt at her job? No, that'd be even more fucked up.

She's going to come get coffee every day believing I'm an asshole, but there's no way we can have this talk at Betty's.

Maybe after we're done at Hay Creek. She'll be too focused at first, and we really don't have much time to get everything done. Yeah, when we get away from the site we'll be riding high. I'll explain before she decides we can never be seen talking again.

"Woo hoo! Got one, boys! First blood to Jordan."

We both spin around at the shouting. Jordan is holding his rod overhead in one hand, with a trout wriggling in the other.

Ewan moves first, walking upstream while hooking his line to his rod. Apparently, he's given up trying to fish for the morning. "Nice. What is that, a fourteen-, fifteen-incher?"

"Hell yeah! I'm eating good today. Isn't that right, Tre?"

"Yeah, bud. You won, so I'm cooking," I call back, wading across to try my luck near the far bank. "Let's see if I can match you."

Chapter 11
Clinical Language Barrier

FIONA

"Good morning, Mrs. Ibarguen," I say when I arrive at the clinic at seven and find her already standing at the door, waiting for me. It's the first of June, but there's a bit of a chill in the air, and we're both wearing jackets.

"Good morning, Dr. Carson," she replies. Her greeting is more enthusiastic than mine was.

I didn't have time to stop and get coffee this morning. Not that I'm sure I would have even if I'd had time. I don't know if I'm masochistic enough to go back to drinking that gas station swill, and the thought of stopping into Betty's and seeing Tre… What was I thinking?

Thirty-three years of life and I've never done anything as stupid as kissing Richard Alan White the Third. I hate myself, and I hate him. And I *really* hate that the kiss has been intruding on my thoughts for most of the weekend. I wish I could call this whole thing off, but I don't want Henley and Montank and their five-hundred-room resort in Kalomish any more than Tre does.

"You can call me Fiona," I tell Mrs. Ibarguen distractedly.

"Oh. Alright. Fiona," she says, like she's testing it out. "You can call me Jean."

"Okay, this way." I lead the way to my office, and Jean Ibarguen follows.

"You know," she begins conspiratorially, "I've always thought you were nicer than people said."

I say nothing, refusing to release the pent-up sigh that wants to escape from my lungs as I wonder how long it will take people to get over the fact that I didn't immediately move back to Kalomish at the first opportunity. Like there's not an entire world out there.

"A lot of people don't like that you left for so long," she tells me, seeming to know exactly where my thoughts have gone.

I don't bother letting her know that I'm already well aware of that. "Take a seat," I say instead, gesturing to the office chair behind my desk.

"But my boys left too. Some people just need to see what's out there."

"Mhmm." I drag a chair around my desk and place it next to hers. Once I'm seated beside her, I begin showing her how the computer works and, fortunately, the subject of my personal likeability fades from focus.

We spend the next forty minutes going over how to enter the files into the computer system. And while she started out timidly, she's a quick learner. I think she's better at reading Dr. Restin's handwriting than I am, too.

"It seems like you've got the hang of this. I'm going to get a cup of coffee. Would you like anything?" I ask.

"No thanks," she answers, focused on the computer screen. I have a feeling she'll tear through these files.

I nod and leave her to it. Natalie and Carol are in the reception area chatting quietly. "Mrs. Ibarguen—Jean—is in the office. I'm going to go grab some coffee. Do you guys want anything?"

Natalie says she'll take a coffee too, and Carol shakes her head.

I sit in my truck for a moment, trying to decide if I should go to the gas station, which is farther away, or to Tre's diner, where I risk running into him. I'm less afraid of how awkward it'll be, and more concerned that I'm going to see him and realize it wasn't just watching Eddie bang some unknown woman that had me all hot and bothered.

I'll have to see him sooner or later though, and if they've realized anyone broke into the trailer over the weekend, I'm more likely to overhear gossip about it at Tre's diner than at the gas station, so I bite the bullet and drive to Betty's.

When I walk in, Tre is nowhere to be seen, and I'm not sure if the feeling that washes over me is relief or regret. But at least I don't hear anyone talking about a break-in on Henley and Montank's property as I wait in line.

"WHAT'S GOING ON WITH YOU AND TRE?" EWAN ASKS, sitting next to me at Malcolm's.

"What do you mean?" I question suspiciously. If Tre let something about Henley and Montank slip, we're done. Game over. I take a sip of my beer as I wait for Ewan's answer. It's from a local brewery, and it's pretty good—not too hoppy with a smooth finish.

"Well, we were up on the Swammish fishing earlier…"

"Okay? What does that have to do with me?" I guess that explains why Tre wasn't at the diner this morning. It's like he and Ewan are long-lost brothers. It's annoying. I wish they *were* dating. Then I'd have a legitimate reason not to sleep with Tre beyond his just being an asshole. *It's not like he'd be the first asshole I ever slept with,* I think and immediately hate my brain.

"He was asking about you."

"Okay. I still fail to see what that has to do with *me*."

"Sis," Ewan sighs. "He was basically asking me why you hated him, and the *way* he was asking it… it was like watching a fifteen-year-old boy trying to work up the courage to ask someone out on a date."

"I don't know what you're talking about." I want to make a snide comment about how much he and Tre seem to talk about me, but I can't do that without making it obvious that I've been talking to Tre too.

"Please. Something is definitely going on between the two of you. I haven't heard you call him 'that asshole' or 'Dickie' in at least a week."

"That's only because you haven't heard me talk about him at all," I counter.

"Yeah, which is noteworthy in and of itself. So, what's going on?"

"Nothing. Are you sure you didn't get too much sun while you were out on the river?" I ask with raised eyebrows, reaching to press the back of my hand to his forehead.

Ewan rolls his eyes as he dodges my hand. "Fine. Don't tell me, but I'm not clueless, sis. It's pretty clear something is going on between you guys. Anyway, since he asked me why you hated him, I explained about mom."

"Oh. How'd that go over?"

Ewan shrugs. "He didn't remember saying it, but he also didn't deny it. He apologized to me. He'd probably apologize to you too. If you'd let him."

"Whatever," I mutter, then change the subject. The last thing I need is to hear Tre tell me he's sorry. "You're still coming with us over the Fourth, right? Kelly was asking when we were climbing yesterday. I guess Tess told her."

"Yeah. Tre threw a fit about it, too."

"Huh? Why? Why would he care?"

"Normally, we go on a rafting trip with a few other guys that weekend, and I'm the guide, so I had to pull out. Tre was pissed about it even though Kyle is going with them instead."

"Oh. Sorry. I didn't know. You could've said no when Tess asked if you wanted to come. You didn't have to go just because of me."

"Eh. Whatever," Ewan says with another shrug. "I'll go climbing with you guys this year and go rafting with Tre next year. It's not a big deal. How's Kelly? I haven't seen her in a while."

"Busy. She's managing the climbing gym over in Nakton now."

"The one that's really popular for kids' birthday parties?"

"Yeah."

"There's not enough money in the world," Ewan says, and I laugh.

He's not wrong, but if Ewan were motivated by money in any capacity, he wouldn't be working as a river guide.

"Whatever, you know that's right up her alley."

Kelly and I were briefly part of the same climbing team when we were younger, but she outclassed the rest of us so fast that she ended up climbing with the older kids almost immediately. She messed around on the pro-climbing circuit for a bit, but she's kind of like Ewan—too laid-back to really want to compete. If I were anywhere near as good as her, I'd be in Austria right now climbing in the Alps, but she loves Kalomish and teaching climbing more than being on sponsored teams and in magazines.

"That's true."

"Do you think dad might be dating again?" I ask, changing the subject.

"No idea. If he is, he hasn't said anything about it to me. Why?"

"There've been a few nights where he hasn't come home. I just figured maybe he was seeing someone."

"If so, it's about time," Ewan says.

"So?" I ask my dad, who's sitting next to me at the long workbench in the storage unit.

It's a bit after eight on Wednesday night, and a large printout of the picture I took of the condo blueprints is on the tabletop in front of us. We've been silently staring at them for the past twenty minutes, and I'm starting to get bored. They're structural blueprints, so it's one big grid of intersecting lines that means nothing to me.

My dad sighs, his chin propped on his fist. He grabs a red felt-tip marker with his free hand, pops the cap off, and says, "These seven," as he begins circling a series of squares where the grid lines intersect. "Each of these is an I-beam that serves as a structural support. If you take out these seven," he states, tapping the square in each circle, "it'll be enough to crumple the building. It won't completely collapse the structure the way we would typically do for something like this, but it'll force them to demolish it and start over. If you take out any fewer than that, there's a chance they could salvage some of what they've built."

"Okay," I nod, my eyes focused on the printout.

"Fiona. You won't be able to do it. It's too much work for one person who's never done this type of setup before to get through in a single night. And I know it might seem like it's only the sheriff's department that's looking into what happened at Bridal Mountain, but I guarantee it's not. The feds are definitely in the loop. They've probably already been to check things out, even if word hasn't made it all over town yet."

I look up to meet his blue eyes. His eyebrows are drawn together, and the muscles along his jaw are tight. "Have you ever known me to fail at something, dad? Has there ever been anything I've set my mind to that I've failed to accomplish?"

"There's a first time for everything, Fi. And this," he says, waving at the blueprints in front of us, "is hubris. This is Icarus shit."

I shake my head. "No. It's not. I can do it."

"Walk me through how, *exactly*, you think you can pull this off on your own."

I force myself to remain still and meet his gaze. "I'm going to use an oxyacetylene torch. I should be able to burn through each I-beam in a matter of minutes. I'll have plenty of time to set the charges," I lie. I knew this would come up, and I can't tell him I'm going to have Tre helping me with the prep. That would definitely be a mistake. So I did some research and watched some videos to figure out the fastest way to cut through steel.

"And how the hell are you going to get an oxyacetylene torch out to Hay Creek?"

I shrug. "I'll get a trailer for my bike and tow it out there along with everything else. It's only seven beams, dad. That's doable. I'll wear a mask, and there will be *nothing* at the scene to identify me." I wait for him to contradict me. I'm prepared to argue the point if he tries to tell me I'm wrong, but he only lets out a long exhale.

"When you notch the I-beams, you have to do it right, so that there's no chance of the beams remaining stacked on each other when the charges detonate. If they don't slip apart, they won't pull the building down on itself."

"Okay," I agree as he sketches how each beam needs to be cut.

"You still owe me five thousand dollars for supplies," he says when he's done.

"I'll get it to you by this weekend."

It's Friday before I actually run into Tre working at Betty's when I stop in for coffee, and he looks as uncomfortable as I feel. I can't help but wonder if it's because he's remembering having me pinned against the wall of the trailer at the construction site, or if it's because Ewan finally told him why I hate him. Maybe both.

Seeing him standing behind the counter with his bright grey eyes —which are *definitely* tracking my walk up to the register—and his slightly mussed hair is bringing back memories of the trailer. I stop myself from folding my arms over my chest. Surely my bra is hiding the fact that my nipples are suddenly rock hard, and I wonder if... *Nope. Not doing that.*

"Hi Fiona," Tre greets.

"Hi. Can I get a cup of coffee? Please," I tack on as an afterthought when I set my stupid to-go cup that he made me buy on the counter between us.

"Yeah, sure," he says, jerking his eyes back to my face. I'm pretty sure he was staring at my tits, and that knowledge does nothing to cool the heat that's coiled between my thighs.

He grabs the cup and walks toward the coffeepot, unscrewing the lid as he goes. There's a small copy of the blueprints inside. There are seven beams circled in red felt-tip marker and a note, which says, '*We need to cut through these I-beams*' with a drawing showing how we need to cut them to create the right geometry for them to slip apart once the explosives detonate. According to my dad, without that, they can stay stacked together like Jenga blocks, which isn't what we want.

Tre pulls out the paper, subtly pocketing it before filling the cup.

I hand him a five-dollar bill when he comes back. There's a slip of what looks like receipt paper already wrapped around the cup when I take it from his hand, carefully avoiding touching his skin.

Unfortunately, his stupid face is distracting me when I reach out for my change, and his fingers brush across mine. I say nothing as I turn and head for the door.

Once I'm back inside the safety and solitude of my truck, I peel away the receipt that's wrapped around the cup.

Goddamnit. Ewan was right. We're passing each other notes like we're back in high school, and I'm not sure it matters that they're about blowing shit up. His note says, '*I need a distraction at Columbia Auto Repair at 1 PM on Tuesday.*'

Does he not realize I have a job? I have patients? And seriously? He couldn't schedule this at noon so I could at least try to turn it into a long lunch thing? He is the worst! I fume as I crumple his note and throw it on the passenger floorboard.

Chapter 12
Smooth Criminal Behavior

TRE

"Heya Tre," Donnie greets over the tinkling of the bell hanging from the door as I walk into the reception room of Tony's garage.

"Hey Donnie. I'm here to meet with Tony."

"Yup, he's expecting you. You can head on back to the office, just watch your step going through the bay."

I nod and walk past him through the door marked *'Employees Only'*. The cavernous garage bay is clean, but smells faintly of motor oil. On my way to the single office door set into the left wall, I note a skid-steer and a front-end loader in different stages of repair. The loader is the same brand I saw on our blueprint run at Hay Creek.

He should definitely have some keys around, then, I think as I step into the office.

"Good to see you, Tre. Grab a seat." Tony shakes my hand across the small, metal desk in his bare, white-walled office.

"Yeah, you too, Tony. It's been a while, man. Thanks for making the time."

"No problem. It'll be an extended lunch hour today," he replies, then crumples an empty sub wrapper into a ball, dropping it in the trash can beside his desk. "What do you need help with? It's not the alternator again, is it?"

"Oh, no. The car's running fine. I could always just drop it off if it wasn't. Nah, I wanted to talk to you about converting it to biodiesel again."

"Wow, okay. I thought you decided not to do that years ago," he states, a note of surprise in his voice.

"Well, yeah. But I've been reconsidering it lately. I've got the loft above Betty's now, which means I don't drive as much as I used to. I could probably manage with the oil the diner uses, more or less. And with climate change getting worse every year, I want to do everything I can. Seems like it's worth looking into again."

"Alright. I hear you. I mean, I'm always glad to help. There are two main ways to handle it." Tony spends several minutes explaining the options, and it's nothing new. When I asked him about converting in the past, I actually meant it. Unfortunately, it's not really feasible for me. Today, I simply need a reason to be here.

I spend the time nodding politely and pretending to listen, but I'm also surreptitiously checking the corners for cameras. When I entered, I briefly scanned the room and didn't notice any, but I need to be sure.

Eventually, Tony winds down and asks, "So, what are you thinking?"

I pause before answering, gazing off into the middle distance as though I'm contemplating my decision. It's the perfect opportunity to sneak a glance out the office door to my right. When it's clear my distraction isn't happening, I reply to buy time.

"Well, without a yard, or even a shed, processing my vegetable oil into biodiesel isn't much of an option, so I guess it's pretty clear I can't do the full conversion." I pause again, still hoping for a distraction. "The combined diesel and raw veg oil could work. I don't mind following the extra steps to start up and shut down, switching the fuels, since it helps the environment. How much would it cost to do all that work?"

That should buy a minute. *Come on, Fiona. I gave you the appointment time.*

"Well, the equipment isn't anything special. I have most of what we'd need already. I'll probably special order the diesel tank..." Tony trails off and considers whatever logistics he needs to account for. "As a ballpark, you're probably looking at—"

"Hey Tone!" Donnie sticks his head in the office door. "Got a customer demanding to speak to you."

"What do they want?"

"I told you. He wants to speak to you."

I raise my eyebrows in surprise. *He?*

"Thanks, Donnie," Tony says sarcastically.

"No problem," Donnie answers before disappearing as quickly as he arrived.

I'm smirking as Tony shakes his head. "Excuse me a moment, Tre."

"Of course. You're the boss. Do what you need to do."

As soon as he's through the door and out of sight, I much more obviously peer around the office, searching for security cameras. Finding none, I pause for a moment to listen at the door. Faint voices echo through the bay from the customer lobby. Good enough for me to decide I can make my move before Tony comes back.

I rush to the other side of the desk and pull open drawers at random. The third one I check has multiple small keys attached to tags with company logos rolling around. Score! I spare a quick glance at the door before snatching one key for the heavy equipment and one for the skid-steers. I double-check that there's still at least one key for each model. When I'm satisfied Tony won't notice I've taken anything, I make sure all the drawers are closed, then return to my seat like nothing ever happened.

A couple of minutes later, Tony walks in, frustration scrawled all over his face. He's never been one to hold back his thoughts.

"All good?" I inquire innocently.

"Pfft. This guy comes in here raising hell about how we screwed up his sister's car when she brought it in last week. Takes forever to get enough detail from him to look it up, he's so busy demanding refunds and free repairs." Tony shakes his head. "Turns out we're not even the ones who serviced the car. She must have gone to A1 Auto, and either she didn't know what shop she used or he just assumed it was us when she told him about it. I tell you, I'm not sure it'd be worth the headache to work on her vehicle if she does come in."

I laugh and get to my feet. "Well, it sounds like your day is picking back up. I'll get out of your hair. Thanks for the info. I'll call you if I pull the trigger on converting."

"Alright. We can take care of it whenever you want. Here, I'll walk you out." Tony steps into the garage bay, and sounds of his technicians resuming work after the quiet of lunchtime filter into the office.

Hah. This went even smoother than I had hoped. I'm getting out of here early, and I didn't have to agree to any work from the shop.

As soon as I step out, my attention is drawn to a bright flame at the front-end loader. I stupidly stare straight at it and, even at this distance, my vision floods with spots. I quickly turn away, blinking like the idiot I am.

"Didn't your dad ever teach you not to look at a cutting torch, Tre? You should know better than that," Tony admonishes.

"Yeah, I know. They're just badass looking. Can anybody buy one of those?"

"What do you want an oxyacetylene torch for?"

I can't tell him I need to investigate methods for cutting steel beams. It's not what I came for, but since I'm here already, I may as well multitask.

"I told you. They're badass. Do I need a better reason?" I grin and resume walking.

"Well, actually, yes. They're incredibly dangerous if you're not trained in how to use them. But you also need to understand how to store and maintain them. You have no business buying one, Tre." Tony is looking at me like he's suddenly reconsidering his entire opinion of me.

"Oh well. No harm in asking, right? Thanks again, Tony. I'll catch you later."

"Yeah, later." Tony is shaking his head as I walk out the door into the bright afternoon sunshine.

"Mr. White. You can come back now."

"You go ahead, Tre. I'll bring some of those muffins by the diner tomorrow morning," Carol tells me.

"I won't say no to that," I answer with a wink, then rise to follow Nurse Machado.

"Nice to meet you, Mr. White. I'm Nurse Machado. Please follow me to exam room two." She offers these statements flatly as I approach and begins walking down the hallway without waiting for a response.

"Um, we've met. Last time I was here? I'm Tre."

Nurse Machado stops at an open doorway and gestures for me to enter. She follows me in, closes the door, and then consults the clipboard in her hand. "Ah, yes. It says here that you had a shoulder injury two weeks ago. How is your shoulder feeling now?"

I hop onto the exam table, the paper cover crinkling under me. "That's why I'm here. I wanted to have a follow-up. It seems okay to me, but I want to get cleared by the doc." I hesitate but continue, "I told all of this to Carol when I made the appointment. Isn't it in there?" I point at the clipboard.

"Yes, I see it here. Thank you. Please step on the scale."

Although we go through the standard routine of measuring my vitals, this conversation remains anything but normal. *How can she not at least remember me being here? Oh, I know. I couldn't quite connect with her before Fiona interrupted. Fiona's surprisingly good at interrupting me. No, don't get distracted by her when she's not even here,* I think, but my brain betrays me anyway, as the vision of Fiona bent over the desk in the trailer flashes in my memory.

"Your heart rate's a bit higher today than last time. Any stressors?" Nurse Machado's question brings me back to the present.

I clear my throat. "No, nothing I can think of."

I flash her my biggest 'I can be your best friend' smile, but she turns away to enter my information into the computer. "So, the last time I was here, you mentioned you hadn't been hiking because you recently moved to town. Where did you move from?"

There are two loud knocks on the door, and Fiona enters before

Nurse Machado can answer. *Son of a bitch! How does she always find the most irritating thing to do?* I look at Fiona as she walks in and suddenly forget my irritation. Her brown hair is tied back in her work ponytail, and her eyes lock with mine for a second, instilling a confusing new layer of guilt on top of the lust I'm already wrestling with. I quickly turn my gaze to the floor as Fiona moves to stand beside the nurse at the computer.

They converse in hushed voices for a minute before Nurse Machado hands over the clipboard and leaves. As she walks by, I glance up and think I notice a hint of a smirk on her face for a split-second before she's past me, then out the door.

"Okay, Tre. What've you found out?"

"Hi Fiona. Nice to see you too. I'm doing well, thank you."

She merely stares at me, waiting. As soon as I make eye contact, the guilt rises again, and I look away.

Idiot. Don't be a smartass. You're trying to fix things here.

"Right. Debrief. When we go, the condo building will be framed up, but it shouldn't be walled in yet. They're supposed to be running electrical and plumbing, which means we'll have an easy time getting inside, and I can cut a few of the timbers to make room for the vehicles. That's assuming we still want to put them inside before bringing the building down."

"I'm not a fan of *shouldn't* and *supposed to*. Or have you forgotten the lock on the trailer door?" Fiona counters.

I haven't forgotten *anything* about the trailer, though I don't say that. I only shrug. "I understand, but it's two weeks in the future. Nobody can guarantee anything."

"Fine. What else?"

"To prepare you in case the 'supposed to be' is wrong, the next stage would be for them to wrap the whole building in insulation. After that, they start putting up the drywall inside. Even if they get ahead of schedule, that's easy for us to get through. We'll just be slightly inconvenienced at the beginning."

"Good to know." She may as well be tapping her foot, she's so impatiently waiting for me to share everything.

"I haven't heard anything about anybody noticing a problem with the trailer or their documents. Security seems to be the same."

"Excellent. Have you solved the problem of cutting those I-beams?"

"Actually, yes. I've checked a couple of different options, and I'm sticking with the simple, easy route. I'll have all the equipment before we go. And yes, I'll be careful. I remember what we discussed," I rush to insert before she lectures me again.

Fiona simply nods and waits for me to continue.

"Speaking of cutting beams, did those blueprints give you everything you need?"

"Yes, it's all fine. Thank you." From the strain in her voice, that may have physically pained her to say. "But on the subject of secret notes, don't get in the habit of passing me messages on receipts. Once, nobody will notice. Probably. If you keep doing it, we're liable to get caught."

"I'm aware. It's not like I do it every day you come for coffee. I needed a distraction to get the keys. And by the way, I thought we *weren't* involving Ewan."

It's Fiona's turn to shrug. "I'm busy during the day." She waves her hand vaguely. "There aren't many rafting trips on a Tuesday afternoon. He doesn't know about cars any more than I do. All he knows is he tried to help his sister, so he just thinks I made a dumb mistake. It's fine. Did you get them?"

"Yeah, it worked like a charm. Thank you… and him, I guess."

Fiona nods. "How long do you think it'll take you to cut through the beams?"

"Probably about thirty minutes per beam."

"Probably?" she says sharply.

"It's not like I've been able to test out that part of it, Fiona."

"Fine," she grumbles. "Anything else I need to know?"

"Nope. I think we've accounted for what we need. Are we still going with the same plan for meeting up that night?" It's two weeks away, but I don't want to make a mistake and give her a reason to get cold feet.

"Yes, but I want you to meet me the day before at this address, at seven-thirty so we can walk through the plan and make sure we both know *exactly* what we'll be doing the entire time. We have a lot to do, and we need to be efficient."

I unfold the paper she handed me, looking at the address. "Isn't this a storage place?"

"Yes. Is that a problem?"

"No. I'll be there."

"Alright. Make sure you come on foot. *Try* to be inconspicuous. Barring an emergency, we keep our distance until then. If anyone asks about your shoulder, I cleared you for all activities. You're back to normal."

"Are you going to be at the town hall tonight?"

"Obviously," she replies, heading for the door without so much as a goodbye.

"Hey Fiona," I call before she's gone. "Is that nurse... does she have memory problems?"

"I don't hire incompetent people, Tre. Her memory is fine." And with that, she opens the door and leaves me sitting on the exam table all alone.

"WE CLOSE IN FIVE MINUTES. TIME TO CLEAR OUT!" I shout to the diner from behind the counter. June's town hall starts soon, and as has become routine over the past year, Betty's is crowded with people killing time beforehand. I love hearing everybody get so fired up, but I need to close early enough to attend myself. I've already stopped serving food and taken care of the grill. The tables have been bussed, and the dishes are in the dishwasher. The remainder of the cleaning can wait until the morning.

The city council obviously won't lock the doors to keep people out if they're late, but I'm sure that pissant Jacob has some way to keep me from joining if I'm not on time.

Chairs squeak as people stand, and the bell above the door jingles as they file out. Eventually, I'm the only one left in the diner, and I lock up before rushing down the sidewalk to the meeting.

I nod to the deputy standing idly outside the main entrance as I walk in. A brief scan of the room confirms that, as usual, all the seats are taken. The room is fuller than I can remember it being, but after word got out about Bridal Mountain, I'm not surprised. Lucas waves at me from the back wall where he's saved a space. I nod as I stand next to him, waiting for the city council along with everyone else. Jacob is such a prima donna, always needing to be the center of attention. We can't just have a meeting. He has to make an entrance.

I check my watch. Two minutes to seven. I survey the room more closely, hoping to judge people's moods. Most of Kalomish has been pretty steadily against Henley and Montank, but there's been plenty of wild talk since the bombing. Many of the people along the walls were just down at the diner, and they're all staunchly anti-developer.

I still haven't found the one face I'm hoping to see, but I suppose she does always sit near the front and center, like a proper little follower. *Damn, she's good,* I think, not for the first time. *If I hadn't run across her up there, I still wouldn't have a clue what she's really like. She's so worried about my being a suspect, she might not want me to make a scene, but can I afford to stay quiet now?*

As if my thoughts summoned her, I see a head in the third row swivel and find me. Then just as swiftly, she spins again to face front.

The conversations have been building to a low roar, and snippets of gossip about what actually happened up at Bridal Mountain intrude on my worrying. Now that I've seen Fiona turn around, I notice people glancing at me and then looking away. Maybe she was right. Maybe I'm more of a suspect than I thought.

Shit, I guess I should keep my mouth shut tonight.

The council members file in from a side door and take their seats. The conversations quickly die out, leaving silence for Jacob to speak.

"Hello. Thank you all for coming tonight," he begins. "I expect many of you are here for one reason, so we'll begin with the most pertinent topic.

"It's true that there was an act of vandalism at the project site on Bridal Mountain. There was significant damage to the construction there. The sheriff's department is actively investigating. In due time, the perpetrator will be apprehended, and further details will be made available."

People throughout the crowd start muttering, interrupting Jacob's moment.

"Please, settle down. We'll have time for questions and answers at the end. For now, it's important to remain calm and not engage in unfounded speculation or baseless accusations." Jacob is looking directly at me, with a smug grin on his stupid face. "That doesn't benefit any of us. If anyone has relevant information that can aid in the investigation, the sheriff's department will provide the number for a tip line."

How does Fiona keep her mouth shut during these meetings? I don't know how much of this bullshit I can stand, I fume.

He continues droning on, restating that something happened and they have no idea who did it. He's using fake politician-speak so it sounds important. As long as you don't think about it. Eventually, he shifts into his corporate mouthpiece role.

"Henley and Montank have reassured the council that they remain committed to their contract and invested in their project to boost—"

"That's not reassuring at all," I interrupt. "Clearly, people don't want them here."

Heads turn in my direction. I don't dare look away from the council to find her face, though. There's only so much BS I can sit through. *Sorry, Fiona.*

"Once again, this is not the designated period for questions and answers," Jacob replies, eyes narrowing.

"If their contract is up for discussion, it shouldn't just be with you. Let's put it to a referendum!" I state. This is met with a smattering of agreement around the room.

"The council is not accepting motions from the floor at this time.

Deputies, please escort Mr. White from the assembly." That shit-eating grin is back on Jacob's smug face.

As two deputies walk down the aisle from the dais toward me, I seize my last moment to speak. "If their contracts affect our land and our water, then we should get to decide!"

I let them seize my arms. As they begin walking me out, I call over my shoulder, "Put these contracts to a vote! Let the people decide."

And then I'm through the doors and heading down the building's front steps. They walk me right past the lone deputy standing outside, serving and protecting the sidewalk very productively.

"Sir, you're not allowed to reenter the building for the remainder of the night. Please move along."

"Sir? Yeah, I know the drill, Dan. You should unwedge that stick from your ass before you hurt yourself," I grumble before walking to the corner and making my way across the street to Malcolm's bar.

I heard everything the council was going to say in that meeting. They don't know anything. And they also aren't listening to anyone. But Fiona and I will make sure they get the message.

Chapter 13
Blow It Up,
Up, and Away

FIONA

AT EXACTLY SEVEN-THIRTY, THERE'S A BANG ON THE outside of the storage unit's roll-up door, and I lift it enough for Tre to slip under. When he stands, he's suddenly way too close, and I have to stop myself from hurriedly stepping back to put some distance between us. He already called me jumpy once, and I don't want to give him another excuse to mock me. So what if I'm 'jumpy'? I'm only jumpy around him. This close though, I can't help but notice that we're almost the same height. He's only a few inches taller than me. Not that he's short. He's not. I'm just tall.

Tre surveys the space. "So, this is your... secret lair?" he asks finally.

I shrug. "It's not like I'm going to build a bomb in my dad's basement."

"Why are you living there anyway? You must make more than enough money, being a doctor and all. Why not get your own place?"

"Not all of us hate our families, Tre. Anyway, I didn't invite you here to talk about my life," I tell him shortly.

"Why *am* I here?"

"We need to go over the plan. We both need to be able to trust that the other is doing what they're supposed to be doing for this to work, and I have a hard time trusting you. Especially when you keep doing stupid shit like getting yourself thrown out of every town hall," I chide, even though I promised myself I wouldn't mention it.

He sighs as if he was just waiting for me to say something about his latest confrontation with Jacob, which annoys me. "It'd be stupider if I started behaving differently now."

He has a point, and I know he has a point. I already thought of it, which is why I told myself I wouldn't say anything. Old habits die hard, though.

"Fine. Sit down." I gesture to the stools in front of the workbench where a large copy of the development's blueprints is sitting. He takes the stool closest to the door, so I sit to his left, between him and the rear wall of the storage unit. I wish this space were bigger and he wasn't so close. "These columns," I begin, pointing to each in turn, "are the ones we have to cut. You know how they have to be cut?"

"Yes," Tre murmurs, glancing up to meet my gaze.

"Draw it for me," I order, extending a pencil toward him.

"Fiona, I know how they need to be cut."

"Then draw it for me. For this to work, I have to be able to trust you. So prove that I can trust you, Tre."

He takes the pencil from my fingers, carefully avoiding touching them, with a muttered, "Fine," sketches the shape of an I-beam, and then draws the cuts that need to be made in it. "Satisfied?" he asks, looking back at my face when he's finished.

"Yes." I swallow. "Okay. So you'll cut those. The guard isn't checking inside the buildings at all, right?"

"No. Just the exteriors, and still only a quick drive-by. Like before. Or maybe… shit. I don't know. It's *supposed* to be a quick drive-by. But Eddie…"

I nod, trying not to think about Eddie squeezing chocolate syrup onto that woman's tits—or the inevitable memory of Tre's hips grinding into mine that goes hand in hand with it.

"Alright. Anyway." I clear my throat. "I'll keep watch while you're cutting the beams. If each one takes thirty minutes, that's three and a half hours. Security will come by at least a few times, and we need to make sure everything is dark and quiet when they do. After you're done, we'll switch. You'll keep watch, and I'll set the charges. That'll take around an hour. When I'm done, we'll switch again. I'll keep watch, and you'll drive the construction vehicles into the building.

Then we'll blow it all up and get the hell away before anyone has a clue what's happened."

Tre nods in agreement.

"Okay. Tell me what the plan is," I order.

"We just went over the plan, Fiona."

"Tre. If you want me to trust you, tell me what the plan is."

He sighs, but repeats everything I said.

I make him do it three more times, then ask, "Do you have a bike?"

"A bike?"

"Yeah. A bike with pedals. Typically, people ride them to get to and from places."

"Yes. I have a bike. Why?"

"Ride it tomorrow," I tell him.

"Is this how you got up Bridal Mountain?" Tre asks, huffing behind me.

"Yes." It's right after nine-thirty on Friday. I could be hanging out in a bar, looking for someone to get lucky with. Instead, I'm pushing my bike up a particularly steep hill on one of the trails that leads out to Hay Creek. To make matters worse, I'm wearing a ski mask—because you can't be too careful with people having trail cams everywhere these days—sweating my ass off, with a backpack full of explosives strapped to my back.

"That's a long bike ride."

"Yes. I know. I did it," I reply shortly.

"Just making conversation."

"What is it with you needing everyone to be your friend?" I resist asking if it's because mommy and daddy didn't love him enough. I'm trying not to be a total ass. It's not Tre's fault I'm frustrated. Sexually or otherwise.

"Who *doesn't* want people to be their friends? Besides you, of course. Even your brother wants people to be his friends."

"Yeah, but Ewan doesn't really care. It's pathological with you. Well. Except with Jacob Nammier." I smirk.

"That guy's a douchebag," Tre mutters.

"No argument here."

"You're really good at making him think the sun shines out of his ass," Tre says with what seems to be forced neutrality.

"Mhmm."

"You guys dated in high school, right?"

"Me and Jacob?" I ask as I *finally* crest the hill and sling a leg over my bike.

"Who else?" he says flatly.

"We went on a couple of dates. Why?"

"Just wondering," Tre says, falling silent.

Thirty-five minutes go by before we make it to the Hay Creek site, ski masks on the entire time. We leave the bikes in the tree line and make our way across the site to the condo building, which is framed but not walled in. Exactly like Tre said it would be. Hopefully that means the rest of his intel is good.

"Okay. Start cutting, and I'll watch the road."

"Alright," he agrees. "It's going to be noisy, though. I might not hear you if you're talking to me."

"I'll make sure you know when the security guards are checking things out," I promise as I glance at my watch. It's a bit after ten. "You should have around forty minutes before the next security check."

"Want to help me find an outlet?" Tre asks, pulling a saw from his own very full, very bulky backpack. "I can use the cordless saw if I need to, but it'll go faster if I can use the corded one."

"Fine."

It takes almost ten minutes of searching before we find what appears to be a temporary electrical box for the builders to use during construction. Then I return to an opening in the framing to watch the road leading to the site.

The night is dark, and the moon is obscured behind a thick cloud layer. The noise from Tre's saw cutting through the I-beam behind me is unbelievably loud, and I wonder how far the sound carries. I'm trying to reassure myself with the fact that light travels faster than sound, which should mean Eddie won't be able to hear us before I can see the lights on his truck, but I'm not so sure that will hold true given the craggy mountain terrain and the twisting roads that lead here.

I'm shifting my weight back and forth when I see the faintest glow in the distance. It's almost eleven. I run across the floor to Tre, grabbing his shoulder. "Stop," I hiss when he looks at me.

He nods and shuts the saw off as I study his work. He's almost done with the first one. It's going slower than he anticipated, and I adjust my expectations about how long this will take, beginning to calculate a new timeline. Call it another four hours to get through the beams. So, probably around three in the morning. Then say, forty-five minutes for me to set up the explosives. That brings us to four in the morning with having to pause for the security sweeps. Then another thirty minutes to get the construction vehicles into the building… Most likely it'll be around five-thirty in the morning when we blow it up. Just as the sun is rising. There'll be no cover of darkness to escape under. And it'll be Saturday morning. It's likely there will be some hikers and joggers out on the trails.

Shit. My dad was right. There's not enough time.

"Hey," I whisper to Tre. "It's taking too long to cut through the beams. At this rate, it'll be light when we blow up the building."

Tre looks from me to the I-beam and back to me. "I'm going as fast as I can, but we can't leave it like this! They don't do a ton of work on the weekends, but someone is bound to come out to the site. They'll definitely notice the giant cuts!"

Shit. He's right too.

"What if we only cut four of them instead of seven?" Tre asks.

I shake my head. "No. It has to be seven. Seven is the minimum number." My dad was emphatic about that. It has to be seven, and it has to be *these* seven.

"Well then, what do you want to do?"

The security truck's headlights sweep across the building as it drives past, and I jump.

"Fiona," Tre says, reaching out to grab my elbow, bringing my attention back to him. "What do you want to do?"

"I..." If we leave without having completed the plan, this will all have been for nothing. Someone will show up to the building during the day and notice the sabotage. We won't get a second chance. "I think we're going to have to risk it. We can split up when we leave the site. If we're lucky, we won't run into anyone. It'll still be early. Maybe no one will be out...?"

Tre nods. "Okay."

"You're sure?"

"Yes. After we detonate the bombs, we'll split up. You go one way, I'll go another. If we're careful, we might be able to hear anyone coming and hide before they see us. Otherwise, just act like you're out on a ride before the day gets too warm and muggy."

"Alright," I agree. I've got a bad feeling about this, but I'm not about to let the opportunity to destroy Henley and Montank's site pass me by.

The security truck disappears, and the glow of its lights steadily fades away. Once they're no longer visible, Tre returns to cutting the beams, and I take up watch again.

It's one in the morning when the security truck comes and goes for the third time. I break our plan and begin rigging the explosives on the four I-beams Tre has managed to cut through so far. He definitely notices when I do, and I can tell he wants to say something about it. He doesn't, though. The truck won't return for another fifty minutes, and I can get these four set up in twenty or thirty minutes and then go back to playing lookout. Plus, it'll save us a bit of time. We might be able to leave during the dawn instead of at sunrise this way, and I feel like we'll need every single minute we can get.

The next time I stop Tre, it's just before two. The security truck is back again, and he's halfway through the sixth column. We take a seat on the concrete floor, and Tre offers me a bottle of water.

"Thanks." I take a sip and then pass it back to him. He's long since removed his ski mask, and his face is smudged with dirt and flecks of steel dust. There's a sharp contrast of clean skin around his eyes, nose, and mouth from the safety goggles and mask he's been wearing. "You'll probably be finished cutting the beams before three, right?"

Tre nods.

"Okay, once you finish, you can keep an eye on the road, and I'll rig up the last of the explosives. By the time I'm done, it should be close to three. As soon as the truck is gone, start bringing the vehicles in, and I'll get the detonation cord set up outside. Bring in as many vehicles as you can before three-forty. After that, we'll bring the building down on whatever is inside. Everything else, we'll just have to leave."

"Alright," Tre agrees.

Not having someone watching the road constantly is risky, but not as risky as waiting until five-thirty in the morning to blow up the building.

When the truck leaves, Tre immediately returns to sawing through the I-beams, and I impatiently shift my weight from foot to foot. I want to tell him to hurry, but I know he's going as fast as he can.

It's two-forty-five when he finishes, and I begin putting the remaining charges in place, running at a forty-five degree angle through the squares Tre cut in the center crosspiece of the beams, abutting the outside crosspieces.

When the charges blow, they'll cut the beams at an angle that should lead to the second floor falling directly on top of the first and bringing the others with it. It's not how actual building demolition would be performed—a fact my dad mentioned no less than a dozen times as we were working through the plan—but it'll be so damaged they'll have no choice but to clear the site and start over.

It should delay them by almost a year.

Tre grabs my arm, startling me from my thoughts, and I don't jump, but I definitely flinch. He notices and quickly lets go, saying, "He's back," with a pained expression marring his face.

We stand in the deepest shadows of the building, waiting for Eddie to drive past on his security sweep, and Tre continues darting glances at me throughout the process. He looks like he wants to say something, but there's no time, and I don't want to hear it. As soon as the truck is out of sight, I return to setting up the last of the charges, and Tre leaves the building. A few minutes later, an engine rumbles to life, and then a minute after that, a little tractor—a skid steer, Tre said it was called—comes in.

By the time I'm standing in the tree line with the detonating cord in my hands, Tre has moved over a dozen small construction vehicles into the building. The cloud cover dissipated during the time we spent inside, and moonlight is bouncing off his hair as he walks across the site to join me.

"Are you ready?" I ask when he reaches me.

He grins. "Hell yes. Let's do it."

I set the cord down, pull a lighter from my pocket as I kneel, and hold the flame to it. We're over a thousand feet away from the site, and we both track the flame as it races up the cord.

"Hell yes," I whisper—echoing Tre's words—when the charges go off and the center of the building sinks in on itself in a groaning cacophony. The smile on Tre's face matches mine. "Let's get out of here."

Chapter 14
Got the Last Word
on the Street

TRE

"Let's get out of here," Fiona says, joy lighting her eyes behind the mask as she turns to her bike.

I sling my backpack over my shoulders and grab my own bike.

"Mask on, Tre," she reminds me before I can take off. "We're not done yet. We still can't let our guard down."

I don't bother replying. I simply dig my ski mask out of my pocket and pull it over my head. As desperately as I want to apologize to her, even I recognize that standing near the building we just destroyed isn't the time or place. "It's still dark. Let's stick to the original plan. I'll follow you," I tell her.

She nods and leads us back through the woods faster than when we arrived. We fly down the trail, powered by adrenaline and a strong desire not to go to prison. It's dangerous in the dark, but Fiona's no longer carrying a condominium's worth of explosives, so I have to trust that she's managing her pace while watching for obstacles. I focus on following where she goes and not falling behind.

I still can't believe she biked up Bridal Mountain with a heavy pack in the middle of the night. I'm breathing hard keeping up with her on this much flatter trail.

I guess I shouldn't be surprised she's so fit. Look at those legs. As dawn lightens the sky, I can make out more details, and the muscles under those tight pants are rippling. *No, damn it. Focus before you crash and break your neck.*

As the miles wear on, the elation of success fades, replaced by sheer determination to get clear before sunrise. When this ride ends, I may never get another chance to apologize to Fiona in private. I mentally rehearse the best I can, but my attention remains focused on the ride.

Eventually, she slows to a halt, making as much space as possible for me on the dirt path. Through the trees to our right, I can make out the gravel parking lot of the trailhead. The forest keeps most of the dawn light out, but past this tree line we'll be fully visible. Not many people should be in this remote area at five on Saturday morning, but there's no reason to risk being seen.

"Alright, we're here," Fiona says. She's breathing hard, but not the way I'm huffing and puffing. I shift my focus from her chest as it rises and falls and meet her gaze. Her eyes still have a fierce gleam, and she's all business. "We're a bit behind schedule, but we should stick to our planned exits."

"Fiona, before—" I try to interject, but she keeps talking right over me.

"I'll ride out first and take the road east two miles so I can turn down the county road back to town. Wait here at least five minutes before coming out and taking the south trail."

"Listen, Fiona. There's something I want—"

"You did a good job out there tonight, even if it was slow. You'll wait here, like we agreed, right? We need separation."

"Yes, of course. Before you go, I have to talk to you about—"

"We're already late, Tre. It's getting lighter by the minute. No time to talk. If we need to do this again, I'll contact you when the coast is clear. Remember, we're back to business as usual in town. You hate me, I hate you. No one knows anything about us," Fiona explains, then shifts her weight to start pedaling.

"I'm sorry about your mom!" I blurt out.

Fiona freezes, her entire body rigid.

Shit, not like that. Idiot! Too late now, get it all out there.

"I'm sorry for saying such mean things after she died. I was an idiot back then and—"

She turns to glare at me. I immediately stop talking and lean away.

"Don't you ever talk about my mother," she demands, ice coating every word. Then she launches forward and rides around the bend, through the gravel parking lot, and out of sight.

My stomach plummets as I realize I should've just left it alone. I could've found another time.

Fuck. If only she'd let me get a word in. If I could have explained… How the hell do I fix this?

THE BELL ABOVE THE DOOR RINGS AN INSTANT BEFORE Ewan nearly shouts, "Holy shit, Tre! Tell me you know what's going on!"

I turn from the coffee maker, having just started a fresh pot, to see him rush up to the counter. "Hey."

"We just got back from a weekend trip and heard about Hay Creek! What's the word? Fill me in."

I force my face to remain neutral as I scan the restaurant. At three on Monday afternoon, it's nearly empty. Sandy is wiping down a table against the back wall. The sole customer is a middle-aged man with a crew cut sitting at a corner booth on his laptop, sipping the coffee I've been refilling for the past couple of hours—Connor, from Portland, he told me earlier.

Kyle walks in and takes a seat on a stool next to Ewan, who's still standing.

"Well, it's all anybody's talking about today. Hey Kyle," I say.

"Hey," he replies, flipping his sandy brown hair out of his eyes.

"Yeah? So what the hell happened?" Ewan presses.

"The only thing anyone really knows is probably what you've already heard. There was an incident out at the condo development on Saturday. They say the main building was blown up, but all the construction guys tell me it wasn't even done being built, so I don't know how that works."

"They didn't see who did it? I thought they had security after the gondola thing."

I shrug, but my eyes dart to a car parked down the street. The Henley and Montank suit is sitting behind the wheel of a nondescript sedan with out-of-state plates, making no effort to hide the fact that he's watching the diner.

"There were security guards, but they must not have seen anything. Everyone keeps spouting stupid theories about who's behind it, but if anyone actually knew, we'd all have heard by now."

"That's it? This is probably the biggest thing that's happened around here in our lives and all you know is something took place on Saturday? I thought this was gossip central!"

Connor is watching us now. Sandy carries two glasses of water to the counter, and Ewan finally sits.

"Hey, all I know is what people tell me, and it sounds like they don't know shit. It only just happened. If you really want, you can try asking some of the deputies. They've been in and out of here getting coffee and takeout all day."

Kyle raises one eyebrow at that, but continues staring at Connor, who returns his focus to his computer.

"You know him?" Kyle asks.

"Not really. We just met today. Connor's in town from Portland for work."

Kyle snorts and looks at me skeptically.

"What? We talked earlier. He's been here long enough he could probably tell you as much about Hay Creek as I can."

"It's Monday afternoon."

"Huh," I murmur. "Hey Connor, these are my friends, Ewan and Kyle. I was just mentioning you're in town for work, but when we were talking earlier, I was so busy telling you about the good places to stay, I think I talked right over you. What was it you do again?"

"Nothing exciting."

Ewan chimes in, "I assume you're not with Henley and Montank, or you'd be at their sites rather than hanging out in here."

Connor gives a thin smile. "No, I don't work for them. I'm a technical specialist. I do chemical analysis, material tracing, things like that."

"Isn't that what you went to school for, Tre?" Ewan asks.

"No, nothing that advanced."

I return my attention to the newcomer. "I don't mean to pry, but you've got me curious. We don't have too many big companies in the area that would bring people in from out of town. Are you with the lumber mill or the factory over in Green Valley?"

"Actually, I work in the public sector."

"You're a fed," Kyle states flatly.

"That's one way to put it. I work for the Bureau of Alcohol, Tobacco, Firearms and Explosives."

Chills run down my spine.

Ewan perks up. "Why the hell am I wasting my time asking this guy, then? You have to know *everything*. Since it's all rumor going around, fill us in on the facts."

"I'm sorry. I can't comment on an ongoing investigation."

"If you're in town to investigate, why are you here?" I raise my hands to indicate the diner.

"I was informed that this is what your friend called 'gossip central.'" He smiles again. "You don't mind if I work here for a while, do you?"

"No. That's fine," I say, forcing myself to sound unbothered. I turn back to Ewan and Kyle at the counter. "You guys actually ordering something or are you just here to talk?"

Kyle smirks. "Reuben, please. With fries."

"Cheeseburger and fries for me," Ewan says, and I turn to start making their food. "We came all the way downtown to find out what we missed, and we struck out twice."

Chapter 15
Get Your Rocks Off Kilter

FIONA

IT'S SIX-TWENTY WHEN I PULL INTO THE DRIVEWAY BEHIND my dad's station wagon, and the dark, nondescript sedan that's been following me for the past few blocks parks at the curb. A white guy with short light brown hair gets out of the car at the same time I get out of my truck, and my heart rate increases noticeably.

"Can I help you?" I ask when his eyes land on me.

"I'm looking for Thomas Carson," he says, giving me a once-over.

Shit. "And you are?"

"Special Agent Connor Smith. I'm with the Bureau of Alcohol, Tobacco, Firearms and Explosives." He reaches into his pocket and pulls out a badge.

I raise my eyebrows. "And you want to talk to my dad because…?"

"Just some routine questions."

I fight to keep from rolling my eyes as I say, "Well, come on then."

He trails behind me, and I unlock the door. Hopefully, my dad's not in the basement. There's nothing in the house, but still. A sixty-year-old white man, alone in the basement with a soldering iron in a small town in the mountains? Special Agent Connor Smith will take one look at him and think: Ted Kaczynski.

Fuck.

"Hey dad," I call out as soon as the door cracks open. "The ATF is here to talk to you."

The TV pauses, and I breathe a sigh of relief. My dad stands up from the couch as I step into the house, and then his hand is extending toward Connor as I move out of the way.

"Thomas Carson?"

"Just Tom," my dad says like it's any other Tuesday and there's nothing to be concerned about. I wish I felt half as calm.

"Okay," he replies with a nod. "I'm Special Agent Connor Smith with the Bureau of Alcohol, Tobacco, Firearms and Explosives."

"Let me guess. This visit is about the 'explosives' part."

"Yup. Your name came up on a shortlist of people in town who would have the requisite knowledge to build an explosive device similar to the ones that were used on Bridal Mountain last month and at the Hay Creek site this past weekend."

"Sure," my dad agrees. "Me and a couple dozen other guys who worked for White Construction over the years. Can't do much around here if you can't clear rock."

Connor nods. "Because of that, I have a couple of questions."

"I'm not going to be much help, but go ahead," my dad says, inclining his head toward a chair as he takes a seat on the couch.

I meander toward the kitchen, as if I don't have a care in the world, and then I stand there listening.

"Where were you Friday night into Saturday morning?"

"I was at a poker game at my buddy Kenny's place. It got late, and I ended up crashing on his couch."

"That would be Kenny Meltzer?" Connor asks.

"Yeah. Me, Kenny, and a few other guys were there most of the night. We try to get together for a card game at the end of every month. Good way to keep in touch," my dad replies.

There's a long stretch of silence. "Any ideas about who could've been behind the attacks?"

"No, not really. No one in town is happy about what's been happening, but I also can't see anyone blowing stuff up over it either."

"Alright. Thanks for your time." The floorboards creak, and then there are footsteps followed by the sound of the door opening and closing, and the lock slotting into place.

I wait a minute before stepping out of the kitchen. "Tess's dad?" I ask.

"He needed an alibi too. Got the whole crew together," my dad tells me, grinning. "Connor Smith is going to have a helluva time finding a suspect."

"FILL ME IN ON WHAT'S GOING ON," CATH SAYS AS SOON AS her seat belt buckle clicks.

"With what?" I ask. Tess, Cath and I are all crammed into the back of Kelly's SUV. Kelly is driving and Ewan is riding shotgun. Between the five of us and our camping and climbing gear, space is tight, but driving out to the Gorge together is half the fun.

"The bombing at Hay Creek! I was gone for work for two weeks. I only just got back into town last night, and I need to know everything!" Cath demands, her pale blue eyes wide.

"An ATF agent came to talk to my dad about it earlier this week," Tess says.

"Yeah, mine too," I supply. "I guess they're talking to anyone with the right know-how, which means they must not have any idea who did it."

"Connor?" Ewan probes.

"How do you know his name?" I ask, confused. This is the first time I've seen Ewan this week, and I doubt my dad would've mentioned Connor's name even if he'd bothered to tell Ewan about the visit.

"He was at Betty's when Kyle and I stopped in earlier this week."

Fucking Tre, I fume, crossing my arms. He didn't say anything about an ATF agent snooping around. Not that I've been in for coffee since he ambushed me with his 'apology' after Hay Creek. I've been avoiding him like my life depends on it. But still. He could've found a way to let me know.

"Did you get his number, Ewan?" Kelly asks with a teasing note in her voice.

"Nah, Kell. You know how those out-of-town guys are," my twin replies with a smirk. "Always too eager to get back to the city."

I roll my eyes. "What was he doing at Betty's?"

"Investigating, I guess." Ewan shrugs. "According to him, he heard the place was a good spot to overhear the latest gossip."

Great, I think as the others resume discussing who could be behind the bombings. *Just fucking great.*

"Come on, Ewan!" I shout. "The next handhold is about two feet above your right hand. One big push."

We've been here since we all spilled out of Kelly's SUV yesterday afternoon. It's around six-thirty in the evening, and the sun is at my back, a fact I'm thankful for—otherwise I'd be burning my retinas, staring directly at it as I tried to watch Ewan's route up the wall.

"You got this, Ewan!" Cath screams from about two feet behind me.

"Jesus Christ, Cath," I complain without taking my eyes off Ewan. "I don't think they heard you in the next valley. You want to try it again? You haven't ruptured my eardrums yet."

"Shut up, Fi. He needs to move."

"Yeah. I know," I tell her. Then, calling up to Ewan, I say, "Switch your left hand to mantle the rock where it juts out and hook your heel on the lip next to your right hand."

"Sure. Let me just pull my leg behind my head while I'm at it!" Ewan shouts back. "You think I joined the circus while you were gone, sis?" His words immediately make me remember Eddie and his date—and the trailer and Tre.

I'm still pissed Tre didn't let me know about Connor the ATF agent being in town. And that he brought up my mom. It's like he believes he can say, *'Sorry, my bad,'* and I'll let it go. Like it absolves him of being a complete fucking asshole. The problem with that is that I'm great at holding grudges and terrible at forgiving people. Ewan forgives people too easily, and I don't forgive them at all. We'd both be better off if we could be a bit more like the other in that regard, but neither of us has ever been able to figure that out.

I think Tre actually meant it, though. He did seem like he'd take it back if he could. But he can't. And I know I should say, *'It's okay. I forgive you.'* But I can't. So we're at an impasse. Only every time I see him, I flash back to the trailer, and I think about kissing him. And I hate him and I hate myself for wanting him and for not being able to figure out how to let it go. *Because if he's half as good in bed as he is at...*

Nope. Not doing that.

"See if I try to help, then!" I yell.

I need to get laid. But there aren't exactly a lot of options here at the moment unless Cath, Tess, or Kelly have switched teams since high school, and I'm pretty sure they haven't. We are right next to the river though, and I've seen several groups of kayakers and rafters go by. Maybe I'll get lucky and a group will stop here for the night. Then I can find someone to have a one-night stand with, and hopefully that will get Tre out of my head. I'm sure the only reason I keep reliving that moment with him is because he's the only person I've made out with in months.

Ewan pulls his left hand from the wall long enough to give me the finger, and I laugh. When he puts it back, his palm is flat against the rock and his fingers are pointed downward to give him leverage to push off. He ignores my advice about the heel-hook though, and jumps for the next hold. His fingers brush against it, and for a second it looks like he might have it. Then he's falling.

I lock the rope down as I hurtle into the air. The force of Ewan's fall, combined with the extra weight he has on me, pulls me up and toward the wall before the opposing forces equalize and my feet hit the ground again as he dangles above me. He only fell about twenty feet.

"You gonna try again?" I shout up at him.

"No. Let me down. My forearms are shot."

"You've been spending too much time on the water," I tease when his feet touch the earth.

"Yeah, well, I'd like to see how well you do rafting," Ewan mutters, glancing toward the river. "You can come talk to me after I have to fish you out of the water."

"You almost had it, Ewan!" Cath says, her red hair glowing in the sunlight as she claps him on the shoulder. "I bet you'll get it if you try again tomorrow."

"Thanks, Cath. Fiona, this is what encouragement looks like, in case you were wondering."

"Whatever. At least I caught your heavy ass. We all know you'd let me float a quarter of a mile down the river before you pulled me out. If I were clumsy enough to fall out of the raft, you'd tell me it was my fault. Hell, you'd probably spout some bullshit about how the universe obviously thought I needed to cool off, or something."

Ewan laughs, and I look over to where Tess is belaying Kelly. Kelly's climbing a 5.14b and making it look easier than I could ever dream of. Even forty feet up in the air, I can see the muscles in her forearms rippling under her dark skin.

I wasn't really sure I made the right decision moving back to Kalomish, but these granite cliffs next to the river beat the facades of downtown Seattle any day of the week, and especially on a holiday weekend with friends.

Another few minutes go by, and Kelly tops out. "Hell yeah, Kelly! You're a badass," I shout as Cath and Ewan cheer her on.

"Ready to lower," Kelly yells.

"Lowering," Tess responds at the same volume. More quietly she remarks, "Kelly's incredible. I can't even look at something this technical without feeling like I have no chance of making it to the first bolt."

"You and me both," I say.

"You could totally send The Old Man's Beard, Fiona!" Kelly comments as her feet hit the ground, having heard our conversation.

"Please, Kelly. I haven't done anything that technical in years. There's no way."

"It's not that hard—"

"Says the pro-climber," Cath quips.

"It's not! I swear. I think they got the rating wrong," Kelly says, and I begin laughing. "Seriously, Fi. Try it. Prove me wrong!"

"Ugh," I grumble. Kelly knows exactly which buttons to push. That's the problem with being friends with someone since you were eight.

"You were giving me shit for being out of shape. Put your money where your mouth is, sis," Ewan dares.

"Fine. Who's belaying?"

"I'll do it," Kelly volunteers.

"Alright," I agree as she unties herself and pulls the rope down. She passes it to me as she sets up, and I tie in. "On belay?" I ask a minute later.

"Belay on."

"Climbing," I say, going through the ritual.

"Climb on."

Kelly spots me as I make my way toward the first bolt. It's just out of arm's reach and takes a couple of moves before I can clip into it. As soon as I do, her feet scuff over the ground as she moves back and begins feeding out rope. I make it to the second bolt without too much trouble.

The rock bites into my fingertips as I pause to look for the next move, but everything within reach appears as smooth as glass. "Where the hell do I go from here?"

"Move your left hand up," Kelly says. "There's a small seam about two feet above where you are now. Then smear off the wall with your left foot. Use that for leverage as you go for the crack with your right hand. It's kind of jammy. Then your right toe will go where your right hand is now."

"Are you kidding? If I fuck that up, I'm going to break a finger!"

"You can do it!" Cath yells encouragingly at the same time Ewan shouts, "Don't fuck it up, then!"

"I thought you said it wasn't that technical!"

"It's not. Just go for it," Kelly replies.

"Just go for it," I mimic sarcastically. Kelly has no idea how good she is. Still, I put my left hand where she said. The seam she mentioned is more of an idea than an actual feature of the rock face. I take a deep breath, then surge upward, jamming my first three fingers into the crack, feeling the granite scrape against my skin, and pressing down hard as my right foot finds the spot my hand was crimping. "It worked! It fucking worked!" I cry.

"Told you!" Kelly says above a chorus of shouts from the others.

I reach into the chalk bag at my waist. From here, the next couple of moves should be pretty easy. After that, I guess I'll do whatever Kelly tells me.

As I reach for the next hold, someone says, "Ewan? What are you doing here?"

My stomach lurches, and I almost miss it. My heart is thundering in my chest as I firm up my position and then glance down. Shit! I was hoping I'd imagined it. But I didn't.

It's Tre. Tre's *here*.

"What the fuck, Ewan?" I roar. "I'm going to fucking kill you!"

"You gotta make it to the top first, sis," Ewan yells back, sounding incredibly pleased with himself.

Chapter 16
No Rest for the Wicked Game

TRE

"It's going to be sunset soon. How much longer to camp? I'm starving."

"Just around the bend," Kyle answers, steering us through a long, peaceful stretch of river as we slowly paddle.

"Oh, come on, Kyle. Don't give us that tourist crap," Cade demands. "I'm surprised you can't hear my stomach echoing off the cliffs."

I point ahead, up in the sky. "Hey, look at that!"

"That's not camp. I don't see anything."

"Oh, you just missed it. That was the last fuck anyone gave about how hungry you are."

Cade's paddle slaps the river loudly a split second before a stream of water sprays me.

I grin and continue paddling. "I'll tell you what. You set up my tent for me when we hit camp, and I'll start making dinner right away. I'll even make sure you get the first plate if you put my tent as far from yours as possible."

"What, my stomach was so noisy it kept you up last night?"

"You definitely kept me up half the night, but it wasn't either of your stomachs." I smirk at Cade and Jordan.

Lucas and Cade both laugh while Jordan blushes, saying, "Sorry."

As we paddle around the next bend, Kyle announces, "There it is."

We steer out of the slow-moving channel in the center of the river to a pebbly beach on the right bank. It gently slopes up to a sandy clearing above the high-water mark, leading to a thin tree line. We won't be alone tonight. There are a handful of climbers illuminated against the cliffs by the late afternoon light.

Once the raft is close enough to the bank, Lucas and I hop out to pull it ashore. The hip-deep cold water is refreshing in the summer heat.

We set about unloading the gear onto the beach and then move the raft above the waterline. Kyle helps me set up the camp kitchen while the others allocate our individual gear to tent spots they're choosing at the edge of the tree line.

I'm about to grab some food from the coolers when I hear a voice shouting from the cliffs that sounds strangely familiar.

Wait… climbers? No, there's no way. I rush across the beach to the cliff wall. The group of climbers comes into sight as they erupt into cheers. Apparently, somebody up there is impressive.

Holy shit, that is him, I think an instant before asking, "Ewan? What are you doing here?"

He's standing at the base of the cliff with three women who look vaguely familiar, and his head whips around at my question. *If Ewan's here, then where's—*

"What the fuck, Ewan? I'm going to fucking kill you!" comes roaring down from the cliff above, which seconds ago was the source of celebration.

Ewan has the most annoying shit-eating grin on his face as he yells back, "You gotta make it to the top first, sis."

My stomach drops through my feet. I look up and my head spins. I'm not sure if it's from the sudden shift in perspective or the anxiety strangling my heart. I haven't seen her since I screwed things up, and now she's *here?*

Fiona calls down, "Oh, you think so?"

"Yeah!"

"Ready to lower!" Fiona sounds even more furious, if that's possible.

"Lowering," the Black woman holding the rope calls out.

"What? Kelly, no!" Ewan hisses.

"When the climber wants to come down, you let them down, Ewan," the woman says. "You know the rules."

My vision clears, and I see *that* ass lowering toward us. Thin athletic shorts that reach halfway down her muscular thighs are pulled taut against her skin by the climbing harness. The straps of the harness seem designed to highlight each ass cheek as she sits into it, making her descent. Muscles in her back and shoulders I've only imagined are visible as she gets closer.

"Hey. Hey, numb nuts!" Ewan shakes my shoulder. "Let's go."

"Huh?" I eloquently interrogate.

"Hurry up before she gets down here."

I follow him as he races to the beach. "What the hell's going on, man?"

"Look, I told you before, if you two spent some time together, you'd get over fighting with each other. You'd probably be friends. But that wasn't happening since you're both stubborn dickheads, which sucks for me because that means I have to listen to both of you complain about the other. When they asked me to join their trip, I saw a way to force you to hang out."

"You planned our rafting trip, so you knew what campsites we'd stop at," I realize.

"Yeah. And then I made sure her group decided to climb these routes today, and here you are."

"I take it she didn't know either?"

"Of course not. She'd probably rather have canceled the trip than spend an entire night around you. But that's the point, Tre. If you just be normal you and not the you who constantly argues with Fiona, this shit'll end, and neither of you will hassle me anymore."

We reach the camp kitchen, and the other guys are off in the trees with the tents. *The tents... Okay, I can work with this*, I think. "Alright, man. We're all on vacation, so let's just have a good time. But this is a fucked-up way for you to go about this, so your penance is to set up my tent for me. I have to cook for everybody, and I need to get started while there's enough light. Have your group come join us."

"They're making you cook on your vacation from cooking?" Ewan asks.

"I was outvoted, so yeah, that's what's happening, and I need you to set up my tent. When you get over there, tell Cade I said 'new deal.' You handle mine, but show him where Fiona's is because Cade has to put his next to hers."

"Why would—"

"Just do it. If you want us to spend time together, then that's the deal." I stare straight into his eyes.

"Alright, whatever," Ewan replies and walks off toward the trees.

I PULL MY CAMP SHOES ON AND STEP OUT OF MY TENT, zipping it closed before walking into the woods. When I've gone far enough that I won't unintentionally attract any wild animals, I unzip my fly and take a leak on the nearest tree.

Now that I'm free from that immediate need, my mind replays dinner, desperately searching for any sign of interest from Fiona. The situation is hopeless.

Angry chittering interrupts my thoughts, and I look up into the boughs above me. In the fading dusk light, I can make out the bushy tail of a Douglas squirrel.

"Oh hey, little guy. Is this your home? Sorry, I'm just about done," I tell it.

The noise continues, its tail twitching.

"Fine, fine. I'll leave your tree alone," I reply, giving myself a couple of shakes and then zipping up. I glance around, but there's nothing to serve as a seat, so I walk to the next closest tree and sit against the base. The chirruping dies down.

I look up into the branches where I last saw the squirrel, struggling to make it out in the growing darkness. "What do you think, little guy? How do I handle things? Fiona was pissed when she left after…"

I don't finish but take a moment to look around for anyone who might overhear, which is absurd. There's no one out here. "She's kept away from me since then. She hasn't even been getting coffee. I don't want to be that prick who hurt her in high school, but if she's avoiding me, what can I do? The whole time I was cooking, I only saw her as she walked to her tent, and she still looked pissed. She didn't come close enough to get dinner. She just had one of her friends pick up her plate. They sat on a couple of rocks with no room for anyone else, so I couldn't even eat near her."

I pick up a small stick and begin breaking off sections.

"I want to make things right, but I can't. And I can't get her out of my head, either."

The squirrel chitters at me from its low branch.

"Talk to her while she's angry? Yeah, I guess that's what I'll have to do. Thanks, buddy."

The chittering continues as I stand and walk back to my tent.

"You totally did! I swear I thought Kyle was strangling a cat, you were screeching so loud, Cade," I say.

"Yeah, and you looked like a drowned rat when we hauled your ass back in," Jordan adds with a smirk.

"Whatever. I'd like to see how cool you are tumbling through a rapid," Cade mutters good-naturedly.

"We'd have to actually fall out first," Lucas rumbles without even turning to look at him, and we all burst out laughing.

Next to Lucas on the log, Kyle leans forward to poke the wood in the campfire, sending a wave of sparks flying up with the smoke.

"That's like this one." Tess nods her head at Cath, on her left. "Try giving tips to your climber with this banshee shrieking 'You can do it!' in your ear."

"Yeah, Tess, you were helping Kelly so much up there. She'd be lost without your tips," Ewan says with more than a hint of sarcasm in his voice.

"Fi knows what I'm talking about. You had her help and still couldn't top out. Isn't that right, Fi?"

"Yeah," Fiona replies tersely.

"Excuse me for trying to be encouraging," Cath answers in mock-indignation.

"I prefer telling people they're screwing up when they screw up," Fiona says, but she's staring hard at Ewan, not Cath. Nobody quite knows how to respond to that, and we sit in an awkward silence. Fiona glances around after a moment, then excuses herself with a clipped, "I forgot something in my bag. I'll be back."

The fire crackles amid the lack of conversation. I drain the last of my beer and get things started again. "So, Kelly, I take it you're pretty good, then?"

"Well, I've done the routes around here a bunch, so I'm kind of used to them," she deflects.

"Please. Knock that off, Kell," Tess says. "She was actually a pro climber for a while…"

As the chatter picks back up, I quietly stand to make my own exit, but Ewan notices. "Here, Tre, I've got more in this cooler."

"Uh, no thanks, man. Bathroom break." I raise my eyebrows and incline my head in the direction his sister went.

As I stride off, Cade calls after me, "Try not to get eaten by any bears!"

I walk a short distance through the trees before turning in the direction Fiona headed, deliberately making noise as I walk. As jumpy as she is, she wouldn't appreciate thinking I snuck up on her in the dark.

The long zip of a tent flap comes from slightly ahead and to the right. My pulse is pounding in my neck as the nerves kick in. *Don't be stupid this time. Don't fuck this up again.* I make my way in that direction, softly calling out, "Fiona?"

"Yeah, I'll be there in a minute. You can go back," she answers from the darkness. The light from the campfire is merely a suggestion of color on the trees behind me at this point.

"It's me. It's Tre. I'm, uh, not asking you to go back. I wanted to talk to you in private, actually."

"Oh, *now* you want to talk, but you didn't bother to tell me an ATF agent was in town? At Betty's!"

"When would I have told you? The only way we can communicate is through notes, and you didn't come in for coffee all week."

"Fine. Whatever."

"I would've told you if I could, but I didn't know how. But that's not what I want to talk about."

"I thought I made it clear already. We can't be together. We can't be seen together, I mean." Her voice sounds closer now.

"Well, nobody is seeing us here. And everyone is hanging out tonight, so even if any of them notice, it won't matter."

"Look around, Tre. Does it seem like I want to talk right now?" Fiona snaps.

"Yeah, I get that. How about I talk and you just be there? And, so you know, you hadn't made anything clear about why you've had a problem with me." I hasten to add, "But I did find out from Ewan, and I get it. I wanted to talk to you ever since, but there was never an opportunity. I had hoped to apologize last weekend, after... But we were in such a rush that I couldn't, and it came out all wrong, and I'm sorry."

I pause, expecting her to yell at me, but the woods are silent. If my eyes hadn't adjusted to the dappled starlight filtering through the trees enough to let me make out her silhouette a few feet away, I'd be afraid she'd left.

"Fiona, I'm sorry for the awful things I said after your mom died. It was mean and cruel, and I was an idiot."

"Oh, well it's all better now."

"I realize 'sorry' doesn't actually fix anything, especially after it's hurt for this long. I wish apologizing wouldn't open an old wound, but until Ewan explained, I had no idea. I completely forgot I ever said anything, much less something so terrible. I guess that probably makes it worse…"

"You really have a high opinion of yourself if you think I've thought about you at all before six months ago."

I expected she'd lash out, so I ignore the jab and continue. "I've spent the last decade trying to be the opposite of that asshole and to not be like my family, which is where I think I got that from in the first place. Actually, it doesn't matter where I heard it. I never should have repeated it, and I definitely don't think it's true. I'm certain it's not true, I mean. Shit. Look, I'm not dumb enough to believe we can take back the words we've said. There's no starting over."

"If we could go back, your stupid words wouldn't be anywhere close to what I'd change," Fiona says softly, voice full of emotion.

"I get why you're always mad at me. If I were you, I'd still hate me too. I'm not asking you to forgive me. I just need you to know that I'm sorry for being so cruel and stupid. I wish I had never said it. I understand if you can't be my friend, and I'll leave it alone from now on."

I don't know what else to say, so I fall silent. After a few moments, a stick cracks under her feet as she steps closer.

"What did Ewan say after he told you what we heard? Since you two are such annoyingly close friends."

"Well, I was shocked at first, and I apologized. But he said he knew I wasn't like that anymore, and that's why he was trying to get you and me to be friends. I didn't think of it in the moment, but since then I've kinda been disappointed in Ewan."

"You're disappointed he forgave you?" She's close enough now that I can see the shock on her face matches the incredulous tone of her voice.

"Not that he forgave me last month. I'm disappointed he let me off the hook *before* I ever apologized. I'd sure as hell hold a grudge in his place. I still hold grudges against my family."

Fiona scoffs. "Yeah, I told him pretty much the same thing."

I pause long enough to be sure she's done, then I grin. "So, you talk to your brother about me?"

"Oh my god. You're such an ass."

I don't hear the same angry edge to her voice now. That might even have been amusement. "You've always said I was a Dick," I tease. I can't make out her gorgeous eyes in the darkness, but I'm certain she just rolled them.

More seriously, I ask, "Do you think we might be able to become friends?" I reach for her right hand with my left, clasping my fingers around hers. Amazingly, she steps slightly closer. Progress. "We've worked well together, we obviously have some shared interests, and it felt like we even had a connection once."

I take a small step. There are only a few inches separating us when I lean forward, and my mind is swirling. Half of me is dying to kiss her again the way I've imagined so many times, half of me is worried about driving her further away, and half of me is waiting to get slapped in the face.

Our lips touch, and I'm not sure who closed the final gap between us. Conscious thought falls away. Heat rises in my face, and then in my dick. Fiona kisses me back, and I run hot all over. I drop her hand and slide mine across her back. The other is already in her hair. I want to hold her so tightly that this kiss can't end. The pressure in my dick is so strong that it flexes rhythmically, trapped in my pants. She presses her hips against mine, making me groan against her mouth.

I start to raise her shirt, but suddenly she presses a hand to my chest, breaking the kiss and stepping back. The abrupt end leaves me breathing heavily, and the aching throb of tension with no release is back between my legs.

"I don't know what to feel about you, Tre. But I do know we're not doing this. And I'm not doing anything with you out here."

I growl in frustration, but I'm unwilling to jeopardize whatever happened here by pushing for more. "Alright. Well, I meant what I said. I'm so sorry. If you want to talk, my tent is the red one at the end. If not, hopefully I'll see you at breakfast. Everybody knows I make some mean eggs."

I turn to leave, but she says, "You cook for other people every day, and you're still cooking for everyone on vacation? Why?"

I simply shrug. "We all do what we can."

Chapter 17
Suck and Blow Off Some Steam

FIONA

I watch Tre walk away from me, his silhouette growing less and less distinct until he's nothing more than a smudge that vanishes from sight.

"What the fuck are you doing, Fiona?" I murmur to the night, hoping it will have a clue, because I definitely don't. Tre's an asshole, and yet… I keep kissing him. Or letting him kiss me. I'm not even sure who started that. I'm also not entirely sure why I broke it off. Part of me says that maybe I should just sleep with him and get it out of my system. Then I remember sixteen-year-old Tre telling his friends that my mom hated her family so much she deliberately drove her car off a mountain.

Sure. He apologized, but that doesn't negate the fact that he said it in the first place. At least I'm trying to tell myself it doesn't, but more and more it feels like I should let it go and accept that he's changed. That he's a different person. But I don't know if I truly believe it, or if I only *want* to believe it because of the way my stupid hormones react whenever he's within five feet of me. It's like every nerve ending in my body lights up, and all I can think about is touching him or having him touch me. I'm not sure I've ever wanted to sleep with someone as much as I want to sleep with Tre. The only problem is that I can't say for certain if I *actually* want him or if I only think I do because it's been so long since I've slept with anyone.

I stalk back to the fire, growing more and more frustrated with every step. *I don't owe Tre anything. We've kissed exactly twice. Nothing more than that. It doesn't mean anything,* I tell myself. *I can sleep with anyone I want. And maybe if I do, it'll help me figure out if I want Tre, or if I just want someone to fuck me so hard I can't think about anything else for a few minutes.*

"Want a beer, Fi?" Cath asks when I return and take a seat next to Kyle.

Tre is already there, but I can't with him right now. Or with Ewan. I hope my twin gets crabs. It would serve him right for being such an ass. Even if he means well, he needs to learn to mind his own business. I have no idea if he's trying to get Tre and me to be friends so that the three of us can sit around the campfire making s'mores and singing *Kumbaya* together, or if this is him playing matchmaker. Both options seem possible, and I didn't ask for either.

"Sure," I agree, extending my hand to take the can she passes over. The outside is wet, and I hold it away from myself as I open it so that it doesn't drip onto me. I take a swig and focus my attention on Kyle. The other guys are all Ewan's and Tre's friends. They're traitors by association. Kyle's neutral, though. He's just here covering for Ewan. "How do you like being a rafting guide?"

"It's fine," Kyle says with a slight shrug of his broad shoulders.

"Kyle's not a big talker," Cade tells me.

"Maybe he just doesn't like the company," I snark. A smile tugs at Kyle's lips. Cade laughs good-naturedly, and everyone but Ewan and Tre joins in. "What do you do in the off season?" I ask, refocusing on Kyle.

"Ski tours."

I wait for more, but Kyle says nothing.

"God. He wasn't lying about you not being a big talker."

Kyle's grin spreads a little wider.

"Fiona, come help me with the fireworks," Tess says, pulling my attention away from Kyle.

Despite my best efforts, I wasn't able to talk Tess out of bringing them, and I briefly consider telling her no. I don't want to light off fireworks and pretend I'm having a good time—I don't want to light them off, period—but I don't need to let my bad mood pour over onto everyone else.

The only person here who's actually at fault is my brother. *Tre didn't orchestrate this*, I realize. *This is all Ewan.* I briefly reconsider my plan to get Kyle to spend the night in my tent. I could simply take Tre up on his invitation—because it was *clearly* an invitation: *'The red one at the end.'* But if I do that, I'll never know if it's because I want *him* or if I just want *someone*, and I *need* to know. If I sleep with him without being sure, I'll hate myself forever.

"Fine," I agree as she grabs my hand and tugs me to my feet. I could use a second to think about things anyway.

"We'll get them and meet you guys down at the beach," she tells the group as she pulls me away. "What's going on with you?" she asks as soon as we're out of earshot.

"Nothing."

"You want to try again? You're pissed at Ewan, Tre is looking at you with big giant puppy-dog eyes, but you're refusing to acknowledge him and flirting with Kyle instead! And don't think I didn't notice Tre following you into the woods."

"Ugh. Did everyone notice?"

"I don't know. No one said anything, if that's what you're asking. So what's up?"

I chew on my lip, trying to decide how to answer the question, but Tess already knows just about every bad decision I've ever made, so what's one more? "I kissed him a few weeks ago. And then he kissed me. Just now, in the woods."

"I thought you hated him?"

"I do. I did. I don't know." The frustration in my voice is palpable.

"Ah. Was it good?"

"I don't know," I hedge.

"So it was good, and you're pissed that it was good. Got it."

"It's not… It's just… Listen. I haven't been with anyone since I came back here, and I think I'm just desperate."

"Does Ewan know? About you and Tre?"

"I don't know. Maybe. *I* haven't told him, but I have no idea what Tre has said to him."

"Mmm," Tess murmurs. "And now you want to use Kyle to figure out if you have feelings for Tre?"

"I mean, if he's willing, yeah. Pretty much. Terrible idea?"

"Let me ask you something?"

"Okay."

"Do you think Tre has feelings for you?"

I open my mouth to say, *'I don't know,'* but before I can, I realize that's not true. "Yeah," I admit. And admitting that means I've got to acknowledge that his apology is probably sincere.

"Let's say you sleep with Kyle and then you realize you do have feelings for Tre. How do you imagine that's going to go over?"

I remember our conversation on the way out to Hay Creek and Tre asking about Jacob and me dating in high school. "Not great," I admit softly. "You're saying you don't think I should do it?"

"No. Given that you've spent most of your life hating him, it's probably not the *best* idea to jump straight into bed with him. All I'm saying is that maybe you should be a little less obvious."

"How the hell am I supposed to do that?" I ask as we near the fireworks stacked opposite the tents, next to the base of the cliff where we piled them yesterday.

"I don't know. Wait until everyone is distracted by the fireworks and then ask Kyle to meet you at your tent later? Maybe no one will notice."

"Uh huh. Sure."

"Well, it's better than what you were doing!"

"I wasn't doing anything yet!"

"Uh huh. Sure," Tess echoes my words, not bothering to hide her disbelief.

"Fine, oh wise one. I'll take your advice."

"Good. Let's go back," she says, her arms full. I consider trying to talk her out of lighting them off one last time, especially since the ATF is lurking around and I'm pretty sure setting off fireworks isn't exactly legal where we're camping. But this is the first time in years it's been rainy enough that there are no fire bans in effect and they can set them off without worrying about burning down half the state.

Fifteen minutes later, I'm standing on the beach, staring up at the sky as colored streamers float down and the scent of gunpowder infuses the air. Tre also complained when they lit the first one, but he shut up after Cade called him a killjoy.

Kyle is a few feet away, on the outskirts of the group, and I edge toward him, letting my shoulder bump against his.

He glances toward me, his eyes finding mine when the next boom lights up the sky. His eyebrows are raised in silent question, and I decide to cut to the chase. "Any chance you might be in the mood for some company tonight?"

"Sure," he replies monosyllabically. Cade wasn't kidding.

"Okay. I'm in the blue Nemo tent. Meet me there in twenty minutes?"

"Alright."

I nod and move away, stopping briefly to talk to Tess. When the next firework explosion diverts everyone's attention to the sky, I turn and walk toward the campsites, hoping my departure will go unremarked upon.

TWENTY MINUTES LATER, I'M SITTING ON THE FLOOR OF MY tent, with the mesh door zipped shut, but the privacy door open, waiting for Kyle to appear. I've already dug through my pack to find the box of condoms I always keep in it, and thankfully they're not expired, since I have no idea if Kyle bothered bringing any on an all-guys rafting trip. I'll need to swap them out in a couple of months though, and I'm putting a reminder into my phone when someone clears their throat. I look up to find Kyle standing outside my tent.

"Come in," I say as I finish typing the reminder.

He steps into the tent, zipping the privacy door shut as I climb to my feet and extend a hand for him to take, tugging him toward me when he does. He crosses the space, looping his free arm around my waist as I bring my mouth to his, and I'm definitely not upset that he's not much of a talker. I release his hand and slide mine into his hair, pressing myself against him harder, deepening our kiss, stroking my tongue across his hungrily, telling myself that this is exactly what I need. A quick and simple one-night stand to blow off some steam so I can forget about Tre, and how good kissing him feels, and—*what the hell am I doing thinking about Tre right now?*

I bring my mind back to the present. To the here and now. To Kyle, whose hands have slid under my shirt. The calluses on his palms are rough against my skin as they skim over my ribs. I arch into him as he moves to pull my shirt off, releasing my grip on his hair, which isn't as soft as Tre's, I notice distractedly as I lift my arms. Once my shirt is off, Kyle strips off his own, tossing it on the floor.

I pull our bodies back together, and the skin of his chest is warm against mine. I move one hand to his ass as I drop the other to stroke him through the front of his pants, and he groans. He's already hard and rocks his hips forward enthusiastically. His hands slide under my bra, cupping my boobs and…

There's nothing here. No heat. No thrill. No *desire*.

"Stop. Stop." I pull away and step back as Kyle's hands fall from my body. *Shit. I don't want just anyone.* The realization hits me hard. "Sorry. I can't do this. I thought I could, but… Fuck."

There's disappointment on Kyle's face as he asks, "Tre?"

"Goddamnit," I mutter. "Is it that obvious?"

Kyle shrugs as he bends down, reaching for his shirt and passing mine to me. "Probably not to most people, but I pay attention."

"I'm sorry," I repeat as I put my shirt on. "I thought I could… I thought maybe if I was with someone else…"

"Don't worry about it. It's fine." But it feels anything but fine as he says, "Have a good night," and turns to leave.

It's sometime after one in the morning, and I'm staring out the mesh top of my tent, looking at the stars, trying to contend with a new reality. A reality in which I can no longer deny I want Tre. And maybe for more than a single night. Kyle is an attractive guy, and I had my hand wrapped around his dick, and I felt *nothing*. Meanwhile, Tre looks at me, and my heart beats faster. He kisses me, and it's all I can do to remember to breathe. I'm not even sure I *like* him, but I can't deny I *want him*.

I feel like an ass for inviting Kyle to my tent and noping out on him the second things started to get real, which is stupid, and I *know* that it's stupid. It's only… ugh.

This trip is a disaster.

Goddamn Ewan. Fratricide is wrong, but I'll be damned if I haven't considered half a dozen ways to kill my brother since I've been lying here alone, regretting every decision I've ever made.

"More," someone moans loudly from the next tent.

"Like this?" another male voice questions teasingly.

I press my pillow over my face, but it doesn't drown out the moaning. Finally, I fling it away and shout, "Unless you want to invite me to participate in the fun, I'd suggest you shut the fuck up!"

"Oh, someone didn't get any," the voice—I recognize it as Cade now—calls back, leaving me considering the merits of homicide. *This is clear provocation. Surely a jury would see that?* I think as I grab my sleeping bag and storm back to the firepit.

The fire is out, and I set my sleeping bag down in front of the log I was sitting on earlier and lean against it. Tre's tent is about fifty yards in the distance. It's dark and quiet. I consider going over to it, but I don't. Instead, I simply sit before the burnt-out fire, sulking.

I jolt awake. The sun hasn't risen yet, but the sky is brighter. There's mist hanging in the air and dew coating the outside of my sleeping bag. I push myself upright, away from the log, rubbing the side of my neck where a crick has formed.

There's a loud bang, and I jump. *What the hell?* I wonder, looking around to find Tre standing in front of a cooler he just slammed shut or threw at the ground or whatever he did to wake the dead.

"Could you be a little louder?" I croak.

He mutters something under his breath. I can't quite make out the words, and it's too early for me to care.

"Is there any coffee?"

"No," he snaps.

"God. And I thought *I* wasn't a morning person," I grumble, grabbing my sleeping bag as I stand to walk to my tent. There's some instant coffee in my pack somewhere.

By the time I return, wearing clean clothes with a jar of instant coffee and a camp mug in hand, Tre has rebuilt the fire. There's a pot of water boiling above it. I dip my mug in, filling it, then dump in a generous amount of instant coffee. I stare at the mug dubiously and add in a little more before swirling it. I should've brought a spoon. Oh well. It's going to taste awful no matter what. Instant coffee always does.

"What're you doing?" I finally ask Tre. He's still standing in front of the cooler, only now the lid is open and he's staring into it.

"Nothing."

"You need any help with that nothing?" I inquire. Everyone else is still asleep. Or at least they haven't crawled out of their sleeping bags yet.

"No." Tre slams the lid on the cooler again, and Ewan comes staggering out of his tent.

"What's with all the banging?" Ewan groggily glances between me and Tre. Apparently Ewan and I are both lighter sleepers than everyone else.

"Dunno." I shrug.

"Is there any coffee?"

"Why does everyone keep asking me that?" Tre snarls.

"Here." I toss the jar to Ewan.

He catches it. "Thanks," he replies, coming to sit next to me as Tre stomps off. "What's his problem?"

"No clue. He's been like that since before I woke up. I just figured he wasn't a morning person." I blow on my coffee.

Ewan grunts noncommittally and then wanders off in search of a mug. As much as I'm not a morning person, my brother has more or less built his entire life around never needing to be awake before nine a.m. By the time Ewan returns with Lucas trailing him, Kelly and Cath are sitting next to me on the log.

Ewan looks at the pot of water, then at the jar of instant coffee in his hand, considering it for a moment before dumping the entire jar into the pot.

"Hey!" I complain.

"It's the last day, sis. You can get more," Ewan says as he swirls the pot and then dips his mug in.

Lucas does the same, takes a sip, and states, "This is awful." I nod as he takes another sip.

We're all quiet after that, but the birds get louder and louder until Tess, Jordan, Cade, and Kyle finally join us.

"Where's Tre?" Cade asks, looking at me like I'll know.

"No clue." It seems like I've been saying that since I woke up, and it's starting to annoy me.

Cade huffs in irritation, but it's not my job to keep track of Tre. I ignore him, and eventually he leaves. When he does, I get up and start poking through the cooler. There are eggs and cheese and not much else.

Tre said something last night about making eggs for breakfast, but clearly that's not going to happen, so I grab the nearby bowl and begin cracking them into it. Even I can make scrambled eggs.

Twenty minutes later, we're all sitting around eating when Cade returns with Tre.

"You used my eggs," Tre states flatly, glaring at me.

"Jesus fucking Christ," I snap. "What is your problem?"

Tre says nothing, so Cade answers for him. "His feelings are hurt because he thinks you and Kyle hooked up last night, and he's being a whiny little bitch about it."

Tre rounds on Cade as Ewan looks at me and bursts out laughing. His laugh quickly turns into a cough as he chokes on a bite of eggs. Serves him right.

"They didn't, by the way," Cade adds on.

"Shut the fuck up, Cade," I warn, feeling my face go hot. At the same time, Tre looks from Kyle to me and says, "You didn't?"

"It's none of your business who I hook up with," I tell Tre as I set my plate of eggs to the side. Everyone else has fallen silent, and their eyes are glued to me. I'd rather be anywhere but here.

"She didn't."

"Shut. Up. Cade," I warn again as Tre asks, "Why not?"

"What part of 'none of your business' do you not understand?" I bite out. Not only do I not want to have this conversation, but I especially don't want to have it right now, with everyone listening.

"Because—" Cade begins, and I realize I have no idea when he and Jordan went back to their tent. I have no idea what he overheard from my conversation with Kyle.

"Because I kept thinking about you, okay?" I cut Cade off, my eyes on Tre. "Because I kept wishing Kyle was you!" I turn to Cade. "Someone should hit you in the back of the head and then leave you face down in the river to drown!" I leave my half-eaten plate of eggs on the log and stomp back to my tent.

Chapter 18
Dazed and Confused as Ever

TRE

I watch Fiona stomp away, dumbstruck.

She was going to hook up with Kyle. But then she stopped? Because she wanted me? And she never came to see me? She didn't even want to tell me today. How is Fiona Carson the most infuriatingly frustrating person alive? How come I can't get her out of my mind?

I turn my back to the group and start packing the cooking gear. They can eat whatever Fiona made and live with it for the day.

"Hey wait," Cade calls. "I didn't get any breakfast yet."

I drop the cooler I'm holding and round on him. "You also didn't get any fucking brains!" I step forward and shove him back. "You knew what happened the whole time we talked and didn't say a damn word? You let me be pissed when you could have just told me she didn't hook up with him. But you *were* gonna tell me right here in front of everyone! What the hell is wrong with you, Cade? You wanted to embarrass her on purpose? You wanted to embarrass me? I thought we were friends!"

"Relax man. It was funny."

"Did Fiona seem like she thought it was funny? Do you think I'm having fun right now? Look around. Is anyone laughing? You can starve, asshole."

Jordan walks up behind Cade and puts a hand on his shoulder, pulling him away.

I return to slamming the kitchen equipment around until it's ready to be stowed in the raft. Everyone has finished their food and returned to their respective tents, or at least left the shared space. I take a few deep breaths. Cade was an asshole, but it's not truly him that has me worked up. I look toward Fiona's tent, but I can't see her. Ewan makes eye contact but doesn't walk over to talk. It's for the best. He engineered this get-together. I'll let Fiona take his head off.

I need to pack my gear, but I detour to Kyle on the way. He's stuffing his tent poles into their bag as I clear my throat. "Hey Kyle. I'm sorry about all that." I nod toward the campfire. "Fiona was right. What either of you do, or don't do, is none of my business. I shouldn't have flipped out like that."

"We're all good."

I nod and go break down my tent.

I'm the last to make it to the raft. It's halfway in the water with Kyle strapping everything in place. After I toss my gear in, Jordan elbows Cade, who pulls me aside.

"Look, Tre, I'm sorry about earlier. I shouldn't have treated it like a joke."

"Alright man, thanks. But in the future, not every single thing has to be a joke. If someone's already upset, you shouldn't try to humiliate them. That's across the line from funny."

"Yeah. I... yeah."

"Come on. Let's finish this trip," I say and walk back to the raft. We drag it fully into the river, where Kyle, Jordan, and Cade take their seats in the back. Lucas and I pull the raft until the water is mid-thigh, then join them.

Kyle gives the safety briefing for our final day while we paddle out to the channel to catch the current.

"... And we should reach the take-out landing around one o'clock, so we won't bother stopping today. It's about an hour and a half drive back to town, where we'll grab a late lunch."

"What?" Cade complains. "That's forever, Kyle! I didn't get any breakfast. We need to get some food."

The entire raft resounds with a chorus of, "Shut up!"

I GLANCE AT THE END OF THE COUNTER AGAIN. THE LAPTOP remains closed, and Connor is smiling neutrally at an older couple en route to a table who've stopped to inform him of who they *know* is behind the bombings.

I return my attention to the grill, pulling the next order. It's his. *A cheeseburger with hash browns. Interesting choice.*

Jackie swoops in to add a ticket to the rail, snatches up the waiting plates, and vanishes. At five-thirty on Monday, the dinner crowd is picking up.

When Connor's meal is ready, I carry it to him myself. Walt is grumbling something I can't make out as he vacates the seat next to Connor.

"I don't think you'll get much work done at this time of night," I tell him, nodding at his laptop.

"You're probably right. Safer to keep it with me than leave it in the car, though."

"You seem to be making a lot of friends."

He laughs. "I don't know what I get more of: hot tips about who's responsible or people trying to pry information out of me."

"Well, that's the trouble with being in gossip central," I reply, grinning. "You're part of it now. And we've never had an ATF agent in town before."

"Fair enough." He smiles ruefully. "But I've got to eat somewhere. I can't just order pizza every night."

Everyone's eyes are locked on us. When it's not their turn to talk to Special Agent Smith, they're intent on eavesdropping. "I guess you didn't take my advice to stay at Mrs. Larson's. She'd cook dinner for you."

"I wish, but I'd never get the bureau to approve my expense report for a bed-and-breakfast."

Hmm. Maybe he's not spying on me. Maybe he is just hungry. Kalomish isn't overburdened with restaurants, after all. Maybe I shouldn't be so paranoid.

"Well, good luck fending off the crowds," I say with a nod before heading back to the waiting orders.

"Yeah, thanks."

I CHECK MY WATCH AGAIN. IT'S EXACTLY NINE O'CLOCK. Closing time. No more excuses. Ewan has been hanging out at the counter for the last two hours trying to talk with me. It was easy to avoid this conversation initially, with the end of the dinner rush happening. As time passed and fewer people came in to eat, I've been running out of minor tasks I can use to pretend I'm busy.

It's Tuesday, and he's the only patron left at the counter where Sandy's completing her side work. When I step away from the grill, she's working closer to him than necessary. I imagine she's trying to hint that it's past time to leave, unaware that it's pointless, at least with him tonight. I resign myself to the inevitable and give her a break.

"Hey Sandy, if you take care of the front door, I'll finish up everything else and you can take off."

She pauses, looking at me quizzically. "The door? Aren't you gonna...?" She glances between me and the counter.

"Ewan's here for me."

"Oh. Well you could have said something, Tre." Sandy throws her hands up as she walks to the front door. She locks it and flips the signs while I wait for her at the back. Sandy says goodnight to Ewan and then goes to the small office to collect her purse and jacket.

"There's always someone who wants to hang around until closing," she tells me as she passes. I watch the parking lot until she's in her car and then close the door before returning to the counter where Ewan is still seated, sipping his coffee.

"Okay, you clearly want to talk. It's just us, so talk," I tell him.

"There he is! That's a lot more than the shrugs and monosyllabic answers I've been getting all night."

"Yeah, well, you cause problems and people get pissed at you. That's kind of how it works."

"Alright, fine. I am sorry that my Fourth of July plans led to so much drama. It *really* didn't go the way I thought it would."

"Yeah, no shit," I mutter. "So, if that wasn't what you intended, what was your goal?"

"I told you last weekend. I'm sick of being a proxy for you two fighting with each other."

"Yeah, you said. And I'm sure that's real, as far as it goes. That was a lot of plotting just to get us to stop bitching, though."

"You think I was trying to set you up with my sister?" Ewan scoffs. "My sister, who wouldn't even use your name because insulting you by calling you Dickie amused her? Why did she stop that, by the way?"

I grab a rag and start wiping the counter to buy some time. "I told you a few weeks ago I tried smoothing things over with her," I reply without looking up.

"That's true, you did. You were pretty weird about it, too."

"Just because I decided to make peace, it doesn't mean she has."

"Uh huh."

"I couldn't understand at the time why she kept getting angry no matter what I said. And after you explained, I wasn't able to talk to her again until that night at the campsite," I say, setting the rag down so I can marry two almost-empty ketchup bottles. I can't explain to Ewan that I did exactly that, and botched it, because I can't tell him anything that might lead to him finding out where we've been together.

"Ah, so I was right to set it all up. You're welcome." Ewan grins. "Wait, if I gave you everything you needed, why the hell are you angry at me?"

I close the lid of the ketchup bottle and toss the empty one before looking at him. He's not wrong. Things are screwed up between me and Fiona, and he made a convenient scapegoat, but the problems aren't his fault. "Fiona confuses me," I admit, "and this weekend made everything so much more jumbled up."

Ewan considers for a moment before asking, "Did something happen with you two? Weeks ago, I mean."

"No! You saw how angry she still was out there."

"Yeah, but I also heard what we all heard Sunday morning."

My face heats, and goosebumps rise on my forearms. "Like I said, very confusing. I really didn't expect that either."

His eyes narrow, but stay fixed on me. "But you were extremely upset that morning when you thought she boned Kyle. Like, 'threw a fit and stormed off' upset."

I move over to the still-hot grill and start scraping it clean.

"Then you ripped Cade a new one for embarrassing Fi." After a pause where I don't respond, Ewan asks, "Tre, do you have a thing for my sister?"

I continue scraping the cooktop—which by now is thoroughly clean—with my back to him.

"Holy shit!" Ewan shouts, then starts laughing.

I whip around, and he's doubled over, grasping the countertop to stay on his stool. "What the hell are you laughing at?" I grumble, sounding churlish even to myself.

Eventually, Ewan recovers enough to explain, "You two idiots—" He breaks into another fit of laughter. "Only you two could fail this hard at being so into each other."

He pauses to wipe away tears. "You spent years hating each other, but *somehow* you now magically want to hook up. Except instead of dating like normal people, you avoid each other and get mad at your friends about it." He cocks his head and looks into the middle distance. "Honestly, saying it that way *does* sound exactly like Fiona's type of ridiculousness."

Ewan drains the last of his coffee and sets the mug on the counter.

"Wow. Thanks. Real helpful."

"Seriously. Based on how you were tiptoeing around it that day when you asked me why she was so angry, you've been into Fi for a while. No wonder you tried to 'make peace.' Wait, that means you fell for her when she was still pissed at you. How did that happen?"

"We're not here to gossip about me. We're here because your stupid plan backfired so badly I have no idea what's going on," I say to redirect the conversation into safer waters. I need to empty and clean the coffeepot anyway, so I carry it to the counter and refill Ewan's mug. "I meant it when I told you I didn't expect her to say what she said about Kyle and me."

"Nah. No more bullshit, Tre. Don't treat me like an idiot." Ewan's voice is still mild, but there's an edge to it that says he's just this side of pissed. "As far as I knew, you two never even spoke. Yet you suddenly developed a crush on her and—out of the blue—tried to be friends, which, of course she rejected. But she stopped trash-talking you with no explanation. Only I couldn't leave well enough alone and forced you to be around each other, thinking it would help, and now she's pissed at both of us."

Ewan takes a sip of coffee. I'm scrambling for some kind of response, but he continues before I can come up with anything.

"You followed her into the woods, where you must've done or said something. And after that, she tried to hook up with the only random guy around, which made you super jealous even though you claim you've only talked to her twice. Then Cade tried his half-baked attempt at 'helping,' which forced her into admitting that she wants you. And for the record, she would've rather eaten glass than told everyone that. So what's going on between you and my sister?"

Fuck, I think, desperately trying to come up with a believable story. *I knew this conversation was going to go badly.* "Last month she started getting coffee here before work. Apparently, she had been getting it from the gas station the whole time she's been back, which is insane, but whatever. Between seeing her every day and you pushing me to talk to her, I figured I'd give it a shot. I've got enough to do with fighting Henley and Montank, right? I don't need to be fighting with her too.

"So I managed to meet with her in private a couple of times and realized I didn't have any good reason to hate her. I actually started to feel something for her and found myself thinking about her even when she wasn't around. You know how it goes. Plus—this feels weird to say to you, sorry—just look at her. Damn. She's gorgeous. Of course, she had a reason to hate me, so nothing really changed until last weekend. Now I'm all mixed up and have no idea what she thinks."

Ewan ignores my comments about how hot his sister is and asks, "Well, what happened when you left the campfire to find her?"

"I met her at her tent. She said she didn't want to talk, but I apologized for what I'd said back in high school. We talked for a bit after that, and I kissed her." Ewan's eyes widen, but he doesn't interrupt. "She seemed into it for a minute, then she broke it off and told me nothing was going to happen with us, and I came back. You know what happened from there.

"That's why I'm all twisted around, man. She and I are one way, then we're the opposite, but then we're something else. It's not even hot and cold. She goes in every direction with no warning, and I don't know what's real or what to expect. If she liked me so much, why push me away? If she wanted me instead of Kyle, why wouldn't she tell me that? And then, despite what she said, I haven't seen her since. Not even for coffee in the mornings," I finish venting and simply stand there, staring at Ewan, hoping for any shred of clarity.

"Yeah, I was surprised by everything that morning, including you, although it makes sense now. When Fi's talking to me again, I'll ask about you. See if I can find anything out."

"Oh, god. Things are already bad enough, don't turn this into teenage drama. And what do you mean when she's talking to you? She didn't talk the rest of Sunday?"

"Apart from yelling at me, no we didn't really chat. Oddly enough, she wasn't too happy, and she didn't particularly want to discuss what happened. It's fine. She'll get over it in a day or two. At least with me."

"Wonderful," I groan. "This didn't help *at all*, plus now I'm embarrassed all over again."

Ewan shrugs. "We're good now, right?"

I nod. "Yeah. I guess there's that."

"You doing anything the rest of the night?"

"I'll finish closing up here, then I'm down for whatever."

"Hang out at your apartment, grab a couple of beers, and stream the new Marvel movie?"

"Sounds good to me," I reply, moving to the next task on the closing list.

Chapter 19
Time of Your Life in the Fast Lane

"HEY SIS," EWAN SAYS, DROPPING INTO THE CHAIR NEXT TO mine.

I fold my arms across my chest and let out a huff.

"You can't be mad at me forever. I was only trying to help!"

"Help yourself, you mean," I mutter. "Besides, no one asked for your help, Ewan!" I snap, swiveling to face him.

"Fine. That's fair. I promise to stay out of your love life from here on out. Though I didn't know I was intruding on it. If you'd just told me…" Ewan trails off when he notices I'm trying to kill him with my eyes. Sadly, it's not working.

"I wasn't… Can we not discuss it *here*?" I gesture to the town hall as I turn back to the front of the room. It's still early, and it's only about halfway full, but I have no desire to talk about me and Tre in a room filled with people who would love nothing more than to over-hear some juicy gossip about the town's only doctor.

"Fine. But I talked to him yesterday," Ewan adds, a knowing look in his green eyes.

Part of me wants to ask what he said or if they talked about me. But that's stupid. What *else* would they have talked about? Another part wants to ask if he's going to be here tonight, but that would also be a stupid question. I know he will. He's at *every* town hall, and he'll be just as interested to hear the latest news as I am.

This is the first town hall since we blew up the condo development at Hay Creek a week and a half ago, and things have been surprisingly quiet, which makes me nervous. Of course, there was a lot of gossip, but surprisingly little official commentary. They're bound to make some kind of statement tonight. I'm surprised they haven't brought Tre in for questioning again. I guess they're being more cautious because of the lawyer his dad sent last time.

"You're not going to let this go, are you?" I ask.

"Nope."

"Fine. We can get a drink afterward."

"Good. What do you think they're going to say about the bombing?" Ewan questions.

"No clue. Why?" I ask as my eyes land on Special Agent Connor Smith, who's against the wall, near the dais, watching the room. He sees me and inclines his head.

"Well, they've got to be trying to catch whoever it is, right?" Ewan's gaze follows mine. "And the fact that no one seems to have heard anything about it—other than it's probably Tre—is weird. Most likely, they have no idea who's responsible."

I shrug. "I guess."

"It's got to be more than one person," Ewan murmurs, running a hand through his brown hair, thinking aloud.

"Why? What makes you say that?" I know he has no idea Tre and I are working together, but that doesn't change the fact that I'd like to know why he's decided it's more than one person.

"I'll tell you later," he comments softly, also still watching Connor.

"Whatever," I grumble. The room has been filling, but there's still no one on the dais. The city council loves to make a show of filing in right on the dot. I glance back to check if Tre is here yet, but he's not. He's usually one of the last to arrive. Probably because he has to close up the diner or whatever.

"Are you looking for him?"

"No."

"Uh huh."

"Whatever," I repeat as I return to ignoring him.

Several more minutes pass before the council members enter the room and take their seats. Jacob Nammier waits until the room falls silent, then says, "Good evening, everyone. I'm glad to see so many people here tonight." His eyes linger on the edges of the room, and I turn to look again.

The room is packed. This is easily the most people I've seen show up to a town hall since I've been back. I spot Tre in his usual place—leaning against the wall near the doors. He's wearing a black T-shirt and faded blue jeans, and his eyes are locked on me. I wrench my own eyes back to the front, annoyed that I want to keep staring at him.

"I'm sure many of you are here for an update on the situation with Henley and Montank."

There's a murmur of assent and lots of heads bobbing around the room.

"Are they packing up and leaving town?" Tre shouts from the back. I want to laugh, but I force my expression to remain neutral.

Jacob's eyes narrow at the interruption. "As always, we will have a question-and-answer session at the end of the night, and I request that all questions be held until then. Anyone interrupting tonight's events will be removed.

"To that end, we have the sheriff here with us. He'll be giving a briefing on the situation with the ecoterrorists."

I raise my hand, and Jacob sighs. "Yes, Dr. Carson?"

Every eye in the room is on me, including Special Agent Smith's, but I need to know where things stand. "Sorry, Councilman Nammier, I just want to clarify: this is being considered an act of ecoterrorism? Doesn't that seem a little extreme?"

"At this point, no. Both of Henley and Montank's active developments have been targeted and attacked. In both cases, high-powered explosives were used to destroy property on the sites. There is no other term that applies," he states, his dark eyes on me.

I say nothing and merely nod as if I agree with him.

"Now, I would like to invite Sheriff Morris to speak."

The sheriff lumbers up to the dais. He hasn't been in to see me during the almost seven months I've been back, and I don't know if he has a doctor outside of town or if he avoids doctors altogether, but he's out of shape and middle-aged enough that I wonder about his blood pressure and cholesterol levels.

Jacob hands Sheriff Morris a microphone. It feels like the perfect commentary on our current political system. "As you've all heard, there have been two bombings on Henley and Montank property recently. While there were no injuries to any persons, the damage to the sites was extensive, and I'm told the cost is in the millions of dollars."

"Don't they have insurance?" Tre calls out, being a general nuisance. On the one hand, it makes sense for him to act the way he always has, but on the other, I want to tell his dumb ass to shut up. He doesn't need to paint a bigger target on his back. Especially not with the ATF in the room.

"Yeah, why should we care? They're polluting the environment, and they're not even locals! Good riddance!" someone else shouts. It's a man I don't recognize who looks to be in his sixties.

The roar of people agreeing floods the room, and I look back to see Tre smirking. His eyes immediately meet mine. He really is an asshole. And an idiot.

"Deputies," Sheriff Morris says with a nod, and as with every other town hall, they move down the aisle toward Tre.

This will make seven. It's by far the fastest he's been thrown out.

Like everyone else, I turn to watch. He looks bored. And even though I no longer want to see them throw him on the floor and slap some handcuffs on him, I think *he* might want them to. It would be the ultimate *'Fuck you'* to his father. His father, who is notably absent. But then my dad's not here either.

I asked him if he was going to come, and he said, *'Why bother? They're going to do what they're going to do. You shout until you're blue in the face, and it won't make a bit of difference.'*

I'd say maybe Rich feels the same, but I doubt it. Chances are he figures that whatever they do to Kalomish, it won't affect him. He has enough money to isolate himself from it in the here and now, and he probably believes the long-term consequences don't matter, since he's already in his early-sixties. It's exactly the kind of apathy that lets terrible things go unchecked.

One of the deputies reaches out to grab Tre's shoulder, and Tre twists out from under his hand.

"How much are they paying you, Jacob? We all know you're selling our town to the highest bidder, so how much are they paying you?"

The second deputy grabs Tre and shoves him toward the door. As always, Tre has the good sense not to push it further than that. Even so, it's only a matter of time until he ends up in a jail cell. I'm an idiot for ever even considering getting involved with him. Unfortunately, I can't get the idea out of my head.

Once the door closes behind Tre and the deputies, the room's focus returns to the dais.

"As I was saying," Sheriff Morris continues, "the property damage is in the millions of dollars, and we're taking these incidents very seriously. We've put together a task force that is liaising with the Bureau of Alcohol, Tobacco, Firearms and Explosives, and we will find the responsible parties."

I raise my hand again to ask if they have any suspects, but the sheriff ignores me. I lower it after a couple of minutes despite wanting to interrupt him the same way Tre did. But I have a pro-development, pro-authority, good-girl, lady-doctor image to maintain, so I don't.

"In the meantime, I want to make it known that we will be providing additional security at the construction sites to stop any future events from occurring." His eyes scan the room as if he's hoping to see someone holding up an *'I did it! It was me!'* sign.

After a moment, he passes the microphone back to Jacob, who prattles on about how the construction is a boon to Kalomish and we should all be grateful for the improvements Henley and Montank have in store. Improvements like increasing conflicts with native fauna, which will result in a greater number of bears and mountain lions being killed because they're too close to resort sites that were recently wilderness. Or maybe he means improvements like the algae blooms that are certain to occur due to runoff from the nitrogen fertilizers they'll use on all the grass they'll inevitably plant. Algae blooms that will kill practically every living thing in the rivers, lakes, and streams.

If my dad were here and had any idea what was running through my head, he'd tell me I sound like Tre. Maybe he's right. Maybe Ewan is right, too. Maybe we have more in common than I've ever wanted to admit.

I'm looking for Tre—and trying to pretend I'm not— as Ewan and I walk into Malcolm's, but he's not here. I wonder if he's avoiding me. *Or,* I sigh to myself, *more likely, he's trying to give me space to decide if I want to see him. To talk to him.* I haven't been to Betty's since we got back from that stupid climbing trip.

"You're buying tonight," I tell Ewan. I normally pay because I make a lot more as a doctor than he does working as a rafting guide, but he owes me after last weekend.

"Yeah, fine. Okay," he agrees as we drop onto stools. The bar will be packed in a few minutes, but we snuck out of the town hall meeting early to beat the rush. As usual, my dad was right—by the end, there was a lot of shouting, and not a damn bit of difference being made. Most of the town seemed to be pro-ecoterrorism though, so that was something. By and large, none of us want Henley and Montank here.

"Hey Fi. Hey Ewan." Malcolm raps his knuckles on the highly polished bar.

"Hey Mal. It's going to be busy in a few. I've never seen a town hall so packed," I warn.

"Thanks for the heads up. What can I get you guys?"

"Bring us two of whatever you have on tap that will best serve as an apology to my sister. I'm paying tonight," Ewan tells him.

Malcolm's lips twitch upward as he glances between us. He doesn't comment, though. He simply moves away to fill two glasses.

"So. What's going on with you and Tre?"

"I thought you talked to him yesterday. Didn't he tell you?" I shoot back. I really don't want to explain my feelings for Tre to my twin. Mostly because I haven't been able to untangle them myself.

"Yeah, but I want to hear your perspective."

"It was never supposed to… *I* was never supposed to…"

Malcolm comes and sets two glasses in front of us and then moves away. Ewan raises his eyebrows as he takes a sip, waving at me to get on with it.

"I kissed him, Ewan, and everything went to shit."

"On the Fourth of July?"

"No. I mean yes, but before then, too."

"He neglected to mention that. How'd that happen? *When* did that happen?"

"I don't know. Not long before that day that you told me you'd told him about mom. And… he was there and… I don't know. I knew I'd fucked up almost as soon as I did it, but…"

"But now you keep thinking about him?" Ewan says, repeating my words from that morning near the campfire. Goddamn Cade.

"Yeah."

"So? What's wrong with that? Tre's a good guy."

I sigh. "You don't get it. You forgive everyone for everything. They don't even need to apologize to you! You just let shit go like you're the Buddha trying to attain Enlightenment or something," I grumble. "I'm not like that."

Ewan shrugs. "He apologized though, right? He said he did."

"Yeah."

"So what's the problem? You want him. He wants you. What more do you need?"

"I don't know if I can actually let it go. Every time I kiss him, I feel like I'm betraying mom."

"Oh god, Fiona," Ewan says with more than a hint of exasperation. "Get over it! Mom's dead, but if she weren't, she'd tell you the same thing. Tre was an asshole then, but he's not anymore. People *can* change. Maybe you should try it out yourself sometime."

"Like it's just that easy?" I grouse, finally taking a sip. It's slightly bitter. If beers had feelings, this one might be remorseful. It's a good choice for an apology beer.

Ewan shrugs again. "Try it, sis. I know you. You're so in your head about what you should or shouldn't do that you haven't bothered to actually find out."

"Whatever."

"Consider it at least."

"It's pretty much all I've *been* doing, Ewan," I complain. I *wish* I could get Tre out of my head, but I can't. I've been avoiding him the past couple of days, because how do I walk into the diner and order a coffee like I didn't tell all our closest friends that I want him so badly I was more or less fantasizing about him while I was with someone else before storming off to sulk about it? What do I even say? I don't really have anything to apologize for, but I feel the need to apologize all the same. It almost seems like one more way for Tre to get under my skin, even though I know it's not his fault.

"Anyway," I say, changing the subject. "What were you saying before in the town hall? About it being more than one person?"

"Oh. Yeah. That. Think about it. That condo building was massive. One person couldn't have done all the work for that in a single night. It'd take at least a couple of people to pull that off. Probably more. You know how long dad and his team always had to prep for those kinds of demolitions. It was never a single-day activity."

"Yeah, I guess. Have you heard any rumors about who it might've been?"

"Tons. Everything from Tre to an imaginary militia hiding out in the mountains to Bigfoot. You name it, someone has been running their mouth about it." Ewan takes a sip.

"What's the consensus?" I ask. I know Ewan hears a lot more gossip working on the river than I do in my office.

"It seems like an even split between Tre and the imaginary militia. I don't think either's right. Tre couldn't do it. I don't mean he wouldn't—I mean he *couldn't*. He doesn't know how. Plus, like I said, he definitely couldn't do it alone, and who would help him? And the militia idea... well, we'd know about them if they were close enough to bother doing something like that. They'd have to come into town for supplies, or we'd see them on the river or something. And the ATF would *absolutely* know about them, and I don't think they have any better idea about what's going on than anyone else does. So if you're asking who I think did it, I have no idea. Henley and Montank, maybe. Tre raised a good point back there about the insurance money. Maybe they're over-leveraged and blowing up their own development seemed like an easy out."

"Huh. Maybe." I file the idea away. It'd make for a good rumor if need be.

"I can't believe you lied to me," Ewan says after a moment of silence.

"What?" I ask, confused by the statement.

"That day when I told you that Tre asked why you hated him. I asked you what was going on with you two, and you stared straight at me and said, 'Nothing.'"

"Yeah. Well. I was embarrassed, okay?"

"You could've told me. If you had, I wouldn't have..." Ewan gestures vaguely.

"I know. It's just... It's Tre, Ewan."

"Are you going to give him a shot?"

"I don't know. Maybe," I say, and Ewan grins like I just said yes.

"Hey dad," I call when I walk into the house. The lights are on in the kitchen, so I head that way once I've kicked my shoes off.

"Hey Fi." He glances up from the steaks he's seasoning when I step into the kitchen. "What's the news?"

"No one knows anything. The ATF agent from last week was there, and they had the sheriff up to talk tonight. It was a lot of 'We'll catch whoever's responsible, mark my words' nonsense. Most people suspect Tre, but I guess after Rich sent the lawyer down last time the sheriff tried to talk to him, they're being careful."

"Mmm," my dad grunts. "They came to talk to me this afternoon. Brought Special Agent Smith with them."

"Oh yeah? How'd that go?"

"They asked about where I was again. The fact that I have an alibi annoyed them. It seems like you're right. They have no real suspects, so they're just circling around anyone with the right skills, hoping to get lucky. They asked to look around the house." His blue eyes meet mine.

"Did you let them?"

"Sure. I've got nothing to hide," my dad says with a smirk, and it's true that there's nothing in the house that could tie either of us to the explosives used at Henley and Montank's construction sites.

I nod. "Ewan was telling me he thinks it's more than one person because one person couldn't have—" I bite my tongue, realizing what I said a second too late.

"Because one person couldn't have done Hay Creek in a single night," he finishes for me.

Shit, I think, my stomach sinking as I lean against the wall. "Yeah," I mumble.

"He's right. So how'd you do it?" My dad's eyes are locked on me, the steaks forgotten.

I feel like I'm fifteen again, and I got caught sneaking back into the house after curfew. "I'm really efficient. You know I've got great time management skills," I reply, lying through my teeth.

"Fiona."

"Fine. I had help."

"From?" he interrogates, still staring me down.

"Someone who doesn't know about you, so you don't need to know about them."

"Fiona."

"No, it's better if neither of you knows about the other."

"Are Henley and Montank leaving then?" He folds his arms across his chest.

"I don't know. Probably not."

"Then at some point, you're going to want me to build you another bomb, which I won't do unless you tell me who the hell is helping you."

I sigh and close my eyes. I should've just gone straight to my room. Hell. Maybe I *should* get my own place. I try to decide what to say, but he's right, and if I can't trust him, I can't trust anyone.

I take a deep breath and exhale it as I say, "Tre."

"Tre? You're joking."

"No. He saw me at Bridal Mountain. He was there doing something similar, and… he demanded we pool our efforts. He kind of had me over a barrel, dad. So we planned Hay Creek together."

"Goddamnit, Fiona!" he growls, bringing his hand down on the island with a loud thud.

"It's fine, dad. It's not a big deal."

"You don't think he'll rat you out if push comes to shove?" he demands, still sounding angry.

"No. Actually, I don't. He has just as much to lose."

"He'll cut a deal, and he'll sell you out. He's already their prime suspect!"

"He won't," I state, feeling surer than I have any right to.

My dad rolls his eyes and goes back to his steaks, ignoring me.

"I guess we're done talking then?" I ask, but he says nothing.

Yeah, definitely time to find my own place, I think as I leave the room.

Chapter 20
Well-Kept Secret Meetings

TRE

THE BELL ABOVE THE DOOR JINGLES, AND I GLANCE OVER. *Hell yes! She's here today*, I realize, struggling to suppress a smile. I close the register as Kevin leaves with his morning coffee, walking past Fiona out to his squad car, and turn to face her. I catch myself staring and raise my gaze to her eyes. She sets her to-go mug on the counter without a word, so I ask, "Just the coffee today?"

"Yup."

I hate having to play out this farce of being enemies, never able to have a genuine conversation. Even though we wouldn't have deep discussions in the diner, these visits have been my only interactions with Fiona over the past week and a half—nine days, but who's counting?—and everything between us is confusing. She hasn't even come in every morning.

On a few of the days, her nurse has come in with several orders. I've tried talking to Nurse Machado, but I'd have better rapport with a doorknob. I've never met someone so aloof. She did nod once, though, the first day she tasted her coffee fresh. I guess that's something.

When I pass back the filled mug, Fiona has already placed three singles on the counter. "Here you go." I leave my fingers lingering a few moments too long, hoping for any response. No such luck. She collects her mug and heads back outside to start her day.

The whole camping experience left me beyond confused. I don't know if she's avoiding me because she doesn't want to be around me, because she's equally confused about our situation, or if she's interested but disciplined enough not to show it in public. I'd love for the latter to be true, but if it were, she's clever enough to have secretly contacted me.

While I work through the breakfast crowd, I try to figure out how to talk to Fiona in private, in a way that won't piss her off further or make our situation more confusing. Since it would only be about us, personally, and not our sabotage, I could use Ewan as an intermediary. His interference set up this mess, so she'd probably be angry about including him, but she seems angry now. I'm not sure if that would make things worse for me, and if it makes her angrier at him, well, that's his problem.

Where should we meet? I ponder when Jeremy comes over from a four-top of his coworkers and puts in an order of burger meals to go. "You guys got a new construction project lined up?" I inquire.

"Actually, we're back at Bridal Mountain. They repaired the damage and we're prepping to lay the foundation for the gondola buildings."

"Wow, that's fast. To tell you the truth, I was hoping with all this trouble, they'd decide to cut their losses and leave Kalomish alone."

"Yeah, Tre. But you know how it is. We gotta take work where we can get it," Jeremy replies.

"Oh, I don't have a problem with you guys, J. You know that. You're trying to make a living, like the rest of us. I just wish Henley and Montank would leave the town alone."

"Eh, I wouldn't bet on that. They brought in some bigwigs last week. If anything, they're doubling down."

"Bigwigs?"

"Yeah, some high-up corporate bosses from New York. I heard they flew them out over the Fourth of July and set them up in those big empty houses in your dad's Highland Estates. The foreman and project manager aren't making a move without those two new people telling them to."

"Wow." I shake my head. "Well, I'd better get your lunches ready. You don't need me making you late with all that management around."

Shit, shit, shit! My mind is racing. After the breakfast rush clears out and I'm left with time to focus, I settle on the fact that Fiona needs to know about this. If there is anything to be done, we should handle it together.

I check the movie theater's schedule and lock in my plan to meet with Fiona. I'll pass her a note with her coffee tomorrow saying, *'Problem w/H&M, movie theater 8 PM, sit in back.'* It's not the shortest message, but without a good reason she'll never show. I can't go to her dad's house, and as strained as things have been between us, I doubt she'd want to come to my place. But I can quietly fill her in on what I've learned at the late show on a weekday. It'll be dark, and most likely we'll be the only people there.

If she doesn't get coffee tomorrow, I'll try for the next day—it would be Thursday, so it would still work. A Friday or Saturday night would be too busy, though, and I'd have to come up with a new approach. But I bet she'll come in at least once before then.

"HERE YOU GO, LITTLE GUY," I SAY, TOSSING A PINCHED-OFF piece of my burger bun toward the squirrel watching me. It lands in the grass halfway between us, but that's enough to scare him. His tail flicks up as he spins around, sprinting to the tree he climbed down a minute ago.

Wow, those grey squirrels are fast, I think as I watch, trying to hold still enough for him to risk coming back for the bread.

I've been sitting at the picnic table in Humboldt Park for the past half hour. I finished my shift at two and brought a burger and fries with me for lunch. Since it's midafternoon on a Wednesday, I don't have too many options for getting out into nature—starting a hike this late means making the return descent in the dark, which is always a bad idea. So I settled for walking over to the park. Afterward, I'll probably ride my bike along some of the back roads. I've been working on my stamina since Hay Creek. Letting people see me ride it regularly could help alleviate suspicion if anyone connects me to the morning Fiona and I took out the condo building.

"You're okay, buddy." I try tossing him a fry.

After about thirty seconds of tail twitching from the side of the tree, he sprints down but stops in the grass partway to the fry. The squirrel pauses and looks around—checking that nothing is rushing in to eat him—then sprints to the relative safety of the base of his tree.

"Yeah, I feel you, buddy. I have no idea what to do either. I know what I want, and she's right there, but I can't go after her. She doesn't want me to, even though she wants me. She doesn't even come to Betty's as much, but I don't know how to interpret that. Now there's this new situation with Henley and Montank. Hopefully she'll want to be involved, at least."

The grey tail twitches, and the squirrel chitters at me.

"I'm not going anywhere, little guy. If you want the food, you'll just have to risk it."

We stare at each other in silence for a few moments.

"What should I do? Keep trying to connect with her through all of this…" I wave my hand, "chaos? Or do I leave it alone?"

A furry grey blur streaks to the fry and back to the base of the tree. He pauses to look around again, then disappears up the trunk.

"Hmm. Go for it, huh? Thanks, little buddy. You know, you're a lot better at advice than the Douglas ones," I say.

It's Thursday night, a quarter to eight, and I'm seated in a corner of the back row of the movie theater. I've been here for the past ten minutes, eating popcorn and watching the same dumb ads cycle across the screen while waiting for Fiona.

The theater goes dark at exactly eight, and some trailer plays. My stomach sinks. *She's not coming. Does she think this is too risky? Is she so mad that she doesn't consider a problem with Henley and Montank worth meeting me?* I wonder as the seconds tick by.

Oh, there she is.

She pauses at the bottom of the stairs, looking around the dark room, then walks up to the opposite corner of the back row. Careful as always. I've been keeping watch for nearly thirty minutes, which makes me certain there are no other moviegoers, but I scan the theater again anyway before moving to the seat next to Fiona.

When she says nothing, I lean close enough to be heard in a whisper over the booming audio. "Thank you for coming. I wasn't sure you would."

I'm facing forward as if I'm watching the screen, but I feel the warmth of her arm pressed against mine from leaning in so closely. This is the first time I've touched Fiona since we kissed in the woods on the Fourth of July. A tingle begins at the base of my neck, then runs up and down my spine.

"I don't want to be seen together here. You said there was a problem?" she replies, also speaking low.

"We're alone. I've kept watch. I didn't have any other way to contact you, and I assumed you wouldn't want to come to my place again."

She sighs. I appreciate the sight of her deep breathing in silhouette, but she repeats, "The problem, Tre?"

"Yeah, I found out they've restarted construction up at Bridal Mountain, which isn't surprising. We always knew that was likely. But they're doing things differently now because they've sent some corporate execs to oversee and micromanage the developments out here. We were hoping to drive them away, but they're more invested than ever."

"Do you know how many people they sent?"

"Two senior people, as far as I know. I haven't heard of additional staff either way, but those two are the ones running the show. They've supposedly taken over every part of the developments."

"Do you know how long they'll be here?"

"No, no idea. I'd guess they're planning on staying a while, because they're staying in some of the empty houses in that gated country club my dad built."

Fiona doesn't ask follow-up questions, and I settle back into my seat. I've had two days to think this over, so I'll wait and give her as much time as she needs.

"We have two options."

I turn my head to stare at her. *What was that, five seconds? And she already has plans? Incredible.*

"One is we stop and settle for what we've done. Henley and Montank are sending a message about their commitment to the projects. They're reinvesting, changing their procedures, and they have to be increasing security as part of that. There's no way they haven't already done so. We won't have the same access we had, and the risk has gone up," she continues, looking forward and leaning into my shoulder this time.

My skin warms at the contact—and how effortlessly intimate it feels—while my chest tightens from the dread of losing my link to Fiona.

"And what's the other?"

She finally turns to look me in the eye. "We send a message back and make them understand they're not welcome here."

I grin in the darkness, and the pressure in my chest eases. "You know I'm in."

Fiona slightly waves her hand. "This was decent for meeting without raising suspicion, but we can't plan here. Can we use your apartment tonight?"

My place? She wants to come to my place? "Yeah, of course." *Oh shit, I didn't clean up.*

"Fine, let's meet back there. We need to leave separately and maintain distance, just like Hay Creek. You go first. Pretend to use the bathroom, then go to your car and head home. I'll sit here for a few more minutes and follow. When I buzz the door, be ready to let me in right away. The longer I stand outside, the more likely it is someone will notice."

"Yeah, sure. Okay, I'll see you there in a few," I tell her, my thoughts swirling. *Holy shit, she's coming to my apartment. I was worried she wouldn't even show, and now we're going to spend all night planning together at my place.*

Chapter 21
Humid Nights
and Weekends

FIONA

I DON'T KNOW WHAT I'M DOING. WHEN TRE TOLD ME THAT two Henley and Montank executives had come to town to personally oversee the development projects, I should've shrugged and said, *'Oh well, not my problem,'* and gone home. Instead, I suggested we go back to his place. Which is stupid.

I don't know what I'm doing, except that last night Ewan accused me of sulking and Kelly and Tess agreed with him. According to Ewan, being around me lately has been practically unbearable. I kicked his stool out from under him and told him he could pay for his own drinks for the rest of the night. And this morning, when Tre handed my mug back with a receipt wrapped around it, I was interested in something beyond replaying the events of that morning at the campsite on an endless loop for the first time in days. *'Remember, remember the fifth of July'* isn't nearly as catchy as the original, but I can't stop doing it.

I don't know what I'm doing, beyond seriously considering hooking up with Tre, which is stupid for *every* conceivable reason. First, there's the fact that it's Tre. I've spent most of my life hating him. I'm not sure we have anything in common besides wanting to run Henley and Montank out of Kalomish. And wanting to jump each other's bones. Because yeah, I want Tre, but it's obvious he wants me too. You don't wake up an entire campsite because you're jealous someone else might've gotten laid for any other reason.

I wish he were anyone else. It would make this so simple. But after inviting Kyle to my tent and then backing out because I couldn't stop thinking about Tre, there's no more pretending I just want to get laid and any willing participant will do. I want Tre, and I want him for all the reasons I shouldn't.

I want him because he's willing to cause a scene at every town hall, and then still go out to Henley and Montank's construction site in the middle of the night even though he'd be the obvious suspect. I want him because when he caught me with a bomb, he didn't run away or rat me out. He decided to insert himself into my life and demanded we work together. I want him because despite seeming like a happy-go-lucky asshole who walks around the world expecting everyone to be his new best friend, he's surprisingly intelligent and thoughtful underneath all that. I want him because he could've turned into a carbon copy of his father and grown up to be the same prick he was in high school, and somehow he didn't. I want him because whenever I kiss him, my brain shuts off and I stop thinking about all the other things I should be doing instead.

And I can't have him. At least not until I figure out how to get over my own shit. Otherwise, I'll just screw things up.

I sigh as I get out of my truck and walk up the street, through the humid night air, to the door that leads to Tre's apartment, looking around for anyone who might be watching it. I don't see anyone, but that does nothing to put me at ease because I *know* Tre is still their prime suspect, even if it seems like the ATF has been talking to everyone *but* him. Sheriff Morris thought he was responsible for Bridal Mountain. There's no way the sheriff didn't point Special Agent Connor Smith straight at Tre the second he rolled into town. There's no way the sheriff doesn't believe he also had something to do with Hay Creek.

I press the buzzer for number three, and the door immediately unlocks. Walking up the polished wooden stairs to Tre's apartment has me feeling jittery for reasons totally unconnected to the investigation. Last time I was here, I didn't care what he thought of me, and I didn't want anything to do with him. Now, I do care, and I want a lot to do with him, but—

His door is already open, and he's standing in it waiting for me by the time I reach his landing. In the movie theater, he was just a shadowy figure. Here, though, it's hard to ignore how attractive he is.

"Hey," I say as he steps out of the entry so I can walk through.

The door shuts softly behind me as I look around his apartment. It looks a little more lived-in than it did when I was here before. Apparently, he doesn't keep it looking like it's ready for a magazine shoot all the time. He cleaned last time because he knew I was coming over, and he wanted to impress me. Or stop me from making snide comments about his housekeeping skills—probably both. I wouldn't have if he were anyone else, but he's not, and I most likely would have. Maybe I'm more of an asshole than he is.

"I should apologize," I begin as I turn to look at him. His eyes seem like they're a darker grey than normal, and he looks uneasy too.

"No, you were right," Tre says, but I continue talking.

"I'm sorry for everything that happened at the campsite. For kissing you, and then inviting Kyle back to my tent. I didn't expect you to be there, and I was mad at Ewan, and I was trying to figure out my feelings, and… I didn't mean for you to get caught in the crossfire."

"No. You were right, Fiona. It's none of my business who you hook up with. I'd like it to be, but it's not. And Cade was an asshole. I was too, for that matter."

I nod. "Thanks."

"So did you?"

"Did I what?"

"Figure out your feelings?"

"Not really. Sorry."

"Let me know when you do?" Tre suggests.

"Yeah, sure," I agree. "So anyway, about the new guys being here. I have an idea. Can I sit down?" I incline my head toward the caramel-colored leather couch.

"Oh yeah. Sure. Sorry. Make yourself at home. Do you want something to drink?"

"Sure," I say, mostly because it seems like Tre wants me to. He's already heading for the kitchen.

"I've got—"

"Whatever you're having is fine," I tell him. I really don't need to listen to him list off every beverage in his fridge.

He returns carrying two bottles of cider, handing me one. I try to ignore the way it feels when his tanned fingers brush against mine. Then they're gone, and he's sitting down in the chair across from me. "What's your idea? Because I've been thinking about it, and the cement will still be a problem for them at Bridal Mountain, but they haven't started the new resort site at Talulish Falls yet, and they haven't finished cleaning up the mess we made at Hay Creek."

"I know. You and your dad don't get along, right?"

Tre snorts. "No. I have as little to do with him as I possibly can. He doesn't like me any more than I like him."

"Why?" I ask, finally curious enough to want to know what's behind their mutual animosity. I couldn't imagine cutting my dad out of my life. He's still pissed that Tre is involved—and has told me as much again and again. Letting that information slip was definitely a mistake. Just one more to add to the list. Not that he wouldn't have figured it out on his own and demanded answers eventually. But still. It makes me wonder if I didn't subconsciously repeat what Ewan said *because* I wanted to talk about Tre with someone who's… neutral. And the second my dad said Tre couldn't be trusted, the first thing I did was defend him and say he's nothing like his father.

"You've met him," Tre states, as if that explains everything.

"Yeah, but he's always been an asshole, and you didn't always hate him, so something must've happened."

Tre sighs. "Do you really want to know?"

"Have you ever heard me ask a question simply to be polite, Tre?" I take a sip of the cider in front of me. It's not bad. There's no label on it, and if I ask about it, he'll most likely tell me something about the orchard where the apples were harvested, but I don't care, so I don't ask.

He laughs. "No, I guess not. I told you I went to Northwestern and majored in materials science. I actually double majored in that and construction management because it was what my dad wanted.

There was an expectation that I would come back and take over the family business. Not because I had any real desire to run White Construction Incorporated, but because it was what my dad wanted. I had no idea what the hell I wanted to do, but I had the grades to get into both programs, so I went along with it. I usually did back then. Trying to argue wasn't worth it. He always ended up getting what he wanted."

"You know you take the most roundabout way possible to get to the point?" I question mildly, and Tre grins.

"Believe it or not, most people understand things better with context, Fiona. Just because you can make the jump between disparate pieces of information, it doesn't mean everyone can. Anyway, when I graduated from college and came back here, I did what I was supposed to and started taking a more active role in the business. That lasted until I started dating Dominique—Nikki—Johnson."

"Okay. Should I know who that is?"

"Probably not. She worked in the billing department at White Construction for a while. She moved to Kalomish for the job. She doesn't live here anymore."

"He didn't like you dating someone who worked for the company?"

"No. That wasn't the problem. He didn't like me dating someone who was Black. He fired her. Not for that reason, since that would've been grounds for a lawsuit. But that was definitely the real reason behind it all. She broke up with me and left town after that, and I haven't had anything to do with my dad since then.

"Before college, I never realized what he was like, but then being away and coming back… It was hard not to see it. And once I did, I couldn't stay there and be another yes-man. My grandma never liked my dad, so when I cut ties with him, she offered me a job at the diner. Then when she died, she left it, and the rest of the building, to me, so here I am."

"Okay. Good."

"Good?"

"Well, your dad owns the houses the Henley and Montank construction executives are staying in, right?"

"I'm not sure. He owns the country club, and I'm pretty sure the houses have been unoccupied since it was built, so I think so. Why?"

"How would you feel about blowing them up?"

"The houses?" Tre asks, seeming skeptical.

"Yeah. Why not? We'll make sure no one is in them when we do it, but it might have a psychological impact that vandalizing the construction sites directly hasn't had. Maybe we could even rig it so that the bombs will go off during the next town hall. Then we'll both be there, which will give you a bit of cover. Assuming we can confirm the houses will be empty."

"I don't care about cover."

"Your dad's lawyers won't keep the cops away from you forever, Tre. And do you think he'll continue paying for them if he believes you blew up his houses?"

Tre exhales and leans back in his chair, seeming to consider it. "Yeah. Maybe. How would we do it?"

"Can you figure out some details about the houses? We'll need to know how far away they are from the neighbors'. We don't want to damage anyone else's property. We'll also want to know how big they are so we know where to place the explosives. What kind of locks are on the doors and whether the houses have security systems... It would be good to know what the security at the country club itself is like too, so we can figure out how much time we'll have and how to get away."

"It's a bit less than a month until the next town hall," Tre murmurs. "There'll be plenty of time to figure all that out. I can probably get most of the info from people who work at the country club over the next couple of weeks. If I need to, I can go out there under the excuse of visiting my mom. I don't do it often, but it won't look suspicious either."

"Okay. That works. And once we know that information, we can use the remaining time to figure out exactly what to do. But generally, I think we destroy the houses, making sure the damage stays confined to the ones Henley and Montank are renting. It'll be a nice 'fuck you' to them *and* your dad."

"Yeah. I like that. Are you going to keep coming into the diner for coffee in the mornings?" Tre asks, sounding hopeful.

I nod. "It'll be the easiest way for us to exchange info without drawing attention to ourselves. But we have to be careful with that ATF agent hanging around."

Tre nods. "Okay. Good."

Chapter 22
Friends and Enemies to Lovers

TRE

"Can I get you anything else? More coffee? Maybe a slice of pie before you go?" Sandy asks the two guys sitting at the end of the counter while bussing their plates. They're the last of the lunch crowd on Saturday afternoon.

"No thanks, hon," the smaller one replies. "Just the check, please."

"You got it."

With no more orders, I turn to clean the grill. A few moments later, the jingle of the bell above the door announces a new customer.

I glance over my shoulder in time to see Eddie slump onto a stool at the counter. Sandy drops off the check and grabs a menu from the rack with a sigh before heading over to him. She extends the menu at arm's length. "Do you know what you want, Eddie?"

He looks her up and down, then leers. "You know what I want."

Sandy stiffens, and I walk up beside her. "All good here?" I ask, staring into his eyes, one of which is watery and slightly bulging.

"Uh, yeah. I'll need a minute to, uh, look at the menu," Eddie says weakly, dropping his gaze as he takes it from Sandy's outstretched hand.

She hurries to the register to ring up the previous customers, although I'm sure she'd find any excuse to get away.

"You look pretty tired, Eddie. Are you doing okay?"

He looks up at me, relieved. "Oh man. I just got done talking to the sheriff. They had me there all day."

"The sheriff?"

"Yeah, he and the feds were grilling me about that night at Hay Creek again."

"Ugh. Everything is about Henley and Montank," I declare loudly enough for everyone to hear. "If they're running Kalomish now, they need to show up at the town hall meetings and answer to us directly."

"You know, that's actually a good point," the larger of the two men at the register says.

"I guess we should tell the council members so they make it happen," I suggest.

They both nod thoughtfully and walk outside.

Sandy has taken the opportunity to disappear into the back. Good call.

"So why was the sheriff harassing you? They must have already questioned you."

"I know, right! They asked me a bunch of stuff I already told them, over and over. And then they kept acting like I was involved, like I let those people blow up the building. I didn't do anything except my job! I was checking on the site the whole night—like I was supposed to— but I didn't see anyone."

"Wow, they think you were involved? Did they say who they thought did it? Everybody in town has a bunch of wild ideas, but nobody knows anything real."

"No. They didn't tell me any names. I think they wanted *me* to tell *them* who it was, but I didn't help anyone!" Eddie says, sounding exasperated. "This sucks, man. I took that job because it was perfect, right? I got to work by myself. Didn't have to deal with customers or anybody hassling me, and it was the night shift, leaving every day free. Mostly though, security is the easiest job in the world! You just sit there, and since nothing's happening, you can play on your phone or watch movies or whatever, but you get paid for it. If I ever found anybody, I'd yell at them and they'd have to listen to me, but if there was a real problem, I would call the cops to handle it. That job was perfect…"

I wish I could roll my eyes, or point out that's probably why he never saw anyone, but I should be sympathetic since I'm the reason he lost his job. "Yeah, that sounds pretty sweet. Did you know it was like that because you worked security before?"

"Nah, I tried once, though. Back when I was delivering pizzas, I went out to that rich development a little ways north of town—"

"Highland Estates?"

"Yeah, yeah, that's it. Oh right, your dad's company did that whole place, didn't they? Well, I went out there a few times and always had to be let in by a security guard, so that's when I got the idea. That's not as isolated as a construction site in the woods, but same thing, you know? I figured I could sit in a little shack for eight hours, press a button or talk on the phone once in a while. So, when I got fired from the pizza place, I tried to get a job working security there."

"I never knew that. You didn't end up doing it, though?"

"No, it turns out they make that job a big pain in the ass. Those rich people have a lot of demands. I did an interview and even a tour last winter, but I didn't want to deal with the hassle."

Now that I know Eddie has first-hand knowledge of the security team and a bit of the procedures of Highland Estates, I keep him talking as long as I can. He's happy to complain about how it would have been a lot more work than he expected, as well as how petty and demanding the wealthy homeowners can be.

Eventually, I learn that there are always two guards on shift, one at the gate shack and one at the main security office, which is near the clubhouse. Half of the job of the office guard is responding to calls from bored rich people who are paranoid someone is trying to break into their McMansion, even though it's always just a raccoon in the bushes or a tree branch hitting their window. According to Eddie, the role of the gate guard is annoying, too. They have to pretend to be happy and respectful to all the rich pricks who complain to management over imagined slights. The gate guard also has to answer the phone when their counterpart is out responding to a call, so there wasn't enough quiet for Eddie.

It sounds like security theater—accomplishing nothing but appeasing people who don't think about it enough to understand it's pointless.

"Well, if being a security guard was too much hassle, why did you take the job at Hay Creek?" I ask.

"I got fired from the stupid gym because some asshole members complained about me, so I had to find something. That came available right when I needed it and didn't have any of the problems of working for rich people. It really was the dream job." Eddie shakes his head, greasy brown hair hanging over his face. "Now I'm unemployed again. I couldn't get hired for security if I tried."

"How about a burger, on the house? If I hear of any openings, I'll let you know."

"Yeah, thanks, Tre. That's great, man."

"You can go ahead. Have a nice day, Mr. White," the guard says as the metal gate rolls aside to allow me entry to Highland Estates.

"Thanks, you too," I reply with a nod before rolling up my window and driving through.

I make a mental note of the desk phone in the guard shack and the CCTV cameras covering both entering and exiting traffic. Eddie gave me insight into the security team and some of their procedures, but I'm out here today to learn about the physical security.

I remain below the unnecessarily slow speed limit as I drive the perimeter roads, scouting for likely access points.

The south end would be a terrible option with the highway running alongside those houses. There's way too much exposure and traffic.

I already know we won't be able to enter along the west. That area holds the clubhouse for the golfers, a restaurant, a bar, and a small event space. I wouldn't survive Fiona's scorn if I were stupid enough to suggest it. There are multiple security cameras on the buildings, and both the security vehicle and my dad's oversized white pickup are in the parking lot.

After talking to Eddie yesterday, I texted my mom to arrange a time I could visit without seeing my dad. No matter what I intend, if we run into each other it'll inevitably devolve into a fight. Now that he's semi-retired, he spends most afternoons golfing on his own course with whatever neighbors can put up with him that day. My mom was right about when he'd be gone, so it's safe to stop by. Well, as safe as talking to her ever is.

Not only did my dad ensure his house was the largest in the entire development, but he also placed it in the center at the rear, forcing anyone visiting to see as much of his creation as possible.

And people wonder why I fell out with the man.

I turn up the driveway and park next to my mom's very modern Mercedes. The contrast between our cars is stark, and I revel in the thought that it tarnishes their image a bit.

I'm here, I text. Then I realize that these houses share a lot of construction, meaning the windows and locks probably match the ones where the Henley and Montank execs are staying. I get out of my car and snap a few pictures. I'm taking a close-up of the lock and handle when my mom yanks the front door open.

"What are you doing, Richie? And why are you texting me like I'm one of your friends you're picking up to go to the movies? You have a key. You should let yourself in."

"Hi mom. Nice to see you too. I'm fine, thank you for asking," I respond with extra politeness.

"Yes, yes. Come in. Wipe your feet."

I do as requested, closing the door behind me.

My mother starts in immediately with, "So what brings you out here this month? More trouble with the police over those developers?"

I count to three, resist sighing with superhuman willpower, and reply, "Sheriff's department, mom. And I never asked for help with that. Dad just did his usual thing, inserting himself where nobody wanted him, and made a call to have someone else actually handle it."

The scowl has already formed on her face when I say, "I wanted to come out here *because* of the trouble going on. I thought I should check in on you to make sure everything's alright."

"Of course we're alright, Richie. Don't be absurd. Nobody's after *us*, just those East Coast developers. There hasn't been a whiff of danger, or any kind of excitement, since your father built this place."

If I find the right angle, she'll start ranting about everything that's happening, and then my only job will be to steer the conversation occasionally. Before I decide on my next comment, she continues.

"Although, Henley and Montank rented out a couple of houses for two of their newest. Lovely people. We visited them when they moved in. It's so nice to have some people of culture around. They're from Manhattan, you know."

"They're staying here?" I ask, already knowing the answer, but fishing for details Fiona and I will be able to use.

"You don't have to say it like that. This is the nicest neighborhood in Kalomish. We set them up in a pair of homes over on Cedar Avenue, the ones near the highway. Those were the only places next to each other. Although we have no shortage of empty houses. I told your father the plans for the Estates were too big, but of course he knew better. You know, we never sold a third of the properties? But we can't lower the asking prices. That would attract the wrong sort..." She continues with the stream of consciousness, but my mind wanders to planning next steps since I have the info I came here to get. The two execs are staying in houses bordering the eastern edge of the development closest to the highway.

After nodding along and dropping the occasional "Uh huh," or "Really?" I seize on a pause in the judgment-filled gossip to extricate myself. "I'm glad things are mostly normal, then, and you two are doing fine. I guess if you don't need any help, I'll get out of your hair."

"Leaving already? You know, you have to fix things with your father. This rift is ruining our family. I know he'd be thrilled to have you back. You're meant for more than just working at your grandmother's restaurant."

"There's nothing wrong with people doing actual work or being involved in the community instead of hiding away, mom." I step forward and give her a brief hug, then walk outside.

Once I'm back in my car, I adjust my route to drive past those houses on my way out. I need to get their addresses and ensure we can access them without being seen.

When I finally approach the southeast corner, I slow down and snap some pictures of both houses, making sure the street numbers are included. The windows and one of the front doors look the same as my mom's, but the second house has a more ornate glass door than the classical wood style. I zoom as far as possible, but I doubt the lock will be identifiable.

I don't want to stop in front of the houses, so I drive on, having gathered what info I could. I'll look up the rest online.

Time to get to work.

THE DOOR BUZZER BLARES. IT'S FIONA. I PRESS THE BUTTON to give her access to the building. She seemed annoyed by my standing in the doorway previously, so I unlock my apartment door and return to the kitchen. I've spent the last few hours cleaning and cooking. I place a pair of plates and two sets of cutlery on the counter to do something with my hands as much as to be ready when the oven is done.

There's a light knock at the door. "It's open," I call out. When I turn, Fiona is stepping into my apartment. She's wearing a deep green shirt that contrasts perfectly with her brown hair—which is down, fanning around her shoulders—and accentuates her eyes.

After she closes and locks the door, she turns to face me, smirking. "Something wrong, Tre?"

"No, no. That's just a really good color on you. Highlights your eyes," I explain.

"Right. That's what you're staring at, my eyes."

"Um, anyway. Thanks for coming," I say with a small wave. *Why did I wave?* I wonder, feeling dumb.

"Yeah, your note said you have info you couldn't pass along at the diner."

"Right. It's all over here." I point, walking to the kitchen island.

Fiona's eyes scan the apartment as she makes her way over. "Whatever you're making smells good."

A legitimate compliment. *Nice, I'll take it,* I think. "Thanks. I figured I should make dinner, since I'm taking up your evening. And before you say anything, no, it's not a date. I heard what you said, and it's like I told you the first time: I asked you here to plan during dinnertime, so I'm providing food. It's not a big deal. No ulterior motives."

"How long do you expect this will take? I thought I was picking up some files." She's definitely side-eyeing me now.

"You are." I point again to the folder. "But we never have a chance to talk about any of this, so I figured you could look it over, ask me questions, let me know what I missed, and talk about what we do next if you have enough info."

As if on cue, the oven timer beeps. "Take a look while I grab this," I tell her as I put on the oven mitts and pull the baking dish out, setting it on the stove. Paper rustles behind me while I plate food.

"Is this... hand-drawn?"

I glance at the paper on top and reply, "Yeah. I don't own a printer, so I used a ruler and a pencil." I shrug and gather the plates, setting them on the island and pouring us each a glass of Chardonnay. "Plus, I've heard that every printer can be traced. I was thorough."

Fiona's absorbed in the files and doesn't look at the food until I take a seat next to her. She glances at the plate and returns her focus to the paper, then does a double-take worthy of a cartoon.

"You made this? It doesn't seem like no big deal."

"It's only roasted chicken and potatoes. You don't have to eat it."

She looks at me silently for a moment and then reaches over to try some. I wonder if she's simply taking a pity bite to get me to leave her alone, so I make myself useful while she's busy, explaining about the information Creepy Eddie had, plus what I learned from my mom. Then I direct her attention back to the folder.

"You've already seen that I drew the layouts of the two houses. The dimensions are in feet for each wall and the property lines, as well as the distances to the nearby houses, the road, and the forest. On the other side, there's a less detailed map of the development and surrounding area, measured in miles. The neighborhood is encircled by the highway to the south, the golf course on the north and west, and state forest land to the east. The two houses we want back onto the forest, and I've marked a trail we can use to get close."

"We can just walk into their yard from the outside?" Fiona asks skeptically.

"The perimeter is surrounded by a five-foot-tall wrought-iron fence, so basically, yes. I've included a page of notes about the security guards and cameras, but as long as we don't scare anybody, they'll never know we were there."

Fiona washes the chicken down with the last of her wine and slides her plate aside. She's all business now. "What about the houses? Do they have alarms?"

I pause with my forkful of potato halfway to my mouth and shake my head. "The whole place is way more interested in security theater to make the residents feel like they have personal security than actually being competent. Each house was built with a landline straight to the office—I guess having concierge guards is appealing— and supposedly there's some sort of panic button they can press to send an alert to the security office, but nothing that would automatically trigger. These two houses never sold and have only been rented for a couple of weeks, so nothing has been customized or updated."

"Okay. No cameras and no alarm systems to trip. What about motion-activated lights outside?"

"That's one thing I'm not certain of. There were floodlights on some of the other houses, but not on any of the unused ones, so the best I can say is probably not. I obviously didn't get out and walk into anyone's backyard to investigate, but from what I see on street maps online, it doesn't look like it. Those aren't high-resolution close-up shots, though."

"Online street maps? Is that where you got the layout details, too?" Fiona asks.

"No, there's a ton of information available about every property in county records, which you can search online. I put details about each house on separate pages in the folder." I reach across her to flip the edges of pages down to show one in the back, pressing against her arm as I do. Warmth spreads between us, and my face flushes.

Fiona turns to me, and although we're too close now, she doesn't pull away. "Is there a record of you looking those up?"

I shake my head again. "I used a VPN and an anonymous browser, like you said. County records don't require an account to search. I looked on maps, but never actually put in addresses. I just scrolled and zoomed to what I needed."

"This is really well done, Tre."

I raise my eyebrows. "Thank you."

"What? I give credit where it's due. This is better than I expected the first time I was here." Fiona smiles. Her eyes are piercing right through me. We're close enough that I can see her pupils widening.

Say something, idiot. It's your turn to talk. Don't screw this up.

Fiona continues, "Speaking of which, your place is back to looking like it's been staged for a magazine shoot." The smirk is back on her face. That look used to infuriate me, but right now I'm struggling not to kiss those mocking lips.

I let go of the files and let my hand rest on her forearm. "I knew you were coming this time."

"And you wanted to impress me?"

"Yes."

"Congratulations. You succeeded," she says softly, then leans forward and presses her mouth to mine.

My eyes go wide as I part my lips, then close as her tongue glides over mine. I slide my arm around her waist. My face is burning now, and I desperately want more.

Fiona's hand is gripping the back of my head as she pulls me toward her. I reach for the bottom of her shirt with my other hand and feel the soft skin underneath. My cock is hardening as my fingers graze her ribs.

Then I drop away from her face, and my hands fly loose as I fall to my knees. I kept getting closer and closer and slid right off the damn stool.

"Shit! Sorry," I mutter, refusing to look up at her. *Idiot!*

All I hear is laughter as Fiona leans back. My face is on fire for an entirely different reason as I rise to my feet.

She stands up as well and takes hold of my hand.

"Does this mean—"

She cuts me off. "Shut up and kiss me."

Chapter 23
Fuck Around and Find Out of Body Experience

FIONA

"And you wanted to impress me?" I ask, staring at Tre, who is too close. I should move away. But I don't. Coming here was a decision.

"Yes." Tre's pupils are blown wide. He's focused only on me.

I should get up and leave. But I don't. Staying and eating dinner with Tre was a decision.

"Congratulations. You succeeded," I tell him, and his eyes widen slightly, like I'm impossible to impress.

I should *really* stop flirting with him. But I don't. Saying *'Fuck it'* and kissing him—here, in his apartment, after he evidently spent all day cleaning and cooking because he knew I was coming over—is a decision. It might be a terrible one, but I lean forward and do it anyway.

His body stiffens as my mouth finds his. Then, all at once, he relaxes and his arm wraps around my waist as his lips part under mine. Fire races through my veins, reminding me of the times I've stood next to Tre and watched a flame race up a detonating cord. My body feels exactly how that looks as I run my hands up the back of his neck, entwining them in his hair, tugging him closer to me as I slide my tongue into his mouth.

Tre's hands slip under my shirt, running over my stomach, and the fire in my veins intensifies. The clenching sensation of need fills my body, hardening my nipples and sending waves of desire emanating from my cunt as I pull Tre closer, stroking my tongue across his.

Then his hands slip from my body. His mouth disappears from mine, and there's a hard thud. I open my eyes to find Tre on his knees on the floor in front of me. Laughter bursts from my throat. I guess it's safe to say he's just as into this as I am.

His cheeks are bright red as he rises to his feet. A dozen smart-ass comments flit through my head. But he's already avoiding my gaze, clearly finding the situation more embarrassing than funny, so I don't say any of them as I reach for his hand and step closer.

Finally, his smoky grey eyes meet mine. "Does this mean—"

"Shut up and kiss me," I say, cutting him off, not wanting him to finish the question because all I know for sure at this point is that I want to sleep with him. I don't know what will happen after that. But I can't stop thinking about him. About how attractive he is, and how brazen he can be. About how thoughtful he is, and how every time he touches me—

Tre's lips are back on mine, chasing the thoughts about tomorrow from my head as his tongue plunges into my mouth and his hand drops to my ass, drawing me closer. My breath catches as I wrap my arms around his waist. I arch into him, feeling exactly how much he wants this. He groans when I grind my hips against his, and his hands slip under my shirt once more, sending heat rising up my spine as he raises my shirt higher and higher. I lift my arms so he can skip the buttons.

"Are you sure about this?" Tre asks as our mouths break apart and my shirt goes over my head. "Because I don't want to do this if you're going to regret it tomorrow."

I want to tell him that I'm sure and leave it at that. But as hot and cold as I've been, it's a fair question that deserves a real answer.

My skin cools as I stand shirtless in front of Tre. If I thought he'd waited until he had me at a disadvantage to ask the question, I'd be pissed. But I know he didn't. I know I didn't really give him a chance to ask it before now.

"I've spent the last week thinking about this. Actually, it's been longer than that. Since the campsite. Since that night at the trailer," I admit. "So no, I won't regret this tomorrow."

"What changed?" he asks quietly, apparently needing to be convinced.

"I…" I sigh. "Last week you said to let you know when I'd figured out my feelings, and the truth is I haven't. Not really."

Tre's face falls, and he retreats half a step.

"But," I hurry to add, stepping forward and closing the distance between us, "I know that I want this—you—now, and I won't regret it tomorrow. You're obviously not the same asshole you were in high school. That much is clear. But maybe I am.

"Ewan told me I should spend less time in my head thinking about what I should or shouldn't do. And he's right. That's pretty much all I've been doing for the past two months. He also said something about how I'd be better off if I just tried it and found out. So this is me trying to be a different asshole than I was in high school, too," I say, beginning to feel like I'm babbling. "I can't promise that I'll ever want to do it again, but I can promise I won't regret it tomorrow."

"Ewan literally told you to fuck around and find out?"

"Not exactly those words, but more or less."

"God," Tre mutters. "That sounds like him."

I shrug. "So. Would you like to fuck around and find out with me?"

Tre's gaze goes fuzzy as he considers it, which is fair since it's all I've been doing for a while now. After what seems like forever, but is probably only a few moments, his grey eyes refocus on my face, and his hand skates across my waist. "Yeah." He grins. "Sounds like fun."

I close the last bit of distance between us. "Good. I didn't know if you had condoms, so I brought some."

"Oh, so *you* did come here with ulterior motives," he comments, and the heat in his voice is unmistakable as his arms wrap around my waist. His fingers move lazily across my back, leaving a trail of goose-bumps prickling my skin.

"Yes. I did. When I say I've been thinking about this for a while, I mean it. And I like to be prepared. So will you shut up and kiss me now?" The words have barely left my mouth when Tre slides his left hand up my spine, locking it in my hair, bringing our mouths together.

His tongue snakes into my mouth as his right hand glides across the side of my boob, gently caressing it, and I moan softly. I slip my hands under his shirt. His skin is warm beneath my fingers, and I'm all but certain the same electric tingles are flowing through his body as my palms run up his sides.

Tre steps backward, and I follow without breaking off our kiss, running my hands over his chest. His pecs are firm beneath my touch, and he gasps when I rake my nails over his nipples. I tug his shirt upward, and he raises his arms.

"You know you have beautiful eyes," I murmur as his gaze locks on mine. "They remind me of a thundercloud. I've always liked your eyes. Even when I didn't like you." I bring my mouth to his neck and drop my left hand to trail across his stomach.

There's a sharp inhale as my fingers dip lower, hovering above the waistband of his pants, and we take another step. We're about halfway down the hallway that must lead to his bedroom. I want us to walk faster, but I also want to drag this out as long as possible.

"Just my eyes?" His voice is breathier than I've ever heard it. The sound sends desire flooding through me. I'm already wet enough that he could spin my back to the wall, strip my jeans off, and plunge his dick into my cunt, and the only thing I would do is beg for more.

I nip at his neck. "No. I love your hair too," I say, raking my nails down his chest, leaving faint red lines behind as a memory before winding my hands into his hair. "It's so soft."

I tug on it lightly, and he gasps, his eyes fluttering shut.

"Do you like that?" I question.

"Yes. You pulled on my hair when I boosted you into the trailer." His eyes are on mine again.

"I know." We take another step, and I drop my right hand to undo the button on his fly.

"Your eyes are beautiful too," he replies. "Like emeralds. Or a flame when you add copper to it. Yeah, a flame when you add copper to it. Hot enough to burn, but beautiful all the same."

The sound of the zipper coming undone seems to echo through the hallway like a distant avalanche as I yank it down.

We take another step, and his hands slide over my shoulders, slipping my bra straps down my arms. I let go of Tre and pull them free.

"I've wanted you since you disappeared into the night and left me standing alone on the side of Bridal Mountain." It's impossible to miss the need in his voice, and desire coils even tighter between my thighs.

"A little civil disobedience gets you off," I joke as his hands move to undo the hooks on my bra. He lets it drop to the floor, just one more piece of clothing strewn in our wake. "I should've figured." I gasp as his hands run up my torso, gently caressing my boobs, his thumbs stroking my nipples. Desire flows through my body, spreading outward in tingling waves, amplifying how much I want him.

"*You* get me off, Fiona." His eyes are boring into mine. "You're beautiful, but you're also smart. And fearless. And infuriating in the best possible way," he adds, drawing me to him, his mouth on mine once more. We take another step, and I drop my hand to run over him, shoving down the boxers that are in my way until I can wrap my hand around his shaft. He lets out a long, low groan against my mouth when my skin touches his, and the sound travels through my body.

My cunt has its own percussion line, drumming a pulsating rhythm of need. We take another step. His bedroom door is only feet away now.

I pump my hand along his very large, very erect dick, pulling my mouth from his long enough to say, "You get me off too. It's going to feel amazing having you inside me. I think..." I hesitate, unsure how much I want to reveal. Unsure whether I want him to truly know how much time I've spent imagining—no, *fantasizing* about this.

"You think...?" Tre asks with a low rumble of demand in his voice. We take another step, and he reaches behind him, fumbling for the doorknob with his left hand as his right works the button of my jeans undone.

The door opens, and then we're taking another step as Tre hits the light switch, turning on a pair of softly glowing bedside lamps.

"I think I've wanted you since you invited me here the first time."

Tre smirks, and we take another step. "The lasagna?"

I increase the pressure I'm using on his shaft. His hand spasms on my waist as his eyes float shut, and he gasps in pleasure. The sound reverberates through me and makes my entire body clench. I want to hear him make that sound again.

"Yes, the lasagna, you ass." I move my teeth to his earlobe and rake them across it. "It was the best fucking lasagna I've ever had."

Tre's eyes open, and he pulls me toward him as he spins, reversing our positions. We take another step, and then his hands drop over my ass to the back of my thighs. He picks me up, and we're falling.

I let out a gasp when my back hits the bed. Tre's arms are on either side of me, caging me in. It's impossible to ignore how attractive he is from this position. Or any position, if I'm being honest.

I should've done this forever ago, I can't help but think. *I should've screwed him in the woods on the Fourth of July. I should've gone to his tent. I should've—*

"You said it was only, and I quote, 'Okay.'"

"Yeah. Well. I was surprised. I didn't want to say something I'd regret."

He snorts as he lifts one hand to run between my breasts, over my sternum, and down my stomach before pushing his other hand off the bed and kneeling between my thighs, his hands on the waistband of my jeans, grazing my hip bones. My entire body feels like it could burst into flames at any moment.

"Something like, 'Hey Tre, thanks for making dinner. It was really good'?"

"Yes. Something like that," I agree breathlessly as I lift my hips so he can drag my pants over my ass. "The food you made tonight was really good, too."

"Are you just saying that because you want me to fuck you?" Tre asks as cold air hits my thighs and then my calves. I've never been so desperate to have someone before.

"No, but could you please hurry up and fuck me?" I demand from where I'm lying on his bed, which is covered in black sheets—it's a mood, and not one I expected from Mr. Happy-Go-Lucky—wearing only a pair of red lace underwear that are completely soaked.

"No. Sorry." Tre sounds entirely unapologetic as he removes his own pants. "I will not *'hurry up and fuck you,'*" he says, mimicking my voice.

"I—"

"You already said you have no idea if you'll want to do this again after tonight, and that's fine," he rushes to add, his hands held up before him. "No strings. But if tonight is the one chance I get to be with you, Fiona, I'm not going to rush through any part of it."

I swallow hard, my heart thrumming in my chest. "Okay," I agree, meeting his resolute gaze. I want him. There's no two ways about it. He could drag this out for hours, and I'd let him.

Tre nods, and then he's kneeling at the edge of the bed as his left hand runs up my calf, his fingers massaging the muscle as he brings his mouth to my leg, his tongue tracing over my knee, lingering at the bottom of my quad as his right hand trails along my inner thigh. I gasp as his mouth seals against my leg. His hands move to my hips, and he drags me to the edge of the bed before his fingers slip under the red lace and he strips my underwear off.

Then his hands are running up my inner thighs, and his lips are trailing behind them, leaving an imprint of heat at each spot they touch. I moan as his thumbs glide over my labia with the lightest of touches. And then his face is right there, and his breath is ghosting across my clit. I shiver as the pause draws on, looking down my body to find his eyes locked on my face, watching me. The moment seems to stretch until Tre drives his tongue into my cunt without warning.

"Oh fuck," I gasp, my fingers clenching at the sheets as I fight to keep my hips from bucking against his face.

His tongue withdraws, and then it's running up me, flicking over my clit as his fingers circle my opening, setting my nerve endings on fire. I trade my grip on the bedsheets for his hair, locking his mouth in place, and he releases a soft moan that thrums through me.

"Keep going," I beg, staring into his deep grey eyes, which somehow seem to be lit from within. His fingers slide into me ever so slightly as his tongue strokes my clit faster and faster.

My body is trembling as the orgasm builds deep in my pelvis. It's like a riptide, pulling me further and further into dangerous currents.

Finally, I can't take it anymore, and I reach down to find Tre's hand, wrapping my own around it, pushing his fingers deeper into me before re-gripping his hair. He curls his fingers against the walls of my vagina, his tongue flicking across my clit even faster.

Then, all at once, I'm coming, my hips rolling beneath Tre's face as a ragged, "Oh, yes, Tre! Yes!" tears from my throat. Just as I'm nearing the end of the orgasm, he seals his mouth on me, sucking on my clit as his fingers are still deep inside me. I shout wordlessly as a second orgasm floods through me, leaving me quivering and panting.

By the time I'm capable of looking down, Tre is wiping his mouth with the back of his hand. Then he's on his side, lying next to me on the bed, his head pillowed on his arm. I feel more relaxed than I have in months. Even my mind is momentarily quiet.

"Good?" he asks softly, his eyes glued to me as he trails a hand up my ribs.

"Amazing," I reply, and a slow, satisfied smile spreads across his face.

"I aim to please."

"You really do, don't you?" I murmur, rolling onto my side to face him, resting my right hand on his hip before letting it slip across his stomach. His abs flex under my touch, and he inhales sharply as my fingers dip toward his cock. I reverse the motion, and he releases a soft exhale, his eyes almost fluttering shut. I repeat the process and am rewarded with the same sharp inhale. This time, I wrap my hand around his shaft and stroke him as I slide closer, draping a leg over his hip. His mouth finds mine, and I taste myself on his tongue as he palms my boob. I gasp when he pinches my nipple, and he immediately does it again. It's all I can do to stop myself from sliding him into me, and if he were wearing a condom, I would've already done it.

Instead, I push against him, and he rolls onto his back, taking me with him, leaving me straddling him. My hair is spilling forward, shrouding us as I begin kissing my way down his jaw.

"There are condoms in the nightstand," Tre says softly as I move my lips from his jaw to his neck.

"I was going to repay the favor first."

Tre smirks, already looking satisfied. "I'm optimistic there's going to be a next time, and I want something to look forward to."

"Are you sure?"

"Yes. Plus, it's been a while. If you go down on me right now, I don't know that there will be anything after that."

I grin. "Okay." I move off him toward the nightstand. He stays on his back, but his eyes watch me hungrily. I open the drawer and remove the box of condoms.

"What are you doing?" Tre asks as I flip the box over.

"Checking the expiration date. You said it's been a while."

"Not that long, Fiona," he scoffs.

"So I see." I take a condom from the box and return to straddling him before tearing the wrapper open. I place the condom over his dick and slowly unroll it. Tre's hands are running up and down my thighs, but his eyes are focused on my fingers skimming over his shaft.

"I never thought watching someone unroll a condom could be so hot," Tre growls, as I line the head of his dick up with my cunt and sink down onto him.

Then his hands are on my hips, pulling me down even more, and we both groan as I quiver around him.

"God, you feel amazing," Tre says, his hands running up my sides and over my ribs. His fingertips graze my nipples, and I grab his hands, interlacing my fingers with his before pinning them to the bed just above his head. I shift weight onto our hands as I lift off him and slide back down.

My breath comes in short, ragged bursts punctuated by soft moans escaping Tre's lips as I ride him faster and faster. I've already come twice, but I'm still right there, teetering on the edge. "I'm so close, Tre," I whisper, staring into his eyes, which haven't left mine for a single second.

He pulls his hands out from under mine, grabbing my waist and rolling us over without missing a thrust. His arm wraps under my hips, lifting me as he slides a pillow under my ass for a better angle.

He places a hand near my shoulder to brace himself, and the bed sinks slightly. His other hand presses down on my pelvis just above my pubic bone as he increases the speed, and it's like every thrust is coming from above and below. I come for the third time, screaming his name as my nails rake from his shoulders to his elbows. All I can do is hold on, my nails imprinting deeply into his skin, as his movements take on a frenetic quality. Then a wordless roar rips from Tre's throat, his hips jerking as he climaxes, his hand still pressing into my pelvis. By the time his body falls motionless, I feel like I'm made of Jello. He's collapsed over me, and his forehead is pressed heavily against mine, but his weight is braced on his forearms to either side of my head.

I trace my fingers along his jaw, and Tre turns his head to plant a kiss on the palm of my hand.

"Was it as good as you imagined?" I ask.

"Better," he whispers. "You?"

"Yeah," I agree. "Definitely better."

"What?" I ask when I look up from the chart I'm scribbling some notes on and find Natalie staring at me.

Her dark eyebrows scrunch together. "Weren't you wearing that shirt yesterday?"

I glance down at myself like I have no idea what I'm wearing. "Oh, this? No, I guess they do look a lot alike, though," I lie.

The nod Natalie gives me says she's not convinced, but she's also not going to press the issue.

I return my focus to the chart as if it's occupying my attention. It's not. I ended up spending the entire night with Tre, and when my alarm went off at seven, there wasn't time for me to make it home before work. I settled for showering at his place and putting the clothes I wore yesterday back on, hoping no one would notice, which was stupid. Of course Natalie noticed, because I wanted to impress

Tre, so instead of wearing a plain black or white top, I wore a jewel-toned green silk shirt.

But waking up with Tre's body spooned around mine wasn't the worst thing ever. It was almost nice enough to make it worth Natalie's scrutiny.

"We have a gap in patients. I was thinking about doing a coffee run. Do you want anything?" Natalie asks.

"Um, sure," I agree, even though Tre made coffee while I was in the shower. By the time I got out, not only was there coffee, but he was in the middle of making pancakes. They smelled amazing, and I could've spent five minutes waiting for them to be done, but I left with a mumbled excuse about stopping by the diner for breakfast this weekend.

Not because I regret last night—I don't. I meant it when I told Tre it was better than I'd imagined. But letting him cook breakfast for me after spending the night with him felt too intimate, and I'm not sure I'm ready to go there.

Instead, I picked up the folder we left abandoned on the kitchen island and made a break for the door wearing yesterday's clothes.

"Just a plain coffee is fine," I finish, remembering the look of disappointment that flashed across Tre's face as I stepped out of his apartment.

My keys jingle softly as I unlock the front door. It's barely after six-thirty, and there's still plenty of daylight. I spent the past twenty minutes sitting in my truck, parked in the driveway, staring at the bumper of my dad's station wagon with a folder full of Tre's handwritten notes on my lap, trying to decide what to tell my dad so that he'll build me another bomb.

The past two weeks have been... tense. He's still not thrilled that Tre knows what I've been doing—that Tre has been *helping* me do it—

and we've been cautiously dancing around each other since I let that info slip.

I take a deep breath and twist the knob. There's nothing I can say that will make him like this.

The living room is empty when I step inside, and he's not in the kitchen either. I open the basement door to find the light on.

"Hey dad," I call as I start down the steps, receiving a wordless grunt in response.

He's at his workbench, and I move to stand beside him, making sure not to block the light. I've been chided about that enough throughout the years. He doesn't look up, staying focused on the pins he's soldering into place on a small circuit board, and I stand next to him, silently watching him work. It's a deeply familiar experience. I can't count how many nights during my childhood were spent exactly like this—although as often as not, Ewan would've been standing here with us.

Eventually he finishes what he's doing and turns off the soldering iron, setting it and the board aside before giving me a once-over. He lets out a small, derisive snort when he does.

"What?" I ask.

"Nothing."

"No, we've been dancing around each other long enough. Just say whatever it is."

He folds his arms over his chest and raises his eyebrows.

"Go ahead. Say it," I prod.

"Didn't hear you come home last night." His tone sounds neutral, but I can feel the judgment rolling off him anyway.

"Do I ask you where you spend the night when you don't come home?"

"No."

"Okay then." I slap the folder down on the workbench in front of him.

"What's this?"

"What do you think about pissing Rich off?" I ask, and my dad's eyes flick from the folder back to me.

He tilts his head slightly as if to say he's not opposed to the idea, then picks up the folder, opening it and flipping through the pages. "Highland Estates?" he mutters, looking at the map Tre drew. "Why?"

"Henley and Montank flew a couple of executives from New York out here, and that's where they're staying. Like the asshole he is, Rich cut a deal with them. So I figured we could kill two birds with one stone. I'll make sure the houses are empty, of course."

"*You* figured?" His eyes are still fixed on the info Tre put together.

"Yes, dad. *I* figured. It's my idea, but Tre has been helping me."

"Tre." He spits the name out like it's a curse, shutting the folder. "No."

"I'll do it without your help then. But it'll be a lot less well-contained if I do," I warn.

"Then do it without my help, Fiona." He slides the folder toward me and picks up the soldering iron.

"Are you—"

"Yes. I'm serious. As long as Tre is involved, I'm not going to help."

"Fine." I grab the folder and head for the stairs. "I'll figure it out myself."

Chapter 24
Big Bad Wolf in Sheep's Clothing

TRE

"YOU'RE GOING TO LOVE THE VIEW UP THERE," THE WOMAN says, bouncing along the trail, as Ewan and I stand to the side on a boulder, leaving room for them to pass. Her hiking partner, a tall man sweating profusely despite heading downhill, simply nods politely and returns his focus to the dirt path underfoot.

"Awesome," I reply with a smile.

We're about two-thirds of the way up the mountain, and these are the first people we've encountered. It's a little after eleven in the morning on Tuesday, and we're hiking one of the steeper, less popular trails in the area. Ewan doesn't know it, but that relative seclusion is deliberate.

I take the lead as we resume trekking, still surrounded by the thick pines that dominate the slopes in this area. After a few minutes, we emerge from the forest onto a rocky section of hillside. The temperature difference hits immediately as the sun beats down on my face, and the heat is compounded by being on the leeward side of the mountain, where there's no breeze.

"Oh wow, look at that view," Ewan says behind me, stepping into the clearing. "Hang on. I want to get a picture."

There are a few peaks in sight, but his breathing sounds labored, and I suspect he wants a break more than he wants a picture. Between the heat and the elevation change, I can understand why that other guy was so sweaty. Ewan's likely to look the same before we're done.

Amazingly, I haven't felt the strain of the hike like I expected. I'm barely breathing hard. I guess all that bike riding is actually working. One more reason to be glad I ran across Fiona on Bridal Mountain.

Fiona.

I immediately think of her in my apartment.

In my bedroom.

In my bed.

Since that night, we've only seen each other at the diner. She's back to getting coffee before work most days, and on Sunday she actually came in for brunch. She sat in a booth along the back wall where I could see her the whole time without having to look around. It was torture pretending not to care that she was there. I would've liked to go sit across from her, but people would talk, and I know she doesn't want everyone to know we're... I don't even know what we're doing. We haven't really had a chance to discuss it.

Ewan hasn't said anything about it either. So he must not know.

Well, I ought to rip the Band-Aid off, I think. *He's bound to find out sooner or later, and maybe this way he'll stay out of it.*

"Hey man, you'll never guess what happened," I start and immediately regret this approach.

Ewan makes a show of staring at his phone like he's reviewing his pictures, drawing out the break. "Yeah, what's that?"

I press on anyway. The last thing any of us needs is a repeat of the Fourth of July because he doesn't know what's going on and decides to get in the middle of it. "Fiona and I hung out last week."

"Last week? How am I just hearing about this now?" Ewan spins to face me, phone forgotten.

"What, I should shout it across Betty's during dinner?"

"Whatever, dick. You can text. We hung out a few days ago."

"I didn't really want to talk about it in front of the whole crew, especially after what happened over the Fourth. And I'm not big on texting, you know that. It's easier to just talk."

"Whatever," he repeats. "So what happened? You're not throwing a fit, so I assume it went okay."

"Uh, yeah. Pretty good."

"Well, that's cool. How, exactly, do you two 'hang out' since you're so weird about each other?"

"I asked her to come by my apartment, and we spent a while talking. I made some food. You know—"

"Wait, you asked Fi on a date?" Ewan's voice rises in pitch.

I look around to make sure nobody has magically snuck up on us in the last ten seconds. "Well, I didn't mean for it to be. But it kinda turned into one, yeah."

"Tre, that's more than hanging out. How the hell did you get her to agree to a date? At your place, especially."

"It really was supposed to just be talking things out, discussing shared interests, that kind of thing. And then it turned into more," I finish sheepishly.

"Seriously? After all the shit you gave me, you two hooked up?"

"What? You complained when you thought something had happened and I didn't tell you. I'm telling you now, and you're pissed about that too?"

"No, jackass. I'm annoyed with you two idiots. I've been stuck between you for six freaking months, telling you both to just get over yourselves and talk. Suddenly you think it's your idea and you're all over each other. You're a real pain in the ass sometimes," Ewan finishes, but he's grinning as he says it.

My shoulders relax and my jaw unclenches. "So, you're okay if we… get together?"

"Dude, it's none of my business who either of you sleeps with. As long as Fi doesn't date some shithead, I don't care who she picks. Honestly, I'm just glad she finally got it out of her system. She's been wound so tight I was worried she was going to snap."

Oh good, I'm important enough to count as blowing off steam. And since he didn't know, that means Fiona didn't talk to him about us. Shit, maybe that was the only time. Maybe she did get me out of her system. Fuck.

My thoughts begin to spiral down a vortex of self-doubt when Ewan says, "Well, should we get moving? I'm starting to bake under this sun."

My eyes come back into focus to see him sip from his hydration pack and wipe his forehead with the back of his hand.

He walks past me to lead the way across the rocky clearing back into the cool shade of the pines. "I hope there's a breeze up top."

"And that's exactly why we need to make them listen, or they'll keep selling off our town, one corporate deal at a time," I assert over the background noise of the diner as the Wednesday morning breakfast crowd is winding down.

Bob gives me a mock salute with two fingers pressed to his forehead, the others wrapped around his receipt. The bell above the door jingles, and he steps out into the sunlight.

As the door swings shut, I turn away from the register to check for another ticket, but Walt pipes up from the end of the counter. "We've already told all the council members they need to put Henley and Montank in the hot seat at the town hall next week."

Beside him, Henry nods firmly, his face resolute as though he's trying to convince them right now.

They both retired a few years ago, and they hang out here gossiping for several hours two or three days a week. Apparently, they rotate between a few spots around town so they don't get too bored with all of their free time and no idea how to spend it.

Behind them, in the corner booth, Special Agent Smith looks up from his laptop. He's still been showing up here for breakfast or dinner at least once every few days.

"All of them, huh?" I inquire.

Jackie hustles over with the coffeepot and tops off their mugs. They've probably downed a whole pot between them.

"Perks of being retired, kid. You got all the time in the world to be a pain in the ass," Walt answers with a grin stretching across his weathered face.

Connor returns his attention to his computer with a hint of a smile on his face.

Another jingle of the bell makes us glance at the door, and suddenly I'm not listening. Fiona is standing in the doorway, backlit by the midmorning sun.

Holy shit, she showed up today after all, I marvel. It's later than she's normally here.

Fiona walks directly to the register and sets a trio of travel mugs on the counter. "Three coffees. Please."

Jackie calls over, "It'll be a few minutes, Dr. Carson. I've got a new pot brewing." She lifts the nearly empty pot in case anyone doesn't believe her.

"Just Fiona, please."

I realize I haven't moved since she appeared, and I'm staring.

Walt folds his arms over his solidly built chest and continues where he left off. "We've been spreading the word around town for you, Tre. The ladies who meet up at the library for their knitting club were especially keen to talk to the council. We'll get those bastards to answer for themselves."

Fiona's gaze darts to Connor before she makes eye contact with me, her face intense but inscrutable.

I'm supposed to make sure the execs are out of their houses during the town hall. I know this is super visible, but it's not like I can be their favorite suspect more than I already am. Backing off now would be suspicious, so I may as well lean into it, I think in her direction, wishing she could read my mind. Wishing I could tell her all of this, but there's no way for us to talk here.

If only we could meet at my apartment again. We could talk over dinner. And then... My pulse starts throbbing in my neck, and then my dick follows suit. I look away from Fiona, busying myself with straightening napkins that are already stacked.

Jackie walks back behind the counter from the other end, hands full of dirty dishes. "My mom has been complaining about it. Apparently, people keep coming to her accounting firm to demand the same thing. They're not causing a scene or anything, but she says it wastes a lot of time. She spent like half of dinner last night talking about it."

"If she wants to be on the council, she needs to listen to the people," Walt responds.

"How about you, doc?" Henry adds, the light shining off his still mostly black hair.

"What's that?" Fiona turns to look at Henry and Walt.

"Are you gonna demand the council bring Henley and Montank to the next town hall meeting to hear from us directly?"

Walt answers for her. "Henry, haven't you been paying attention? The new doc *wants* them here."

"Even if she supports them, she should want them to come talk to us. If they were doing good, they'd be able to explain it. But they have to be there to make their case."

They begin bickering, seeming to forget they were talking with the rest of us.

Fiona gives me serious get-me-out-of-here eyes and surreptitiously sidesteps away from the fired-up retirees.

I guess I don't have to brief her on how things are going around town, I chuckle to myself.

I press against the counter as close to Fiona as I can, and in a low voice say, "You're here late today."

She shrugs. "I was a little behind this morning. Now I'm doing a coffee run for the office. Seems I picked a bad time." Her emerald eyes are piercing through me, and I can't look away. Heat is rushing up my neck into my face. "I guess Henley and Montank will be at the town hall, then."

"Uh, yeah. People are being very vocal," I reply uselessly.

We stand for a few moments in silence, and I'm trying to look like I'm not staring at her.

"So, how's that coffee coming?" Fiona prompts.

"Right. Fresh coffee coming up," I say without actually checking that it's ready. I grab the three mugs and head to the coffeemaker. One pot is done. After filling the mugs, I return them to Fiona at the register.

She's already left a ten-dollar bill on the counter, but when she collects her drinks, she traces her fingers along mine. A shiver runs up my spine, then she turns away and walks outside, leaving a sad jingle in her wake.

THE BLUE SEDAN WAITS FOR ME TO TURN OFF THE ROAD before leaving, since the entrance to the parking lot is little more than a single car's width. I give a small wave as I drive past, then pull into the nearest spot. Fiona's truck is parked in the far corner. It's one of three vehicles in the lot.

I never bother coming to White Rock Lake Park because it's a twenty-minute drive east of Kalomish with a simple loop trail. The lake is pretty enough, but there are better hikes.

I get out and pretend to stretch for a moment, scanning the park for Fiona. There's a large, flat section between the cars and the tree line that contains a few picnic tables and benches, but Fiona isn't out in the open.

Her note this morning only said, *'White Rock Lake Park, 8:30.'* I stand there for a moment, trying to decide where to go, when a couple walking two black labs appears at the western trailhead where the path wends along the shore. I don't want to run into them, so I veer toward the eastern trailhead that leads through the woods within the park's boundary. I just have to trust that she knows a good location, and I'll stumble across her eventually.

When I reach the trees, I see a woman sitting on a bench offset from the path in the fading light.

Fiona.

She stands as I approach, and her soft brown hair falls over her shoulders, contrasting nicely against the green tank top hugging her curves. Where the tank top ends, form-fitting blue jeans take over.

I can't decide where to look. Those legs that felt so warm and soft with my face buried between them? Those toned, tanned arms and the well-muscled shoulders that are visible under the cascade of straight, chestnut-colored hair? Or the smooth skin on her chest contoured by her tight top?

"Something wrong with my shirt, Tre?"

I jerk my gaze up to her face. Her smile has turned into that mocking smirk I can never get out of my mind.

Her eyes! That was the right answer. Damn it! I berate myself for screwing up our first private meeting since the night she spent at my apartment. I sigh in disappointment.

"No. Sorry. That is a really good color on you, though."

She rolls her eyes before glancing over my shoulder. Then she turns to join me in walking along the path, deeper into the forest. "Right. I forgot what a fashionista you are," she says, and I'm unable to get a read on her mood.

I have no response, so we walk in silence for a few seconds, then I probe, "So, you wanted to meet out here…?"

"Yeah. I figured outside of town would be better, and the parks tend to be pretty empty this late."

"Right, I understood about the time and place. But I'm wondering why you wanted to meet," I say, turning to look behind us. There's nobody else in sight. "Did you want to talk about next week's plans here?"

"No. There's not enough privacy for *that*. We'll meet the night before at the storage unit to go over the details. Same as last time."

"Okay. Sounds good…" I trail off, waiting for the conversational ax to fall. If we're not here to talk about the plans, we must be here to talk about us. The silence stretches, and we come around the back end of the loop to see the lake ahead.

"You told Ewan about us?" Fiona finally says, and I can't really tell if it's a question or an accusation.

"Oh. Yeah."

"That's it? Yeah?"

"Well, I wanted to make sure he wouldn't interfere again. The last thing we need is another public debacle, so I thought I should tell him before that happened."

"Fine, but you couldn't let me know? He ambushed me about it at Malcolm's last night."

"I only told him the day before, and you didn't come in to Betty's at your normal time yesterday morning. It's not like we can talk there anyway, but I was surprised when you showed up. There was kind of a lot going on around us right then." It sounds like I'm making excuses, but it's all true.

She pauses facing the lake, but turns her head to glare at me. "Speaking of. What made you think it was a good idea to lead a people's revolution against the city council when you know you're the main suspect?"

"It's not *that* big of a deal. Plus, your whole plan depends on those execs being out of their houses during the town hall, so I've been trying to make sure that happens. Also, there are a lot of people around Kalomish who are on our side," I reply with a grin.

Fiona stares at me for a few moments. "Actually, I've been kind of surprised by that. There are plenty of people who complain, of course, but I didn't know so many were supportive of… direct activism."

"They may not be ready to take the same risks, but people like to do what's right."

"Maybe. But you've definitely made sure the sheriff is going to stay focused on you."

"Yeah, but that was never going to change. Being loud won't make things worse, but suddenly acting differently and pretending not to want Henley and Montank gone would be really suspicious." I pause, then add, "You know, I wanted to explain all that yesterday. I wish I could talk to you more."

"That's how we get caught, Tre." Fiona starts walking again.

I move to the inside of the trail so she can see the lake and what passes for a sunset when the peaks block the horizon. "I know. Obviously I haven't done anything else. It'd be nice if we could use burner phones, or something, though."

She sighs. "There's no way we're doing that. The cops are going to pick you up again at some point. If you have a burner phone on you when they do, or if they search your place and find one, they're going to know you're hiding something. Plus, even if they wouldn't have my name, they'd have any texts we send and any call history, which means they'd know you have an accomplice."

My shoulders slump. I can't fault her logic. "I know. You're right. I'd like to at least be able to talk to you, though. Even if it's not about that stuff."

I guess she thinks I'm trying to justify having burner phones because she responds, "No one would ever believe you if you tried to explain that you weren't doing anything illegal. 'I was just talking to my secret girlfriend, who I can't talk to on *my* phone for no reason at all, officers.'" She laughs as she finishes mimicking me, not noticing that I've stopped dead in my tracks.

"Secret girlfriend?" I ask, and Fiona whips around to face me. "Is that what you are?"

"No! Shit. I was just trying to point out the absurdity of it. I'm not... I mean we're not..." She takes a deep breath. "I have no idea what we are or what's going on between us, Tre. I told you before that I haven't figured out how I feel. I had a great time that night, but I don't know if that's enough to try being more. I have a lot to get over.

"Add in everything else, and we are so far beyond complicated. I'm not sure I want that. I didn't mean anything by it. I just wanted to point out why burners wouldn't work. I'm sorry."

I nod and catch up to walk beside her again, trying not to feel rejected because technically nothing's changed, but the surge of hope I felt when she called herself my girlfriend just crashed hard into reality.

"Before we get to the end of the trail, what else did you want to talk about?" I ask.

"That's pretty much it. But now that Ewan knows about us, be extra careful with him, too. You two already talked about me enough when there was nothing to know. You can't let anything slip. He may seem like some wannabe-Buddha, but just because he's chill doesn't mean he's dumb. No one can know what we've been doing."

"I know. I only told him to prevent problems." When Fiona doesn't respond, I add, "That's everything?"

"For now," she confirms, ambling back toward the trailhead and the parking lot.

I glance back, making sure nobody is around to see us in what remains of the dim light. We're alone, so I place my hand on the small of Fiona's back while we walk. She doesn't pull away, but we split up before we reach the tree line, leaving the same way we arrived. Alone.

Chapter 25
Curiosity Killed the Cat Burglar

FIONA

"I THOUGHT WE WERE GOING TO MEET TOMORROW NIGHT," Tre says as he ducks under the door to the storage unit and helps me push it back down. Like last time, he's too close when he stands up. But unlike last time, I have to stop myself from moving toward him rather than stepping away.

Aside from the thirty minutes we spent walking along the trails near White Rock Lake, I've been keeping my distance and trying to be smart. Special Agent Connor Smith is still skulking about. I've seen him in the diner more than once when I've stopped to grab coffee before work, so my interactions with Tre have been limited to those brief exchanges coupled with stolen glances when I've gone into Betty's on Sundays for brunch. All three of them.

Ewan had the day off on the last one. I guess the river was too low to run rafts, so he came with me. Amazingly, he didn't make a single remark even though he definitely noticed me staring at Tre.

Exactly like I'm doing right now.

Shit, I chide myself as I retreat toward the workbench near the wall.

"Um, yeah. Tomorrow," I say, swallowing and averting my eyes. "We actually need to get into the houses tomorrow night to get everything set up, so I wanted to go over the plan tonight."

"Tomorrow night?" Tre's voice is sharp.

"When else would we do it? We have to set everything up before the town hall, so we can both be there like normal, and we can't do it during the day. Someone would be bound to see us."

"So we're going to… break in? While they're home?"

I nod. "Yeah. Unless you've got some way to get them out of their houses in the middle of the night?" I really tried to come up with something, because I'm also not thrilled about the idea of breaking into occupied houses—even if they'll never know we were there, it feels wrong in a way the stuff we've done up until this point hasn't.

"I…" Tre begins, then pauses, eyes downcast. "We… No. That won't work," he mutters.

"If it makes you feel better, I couldn't come up with anything either. If you think of something in the next twenty-four hours, though, let me know."

"How? We're supposed to be keeping our distance, right?" He doesn't sound any happier about it than I am.

"Call my office. Ask to speak to me. If Carol says I'm busy, leave a message saying that I left my wallet at the diner, and I'll call you back."

"You just came up with that now?" he asks, eyebrows raised, a skeptical look in his grey eyes.

I shrug.

A grin spreads across his face. "You've been thinking about me," he says, sitting down on the stool closest to the storage unit's door, leaving me with the one between him and the wall, same as last time.

Unlike last time, the bombs we'll be using are different because I had to build them myself. I tried more than once to get my dad to change his mind. But his answer was the same every time: not as long as Tre's involved. I'm lucky he never bothered asking for the key to the storage unit back, so I at least had a place to work.

"Anyway," I state, trying to force the conversation back on track. "I'd like to go in around two in the morning. People have usually been asleep for a couple of hours by that point, and it'll give us plenty of time to get away. Once we're inside, it'll take me about fifteen minutes to get everything wired up."

"How are we getting in?"

"I've got a lock-picking gun."

"You've…" Tre shakes his head. "MacGyver would've picked the locks the old-fashioned way."

My laughter bounces off the storage unit's steel walls. "Yeah. You're right," I agree after a moment.

Tre sits beside me in silence as I explain the rest of the plan. "Okay," he finally says when I'm done. "Want to spend the night tomorrow?"

"What?" I ask, the question taking me by surprise.

"You should spend the night. We're already going to be together for most of it. Come to my place when we're done."

"I… Yeah. Okay."

I SQUEEZE THE HANDLE OF THE LOCK-PICKING GUN, AND A sharp *snap* echoes through the night.

"Jesus," Tre murmurs as I flinch. "You didn't mention how loud that thing is."

I squeeze the handle two more times as I continue applying torque to the lock. I turn up the tension gauge on the gun and squeeze the handle another couple of times before the lock rotates, the bolt softly clicking over.

I turn the knob, waiting to see if an alarm goes off. Waiting to see if we need to make a break for the trees. I was careful when I built the bombs, and we're both wearing gloves and masks now. If we need to leave it all and run, they won't be able to get fingerprints off anything.

But the night is quiet, and the lights in the house stay off.

"We're in." I bend to pick up the container on the ground next to me. It's a sealed paint bucket with wires coming out of it. It's small enough that if I stash it in a closet, behind some coats or boxes, it should go unnoticed.

We step through the door, and I gently close it behind us. In unspoken agreement, we pause again to listen, but the house is silent. I take slow, sliding steps, trying to avoid bumping into anything as I move further inside, heading for the hallway where Tre's drawing indicated there should be a small interior closet.

When I open the first door on the left, it's pitch black. I can't tell if it's the closet I'm looking for or something else entirely. I hit the button on my headlamp, turning it on to the red light mode. Muted crimson floods the space. Tre's drawings were right.

Hopefully the same will be true for the second house, I think as I set the container down and move some boxes out of the way, clearing space to slide it under the shelves once I've got everything wired up.

"How does that work, anyway?" Tre whispers.

"Can we discuss bomb-making later?" I reply at the same volume.

"Yeah, sure," he agrees, fidgeting.

I connect the wires coming out of the paint can—which contains discretely packaged gasoline and ammonium nitrate—to the small microcontroller, my hands casting eerie shadows in the bloody light. Having spent my entire childhood watching my dad fiddle with different breadboards and circuit implementations, plus reading at least fifty different DIY articles, made designing my own MOSFET-controlled switch on a timer easy.

I just hope I got the proportions of fuel to oxidizer right, and I hope the explosion and resulting fire will be as controlled as I intend them to be. I checked my calculations multiple times, but I'd feel better about all of this if I'd been able to get my dad to agree to validate them since I've never designed an IED before.

As soon as I've got the paint can wired to the microcontroller, I connect the series of twelve AA batteries to the controller, and the timer starts. It doesn't look like anything—there are no flashing lights, nothing counting down—but in seventeen and a half hours, the circuit will open and energy will flow through the wires into the paint can, where they'll spark against the steel plate inside, and the gasoline will ignite. Exothermic decomposition of the ammonium nitrate will do the rest. The paint can will explode, sending what remains of the gasoline flying onto the house's walls and floor. Then the whole thing will go up.

The houses at Highland Estates are spaced far enough apart that as long as the explosion isn't any bigger than I intend, no other houses are likely to catch fire. And all the lawns are so well watered that there's next to no risk of starting a forest fire despite the droughts the entire state always seems to experience this time of year.

It should work exactly like I intend.

Should.

"That's it. I'm done," I whisper as I push the device closer to the wall and move the boxes in front of it, effectively hiding it from view.

"Okay. Let's go," Tre replies, leading the way back to the door we came in.

As soon as we're outside and the door is shut, I insert the tension rod and lock-picking gun back into the lock.

"Again?" he asks.

"Do you want them to wake up and think, 'Huh, wasn't the door locked last night?'"

Tre shakes his head.

"Then yes, again."

"Okay," he agrees, his eyes scanning the area around us as a series of loud *snaps* reverberate across the neighborhood.

The lock slides into place after a few seconds. "Good?"

Tre nods. "Seems like it."

"Okay. One down, one to go."

We go to the second house and repeat the process, using a utility room instead of a closet this time to set up the bomb. As I'm wiring the battery series to the microcontroller, something brushes across my lower back.

"Shit!" I hiss, jerking away.

"What?" Tre whispers as I twist around. "Oh. Shit," he mutters, his voice gone flat in shock.

We both stare silently at the black cat that's rubbing its face against my thigh, purring.

"You didn't say anything about a cat!" I accuse.

"I didn't *know* there was a cat! Obviously!"

"Did you ask?"

"About cats? Why would I ask about cats?" Tre shoots back. "Who brings a cat on a work trip? I checked to make sure there were no other people living in these houses, not pets."

"What about the other house?"

"What about it? I didn't see any animals. No food or water bowls. Did you?"

"No, but until this cat showed up, I didn't know there were any here either," I tell him as I scratch its ears.

"Well, we can double-check before we leave," Tre says, sounding annoyed. "What are we going to do with this one?"

"I don't know. Take it with us?"

A crease forms between his eyebrows. "You want to steal their cat?"

"Well, we can't leave it here!"

"What if we just put it outside when we leave?"

"So it can get eaten by a coyote?"

Tre sighs. "Fine. We'll take it with us."

"Go check the rest of the house. Make sure there's not another one," I order.

"You want me to—" Tre shakes his head and then turns and walks away.

"That's right," I say to the cat as it rolls onto its back. "You're going on an adventure."

WE'VE BEEN SILENTLY TRUDGING THROUGH THE STATE forest along a series of interconnected logging roads and hiking trails when Tre finally says, "What are we going to do with it?" as he stares at the cat in my arms.

"Batman."

"What?"

"His name is Batman," I clarify. "It says so on his collar."

And Batman is starting to feel really heavy. I've been carrying him for over an hour and a half. Based on the amount of squirming he's doing, he'd prefer if I put him down. I don't know what he'd do if I did though, and we're not that far from my truck now. This time, it actually made sense to drive and then cut across the state forest land on foot. If we'd tried to bike this route, it would've been more than forty miles on the back roads. If we'd taken the more direct route up the highway, we would've been seen. There's no way they'll connect my truck to the houses catching fire with so many hours between the events and so much distance between the locations.

"Of course it is," Tre grumbles. "So what are we going to do with Batman?"

"I don't know. Want a cat?"

"Yeah, I'm sure it'll work out really well for me if the sheriff shows up at my apartment to ask me some questions and sees Batman lurking inside."

I sigh. He's got a point. "I don't know. I guess we'll drive over to the nearest Walmart so I can get a litter box, and I'll take him home with me. Tomorrow I'll see if I can get Ewan to take him for a couple of days until I can figure something out. Rain check on spending the night?"

Tre glares at Batman, muttering something under his breath, and Batman purrs in my arms.

"Sorry, I didn't quite catch that," I say.

"Are you free this weekend?"

"Why?"

"Well, if I'm taking a rain check because Batman had to come slinking out of the shadows, I want to reschedule now."

"Saturday night?" I ask after considering it for a moment.

"Alright," Tre agrees.

Chapter 26
Hard Questions Abound

I STROLL INTO THE TOWN HALL AND SCAN THE ROOM. IT'S nearly as busy as last month. All the seats are taken, but there's more standing room available. When I check my watch, it's ten to seven. I'm never here this early, so more people are likely to show.

Lucas notices me looking around and waves me over to join him. He's standing with Walt and Henry near the middle of the back wall. They were at Betty's this evening, but I closed extra early to make sure I'm present—and visible—before the meeting starts. I stand next to Lucas, trying to gauge the feeling of the crowd.

Several dozen of those standing nearby were with us at the diner, so I know they're riled up and ready to speak out. Many of the people in the seats are talking excitedly. I can't make out individual conversations with so much going on, but the overall buzz is low and intense.

In addition to the usual deputies near the dais, there are two more in the back, flanking the doors. And that's before the sheriff comes out with the council.

Of course the developers get extra protection, I fume. The rest of us have been getting screwed for the last couple of years, and the sheriff's department hasn't done a thing, despite the injunctions against Henley and Montank. But the instant these execs show up, the sheriff is ready to do his job.

I take a breath. If I can't rein this anger in, I'll get myself thrown out before I can be alibied.

Special Agent Connor Smith is standing against the wall nearest the dais. His posture is relaxed, but his eyes are roving over everyone.

At least he's not part of Jacob's games. He's out here early and doing his work in front of us.

I search the front rows for Fiona's familiar chestnut-brown hair while distractedly agreeing with Walt on whatever he's complaining about.

There she is! I spot her in the third row, but not near the center aisle like usual. This place must have filled up fast.

Now that I've found her, I recognize Ewan sitting next to her. She leans closer as she talks to him.

Everything is going according to plan. Just let it all play out, I remind myself.

I settle against the wall, continuing to scan the crowd. My gaze repeatedly returns to Fiona, and we make eye contact several times when she turns to survey the room as well. Heat flushes my face each time, and I commit myself to biting my tongue tonight, even if it raises suspicion. I can't slip up and be the reason she gets caught.

At precisely seven o'clock, the city council members file in, accompanied by Sheriff Morris, and take their seats. The sheriff stands next to them on the dais.

Jacob waits for the noise to die down and then addresses the room. "Thank you all for coming this evening. I'm glad to see so many friends and neighbors here with us tonight." He gives the room a beaming smile as if that will make everyone forget their problems.

When the pause is filled with silence, he continues, "I imagine many of you are eager for an update on the investigation into the ecoterrorism of the Henley and Montank projects. We have—"

"We're eager for them to speak to us themselves!" a man's voice shouts from the crowd to my right.

"We have Sheriff Morris here tonight to brief everyone. We can all feel confident that the situation is under control and we have nothing to fear." Jacob turns and motions to the sheriff, who moves to take the microphone.

"How about Henley and Montank destroying our town!" an elderly woman calls out from along the wall far to my left.

Jacob pulls back the mic. "I will remind everyone that there is a designated question-and-answer period reserved at the end of the meeting. Please hold all comments until then." He passes the microphone to the sheriff, who steps to the forefront.

"My department is deploying its full resources to protect Kalomish from these terrorists. You've seen the patrols on the roads. We have a joint task force with the ATF dedicated to investigating the attacks. We will—"

"What about the pollution of the watershed after the Hay Creek development started? You investigating that?" a man seated in the middle yells.

Morris's face turns to a scowl in an instant. Before he can respond, though, the man to my right from before adds, "Yeah! Did you arrest anyone from Henley and Montank for that?"

I don't bother hiding my grin. It looks like I don't have to speak out tonight.

"I'm not finished," Sheriff Morris says. "We will provide all necessary protection so there are no more terrorist attacks. The criminals will be apprehended."

"Why don't you protect us from Henley and Montank?" a woman seated near the front shouts.

"Yeah, why do you only serve them, Sheriff? We're the ones who elected you!"

"Do they run your department?"

The interruptions are coming from all around now.

"Deputies," Morris begins, but realizes there are too many people shouting. He doesn't have enough deputies to remove them all. The two who are flanking the dais reflexively touch their hands to their belts.

Many of the voices are now directing their anger at the council, bypassing the sheriff entirely. Some people in the seats stand up with calls of "Where are Henley and Montank?" and "Do they run the city now, too?"

I fold my arms and enjoy the show. Hopefully they'll keep this up all night. Council members are covering their microphones with their hands and talking intensely among themselves until Jacob bangs a gavel repeatedly.

Why does he have a gavel? I wonder. *What a prick.*

"Order! Order! Everyone calm down or we'll cancel this meeting!" he practically yells into his microphone. This temporarily overpowers the noise of the crowd, and everyone falls silent. The tension in the air is palpable, but nobody sits down.

"The council has heard your numerous requests since last month's town hall. As always, we serve the interests of the people of Kalomish."

"We didn't want them—" a man speaks up, but Jacob swiftly cuts him off.

"We have invited representatives from Henley and Montank to join us this evening." Jacob pauses with a benevolent smile at the nodding and murmuring passing through the audience. "This council has only authorized contracts that will benefit the people of Kalomish and contain strong provisions for the protection of our environment and resources."

He turns and signals a staffer behind him, near the door the council entered through.

"At this time, the members of Henley and Montank who are overseeing the projects will share some prepared remarks. After that, we will hold the open question-and-answer session where you can address your concerns in an orderly fashion."

Two new people step onto the dais and stand in front of the council seats. A thin man well over six feet tall smiles and waves to the room, while a short woman receives a microphone from Jacob. She turns to the crowd and offers a matching smile.

"Good evening. First, I want to thank the Kalomish City Council for kindly inviting us to join you all tonight. We're very grateful to have this opportunity to connect with you directly."

"Get to the point!" a voice calls out from the standing section, but I can't tell who it was.

Unbothered, the woman continues, "We'd like to introduce

ourselves. I'm Henley and Montank's Director of Operations for the Western Division—"

"You ruined Hay Creek! How are you going to fix it?" the man standing to my right interrupts. *I should find out who that is. I bet we'd get along great.*

Jacob responds before the corporate execs. "We have warned you repeatedly. The time for comments and questions is reserved for the end. Deputies, please escort Mr. Trowbridge out."

The people standing near Mr. Trowbridge step closer and form a wall around him, then a woman in the front row yells at the execs, "You're here to make money off our mountains and rivers. When your condos fail because you ruined everything, you'll just write it off from your skyscrapers. We'll be the ones dealing with the mess forever!"

There's a commotion near the door along the back wall. When I turn to look, the deputy stationed there is pushing his way through the crowd to the exit. The deputy on the other side is already gone.

Other voices have started barking angry demands at the dais. Jacob is looking expectantly at the deputies, but they're looking at the sheriff, who is standing off to the side, animatedly talking into his phone. Both of the execs are standing awkwardly, unable to respond to the gaggle of anonymous people shouting at them.

After another difficult minute passes, the sheriff beelines to Jacob. They confer briefly, but the room is far too noisy to hear anything. I'm not left wondering for long, though. Sheriff Morris leaves his two deputies at the dais and marches down the aisle, his face a storm cloud. He glares at me as he heads for the exit, and behind him Special Agent Connor Smith pushes away from the wall, his eyes narrowed as he follows.

"The remainder of this meeting is canceled," Jacob announces. "Thank you all for attending. We will meet again when we can all act responsibly. For now, please make way for our first responders as you leave. We'll see you at the next town hall."

With that, the council members stand and exit, bringing the corporate executives with them.

The shouting skyrockets as nearly everyone in the room joins in.

Those who weren't angry at Henley and Montank before are now pissed about being dismissed without discussion or having any chance to be heard.

It's impossible to make out Fiona in the crowd, so I slip out while most people are busy yelling after a council that's never listened. At the end of Main Street, a cruiser speeds out of sight, lights flashing.

Well, I guess Fiona's bombs worked. Perfect timing. Not that I'd expect anything less, I think with a smile, walking down the steps. It looks like I'll reach Mal's early enough to grab a seat.

"RICHARD WHITE, COME WITH ME," A DEEP VOICE BOOMS, formally but not very politely. It's the same deputy who escorted me last time. I follow him deeper into the sheriff's department, leaving the waiting area behind.

I'm here alone this time.

Kevin and his partner, Deputy Wasserman, were parked outside Betty's this afternoon. As soon as I left the diner, they stopped me to let me know I was being summoned by the sheriff for more questions and pressured me to ride with them. They weren't arresting me, so I politely declined, but I didn't press my luck by delaying like before.

I called Arthur Kostas on the drive over since he gave me his card for exactly this situation. But just as Fiona predicted, he's no longer any help. He sounded very sympathetic when he informed me he wouldn't be able to assist me in this matter as his firm is retained by White Construction Incorporated, and it would be a *'significant conflict of interest'* to represent a client who is accused of destroying property of White Construction.

Disappointing, but not surprising. That just means I'll be stuck listening to the sheriff all afternoon.

Deputy Voice leads me to the same conference room I was in previously. He waits at the door, and, not having any better ideas, I sit in the same seat again.

After a few boring minutes of the two of us looking everywhere but at each other, the sheriff and another deputy walk in. His eyes flick to the empty seat next to me, and he grins.

Next, Connor enters carrying a manila folder and a notepad. He joins the sheriff at the table as the new deputy sets up a video camera on a tripod.

"We'll be recording this interview," Sheriff Morris announces to the camera pointed down the length of the table. He introduces himself, the two deputies in the room, and then me, using my full name—Richard Alan White the Third. I manage not to roll my eyes. Connor introduces himself as Special Agent Connor Smith of the Bureau of Alcohol, Tobacco, Firearms and Explosives.

"No counsel today, Mr. White?"

"No, just me."

The sheriff's eyes gleam in anticipation. "Mr. White, where were you last night, Wednesday, August twelfth?"

I cock my head to the side, astonished that *this* is how he's choosing to start. "What is this regarding?" I ask, taking a page out of Mr. Kostas's book since it worked so well.

"Don't play games with me, White. You're a suspect in two counts of arson. If you can't provide a credible alibi, I may just arrest you here and now."

I turn my head to stare straight into the camera, trying to highlight for the record the hostility and threat he's applying.

Special Agent Smith's eyes are on me as he taps the butt of his pen against the notepad.

Looking back at Morris, I answer, "'Night' is a long time, Sheriff. I was several places depending on the time. Care to be more specific?"

"No. In fact, you'd better just tell us where you were the entire day." A scowl is firmly ensconced on his face now.

"Alright. I was working at Betty's Diner from six a.m. until shortly before the town hall meeting—"

"You were there the whole time?"

"Yes. I own the place. Most days, I'm there open to close. Hundreds of people see me. Feel free to ask around town."

"Go on," he instructs tersely.

"I closed up and went to the town hall. That ended early, which you know because you left before the rest of us." His scowl deepens. "After that, I spent the remainder of the night at Malcolm's bar until I went home. Half of Kalomish was there. Then I got up this morning and was back at the diner at six."

"Was anyone with you? Can anyone corroborate your whereabouts overnight?" Morris asks.

"No. I live alone. No one was with me."

The scowl eases as he leans forward slightly. "And the night before? You accounted for work at six. Where were you before that?"

Here we go, I think. *Don't screw this up.* "Yes, before work yesterday I was also at home. Once again, I live alone. It's not a crime to be single." *Nice, I didn't even have to lie. I got home at least half an hour before work.*

Morris, however, seems delighted. "So you have no alibi for Tuesday night."

"Whoa, you asked me about Wednesday night, so I told you about Wednesday. Are we going to talk about where I spend every minute of every day? As Mr. Kostas told you before, if you're only fishing for information, I'll just leave."

"We'll talk about whatever I ask you about. If you don't cooperate with this investigation—"

"What? You'll think I'm a suspect? You already do. All I really do is work too much and live alone. Do you have any actual questions for me?"

"Yes. You still need to account for your whereabouts on Tuesday night." His face radiates smugness.

"I already answered that question. And nobody can corroborate because I was alone at home. Like I said."

Agent Smith clears his throat.

Morris glances sideways, then refocuses on me. "When was the last time you were at Highland Estates?"

"Highland Estates…? I visited my mom there maybe three weeks ago. I guess it was the weekend, so maybe three and a half. What does that matter?"

"I'll decide what matters, Mr. White. You haven't been there since?"

"Obviously not, or I would have mentioned that as the last time I was there." The scowl is back in place. "Why are you wasting time asking about what I did almost a month ago? Whatever you think I'm responsible for must have happened yesterday, since that's what you were focused on. You ran out of the town hall meeting last night, then the city council hid from everyone demanding accountability. Is that when this happened?"

"I'm asking the questions here. With your background in construction, how much training have you had in explosives?"

"Explosives? What do you think I am? I don't have any training in explosives. I know about building things, not blowing them up. Wait, are you trying to pin the Hay Creek thing on me, too?"

Special Agent Smith flips open his manila folder and shifts his gaze to the papers inside.

"We're conducting a thorough investigation, and we have to follow all leads. Don't you want the terrorists destroying our town to be caught?"

"I definitely do, Sheriff. But they hold your leash, so you'll never punish Henley and Montank for destroying our town," I say heatedly, standing up.

"You just settle down, White," Morris replies with that gleam in his eyes again.

"Mr. White, how much do you know about steel I-beams?" Agent Smith asks calmly, speaking up for the first time.

"What?"

"You've spoken of your knowledge of construction. Do you have experience working with steel beams?"

"Yes, of course. I've worked with and studied all kinds of equipment and structures. You can't possibly think that's enough to blame me for Hay Creek. I can name dozens of people who have experience working with I-beams, and they're all currently in construction. I've been out of that field for years."

"Can any of those people create and program a MOSFET-controlled switch?"

"I don't know. I have no idea what the hell you just said."

"Surely with your," Smith pauses to look in the folder, "materials science degree you're familiar with circuitry."

"Surely with the research you've done on me, you're aware that I never took a single circuitry class. I don't know how to program anything. I run a diner, and before that I helped manage building sites. My spare time is spent outdoors. The most I use a computer for is to do my business accounting."

Special Agent Smith pulls two photographs from his folder and places them in front of me. They're black and white shots of the burnt-out houses at Highland Estates.

"Mr. White, someone in this community is destroying buildings, and they're escalating. They've moved from isolated, empty sites to people's homes. These two could have easily spread to the entire neighborhood or set the state forest on fire."

I look up from the photos to meet his gaze. "Setting a fire doesn't take a college degree. You were at the town hall last night. Almost everyone was there, and they were all angry and shouting. Are you going to arrest them all?"

I slide the pictures across the table.

"I came here in good faith. I love Kalomish and want to help, so I gave you my time after working all day, only none of you are doing anything in good faith. You want to pin every crime in town on me. Except you can't, because I'm no terrorist. You just want me to say something that you can twist and use as an excuse to blame me for everything." I'm staring hard at the camera now. "I tried to be helpful. If you pull this again, I'll sue you for harassment."

"There's no need for hostility, Mr. White," Special Agent Smith says.

The sheriff leans back in his chair as I stalk past him and out the door.

Chapter 27
Picnic Basket Case

FIONA

"No," Carol murmurs from around the corner. It's seven-fifty, and the office isn't open yet. She's either on the phone or she's talking to Jean, since I saw Natalie restocking the cabinet in exam room three about thirty seconds ago.

There's an indistinct response. Jean then.

"I'm certain Rich is insured, and Henley and Montank must have their own policy to replace whatever their people lost in the fire. It's all just stuff. But I feel so bad that man lost his cat. It's so sad. I'm sure whoever did it had no idea there was an animal inside the house," Carol replies, continuing her side of the conversation. "I heard they brought Tre in for questioning again yesterday afternoon."

I stop in my tracks, just around the corner, still out of sight. Batman the cat is fine. He was sitting on my bed cleaning himself when I left this morning. Not that anyone else knows that. Well, anyone besides my dad and Tre.

This is the first I'm hearing about Tre being taken back in for questioning, though. I haven't stopped by Betty's yet this morning, and Ewan and my waiting room are the only other places I ever hear gossip.

"Not that he had anything to do with it, obviously," Carol rushes to add.

"No, of course not," Jean agrees. "They wouldn't have let him go if he did. He's such a nice boy. He never charges me for my coffee when I go in for breakfast."

I step out from around the corner. "Is the first patient at eight-fifteen or eight-thirty?" I ask Carol, already knowing the answer—it's always eight-thirty on Friday. I have enough time to run to Betty's and pass a note to Tre as I pick up some coffee.

I was planning on that note being a meeting spot for tomorrow night, but if the investigation is focused back on Tre, I should cancel. That would be the smart thing to do.

"Eight-thirty," Carol says.

"Great. I'm going to go grab a coffee. Do either of you want anything?"

Shadows are creeping across the landscape when I pull into the lot at White Rock Lake Park shortly before eight. I seriously considered canceling on Tre yesterday. I sat in the loading zone, staring into Betty's, weighing my options for long enough that I ended up being a few minutes late to my first appointment. But no one from the sheriff's department or the ATF was inside, and instead of canceling, I passed him a note that said *'White Rock Lake, 8 PM'* when I paid for my coffee.

The park worked well as a meeting spot a couple of weeks ago, and it's far enough away from Kalomish that we're unlikely to run into anyone we know. Plus, this late in the evening, the traffic on the single-lane road that leads out here is sparse enough to make it easy to tell if you're being followed.

Tre's car is already sitting in the lot. Aside from mine, it's the only vehicle, which is good, because being seen with Tre right now would be a mistake, and that's the real reason we're meeting here.

My dad made sure to tell me this morning that the sheriff talked to Tre again. My dad, who was apparently warning me off. My dad, who seems to have worked out that my entanglement with Tre is something more than... strictly business. My dad, who's right, of course. About all of it.

But here I am anyway, hoping that they're less focused on Tre than I think they are. Hoping that they haven't been able to make a judge think they have enough probable cause to get a court order allowing them to put a tracker on his car. *But if they had that, they'd have arrested him already*, I think.

I take a deep breath, grab my bag off the seat beside me, and get out of my truck. The echo of the door slamming shut behind me bounces across the lot as I move toward the trees in search of Tre. The breeze is still carrying the heat of the day, and there's a fire ban in effect. All the parks are emptier than they would be if half the state weren't bracing for wildfires.

I was lucky the bombs I planted in the executives' houses at Highland Estates caused exactly the amount of damage they were supposed to, and no more. A fact my dad snapped at me more than once.

The pictures on the front of the local paper showed two burnt-out shells. The surrounding houses were untouched, and despite my dad's reaction, I don't think he could've done a better job.

I meander farther into the woods and find Tre on the same bench where I was waiting for him last time. He stands when he sees me.

"You brought a picnic basket," I say when I'm close enough to make out the shape next to him.

"This time it *is* actually a date," he replies smugly, his grey eyes fixed on me, and I can't help but remember that night in the trailer. Something must show on my face because his smile grows a little broader and his eyes flick toward my chest, but, for once, I don't say anything about it.

"Is it? Is that what we're doing?" The question is, unfortunately, as much for me as it is for him, because I can't figure out what I'm doing.

"Are you seeing anyone else?" Tre asks, seeming to already know the answer.

"No."

"Do you want to?"

"No," I admit, knowing it's the crux of my problem.

"Me neither. So yeah, I think that's what we're doing."

"And how is that going to work when we can't be seen together?"

Tre shrugs, then picks up the picnic basket. He takes my hand and tugs me along the trail toward the lake. I fall into step beside him as he says, "Change your mind."

"Change my mind?" I scoff.

"Sure. Us not being seen together is your rule. Not mine. So change your mind, and then it's not a problem."

"Uh huh. Because the sheriff wasn't just talking to you, Tre. Again," I reply, rolling my eyes. "Because the ATF isn't in town, looking at you as their prime suspect."

I know I should leave. I know I never should've told Tre I'd spend the night after Highland Estates. And I shouldn't have offered a rain check when it became clear I wouldn't be able to. I should've listened to my dad. I shouldn't have come here tonight.

"You're right. He was. And just like last time, he has nothing, and I won't tell him anything. Even if they were to arrest me tomorrow, I still wouldn't tell them anything, Fiona," he says seriously, and the soft buzzing of insects awakening for the night seems to underscore his words.

"You're really going to sit in a jail cell when you didn't even build the bombs?"

"If it comes to it, yeah. That's my plan. The maximum sentence in Oregon for property damage that doesn't result in bodily harm is five years."

"You looked it up?"

"Yes. Before Hay Creek. I know you believe I don't think things through, Fiona, but I do. Even if I don't think them through the same way that you do."

"Okay, fine. But that doesn't mean it would be a single charge. And federal charges could be a max of twenty years," I tell him.

"I know. I looked that up, too. After the ATF agent came into the diner the first time."

"Or that the sentences would run concurrently if there were more than one."

"Fiona, *I know*," Tre says, his thumb running across the back of my hand. "Most likely they would, though. You know you're considering the worst possible outcome as the default?"

"Yes, because preparing for the worst is the *smart* thing to do," I assert.

"Okay, you're not wrong, but it's unlikely they'd get a conviction against me."

"Why? Because you're everybody's best friend?"

"Yes. The same way that you've spent the better part of the past year making everyone believe you're pro-development, I've spent most of my life being *everyone's* friend, and no one wants Henley and Montank here. Those two things combined would make it next to impossible for them to get a conviction."

"You're…"

"Right? You can say it, you know," he states lightly.

"Fine," I grumble. "You're right. No jury in Kalomish would convict you. But that won't matter if they bring federal charges against you."

"It wouldn't matter. I wouldn't mention you," he tells me, and I…

I believe him, I realize. It's the same thing I said to my dad when he told me Tre would tell the cops it was me.

"I… I'll think about it," I say as the lake comes into view.

"Good. How's the cat?"

I sigh. "Ewan wouldn't take him. He's still at my house."

"Oh," Tre murmurs, and it sounds like he's trying to repress a laugh. "How's that going?" He releases my hand and pulls a thin blanket from the side of the picnic basket, spreading it across the ground.

I can't help but remember that woman kneeling in front of Eddie and sliding her mouth over him. Or Eddie licking whipped cream off her face. Or the chocolate syrup dripping from her boobs onto his body. Or Tre saying, '*You know, we could… If you wanted to.*' And the truth is, I really fucking want to. I wanted to even then.

I hope there's whipped cream and chocolate syrup in that picnic basket.

"My dad isn't thrilled," I reply, which is only a bit of an understatement. I'm not sure if he was more surprised to see a cat on the kitchen counter when he woke up Wednesday morning or pissed to learn the *reason* Batman was in the house to begin with.

"What'd you tell him?"

"I... Are you asking if he knows?" I probe, setting my bag at my feet as I drop to sit beside Tre, my shoulder brushing against his.

Tre shrugs, and I'm suddenly replaying our conversation, trying to remember exactly what I've said since I arrived. *They questioned him again two days ago,* I realize once more. *What if the sheriff told Tre that he knew two people were involved in the crimes? What if Tre told them I was the other person? What if they told him they'd cut him a deal if he got me to confess to it on a recording? What if—*

"Fiona?" Tre says questioningly, and clearly I've missed something.

"Sorry, what?" I respond, still distracted as I remind myself that I decided I trusted Tre. I decided that weeks ago. He already knows enough that no one would need him to get me to confess to anything. He could simply take them to the storage unit. They'd cut the lock and bring in bomb-sniffing dogs, which would immediately alert on the space. Then they'd dust for prints and find mine *and* my dad's. Then they'd take swabs and do a chemical analysis, and the entire workbench—at the very least—would test positive for the same explosive residue they found at the sites.

Fuck. I thought I'd thought things through. I thought—

"Fiona?" Tre repeats, and my eyes focus on his, which look... concerned. "You wanna tell me what's wrong?"

"I..." I'm frozen with indecision, caught between the desire to trust Tre—to tell him the truth—and sheer panic, left feeling like a rudderless ship being tossed around a wine-dark sea.

There's no part of this situation that's familiar to me. I don't freeze. I wouldn't have made it through a single day in the ICU if I did. Yet, here I am. Unable to get the words out. Unable to deny it. Unwilling to confirm it.

"Nothing," I say after a moment, and my voice sounds strangled even to myself. "Nothing is wrong. I'm fine."

"You looked more fine that morning at the campsite than you do right now," Tre tells me, refusing to accept the lie.

"You…" I take a deep breath. "You know enough to send me to jail, Tre. And not only me."

"That's nothing— Ah. I see. I'm not going to, though."

"I know," I say, and I'm *almost* positive it's true. "It's just… he realized we were working together last month and things have been tense since then and he's convinced that you're the same as your dad and you'll try to pin everything on me," I blurt out.

"Okay. And he knows that we're…?" Tre asks, his uncertainty about whatever we are finally showing through.

"He doesn't know, but he assumes."

"Well. This isn't exactly how I was hoping tonight would go, but if it makes you feel any better, here's what happened when they had me come in for questioning." Tre explains his conversation with the sheriff and the ATF, ending with, "Then I left. That was it. That was the extent of the interview. He doesn't know anything. Not about me. Not about you. Not about *us*."

I nod, looking out at the lake. The surface is rippling softly in the breeze, and frogs are chorusing closer to the shore, their croaks echoing across the water and bouncing off the stone.

"So. What's the plan for the rest of the night?" Tre asks, giving me an out, evidently willing to let me continue to dance with the decision of whether we're actually doing this, because it's pretty clear what he wants.

It's been clear for a while. And I picked this park for a reason.

I look up at the cerulean sky above us. "Do you know anyone with a house for rent?" I finally ask, giving voice to my next most pressing thought.

"What?"

"I need to move." I interlace my hand with his and lean into him. His skin is warm, and he smells faintly of citrus. The scent is highlighted by the contrasting notes of cooling sunbaked granite and water that are suffusing the night air. Being here with him feels companionable and right in a way I never could've predicted. "I've been back for most of a year, and you were right. I can't keep living with my dad indefinitely," I say, and there's only the smallest hint of irony in my voice.

"I'll ask around. You're going to stay?" he verifies, and the hopefulness in his voice is impossible to miss.

"Yes. I'm going to stay. What's in the picnic basket?"

Chapter 28
From the Outside
In Flagrante Delicto

TRE

"Wʜᴀᴛ's ɪɴ ᴛʜᴇ ᴘɪᴄɴɪᴄ ʙᴀsᴋᴇᴛ?" Fɪᴏɴᴀ ᴀsᴋs.

I nod at the bag beside her. "What's in the bag?"

She reaches an arm across it, covering it.

"I'll show you mine if you show me yours," I offer.

"Alright. But not here. Let's move a little farther down," she says as she stands and hefts her backpack.

I wonder what difference it makes but say nothing. Instead, I scramble to my feet and bundle the blanket atop the picnic basket before joining Fiona on the trail. She loops her free arm through mine and leads me a couple of dozen yards away to a grassy clearing with a bench looking out at the lake.

When it's clear this is our destination, I spread out the blanket again.

"I believe you were going to show me something," Fiona tells me.

"Sure, I'll go first." I drop to my knees, reaching into the basket without letting her look inside. I smile as I raise two resealable bags. "I brought sandwiches."

Her head tilts slightly, and she opens her mouth to say something, but I rush to continue before she can. "Don't worry, that's not all. I also have chips. And water too."

Fiona's eyes have narrowed, her brow is furrowed, and she's staring at me. "Tre, what the fuck?"

"It's a date at a park. I brought a picnic. What's wrong? What did you bring?" I ask, sounding confused.

She stares at me for a few moments before shaking her head. She unzips her backpack, reaches into it without looking, and holds up a pack of condoms.

"Oh… That kind of date," I say, feigning surprise. I pause for a heartbeat, then add, "Well, I guess we'll want these." I lift a can of whipped cream, a bottle of chocolate syrup, and a container of strawberries from the picnic basket.

My grin is genuine now, and I chuckle to myself.

"You ass," Fiona grumbles before barking out a laugh.

"And I do have some of those, too." I incline my head toward the condoms she's holding.

"Yeah, well, I wanted to make sure we have some that won't crumble to dust from old age," she responds with a smirk.

I set everything on the blanket and stand. "Well, I guess if I'm so out of practice, we should do this more often," I state, closing the distance between us.

Heat is already flooding up from my chest, burning my face as I kiss her. One hand wraps tight around her waist while the other slides through her hair to grab the back of her head. All thought of joking is gone, replaced by pure need as I plunge my tongue into her mouth and crush our bodies together. I want to touch every part of her, press myself against every part of her, fill every part of her at once. But it's more than just a physical need. I want to go to sleep next to her and wake up with her every morning. I want—

Fiona responds in kind, grabbing my hair with one hand and my ass with the other, pulling me firmly into this moment. My grip loosens as my attention focuses on our tongues sliding across each other.

I moan, and the friction of our hips grinding together brings me fully erect. I wish we didn't have all these stupid clothes in the way, but I'd have to let go of her to remove them. I slip my hands under her shirt and run them up her ribs, lifting it as I go.

Fiona must not want to pause either. She yanks my head back and to the side, breaking our kiss to shift her mouth to my neck, alternately licking and sucking.

Chills race up and down my spine. I groan and stop trying to remove her shirt. There's no way I'm interrupting this. Instead, I kick off my shoes and unbutton my pants. I get the fly undone as a wave of pleasure runs through me.

"Oh my god. You're incredible," I tell her in a breathy whisper. My dick is throbbing, but I don't want to move and risk ending this sensation. I undo the fly on her jeans while she works her tongue on the other side of my neck.

Her mouth vanishes as she stops to wriggle out of her pants. Normally I'd kill to watch that happen, but I'm so desperate to get free of my own that I yank them down instead. Then I rip my shirt off before staring hungrily at Fiona, who's standing with only her top half covered.

I've waited too long for this, so I step forward, trailing my fingers over her waist and ribs, then pull her shirt over her head. Right when the collar passes her mouth but still covers the rest of her face, I pause, trapping her arms. I hold the shirt aloft with one hand and press my lips to hers again. She leans into me, and her teeth scrape sharply over my lower lip as she bites it. I'm ready to have her this very second. But I don't. I don't know when we'll get to do this again, so I want it to last as long as possible.

I lightly trace her spine up to her neck with my free hand. Her whole body shivers, and I feel her smile through the kiss.

Finally, I pull her shirt off, tossing it aside before unhooking her bra. As soon as her hands are free, she grasps my dick and starts stroking. I pause, closing my eyes and letting out a long exhale.

"I've been dreaming of this," I admit, letting my hands roam over her body. I'm hard enough that I feel like I might burst. I need to be inside her, but I can't waste this opportunity.

I force myself to step back. Her hand falls away, and I groan, missing her touch already as I kneel beside the picnic basket. "The past three weeks have been torture. Knowing what it's like to have you, but not even really being able to talk to you, much less be with you. And I've thought about this every time I've seen you."

"Weeks? I've been imagining this since that night at the trailer."

"Same," I say, holding up the bottle of chocolate syrup.

Fiona grins as I close the distance between us. I gently brush her hair from one shoulder and then drip a line of syrup down the side of her neck and along her collarbone.

"My turn," I declare, then run my tongue over her skin, cleaning off the chocolate.

Her pulse is pounding under her soft skin. She drops her head and moans. After a moment, her hand is on my cock, slowly stroking. It takes every shred of willpower I have not to abandon my plan in favor of rocking my hips into her hand.

Instead, I lean back far enough to squeeze syrup all over her chest, then drop the bottle as the viscous liquid runs down her body.

With my hands free, I simultaneously massage her firm ass and trace my fingers over the soft skin of her well-muscled back. My mouth descends on her chest. I want to consume every part of her. I lick the syrup from her neck down to her tits, then circle my tongue around her nipple until it's a hard peak, and she moans again. When I bite it, she squeezes my cock hard, and it's my turn to moan. Her grip compressing the stiffness feels amazing, and it's heightened by the pressure throbbing in me.

"Do that again," I demand, moving my mouth to her other boob. Instead of licking or biting, I begin sucking. She's squeezing me as I flick my tongue over her nipple while I apply suction in waves. Her other hand is in my hair, fisting tightly as she arches forward. The light pain barely registers amidst the joy of the softness from her ass in my hand and her boob in my mouth competing with the burning desire to have all of her at once.

Eventually, I sink to my knees to follow lines of chocolate down her body with my tongue. When my lips reach her hips, her stomach quivers.

I give one last nip at her abs, then turn to the basket once again. I hold up a large strawberry and maintain eye contact as I trace my tongue over its tip, then bite into it, chewing and swallowing before moving in for another kiss. I've been enjoying the chocolate, but I want to fill her mind with the flavor of strawberries.

When Fiona leans into me, I step back, breaking off the kiss to hold up another. This one I place stem first in my mouth, gripping the top with my teeth. Fiona grips my neck with one hand while the other cups my balls, and she wraps her lips around the strawberry. Instead of biting it, like I expected, she sucks it out of my mouth. Her piercing emerald eyes stare into mine as she draws it from her mouth, tongue slowly trailing across it like a promise.

My dick is *aching*.

Before she can eat it, I snatch it from her hand, grab her ass to bring her close, and lick her neck as I trace the strawberry over her skin and down her body like the syrup earlier, ending on my knees again.

Then I bring the strawberry up from below, teasing it across her clit, which is already fully open. I shift her legs wider and lean in to flick my tongue over her, eliciting a gasp. When I press the tip of the fruit to the opening of her cunt, Fiona squirms and her hands tighten in my hair.

I rotate it against her as I maintain the rhythm of my tongue stroking across her clit. Her breathing comes faster. I pull it out and lean back to look up. Fiona is staring down at me in confusion, and maybe annoyance.

"What's—" she begins as I bite into the strawberry, eating everything but the stem. Then I plunge my fingers into her, and her eyes go wide. I smirk for a moment before putting my tongue back to work on her clit.

Fiona moans, "Yes, yes," as I find my rhythm. I'm stroking the tip of my tongue quickly while slowly pressing two fingers inside her, curling them toward me. The tangy flavor of her wetness blends with the sweetness of the strawberry. It takes a moment to find the rougher texture of her G-spot, but as soon as I do, she grabs my hair again.

"Don't stop," she breathes. It doesn't take long before she climaxes.

"Oh!" she calls out as her body convulses. Her hips are rocking too hard for me to continue using my mouth, but I hold my fingers against her, which makes her cry out more.

I slowly remove my fingers, supporting her as she sinks onto the blanket.

"As good as you remember?" I ask, letting more than a hint of satisfaction creep into my words.

"Amazing. Again."

I trace my fingers over her body as she recovers. Eventually, she shifts to her knees and turns to me.

"Get up," she orders, and I do as I'm told, anticipation already building.

Fiona points at the bench and says, "Sit there."

I follow her instructions. The wood is hard and rough, but there aren't any splinters, thankfully.

Fiona drags the blanket in front of the bench and reaches into her bag. She faces me with a smile and a dangerous gleam in her eye, then displays a coil of rope.

"Ooh, interesting," I murmur as she walks around the bench behind me. I turn to watch, more curious than ever.

"No, just sit there. Give me your hands," she demands.

I reach my arms up, hands near my head.

Fiona lets out an exasperated sigh and grabs one, pulling my arm over the back of the bench. She repeats the process with the other, and then the rope wraps around my wrists.

I'm staring forward, wondering what the plan is. She could've tied my hands without the bench, and even bound like this, I can get up. After a few seconds though, there's a tug to one side, and I can't move to the right any longer. *Huh*, is all I have time to think before I'm pulled the other way. Now I'm barely able to shift my arms. *She tied me to the legs of the bench*, I realize.

Oh shit, what if I can't get out of this? What if someone shows up? How long will it take to get away? What if she ends up disappointed because I can't do enough to make this fun? What if—

Fiona struts into view, her eyes boring into mine. "It's my turn to repay the favor," she says before straddling me and plunging her tongue into my mouth.

"Mmm," I groan and try to wrap my arms around her. Only my hands don't move, and my groan turns to frustration.

Fiona's lips, still pressed against mine, curl into a smile. She leans away to tell me, "Nope, you just have to stay there."

Then she lifts the whipped cream can and sprays a little where my neck meets my collarbone. The cold is quickly replaced by the warmth of her tongue as she licks it off my skin, and my eyes roll back as I let out a deep sigh. All too soon, it's gone, and Fiona pulls away. She adds some to each of my nipples, and I know that means her mouth will be on them soon. That knowledge, combined with the sudden chill, makes them harden and ache. Down below, my dick follows suit.

Fiona licks the cream off my chest, and I gasp in a breath. The pressure is building as my dick pulses with need. I strain against the rope, twisting my hands to no avail.

"Okay, you got me going. Untie me now," I plead.

Fiona sits back and stares into my eyes. "Oh, do you need release?"

She moves to kneel between my thighs, spraying whipped cream all over my cock. She gives me one last smirk and lowers her head.

"Oh, fuck!" I shout, closing my eyes and dropping my head back as she sucks it off me.

I'm unable to do anything but writhe, nearly overwhelmed, as she slowly works down the length of my shaft. Fiona moves inch by inch, licking the whipped cream off me, swirling her tongue all over, sucking as she swallows.

By the time she's taken me fully, there's a tingle building at the base of my dick. I arch my hips to press further into her throat, and I want to tangle my hands in her hair and push her head onto my cock even more, but I can't. I desperately want her to keep going, but I don't want to finish without ever being inside her.

"Oh god, Fiona. I'm getting close," I warn. If she wants to be in control, she can decide how this ends.

She eases off agonizingly slowly, running her tongue over every inch of my cock, leaving me a panting, quivering mess.

"Good?" she asks as she sits back, looking pleased.

"Incredible."

"I aim to please, too." She reaches behind her into the backpack, and all I can do is admire the view and wait for whatever comes next. The crinkling sound of a wrapper precedes her turning back to me with a condom.

"Damn," I breathe softly as she rolls it out over the length of me. "Okay, but you probably want to wait a sec because I am still right there."

"Mmm, then I guess I should join you," Fiona replies in a low voice. She climbs onto the bench, straddling my lap. She reaches her hand between us to align my cock with her clit, then rocks her hips sliding up and down my shaft. The friction is *exquisite*.

I look down to watch, but every time she rocks forward her tits rub against my face, and I can't focus on anything else.

I strain against my bonds again, but the most I can manage is sliding my arms side to side. I never realized how much I relied on grabbing or touching with my hands. Who thought torture would be so fun?

She's so wet as she slides along me, and my dick is throbbing again, although I'm not sure it ever stopped. I growl in frustration.

That must have been the cue Fiona was waiting for because she repositions herself above me, guides the tip of my cock to her opening, then sinks down. I'm enveloped in her warmth as her walls press around me.

She moans at the same time I say, "Oh, yes."

She pauses in my lap, quivering with me inside her. I arch my hips again, pushing deeper. She gasps, and her muscles squeeze my cock in waves.

When her eyes open, she starts bouncing atop me, riding my length up and down. She doesn't bother trying to build up speed. She seems like she's racing to the finish. I've been desperate for release all night, for weeks really, so I rock my hips in sync with her rhythm.

I'm thrusting while she's riding in perfect counterpoint, and the tingle starts rising again. I'm nearly there.

"I'm gonna come," I call out without slowing.

"Don't stop!" Fiona orders.

The first wave of the orgasm hits and flows out from my dick, then the burst of cum shoots out, trapped by the condom. My leg muscles twitch, but I force myself to keep thrusting, although erratically. My cock is even more sensitive now, and each thrust brings a new level of pleasure.

"You feel so fucking good," I tell her just before she cries out, writhing on top of me, her hips convulsing wildly. I want this to last as long as it can for her, so I continue thrusting until she falls still.

My shoulders slump, and I'm panting. But it's hard to say whether it's from exertion, the overwhelming sensation of my need for her having been fulfilled, or sheer stress relief.

Fiona is still straddling me, holding me inside her while she rests against my chest, her head on my shoulder. Suddenly she bolts upright, staring down the trail.

"Shit, headlamps! Someone's here," she says, jumping off the bench.

"What? Untie me, quick!"

She doesn't respond. She's busy grabbing our clothes.

"What the hell? Fiona, come get my hands," I demand, but still no answer.

Ohfuckohfuckohfuck. Why the hell is she leaving me like this? I didn't even ask for this, and she's going to abandon me here? My mind is racing and not the least bit helpful.

"You can't leave me here! It won't take long, just untie me." My voice rises as I beg in desperation.

"There isn't time," she hisses.

"You can't be serious! You're going to leave me tied to a park bench, naked?"

She picks up the blanket, spreading it across my lap. "There. Now you're covered."

"I'm not—What? No! Fiona, they're going to see me!" I plead.

"Just hold still and be quiet. Maybe they won't notice you."

"This isn't *Jurassic Park*," I fume, my heart pounding for a totally different reason now.

"Shh. I'm not here!" she says, disappearing around a tree trunk with our clothes in her arms.

I have to do something. I can't just wait for them to find me.

I already know I can't pull my way out, but I can shift my arms to the sides so there's some play in the rope. According to a Hardy Boys book I read as a kid, when someone is tying your hands with rope, if you flex your forearms and press your hands against each other, you'll be left with a little space afterward that you can use to work yourself free. I did that, as much as I was able, but it doesn't seem to have mattered.

I feel around with my fingers, assessing the knot. Fiona was in a rush earlier, trying to move on to more fun activities. This shouldn't be too bad, only the knot is thicker than I expected. I'm picking at it from every direction, but I'm not making any progress. *How the hell is she some kind of expert in fancy knots?* I wonder.

Muffled voices drift to me, indistinct but moving closer.

Oh great. Not just one person. A chill builds in the center of my chest.

I try twisting my wrists and wriggling my arms, desperately hoping I can slide out of the rope. But it's as unsuccessful as everything else. Footsteps crunch over the rocks on the trail nearby. They'll be on top of me soon.

I'm not going to make it out of these ropes in time, and even if I did, they'd see me run away now. My only option is to freeze and hope they don't notice me, like Fiona said. With my shoulders over the back of the bench, I can't even sink down and hide.

I hold my breath and close my eyes—because obviously that will help—every muscle tense.

The voices slowly move past me deeper into the woods.

"This is fucked up, Fiona! I am *so* going to get you back for this," I whisper once I no longer hear the voices.

She materializes out of the darkness to my right, moving behind me.

"Nothing happened. You're fine. I'll have you out in a couple minutes."

"Nothing happened?" I mutter as the ropes tug against my skin. Eventually the knot loosens, and the rope drops from my wrists.

I spring away from the bench before Fiona rises to her feet. The blanket slides to the ground, and the spent condom falls from my completely flaccid dick.

"You're *never* tying me up again, no matter how hot that was," I declare.

She eyes me up and down before answering. "It was pretty hot, and I would've gotten you out if I needed to."

I waste no time putting my clothes on as Fiona keeps watch. For all the good that does now.

"You know what sucks?" I ask.

"What?"

"The Hardy Boys are full of shit."

"ORDER UP!" I SHOUT.

Jackie adds a new ticket to the rail and scoops up the plates I just set out. Before grabbing the next ticket, I pick up my water bottle and make a show of drinking. I take my time because I'm using the opportunity to stare at Fiona.

It's the height of Sunday brunch, and she's sitting along the rear wall again—in my line of sight from the grill. Over the past month, we've only stolen brief glances while she's been here. It's been better than nothing, and although I've appreciated her coming, it's also been torture. Today feels different, though. She's not bothering to hide that she's watching me. When I smile at her, she doesn't turn away. It's almost as if we're truly spending time together.

The bell over the door rings, calling me back to my responsibilities. I set the bottle down and reach for the next ticket.

"Richard White," a deep voice booms from the front.

My brows draw together in confusion as I turn to look. *Nobody calls me that… except the cops. Shit.*

Customers who've been standing by the door waiting for a table are pressing back, crowding people already seated. A wall of brown blocks the doorway before resolving into a pair of deputies flanking the sheriff. Another two deputies are circling around the counter, shoving people more than necessary on their way to the employees-only area.

"What is this? What's going on?" I ask loudly. I'm used to speaking over the noise of dozens of people eating and talking, but the diner is rapidly falling silent.

"Richard White, you are under arrest," Sheriff Morris replies just as loudly.

That's not the voice that called my name, I think uselessly. Then the first of the deputies reaches the grill, and I recognize Deputy Voice an instant before he grabs my upper arm. *Ah, it must've been him.*

"What? What the hell for?" I demand as both deputies drag me forward. Deputy Voice yanks me down, almost smashing my face against the countertop. The other deputy twists my arm behind me until my shoulder hurts so much I grunt in pain.

"Sir, please stop resisting," he intones while they lock me in handcuffs. *I guess they're putting on a show today.*

"We've been over this, Morris. I didn't do anything, and you know it!"

"You'll have your chance to explain it to the judge. Until then, you have the right to remain silent…" The sheriff recites my Miranda rights to the entire diner as the deputies shove me around the counter.

I try to get one more glance at Fiona before they drag me away. I only find her for a second, and her expression is carefully blank.

Fuck. Exactly what she was always afraid of. She won't trust me anymore. Nothing has changed since I talked to these assholes. Why are they doing this now? My anger is swiftly turning to fear. Fear that I've let Fiona down.

"Sandy, close the place up!" I shout over my shoulder before they drag me outside.

The deputies haul me to a cruiser parked on the curb, but don't put me inside. After a moment, the sheriff struts out too. He pauses in front of me and leans close with the most infuriatingly smug grin I've ever seen. I wish I could punch him.

"We have footage of you riding out to Highland Estates two days before the firebombing. I got you."

Chapter 29
Truth and Consequences Be Damned

FIONA

Like every Sunday during brunch, Betty's is busy. I had to wait a few minutes to get a table near the back, where I'd be able to watch Tre while he's working at the grill.

He's currently gulping down water, staring at me. His throat is moving with each swallow, bringing back memories of last night, and it's making me more hot and bothered than I'd care to admit.

I can't help but remember Tre saying, *'Change your mind.'* I can't help but imagine what it would be like to sit across from Tre and eat breakfast with him, instead of watching him from across a crowded diner. I can't help but wonder if he's right. *Maybe I should change my mind. Maybe it is that simple,* I think as I raise a sausage link to my mouth and take a bite. It's perfect. Crispy and juicy, and—

"Richard White," someone barks over the jingle of the bell above the diner's front entrance, pulling my eyes away from Tre.

Shit. There are five brown uniforms standing in the doorway. The sheriff and four deputies I don't know but have seen at various town halls. My stomach plummets, and I force a blank, disinterested look onto my face as two deputies push their way through the diner toward Tre, who just looks confused.

"What is this? What's going on?" Tre asks.

"Richard White, you are under arrest," the sheriff says from his position near the door as a deputy grabs Tre and throws him face down on the counter. Then the other one is forcing Tre's arms behind his back and locking a pair of handcuffs around his wrists.

The fact that I wished for this very thing to happen a few months ago isn't lost on me. Only now I want to jump between Tre and the deputies and demand they let him go.

They're reading Tre his Miranda rights as they push him toward the door. His head turns, and his eyes briefly find mine. They're full of panic, and I can feel my breakfast threatening to reappear.

They're almost to the door when Tre turns and shouts, "Sandy! Close the place up!"

I throw twenty dollars onto the table as I stand and unobtrusively head for the front. There's a small crowd formed at the diner's entrance, watching the scene unfold, and I push my way through them in time to hear the sheriff say, "We have footage of you riding out to Highland Estates two days before the firebombing. I got you."

Fuck. What am I going to… How am I going to… My thoughts spiral as I stand in the middle of the crowd and watch them force Tre into the back of the cop car.

Then the door slams shut, and Tre's eyes find mine again. He looks as sick as I feel, but he gives me a small nod as the car's engine rumbles to life, and it pulls away from the curb. His eyes stay locked on mine until the angle makes it impossible to see him, and my own words from last night are left echoing in my head: *'I would've gotten you out if I needed to.'*

Did I mean it? I wonder. *Did I really mean it?*

MY DAD IS ON THE COUCH WITH BATMAN IN HIS LAP, watching yet another documentary when I walk in. For all the complaining he did about how I shouldn't have brought *'that cat'* home with me, they look pretty cozy. I glance at the TV in time to see black and white footage of helicopters with guys wearing bucket hats and carrying guns moving across the screen, followed by the narrator saying, "Ho Chi Minh." The Vietnam War, then.

I pick up the remote and shut the TV off. My dad is already glaring at me when I flop onto the couch next to him. "The sheriff just arrested Tre."

"Jesus fucking Christ, Fiona," he growls, his eyes falling closed. "I told you this was going to happen." His eyes open. "You need to find a lawyer."

"He's not going to rat me out, dad."

"He damn well will. As soon as he sees a chance of getting off easy, he will sell you out. None of the Whites has a loyal bone in their bodies."

"He's nothing like Rich, dad. He won't do that."

"Fiona—"

"No, dad. He won't. Plus, I'm going to get him out. It won't even be an issue."

"How? You don't even know what they have on him!" my dad refutes.

"Footage of Tre near Highland Estates a couple of days before the houses went up in flames. Probably from a trail cam or something. I heard the sheriff tell him that as they were putting him into the cop car."

"You heard—"

"Yes, I was at Betty's when it happened."

"Is that where you were last night?"

"Not that it's any of your business, but yes. I was with Tre last night."

"Goddamnit, Fiona!"

"You don't get a say in who I'm involved with!"

"So you're involved with him now?" my dad snaps.

"Yes. I'm fucking *involved with him*! And I want to *stay* involved with him, so I could really use your help!" I shout back. "Especially since I doubt Rich is going to shell out for a lawyer this time."

"Pfft," he scoffs as he stands, dumping Batman into my lap before pacing across the living room. "I can't believe you're interested in Tre."

"Jesus Christ, dad. *Grow up!*" He turns to face me, his blue eyes boring into me as I continue, "Tre is Ewan's best fucking friend. He's been nothing but reliable since we started working together. He's a *good* person. I get that you don't like Rich. I don't like Rich either. *Tre* doesn't even like Rich. But Tre isn't his dad, and *I* need your help."

"For what? How exactly do you think you're going to get him out?"

"It was only the sheriff's department that was involved in the arrest. The ATF wasn't there, so either they didn't know what the sheriff had planned, or they don't think there's enough evidence for a conviction. Either way, I imagine detonating some bombs that are identical to the ones I've already used will go a long way toward getting Tre out. And I can build another one like the one I used at Highland Estates, but I need you to build me one like the ones I used at Bridal Mountain and Hay Creek."

"To blow up what?" my dad asks skeptically.

"I don't know yet."

"Well, I can't build you a bomb if I don't know what it's going to be used on!"

"But when I figure it out, will you do it?"

He sighs. "Yes. But only so Tre won't cut a deal and turn you in."

I roll my eyes but say nothing.

"You should give the cat back."

"Yeah. I know. I've already got a plan for that." I glance down at the black void of fluff who's curled in my lap, purring. "Thanks, dad."

It's just after six, and I'm sitting alone at the bar in Malcolm's with a bottle of cider I've been nursing for well over an hour, zooming in and out of aerial satellite maps around the development sites, trying to determine what I can target when Ewan sits down next to me at the bar.

"Hey sis," he greets with an edge to his voice that's not normally there.

I hit the button on my phone, locking it before setting it face down on the bar. "Hi Ewan," I reply, watching Malcolm walk toward us.

"Hey Ewan, what can I get you?" Malcolm asks.

"Hey Mal, I'll have whatever Fiona's drinking."

Malcolm nods, then moves away to grab a bottle for Ewan. An uneasy silence settles between us, and I make a show of paying attention to Malcolm's movements behind the bar. All too soon, he's setting a bottle in front of Ewan.

"Put it on Fiona's tab," Ewan says. Mal glances at me, and I nod. "Let's grab a booth, Fiona."

I groan but stand to follow my twin. The bar is mostly empty, but Ewan chooses a booth in the back corner—the one farthest from everyone else—and my stomach sinks.

"So," Ewan says when I sit down across from him.

"So?"

"Guess what I heard when I got back from the trip I was guiding today."

"I don't know, Ewan. What?"

"I heard they arrested someone for firebombing the houses out at Highland Estates. I heard that someone was Tre."

"Okay, and?"

"And that got me thinking about you guys. You were there when he was arrested this morning, weren't you?"

I shrug noncommittally, wanting to avoid the question.

"Of course you were. Because you've been there every weekend for the past month. So I want to know why Tre's sitting in a jail cell for some bombs I'm pretty sure you built."

"I don't know what you're talking about," I say flatly.

"Bullshit, sis. The timing of it all has been bugging me for months. All of a sudden, right around the same time Bridal Mountain was sabotaged, you stopped shit-talking Tre. Stopped calling him Dickie, even. And right around that same time, he became interested in you. Then, come to find out that somehow—I wasn't sure how, but I've got a pretty good guess now—the two of you'd been spending enough time together to develop feelings for each other, even before our Fourth of July trip. Strong enough feelings for you to bail on Kyle because you couldn't stop thinking about Tre, which isn't the sort of thing that happens overnight or because you saw each other a few times while you were getting coffee like he tried to tell me."

"What's your point?"

"Tre doesn't know how to build a bomb, Fi. But I could muddle my way through it, which means you could too. Tell me what's going on."

"You know Rich knows all about explosives. Who's to say Tre didn't pick up a few things from his dad the same way we did?"

"Enough, Fiona. My best friend is sitting in a jail cell right now, and I know you have something to do with it, so tell me what the hell is going on and maybe we can fucking figure out how to *fix* it," Ewan demands.

I let out a long sigh. I never wanted Ewan to be involved in this. I never even really wanted Tre to be involved in it. Tre involved himself though, and now it seems like my twin is going to do the same thing. Part of me wants to keep lying to him, but he's obviously figured out the gist of what's happening, and I need the help. I can't go around asking the kind of questions I need answers to without arousing suspicion. Ewan isn't everyone's best friend the way Tre is, but he always knows way more about what's going on around town than I do, and I need information. Plus, every idea I've been able to come up with would work a lot better with two people than with one.

"Fine," I say. "Tre and I sort of... ran into each other that night at Bridal Mountain, and we've been working together since then." I explain about Hay Creek, and then Highland Estates.

"So that cat you wanted me to watch...?"

"Yeah."

"Sis," Ewan scolds, shaking his head.

"I *know*, Ewan. What do you think I've been sitting here doing for the past couple of hours? I'm not just going to let him sit in jail."

Turns out I *did* mean it when I told Tre I'd have gotten him out if I needed to.

"What's the plan, then?"

"Can you find out where the Henley and Montank executives are staying?" I ask. "Without making it obvious that's what you're doing?"

"Probably."

"Okay, good. Do that. And you know that idea you mentioned to me after the town hall when I asked you who you thought was responsible for Hay Creek? About Henley and Montank being involved?"

"Yeah, why?"

"You think you could spread that rumor around a bit?"

Ewan grins. "Yeah. I can do that. What are you going to be doing in the meantime?"

"I'm going to start by arranging the return of the cat. Then, once we know where the Henley and Montank executives are staying, we'll make it clear that Tre wasn't involved, which will hopefully be enough for Rich to send his lawyers to get Tre out."

It's five in the morning, and I'm sitting in my truck with a cat carrier on the seat beside me. Most of the houses on the street are dark, and the ones that aren't still have their blinds pulled shut. Sunrise is a bit more than an hour away. I take a breath, raise the hood of the sweatshirt I'm wearing over the baseball cap on my head, and grab the cat carrier before getting out and shutting the door quietly behind me. I'm already wearing gloves, so I don't have to worry about leaving fingerprints on the carrier.

My destination is five blocks away, but I didn't want to park any closer on the off chance Carol's neighbors have doorbell cameras. Almost no one in Kalomish does—that's a 'big city' thing—but there's no reason to chance it.

The air is cool, and there's a light fog hanging over the streets. We're still in summer's grasp, but fall is waiting in the wings.

Batman is quiet inside the carrier as we walk. I'm sure he enjoyed his little adventure, but I imagine he'll be happy to be back with his person.

Carol's house is a small white bungalow. The lights are all off. She doesn't need to be at the office for another two and a half hours. There's no reason for her to be up this early.

I set the carrier down on her front doorstep before removing the note from my pocket and wedging it under the handle.

"Bye Batman." I reach a finger through the metal grate to scratch his cheek. He begins purring almost immediately, and I totally understand why the Henley and Montank guy brought him along on a work trip. If he were my cat, I'd have brought him too.

I stand up and press the doorbell four times in quick succession, and then take off down the street in the opposite direction I came from, opting to take the long way back to my truck.

Carol will see the letter and immediately call the police to let them know that the cat isn't dead, and that Tre had nothing to do with it. She'll give them the letter, which says they've got the wrong guy. Then she'll tell everyone she runs into all about it for at least the next week.

That won't be enough to convince the sheriff or Rich, I'm sure. But what Ewan and I do next should create enough confusion to get Rich back on Tre's side, at least.

Chapter 30
Thinking Hard Time

TRE

"Richard White," a man's voice calls from the door. I open my eyes, but otherwise don't respond, seated on the bench running the length of the holding cell with my head resting on the concrete wall behind me. It's Deputy Wasserman, although I don't see Kevin. "Get up. Your lawyer's here."

I raise one eyebrow but comply. A small grunt escapes my lips as I stand, joints stiff from trying to nap away the morning sitting upright. They woke me up hours ago, but there are no windows in the drunk tank—and they took my watch along with all my other possessions when they booked me—so I don't know exactly when. Or what time it is now.

"Let's go," Wasserman orders as I stretch my arms overhead. I glance at the corner. The guy they brought in last night is still passed out on the bench with his arm draped across his face. They don't care if he sleeps.

Wasserman cuffs my hands in front of me, then lets me out and leads me to a small, windowless room with a square table. After a few moments, the man from last week's town hall enters, dressed in a suit and carrying a briefcase.

Without glancing at the deputy, he reaches back and shuts the door.

"Mr. White, pleasure to meet you. Sorry for the delay." He extends his hand.

I shake it, awkwardly wagging my other beside it in the handcuffs. "I saw you the other night."

"Nick Trowbridge. Yes. My first Kalomish town hall. I wanted to shake the tree a bit, so to speak. See what I could get them to say in public."

"And you're a lawyer?"

"Yes. Environmental law mainly, which is how I got involved in all this. I work in Portland but was recently hired to help with your town's legal suits against Henley and Montank. When you were so publicly arrested, multiple people reached out. They told me you're a strong voice in opposing these developments."

Ah, that tracks.

After the deputies finished booking me yesterday, I was left alone in the holding cell. I had as much access to the pay phone as I wanted, but without my phone, I only knew a couple of numbers. I called who I could—including Ewan, although everyone at his outfitter was on the river all day—but had to leave messages asking them to call a lawyer for me. Law offices aren't usually open on Sundays, so I knew I'd be waiting. The courts also aren't in session on the weekend, meaning I haven't been arraigned yet. Sheriff Morris timed his big arrest deliberately.

"Well, thanks for coming. How long until you can get me out?"

"Okay, good news and bad news there. Your arraignment is set for this morning, so we'll get to argue for your release very soon. The bad news is we only have a few minutes right now to prep."

Morris was probably hoping I wouldn't be able to arrange a lawyer so quickly.

"I have the list of charges here. It looks like they want to charge you with three different sets of crimes spanning multiple occasions. Don't tell me about what happened and what didn't. There'll be time to work on all of that later. I assume you intend to plead 'not guilty'?"

"Yeah, of course. They don't even—" I begin, but Nick holds up a hand to stop me.

"I'm sorry. I will absolutely listen to your side of the story, but we have almost no time before the deputies transport you to the county courthouse."

"They're trying me here?" I ask incredulously.

"This isn't the trial. Your arraignment is just a pretrial hearing where they inform you of the charges, make sure you have a lawyer, and set your bail. The trial won't happen for weeks, or more likely months, but it seems like they want to handle it locally, yeah. I haven't had time to look into everything since I spent most of the morning driving out here.

"At a guess, I'd say maybe Henley and Montank don't have the same pull in Salem as they do here. It's also possible the district attorney is jumping the gun because the sheriff wants the glory and the council wants to show that everything is safe for the big developers. I've read a summary of the evidence that led them to arrest you. It's flimsy. The closest things they have to incriminating are a lack of alibis for the middle of the night and some evidence that you were on a bike near the houses that got destroyed a few days prior to that incident."

Three loud knocks sound on the door, then it swings open.

"Time to go, White," Deputy Wasserman says.

I look to Nick, who nods. "I'll meet you at the courthouse. Don't talk to anyone."

I SHIFT IN THE UNCOMFORTABLE WOODEN CHAIR IN THE waiting room. The clock on the wall tells me it's ten-thirty. It was the first thing to let me know the time today when I arrived just after nine. The only other people in here have been the officer standing by the door and two other men waiting for the courtroom, the last of whom was escorted out fifteen minutes ago. I haven't seen Nick Trowbridge, no matter how many times I've complained.

An older man dressed like the door guard enters and calls my name. Those aren't deputy uniforms. I guess they're bailiffs.

I stand and follow him down a hallway until he leads me through a small door. We enter the courtroom with my attorney sitting at one table, a pair of lawyers conversing at another, and the judge already seated, watching me. The gallery is empty except for the man from Henley and Montank who came to the diner when Kevin first wanted me for questioning.

Nick stands as I join him. "We only have a minute. These are the charges they're planning to bring against you." He points to an open folder on the desk. There are a handful of papers, and on top, under a court letterhead, is a list of crimes: arson, destruction of property, trespassing, possession of a destructive device, unauthorized use of a vehicle, criminal mischief, and animal abuse.

"The judge will start things off. He'll read the charges and ask how you plead. You answer, but only say, 'Not guilty, Your Honor.' Nothing more, understand? This isn't the trial. This isn't the time to explain or blame someone else. 'Not guilty,' then you let me do the talking from there. Any questions?"

"Yeah, actually. There's nothing on here about terrorism, but these are all about the projects from Henley and Montank. Are there more coming?"

"What? No, there are no terrorism charges. That would automatically be a federal case, and the FBI would be running everything. Despite Councilman Nammier's grandstanding, neither the council nor the sheriff's department has legally expressed anything as terrorism, and none of these charges stem from the ATF investigation."

The judge clears his throat.

Nick glances at him and then back at me. "Anything else?"

I shake my head.

"Remember 'Not guilty' then say nothing."

He turns to face the judge, who asks, "Are we ready to begin, counselors?"

"We are, Your Honor," Nick replies.

"Yes, Your Honor," the older of the two lawyers, a woman who looks to be in her fifties, stands and answers.

The judge goes through a formal introduction of the case in a monotone pattern that makes me think he's done this so many times he could recite it in his sleep. After reading the list of charges, he asks, "How do you plead?"

"Not guilty, Your Honor."

"On the issue of bail, do the people have a recommendation?" the judge asks, looking at the woman who was introduced as the district attorney.

"We request that the defendant be held without bail. He has aggressively demonstrated his opposition to the affected projects, and the crimes are increasing in violence. If he is released, the threat to the people is unacceptably high."

"Your Honor, the people have not provided any substantiation for their claims of my client's involvement in these alleged crimes," Nick states. "Their supposed evidence does not meet the threshold to validate these charges, and the case should be dismissed."

"Save it for the evidentiary hearing, Mr. Trowbridge."

"Furthermore, Your Honor, my client is a pillar of the community and has no criminal history. He owns and operates a local business and is active in local politics. He poses no threat and is not a flight risk. Unless the people can demonstrate *how* he is a danger, we request he be released on his own recognizance."

The judge looks at the district attorney again.

"Your Honor, in addition to his publicly stated goal of making the victims of these crimes flee the state, there is evidence of his presence near the scene of the latest crime in a timeline that indicates responsibility."

"We request—" Nick begins before the judge interrupts.

"I've heard enough, counselors. Given the scale of the damage and the likelihood of further criminal activity, I have determined that the defendant poses a continued threat to the safety of the community. He is to be remanded into custody without bail."

Nick looks frustrated, but the DA has a solid poker face. The judge glances behind us before shuffling papers, and I look back to see the Henley and Montank suit smirking at me.

Nick rushes to reassure me as the bailiff approaches. "Don't worry, there's still plenty I can do to get you out. I'll work on that and meet you at the jail soon."

A LOUD CLANGING ECHOES DOWN THE HALL, WRESTING MY attention away from the thoughts looping in my head.

I look at the door while my cellmate sits up on his bed. "Dinner time," he explains, the first words either of us has spoken. He doesn't get up, so I follow his example and remain on my bed. I've been sitting here since I got processed into the jail. They kept me in a more secure waiting room for inmates at the courthouse for hours until some sheriff's deputies herded a group of us onto a small bus and drove us to the county jail. The last time I saw a clock, it was nearly five, just before they led me to my cell.

Almost the entire day has been spent sitting around, and with nothing to do, I've been stewing over my stupid mistake.

If I hadn't gone out there on my own, I lament for the thousandth time.

After Fiona and I finished prepping at her secret lair on Monday night, I got worried. On our first job, I was certain I knew the trailer's lock and the site security procedure, but I got both wrong. Thankfully, Fiona was clever enough to get us in through the window, because otherwise we would have been screwed by my not being thorough.

We had to get the houses done in one shot. The plan was based around the town hall. We wouldn't get a second chance.

I was worried enough that at midnight I dressed in black and rode my bike down back roads to the state park trail I recommended we use. Nobody was out that late, and I made it to Highland Estates in about two hours. I scouted the yards of both houses to make sure there weren't any motion-sensor lights and the doors looked the same as on my drive-by visit.

It took less than half an hour. I followed a different path home, figuring I could check a backup option and reduce the chance of being seen where Fiona and I would travel the next night. I even made it home with enough time to take a nap before work.

Everything seemed to go perfectly, but there must have been a trail cam along that second path. If the sheriff had footage of both of us in ski masks from Tuesday night, that's what he'd be focusing on. And he wouldn't have been able to identify me. But I was on my bike in the woods while not committing a crime, so I wasn't wearing one. Now I've proven Fiona's fears about me being sloppy right all along. I hope she knows I meant what I said. I accepted that I'd face the consequences of my actions before I went up Bridal Mountain. I won't drag her into this. Our working together was all my idea anyway.

Plastic thunks down inside the cell, and my eyes refocus to see a pair of bored guards walking by, shoving baggies of food through the bars on either side of the hallway.

My cellmate walks over and grabs his first, his beige shirt and pants hanging as loosely on him as mine do on me. My stomach rumbles, and I suddenly realize I haven't eaten today. The deputies didn't give me anything for breakfast before they rushed me off to court, and I was sitting in courthouse waiting rooms the rest of the time. I'd been too preoccupied to notice.

When I pick mine up, I'm not sure what I'm seeing at first. A handful of apple slices are smashed on the outside of a sandwich that looks like a few slices of bologna and some approximation of cheese on white bread.

"Hey man, is this a normal dinner?" I ask. I expected the food wasn't going to be good, but in TV shows and movies you always see guys going through cafeteria lines.

He's halfway through his sandwich. He swallows and pauses long enough to answer. "Yeah. It's always shit."

I nod, and we return to our respective meals. It's not good, but I'm hungry, and I may as well get used to this.

Despite my new lawyer's assurances, I know the system is rigged. I just have to ride this out until the trial. If they're going to do everything locally because they think they have control, I will happily take my chances with a jury.

The sound of urine hitting the aluminum toilet bowl in the far corner breaks my train of thought as my cellmate relieves himself.

Well, this is my life now, I realize.

Chapter 31
Small Town Gossip Network

FIONA

My dad huffs from his position beside me at the workbench in the storage unit. He's been watching me put together another IED that's identical to the ones Tre and I used at Highland Estates, and I can feel the weight of his judgment pressing down on me.

I roll my eyes. "Something you wanted to say, dad?"

"It's not very elegant," he grumbles.

"It worked, didn't it? That's all that matters."

"If you—"

"The point is that it's identical to the last ones we used, so no, I can't."

"Fine," he mutters. "Did you have to involve your brother? It's bad enough you're involved. But Ewan? When the ATF is already sniffing around?"

"Ewan involved himself."

My dad huffs again.

"I told you. Tre is Ewan's best friend. Ewan's not going to let him sit in jail if he can help it. Actually, I think you're just about the only person in town who *doesn't* care if Tre gets out," I say as I finish wiring the batteries in series.

Carol was excited to tell us that someone had left the Henley and Montank executive's cat on her doorstep this morning. *'Tre couldn't have done it!'* were the first words out of her mouth when she came into the office. Then she immediately launched into the story of finding a very traumatized cat who *'must've been locked in that cage for days because the poor thing was so starved for attention!'*

She was convinced the sheriff would drop the charges against Tre and he'd be released before the day was over—which obviously didn't happen or my dad and I wouldn't be sitting in a sweltering storage unit, with no breeze, using bomb building as family bonding time, or whatever it is we're doing.

Not only did the sheriff not release Tre, but according to the gossip Ewan overheard, the cat never even came up during Tre's bail hearing. It doesn't matter, though. Carol told Natalie, Jean, and me about the cat. She's sure to mention it to every patient who comes into the office this week. And Jean also likes to make sure everyone is in the know. I think she doesn't want anyone to feel left out. Between the two of them, it'll be all over town in a day or two. Then the sheriff will have to contend with people *knowing* he's withholding information that indicates Tre might not be behind the attacks.

"I'm just saying—"

"Dad, I'm trying to focus."

"Fine," he grouses impatiently. He's already finished the bomb he was building, and now he wants to lecture me while I'm a captive audience.

I decided on Bridal Mountain's lower passenger terminus as one target, and the Henley and Montank executives' cars as the other.

The passenger terminus is the riskier target, since there may still be increased security at the construction sites, depending on how confident Henley and Montank are that Tre is the perpetrator. I intend to spend tonight watching it.

Assuming it's viable, and I can get in and out without being seen, once Ewan determines where the executives are staying, I'll give him the bomb I'm building to put under their cars and set off in the middle of the night when no one is around. There'll likely be some damage to nearby cars, which is unfortunate, but insurance'll cover it and no one will be hurt. And I'll use the bomb my dad built on the lower terminus and take out its gondola support column, the same way I did at the upper site back in May.

The sheriff won't be able to keep that under wraps, and it *should* be more than enough for even the worst lawyer to use to get Tre out of jail, and hopefully get the judge to drop the charges—*with* prejudice, if we're really lucky.

"Are you sure he's worth it?" my dad asks softly.

I set everything down before turning to face him. "Yes."

The bare bulb overhead casts long shadows on his face as his blue eyes bore into mine. "Tell me why."

"That first night, when we ran into each other at Bridal Mountain…" I sigh. "Neither of us was expecting to see the other there, but Tre especially wasn't expecting to see *me*. I spent every single town hall for months leading up to that voicing support for Henley and Montank. And then I pushed him down the mountain, and despite all that, he instantly adjusted his worldview. Do you know how rare that is?"

My dad says nothing, so I continue. "It took me a lot longer to even begin to consider that he might not be a total moron. Initially, I only heard him out so that he would keep quiet about having seen me, but when I did, when he told me what he was doing at the construction site, his plan was *better than mine!*"

"Ah," my dad murmurs.

"What?"

"Competence," he says, as if it explains everything.

I nod. "All along the way, anything I've asked of him, he's managed to figure out. But it's not just that. I know he seems like he walks around without a care in the world, but that's simply what he lets people see. It only looks that way because he's hyperconscious of everyone around him all the time. He doesn't let that paralyze him, though. He's the only other person in this town actually acting against Henley and Montank directly instead of complaining to the city council and hoping for the best."

My dad grunts noncommittally.

"Plus, he's sitting in a jail cell for me, dad. How could I not be sure?"

He falls silent, and I turn back to the workbench to finish up the wiring. Finally, he says, "Your mother was the same."

"What?"

"She was highly competent and very thoughtful." He shrugs.

"I suppose so. There was nothing she couldn't figure out."

"Yeah."

"She would've sat in a jail cell for you, too."

He nods. "She would've."

It's nearing six-thirty when I walk into Malcolm's and spot Ewan sitting at the bar with Cade and Jordan on one side and Kyle on the other. *He didn't say anything about inviting them*, I think with a grimace. I haven't seen them since that morning at the campsite, and I want to turn around and walk out, even though it makes sense. A little. For Cade, at least. And Jordan goes where Cade goes.

But I have no clue why Kyle is here, and I stare at his back long and hard. Ewan and Jordan are in the middle of the group. I can sit next to Cade, or I can sit next to Kyle.

I don't like either option.

After another second of indecision, I force myself to move out of the doorway toward the bar. Kyle glances at me when I slide onto the stool next to his.

His eyes widen slightly as he inclines his head, but he only murmurs, "Hey Fiona."

"Hi Kyle," I respond as I tamp down on the urge to apologize again. For what happened in July, for sitting next to him tonight. I don't even know. All I know is that I'd still like to punch Cade in the face, so sitting next to Kyle is the safer choice.

"Hey Fi," Ewan says at the same time Cade practically shouts, "Fiona!" like we're old friends. Like he's not at the top of my shit list.

"Ewan," I reply, letting the annoyance creep into my voice,

although I can tell from the laughter in his eyes that he already knows exactly how I'm feeling. Whatever he's doing, it's deliberate. "Jordan."

"Oh, she's definitely still mad at you," Jordan stage-whispers to Cade.

"That's why I'm here," Cade says loudly enough for half the bar to overhear. "To apologize for being an asshole in person!"

"Whatever, it's fine," I grumble, not wanting to rehash that day for everyone. It's Tuesday night, and it's not that busy, but even so. Malcolm stops by long enough to ask me what I want and then moves away.

"Hey sis, I heard your receptionist found the Henley and Montank cat on her doorstep yesterday."

"Yeah, is that true, Fiona? The cat's not dead? Someone returned it after they arrested Tre?" Cade calls down.

My eyes dart to Ewan—who's definitely smirking—and I sigh.

"Yup."

"Tre couldn't have done it!" Cade crows, spinning on his stool. "Did you all hear that? Someone returned Henley and Montank's cat after Tre was arrested, so it wasn't him," he says to the room.

"I bet those executives had the cat stashed somewhere safe all along," Ewan comments.

"What, you think they blew up the houses themselves?" Cade asks as Malcolm sets a pint on the bar in front of me.

Ewan shrugs. "Probably the construction sites too. Think about it, Cade. They had security at Hay Creek. And Highland Estates is gated. They're the only people with access everywhere."

"Why would they blow up their own sites?"

"Insurance fraud," Kyle says softly, surprising me.

"Insurance fraud?" Cade echoes.

"Why not?" I reply. "People who are underwater on their mortgages have been known to burn down their own houses. Why not a company like Henley and Montank? It *does* make sense."

There's a thoughtful look on Jordan's face. "It makes more sense than Tre."

"Insurance fraud," Cade says. But this time, it's a statement and not a question, though he still seems to be shouting it to half the bar.

Ewan, Jordan, and Cade continue loudly speculating about Henley and Montank's solvency for everyone to hear.

"I don't normally see you here," I murmur to Kyle.

"I heard your receptionist found the cat, and I thought it was interesting."

I close my eyes and take a deep breath.

"Anyway, I didn't have anything else going on, and Tre's a decent guy, so I decided to tag along."

"You thought it was 'interesting'?"

"Yeah. I mean, you'd expect the sheriff would've said something about it... right?"

"Mmm." I take a sip of the beer in front of me to buy myself a second to figure out how to respond to that. I'm not sure if Kyle's fishing for information, or if he's worked it out. But it's like he said. He pays attention. "Makes you wonder what else they're not telling us," I eventually say.

"It does," Kyle agrees. "Hey Cade, why do you suppose the sheriff doesn't want anyone to know about the cat?"

"They must be trying to frame him!"

Kyle's lips are turned up when I look back at him. "Like I said, I didn't have anything else going on."

I'm crouched in the tree line about a quarter of a mile away from the lower passenger terminus at Bridal Mountain, sweating my ass off. The ski mask covering my face is uncomfortably plastered to my skin, but I can't risk removing it.

I've watched the site for the past three nights, if you include tonight, and I'm running on fumes. But I'm stuck here waiting because Ewan and I need to coordinate our attacks—it'll make things more confusing, and who knows? Maybe it'll give that militia rumor legs and distract the ATF.

Ewan found out that the Henley and Montank executives are staying at a hotel in Jansen, half an hour outside of Kalomish. Apparently, every hotel within the town limits was 'at capacity.'

They haven't reduced the security at the sites, but fortunately the guard at this one has been spending ninety percent of his time holed up in his truck, which is understandable considering his truck has air conditioning. *And protection from the mosquitoes,* I think as another one whines sharply near my ear, despite the fact that I basically bathed in DEET before coming out here.

Unfortunately, the security guard does walk around the site periodically, and he doesn't do it on any kind of schedule I've been able to figure out, which is going to make this riskier than I'd like.

We agreed that three-thirty in the morning was the best time to act, but Ewan has probably already set up the IED beneath the executives' cars. He immediately understood the design and didn't so much as bat an eye when I mentioned that there could be federal charges if we got caught. He spent more time interrogating me about the storage unit than anything else, and he wasn't any more satisfied with the explanation that it *'belongs to a neighbor'* than I am.

I haven't been able to get any additional details from my dad beyond that, and I've tried more than once. Ewan made a comment about how I'm *'usually better at finding out stuff like this,'* and I snapped at him that *'I've been a little busy lately. Plus, dad is already pissed at me. I don't need to make things worse.'*

Of course, Ewan wanted to know what *that* meant, and the rest of the conversation has been replaying in my head since then.

Me, telling him I really needed to find some other place to live.

Him, asking me why I don't just move in with Tre.

Me, explaining that for one, Tre hasn't asked me, and for two, it's way too early for that.

Ewan laughed. He spent at least a solid minute laughing. By the time he finished, he was gasping for air, and there were tears streaming down his face. He went on to tell me that I'm committing felonies just to *try* to get Tre out of jail, so saying that it's too soon to be moving in together was the most asinine thing he's ever heard.

And I stood there with my mouth hanging open, unable to come up with any response except to mutter again that Tre hasn't asked me.

Ewan rolled his eyes, and I told him we needed to leave.

But...

It's been replaying in my head for the past few hours. Tre hasn't asked, but I don't know what I'd say if he did because, like usual, Ewan has a point.

I blow out a long breath and then pick up the bag of explosives as I stand. The moon has long since sunk below the horizon, and the night is dark, but I move cautiously anyway, trying to avoid attracting notice as I slowly venture out of the tree line.

It takes almost ten minutes to travel the quarter of a mile from the forest's edge to the support column that anchors the lower terminus. It's another ten minutes—thanks to shaky hands—to set up the linear charges around the column and connect the detonating cord.

My dad tried to convince me to use a remote detonator, saying that it was too risky to do this manually, but I insisted it had to be exactly the same as before. He's not wrong. It's insanely risky, and if I'd told him they still had security posted here, he wouldn't have agreed to do it my way. So I didn't mention it.

All that's left to do is unspool the cord and then light it. The truck is far enough away that the security guard should be fine.

Rocks shift beneath my feet as I carefully pick my way across the expanse. The last thing I need is to twist an ankle in the dark because I wasn't paying attention. Getting away is going to be tough enough already. As soon as the charges detonate, the security guard is going to call the sheriff. The woods will be crawling with cops well before I'm out of them. Fortunately, I've spent the past few nights walking these trails in the dark. None of the people they send out will have done the same.

Finally, I reach the end of the spool and turn to check the site. But when I look back, the cab light in the truck is off. It only ever goes off when the guard gets out.

My eyes race over the area, trying to find him. And when I do, he's standing at the base of the support column, staring at it.

Shit. Shit. Shit shit shit.

"Hey!" I shout, pitching my voice low.

He turns, searching for the source of the noise, and his eyes skate past me. I strike the flint wheel on the lighter, holding it up, and his head jerks toward the light.

Only…

Only the dumbass runs toward me, not back to his truck like I was hoping.

Fuck. Fuck!

I stand there waiting. Like prey.

I can't move yet, though. I don't have a choice. The bomb needs to detonate. I can't risk letting the ATF have access to an intact bomb my dad built. The chances of them being able to gather evidence from it—to trace it back to him—are too high.

So I stand there, allowing the security guard who wants to play the hero to close the distance between us.

I need—

There! He's far enough away. He has to be far enough.

I hold the flame to the cord, dropping it as soon as it ignites. I rush to the trees.

There's an echoing boom behind me. I don't stop running until I reach the tree line. When I do, it's simply to look back long enough to check that the guard is okay.

He's frozen, staring at the support column, which is now lying on the ground. Then he turns and begins sprinting toward me again, and I take off deeper into the forest, running at full speed.

I need to get away. It's five miles to the nearest trailhead, but I can't go there. It'll be crawling with cops waiting for me to appear.

No. I have to head for the river. It's farther—eight miles instead of five—but from there I can trek up to Ewan's outfitter.

Chapter 32
Feeling Good to Go

TRE

"Uno," Dave yells as he places a Draw Two card on the pile.

I slap another Draw Two on top of his, and the table erupts in a chorus of "Ooh."

I actually have a Reverse card in my hand, but I'll help my cellmate win, even if he doesn't know it.

"Aw, c'mon man," Little Mike says, drawing four cards from the deck.

Everyone around the table takes their turn until Dave slaps down a yellow Skip shouting, "I'm out!"

He spends a minute gloating as the next dealer collects and shuffles the cards.

"White, your visitor is here," a voice declares behind me.

"Ah, is it ten already?" I ask, standing.

The guard gestures for me to precede him out of the rec area.

"No, please, after you." I give him a grin and a fake bow.

"It doesn't get any funnier no matter how many times you say it. Move."

"Eh, you're gonna crack a smile one of these days. Just watch," I inform him as I walk to the exit.

He leads me down the halls to a grey steel door in a row of grey steel doors. After inspecting me for contraband—*what would I even be smuggling out?*—he ushers me through.

Nick Trowbridge is seated at a small metal desk bolted to the concrete floor. He was in the middle of arranging papers in front of him, his open briefcase resting atop the desk.

Nick reaches out to shake my hand as I sit. "Mr. White, how are you holding up?"

"Like I told you last visit, call me Tre, please. And I'm just enjoying my all-expenses-paid vacation. It's nice to have some time off work," I joke.

"Well, as nice as that sounds," Nick says wryly, "I think I have better news for you. A lot has happened since we last spoke, and it's obvious that you couldn't be responsible for any of the vandalism that's occurred, so the short version is I've petitioned for an emergency hearing tomorrow to get the whole case dismissed."

"Awesome. It's only been a couple of days. What's changed?"

"Where to start? Well, first, apparently one of the Henley and Montank employees brought a cat with him. It'd been gone since the house fires and was assumed to have died. However, on Monday morning, it was delivered to a local woman's doorstep with a letter saying you were innocent."

"Wait, what?" I ask, dumbfounded.

"Yeah, but that's not all. The lady who got the cat called the sheriff's office immediately, but they charged you without disclosing it. We are going to have a field day with them in court."

"And that's enough to get the case dismissed?"

"Well, there's more. Last night—or early this morning, technically—there were more attacks."

My eyebrows shoot up my forehead, and I lean forward. *Fiona, what are you doing?* I wonder.

"I'm sorry. Did you say 'attacks' plural?"

"Yes, two in one night. Whoever set fire to the houses found the hotel where those same execs are staying and firebombed their rental vehicles. It's too soon to have any results from the investigation, but nobody's been identified. The other incident was an explosion at the lower end of the aerial gondola system, seemingly identical to the one that started everything. Again, it's far too soon to know the details, but they did share with me that the security guard on site saw a person ignite the device and chased them into the woods before losing them. You've been here for days. The DA would never be able to make the case that you're responsible now."

Two attacks? Did Fiona remotely detonate the cars the way she did the houses? She could hit multiple targets and make it look like there's a whole group involved. Maybe that's the plan. Creating new suspects helps me… Is she trying to trick people into blaming that imaginary militia? How did she pull it off so fast, though? It took us weeks of prep to do one together.

"Mr. Wh—Tre? I realize this is a lot happening all at once, but it's fantastic news for you. We should be able to get you released as soon as we can get on the court's docket."

I focus my gaze on Nick again. "You've said 'we' a few times. Who else is involved?"

"Right. That brings me to the final development I have for you. I was contacted by another attorney today, Arthur Kostas. Since I'm already your attorney of record with the court, he approached me. He's offering to represent you."

Nick pauses for my response, but this is one surprise too many, and my mouth is hanging open while I simply stare at him.

"I told him I'd speak with you before making any changes. I've watched the videos of your two interviews with Sheriff Morris. Mr. Kostas was representing you in the first but not the second. I also note that you didn't contact him for counsel after your arrest, so I don't know where things stand between you. I've brought the necessary paperwork if you are interested.

"You can sign these forms," he gestures to a few on the right side of the table, "if you want to transfer power of attorney and legal representation from me to him. Or you can sign these," he continues, gesturing to the pages on the left, "if you would like to inform the court and the jail that he will be an additional member of your legal counsel.

"The choice is entirely up to you. I'm happy to continue defending you, but my professional advice is that you should seriously consider utilizing him. As I've mentioned, my background is in environmental law, and he has significant experience in criminal defense. That can really make a difference."

Finally, I find my voice. "Uh, yeah, I know he's very good at his job. He can definitely help out, but I want you to continue as my lawyer. I don't have to worry about you disappearing on me."

"Great. If you just sign these, I'll take care of it."

As I skim the documents, he adds, "Since tomorrow isn't an authorized visitation day, I may not be able to contact you in advance. We're going to get you in front of a judge ASAP, so don't be surprised if they bring you to the courthouse in the morning."

After I sign the papers, I write down a number on the back of one of the unused forms. "When you get it scheduled, can you call this number? Give Ewan the details, please."

I WATCH THE CLOCK ON THE WALL HIT TEN. I'VE BEEN sitting in this waiting room at the courthouse with a guard and three other inmates for the past hour. The door opens, and a bailiff calls my name.

I follow them a few dozen feet down the hallway to a small concrete room with a central divider and one chair bolted to the floor. The divider is concrete on the bottom and a thick pane of glass on top with a metal mesh opening to talk through. It looks like a movie set.

Mr. Kostas enters the opposite side and takes his seat.

"Good to see you again, Mr. White, even under such circumstances."

"You too, Mr. Kostas. I have to say, I'm surprised you're involved…" I trail off, waiting for him to explain.

"Yes. The issues I described during our previous conversation are no longer an obstacle. Since it's clear that you weren't responsible for the fires that destroyed White Construction property, there is no more conflict of interest, and White Construction has tasked my firm with representing your defense again."

"Ah." *Dad. What a vindictive shit. Now he's back to trying to make the family look good.*

"I'm here to prepare you for what you're about to walk into. This isn't a regular hearing. I'll be brief because Mr. Trowbridge is in the courtroom, waiting for our case to be called.

"I've been in negotiations with the district attorney this morning, and we've reached an agreement. We can prove the crime against the cat never even happened. Once we're in the courtroom, the clerk will read the case info, then the judge will ask us about our motion, and the DA will move to dismiss all charges. When that happens, we'll argue for dismissal with prejudice so that they can't try to charge you with these crimes again in the future. Your job is to sit there and say nothing. After we win, you can celebrate."

"I like the sound of that," I reply.

"It's worth noting that it's limited to the same jurisdiction, meaning if a federal investigation wanted to charge you, they could. But as far as I know, the investigation there has taken no action against you. Besides, with all the reasonable doubt available now, I'm confident we can manage any future charges. I've informed the DA that we are prepared to pursue a case of prosecutorial misconduct if she tries to fight us on it. And not only for charging you under such a flimsy pretext but for withholding potentially exculpatory evidence. What they did arguably constitutes a Brady violation."

I must look confused because he elaborates. "Brady v. Maryland. It was a Supreme Court case whose ruling requires that exculpatory evidence be turned over to the defense. They knew the cat had been returned hours before your arraignment and charged you with that crime anyway. Only the person who was at the house could have returned the cat, so there's automatically another suspect plus tremendous doubt about your guilt, never mind the note delivered with the animal that specifically said you were not responsible. Had that been disclosed, as it should have been, you would have walked out of the arraignment free and clear."

"So I just go to the courtroom, you tell the judge all of that, and I go home?"

"Essentially, yes. I'll return if there are any last-minute developments. As always, don't speak to anyone without me or Mr. Trowbridge present."

"Right. Thank you," I say before we head to our respective doors. I can't stop grinning the entire way back to the waiting room.

I sit there for another fifteen minutes before a different bailiff walks me to the courtroom. It's similar to last time, but with a few more people. Mr. Kostas is sitting beside Nick, and Special Agent Smith is sitting behind the DA. The Henley and Montank suit is scowling in the gallery as I walk to my seat, but I pay no attention because Ewan is sitting in the front row behind my lawyers, grinning.

I scan the empty seats again, although it's obvious nobody is in them. *That's okay. Of course she wouldn't come. It would be crazy if she did. Especially right after hitting two more targets*, I think, trying to talk myself out of the unreasonable disappointment I feel at her absence. *I'll see her soon. I definitely don't want her to blow her cover.*

Nick gives me a smile and a nod as I take my seat.

After a minute, the judge asks, "Are we ready to begin, counselors?"

Both sides agree, and everything transpires almost exactly how Mr. Kostas described. The DA initially moved to dismiss without prejudice but offered no arguments when Nick explained the many problems with their handling of the case.

Eventually, the judge declares, "I agree. All charges in this case are summarily dismissed with prejudice. Mr. White, you are free to go."

I turn and hug Ewan. "Thanks for coming, man."

"Of course, Tre. I'll give you a ride home once you're done with all that." Ewan waves vaguely at the lawyers.

"Sir?" someone says behind me.

The bailiff is standing uncomfortably close when I turn.

"I asked Ewan to bring you some clothes. The bailiff will show you to a restroom where you can change," Nick explains, "and he'll collect that uniform. You won't be needing it anymore."

"Thank you so much. Both of you."

Mr. Kostas nods, and Nick replies, "You're very welcome. I'll meet you in the hallway, and we can discuss next steps, but I'm sure you're ready to be home. Go get changed so you can get out of here."

Chapter 33
Soft Launch into Motion

FIONA

I GLANCE AT MY WATCH. IT'S NINE-FORTY-FIVE. EWAN SAID Tre's hearing is scheduled to start at ten.

Soon, I think, over the voice that's been ceaselessly chattering in my head, telling me that what I did wasn't enough. *He'll be out soon. It has to be enough. And not just so that I can get a decent cup of coffee again.*

"How long has this been present?" I ask as I rotate Ellen Pangow's arm.

"A while, but it was only the one spot near my elbow at first. Now it's on my inner arm too, so I thought I should have someone look at it. It itches a lot. I've been trying not to scratch it, but…"

"Do you remember when you first noticed it?"

"I think it was at the end of last year. Around Thanksgiving? I know I should've come sooner, but I was busy, and…" She fidgets, and the exam paper covering the table crinkles beneath her.

"You're here now. Does anyone in your family have psoriasis?"

"Not that I know of."

"Any joint pain or stiffness?"

"No. Just the itchy skin. That's part of why I kept putting off making an appointment."

"Okay." I look up at her with a wan smile. "Well, good news, bad news. Congratulations, you're the first in your family, apparently. You've got bragging rights. That's the good news, unfortunately. Bad news is that this is psoriasis, and psoriasis is a chronic immune-mediated condition, so you're stuck with it, but the symptoms are typically very manageable.

"I would like to get you started on a topical steroid to treat the plaques on your skin—that's what these are called," I say, tapping her arm. "Then, in about four weeks, I'd like you to make another appointment so we can see how that's working. If it works, that's great. If not, we can discuss alternative treatments."

The closest dermatologist is over an hour away, and he probably won't be able to fit her into his schedule for months. Plus, her case is uncomplicated enough that I should be able to treat her here.

"I'll call the prescription in to your pharmacy, and you can make a follow-up appointment for next month with Carol before you leave. Natalie will be back in shortly to confirm your pharmacy details and answer any questions you might have right now," I tell her as I stand. "But feel free to call the office if you have any other concerns prior to your next appointment, alright?"

She nods, and then I'm out the door.

My day is fully booked, but even if it weren't, it's not like I could've gone to the courthouse. What I *want* doesn't really matter because the last thing I *need* is for suspicion to fall on me now. I don't know what I'm going to do. How are Tre and I supposed to be in a relationship if I can't come up with a way for us to be together that doesn't automatically raise everyone's eyebrows? I sigh as I step into the next exam room, resolving to let my subconscious wrestle with the problem, because I've been turning it over like a Rubik's Cube all morning and I've gotten nowhere.

It's two hours later when Carol says, "Dr. Carson?" as I'm walking between exam rooms.

"Yes?" I change my path to head toward the reception desk so she doesn't have to shout.

"Tre called about twenty minutes ago! He got out of jail. Apparently, they *finally* realized he couldn't have done it!"

"Oh, okay. That's good," I force myself to say neutrally, despite the relief washing over me.

"Yes! Anyway, he said that you didn't settle your tab last time you were in the diner and he wanted to know if you might stop by sometime today to do so."

"I paid…" I glance at my watch as realization hits me. It's almost noon. "Can you call him back and tell him I'll stop in at twelve-thirty to settle up?"

"Yes, of course. I'm sure he must be dealing with quite the headache…" Carol continues talking as I consider the merits of trying to pass Tre a note.

THE DOOR IS UNLOCKED, BUT BETTY'S IS DARK WHEN I walk through the rear entrance. And silent. There's always noise.

"Hello? Tre?" I call out to the empty space.

A door to my left opens, and I jump. Tre is standing there, backlit by the light from the office, with a smile on his face, his blond hair seeming to glow.

He's here. Out, I think as I stand frozen, watching him approach. He steps into my space before stopping and reaching around me to flip the lock on the door. Then one hand is on my hip and the other is sliding along my jaw, into my hair, as he presses me against the wall, his mouth on mine. Something more than desire—*need,* I distantly realize—floods through me, and I slide my arms around him, hands slipping under his shirt. He moans as my fingertips brush across the skin of his lower back, and his hand tenses on my hip.

I don't make the decision consciously, but the next thing I know, my hands are running up his body, over his ribs, raising his shirt of their own volition. I glance toward the front of the diner as our lips break apart, and I pull his shirt off.

As soon as Tre's eyes return to my face, he follows my gaze. "No one can see us," he murmurs as his fingertips brush along my cheek. "Promise."

"Okay." I nod. "I don't have long, though. I have to be back by one. Patients."

"Got it," he says, his hands dropping to the hem of my shirt. Air moves across my stomach as he tugs it over my head, and desire ripples through me, settling between my legs.

"Condom?" I moan as Tre's hands slide over my ass, and he lifts me, pinning me against the lightly textured wall with his body. For once, I didn't bring any. This isn't how I was expecting this visit to go, but it seems like maybe we both need this.

"Yes," he answers, and I wrap my legs around him as his mouth lands on my boob. His teeth find my nipple through the mesh of my bra, and I arch into him. The whole thing is going to be soaked, and I can't bring myself to care.

I twine my hands in his hair. *It's so soft*, I think as I let his tongue and teeth work away the worry of the past several days.

All too soon, he's sliding me down his body, setting me on my feet. "God, I love that look on your face," he says, sounding breathless.

"What look? And will you please fuck me already?"

"*That* look. That look that screams, 'Will you please fuck me already?' louder than your words ever could," Tre says, and I kick my shoes off as he fumbles with the button on my pants.

As soon as he's got it undone, I shove them down and kick them away. Then I grab his hand and drag it under the thong I'm wearing, between my legs, as I stare into his silvery-grey eyes. His lips part, and his breathing accelerates as his fingers dip into me slightly.

"Tre," I gasp as my hips twitch involuntarily. "Do you feel how wet I am?" I demand, releasing his hand so I can get his pants off.

He nods, but says nothing, and his eyes stay locked on mine as his fingers continue teasing me, and my breath comes in ragged gasps.

When I wrap my hand around his dick, there's a large drop of pre-cum beaded at the tip. My entire body tightens at the realization of how much he wants this—how much he wants *me*. His thumb glides across my clit as his fingers finally thrust all the way into me, and my knees go weak, my legs turning to jelly.

"I'm so glad you're out," I whisper with a mixture of relief and desire flooding my voice as I stroke the smooth skin along his shaft. "I could do this every day."

It's not until Tre responds, "Could you?" in a husky murmur that I realize what I've said.

"I… Will you please fuck me already?"

His eyes stay locked on me, and momentarily I fear he might force me to answer his question, but then his fingers slide out of me with agonizing slowness—I miss them as soon as they're gone—and he bends to retrieve a condom from his pants pocket.

I strip off my underwear, watching as he unrolls it. My heart is racing as anticipation builds. Then his hands are moving over my ass once more, dipping to my hamstrings, lifting me into the air. I guide him into me, my back pressing more firmly against the wall as he sinks deeper.

"Yes," I groan, quivering around him as his cock flexes.

"I didn't think I'd ever get to be with you again," Tre says softly as he holds me there, buried deep inside me, the heat of his body flowing into mine. His eyes are pinning me in place as much as his body, and the vulnerability in his words is crystal clear. I can't not respond.

"I told you I would've gotten you out if I needed to," I remind him, bringing my hands back to his hair.

He nods before pulling away just enough to thrust into me again, and pleasure begins rapidly building. I'm not going to last long, but I don't think he will either.

"I'm almost there," I warn raggedly after no more than a couple of minutes have passed.

"I know. Me too."

Tre's mouth finds mine right before the orgasm hits me, erupting outward from my core as my hips buck against him, my clit fluttering and my cunt squeezing his dick until it feels like every nerve ending in my body is overwhelmed with sensation. As soon as it begins to slow, Tre is coming and his thrusts lose all sense of rhythm, which pushes me to the edge again.

It's not until he pulls out of me and sets me down some indeterminable amount of time later that he says, "We should talk."

I glance at my watch. *Good thing everyone always expects doctors to be late.*

I have to get back for my next appointment, and I have no idea what to say. "Yeah. I know, and thanks for waiting to say that, but I don't have time right now."

"Okay, when?"

"I'll let you know," I tell him as I gather my clothes from the floor. "I really am glad you're out."

When I walk into Betty's on Sunday morning, the place is slammed. It seems like half the town is crammed into the confines of the diner, and I'm not sure if it's because they're hoping there'll be another showdown between Tre and the sheriff, or if they're simply here to show support.

I suppose there's no reason both things can't be true.

As I stand there, looking at the crowd, I consider turning around and leaving. But there's no one I recognize from the sheriff's department or the ATF, so I don't.

I've been avoiding Tre all weekend, trying to figure out a way to untangle the Gordian Knot I've created. Since he was arrested, it's even more obvious that we can't just start dating. I can't just *'change my mind.'* Both Ewan and Kyle worked out what had happened pretty quickly. It'd be stupid to assume that other people wouldn't do the same. And even if all they'd do is wonder about it, I'd rather never give them the idea. Because while they can't charge Tre again, there's nothing stopping them from going after me, except for the fact that I am, at least currently, a totally implausible suspect. And if we suddenly make it known that we're... together two days after he's been released from jail. Well. I'll go from being a 'totally implausible suspect' to 'most likely to have bombed construction sites' overnight.

I want Tre, and I want to be *with* Tre, but I'm not an idiot.

I still don't have a perfect plan, but I've got something that might work. Maybe.

He's at the grill. Like usual.

Unlike usual, I ignore the first table that opens up. And then the second one along the rear wall where I've been sitting in recent weeks, waving the couple waiting behind me forward, telling them I'll wait for a spot at the counter since it's busy and I'm alone. Finally, fifteen minutes later, an older man at the counter near where Tre's working abandons his seat.

I slide onto it before the space is even cleared.

After another handful of minutes passes, Tre turns with a plate full of steak and eggs. He freezes—plate precariously angled in one hand—when he sees me, and I smirk. When he stays frozen for a second too long, I raise my eyebrows and tilt my head in question, and he springs back into motion. He moves away from me, down the counter, and sets the plate in front of a man around my age. They exchange a few words, and then Tre is standing across from me, gathering up the previous customer's used dishes.

"Hey Fiona. You're… here," he says, stating the obvious.

"Yes. Can I get a cup of coffee?"

"Sure." He dumps the dishes into a bus bin and washes his hands. Then he grabs a mug from the shelf and fills it with coffee. "I meant here at the counter." His fingers brush against mine as he passes me the mug.

"I know. Call it a soft launch," I say, my eyes sliding past his shoulder to the wall he so recently had me pinned against.

His eyes track mine, and he smirks knowingly. I wonder how much time he's spent staring at that wall, thinking about—

"Does this mean…?"

"We'll talk. You should make an appointment at my office." I take a sip of coffee.

"An appointment? For?"

"Your shoulder. I saw the way they wrenched it when they arrested you. It was the same one you hurt earlier this year, right?"

"Oh. Yeah," he says, rolling his left shoulder. "I'll do that. Now that you mention it, it's been kind of achy lately."

Chapter 34
Deep Cover Your Ass

TRE

"Makes you wonder what they were trying to cover up," I finish.

"Oh, honey, I didn't even think about that!" Carol exclaims, raising her hand to her mouth.

"I'm *so* glad whoever returned that cat and tried to clear my name picked you."

"Mr. White, you can come back now," Nurse Machado says from the doorway.

"Me too, Tre. I knew you didn't do those things they said. And I was so relieved that poor cat was safe," Carol says, touching my shoulder as I walk past to follow the nurse.

"Ah, exam room two. Just like old times, huh?" I tease.

"Old times?" she queries, shutting the door.

"Yeah. You know. Like the other times I was here about my shoulder."

"So this isn't a recent injury?"

"It is. It got wrenched last week, and it still hurts. But I was here before. When I hurt it. Before." I'm studying her face for any sign of remembrance as we go through the motions of checking my vitals.

While she applies the blood pressure cuff, she asks, "This pain started last week. Have you been able to use the shoulder?"

"Yeah, it still works, but it hurts when I move it in certain directions."

"Take a look at this chart and tell me which number most closely matches the level of pain you're experiencing."

This again, I think. "Most of the time it's zero, but it can be, uh, six."

She dutifully records my information on the computer but makes no further comment.

"So, how's your week going? Do anything exciting lately?" I'll make friends with her eventually.

"It's fine. How about you?"

I tilt my head quizzically. *Is she not aware? She's not real talkative, but I know how this town gossips, and it's the biggest story around.*

"Well, I was—" I begin when Fiona raps on the door and enters. *Every time!*

I turn to watch Fiona, no longer caring about whatever I was going to say. Her hair is pulled back, highlighting her face. Her malachite eyes are fixed on mine as she crosses the room. She speaks with the nurse quietly for a few moments before taking a seat at the computer.

"Hurting your shoulder twice in a couple of months... Maybe hiking isn't your sport," Nurse Machado comments as she leaves.

My eyebrows draw together, and I whip my head toward her. *I didn't tell her how I hurt it this time—hiking was my excuse last time. So she does remember...?*

"You can stop staring now. She's gone," Fiona says, grabbing my attention.

"Huh. Is she... What's her deal?"

"You're always so concerned about my nurse. Is that what you want to spend our time focused on?" Fiona stands and walks the few feet to where I'm seated on the exam table. She moves between my legs and leans forward, her face inches from mine.

I close the distance and press my lips to hers. I slide my tongue into her mouth while one hand skims along her neck to the back of her head and the other grabs her ass, yanking her against me. We stay locked together for a minute until my dick is so hard it starts pulsating, aching to be touched.

I lean back to pull her onto the exam table with me, but she steps away. Her breath is coming fast as she says, "We don't have *that* much time, Tre." But her cheeks are flushed as she tucks stray hairs in place.

"Hey, all I know is we're almost sort of a thing and you said to come here. Tuesday afternoon was the earliest appointment I could get without a favor from Carol. So what's up?"

Fiona clears her throat. "I've got a plan. For us."

"Of course you do." I grin.

"What's that supposed to mean?"

"Nothing bad. You just have very specific plans for every single thing. Even when people have no idea you've ever thought about something, you have an entire plan for it. I love it." *Oh shit. Did I just use that word? Can I say that? Is it too soon? Am I going to freak her out?* My eyes go wide as my mind pivots from humor to worry, but Fiona seems to take it in stride.

"Right. Anyway. If we're going to be together without making me a person of interest, we need a cover story that will make sense to people."

"A cover story?"

"Yes," she says. "Something that won't make people look at us and wonder how that happened. I was thinking we could volunteer to work on some town project. Something that'll require us to spend time together planning it."

"That... Of all the things I expected you might say, *that* never occurred to me."

"We want to be together, but if I 'change my mind' and we start dating out of the blue, I'll become an obvious suspect. I sure as hell don't want to keep sneaking around forever. Not only do we barely get to see each other, but it's... inefficient."

"Yeah, I get it. We need a safe way to be around each other in public long enough that people won't be suspicious when they finally see us dating," I acknowledge. "You're not wrong. That Henley and Montank investigator is still watching me, and the ATF is hanging around town. Speaking of which, I had an idea that could help."

I hear the skepticism in her voice when she asks, "What's your idea?"

"They're looking for suspects, so we'll give them some. I'll get a couple of prepaid phones and call in some anonymous threats using right-wing ideology talking points. 'Don't tread on me. Free citizens don't follow your corrupt laws. Stay off our land…' all that dumb shit. People are already speculating about some militia being responsible, so it might send the investigators down that path and make them less likely to ever consider you. It'll provide more reasonable doubt if there are any future charges.

"And maybe they'll back off a little if they think that's who's behind it all. They're dying to paint environmentalists as terrorists, but the extreme right gets free passes on everything. They might treat it like the Cliven Bundy standoff and drop the whole thing."

"Hmm, maybe. Just let me know *before* you do it, okay? If you don't do it right, they'll trace it to you and you'll be screwed."

"Fine, I won't do it yet. But I'll probably start working on the wording of my 'manifesto,'" I reply, grinning.

"Right. So, any ideas about an event we could use as a cover story?"

"You just assume I know everything that's happening in—okay, yeah, fair enough." I consider it. "There's nothing good coming up soon. Everybody does their own thing for Labor Day. There's the Homecoming parade, but the high school puts that on, so it doesn't make sense for us to get involved," I say, and her face falls. "What if we create one?"

"Okay. What do you have in mind?"

"What if we did a harvest festival? Plenty of towns have something similar, so it'll be easy to sell. Most of Kalomish is united against the developments right now, and I don't want to lose that. This could help keep people connected." I pause, thinking. "If we're going to sell it as a harvest festival, we should hold it in late September or early October. That'd give us five or six weeks to work together openly, which is enough to make dating afterward believable. Plus, it'll give everyone a chance to see you as part of Kalomish again, instead of as someone who left." I nod. "It's a good plan."

"I don't want a second job, Tre. Just a cover story."

"Please. I'm going to get tons of people working on this. All we'll have to do is keep the ideas flowing and coordinate everybody. It'll be great!"

"Do you really think the city council is going to approve a new festival? Especially if it's your idea?" Fiona asks, frowning. "Jacob hates you, and the rest of them follow his lead."

"I don't give a fuck about Jacob. I'll work around him. Same as always," I tell her with a shrug. "There's no reason to change tactics now. I'll spread the word and get everyone excited first. Then we'll make it official after the town's already behind it. You can even pipe up in the next town hall about how you think it's 'such a great community-building idea,'" I finish with a smirk.

"Alright," Fiona says, rolling her eyes, but she's smiling when she does. "I guess that settles that. I'm looking forward to spending the night more than once a month."

"Yeah, and without being afraid I'll get arrested for public indecency."

She shoves my shoulder, grinning, and then stays in my personal space, eyes locked on mine.

"Oh, that reminds me." I reach into my pocket and dig out a napkin, killing the moment. "I heard of a house you can rent. You remember Mrs. Walker, the math teacher? Well, she passed a few years ago, and her son owns the house. But he's a professor over in Eugene, so he rents it out. You could probably move in whenever you're ready because it's been available for a couple of months."

"I'm amazed you found something already."

"Yeah, I haven't had much time, so it's just the one. Sorry. I'll keep looking and let you know of anything else in case that doesn't work out."

The bell above the door rings as I walk out from the rear of the diner carrying a stack of freshly washed plates.

"Hey. You can grab a—" I stop dead in my tracks. "Dad? What are you doing here?"

Richard Alan White the Second, as he likes to be called—or Junior, as I prefer to think of him—stands in the doorway surveying the diner. He's got two inches and probably fifty pounds on me. He's making no effort to hide his opinion, with his brow furrowed and a slight sneer on his face. At three-forty in the afternoon on a Wednesday, he's the only other person here besides Jackie, who's having a meal in the back. The lunch crowd is long gone, and it's way too early for dinner.

I set the plates down on the nearest surface and wait for a response.

"I haven't been in here in years. Looks exactly the same as it used to."

"Thank you."

"That wasn't a compliment," he snaps.

"Okay. Well, you've seen it. If you only came here to shit on the place, or trash talk Grandma Betty, you can leave now," I warn.

"I shouldn't have to come here at all, Richie. I've been expecting *you* to come to the house."

I recoil. "Why the hell would you expect me to come visit you?"

"To say thank you!" his voice booms. "I saved your ass from prison. You're walking free right now because I gave you the help you obviously couldn't get yourself."

"You think you—"

"You're damn right I did! Do you think that Greek fella stepped in and beat the DA because he's nice? I only deal with winners, and whatever schmuck you had wasn't getting you anywhere. Your mother told me you came to visit after I protected you from the sheriff the first time. You never said a word of thanks then, either! I swear I don't know how she raised such an ingrate."

"What the fuck is wrong with you? You never helped me. You never do anything unless it benefits you!" We're both shouting now.

"And the second you thought I damaged *your* property, you made sure your lawyer wouldn't help me. Not that I—"

"Yeah, after Morris arrested you, I actually believed you did it. And I almost respected you. At least then I thought you had finally accomplished something, even if you did fuck it up enough to get arrested."

My mouth is hanging open. There are so many things I want to yell at him I can't pick one.

"It turns out the only thing you're good at is being a disappointment."

"I didn't need any help from you, and I sure as shit never asked you for anything! You can get the fuck out of my restaurant. And feel free to tell mom you're the reason I won't visit her anymore. I'll never set foot in your fucking house again," I declare.

"Always so sensitive. And whiny. You're lucky I saved—"

I reach behind me toward the grill, hefting a frying pan in my right hand and lower my voice. "Get. The fuck. Out."

He stands there, eyeing me for a moment, then shakes his head. "You little shit," he fires off before turning and slamming the door open on his way out.

I'm still holding the frying pan at the ready when Jackie hesitantly pokes her head out from the back. "Tre, are you okay?"

I let out a sigh and set the pan down. My hand is shaking now that the adrenaline and anger are fading. "Yeah, thanks."

"I'm sorry," she offers.

"Yeah. There's a reason I work here and not with him."

I DROP MY PLATE IN THE DISHWASHER ON MY WAY TO THE front of the diner. I've been killing time, waiting for Nick Trowbridge to show up since my shift ended. Only when I scan the room for him, he's not here yet. Special Agent Connor Smith of the ATF still is, though. He came in for lunch, but that was a couple of hours ago, and the restaurant has emptied out since then.

Is he here to watch me? Or to listen to gossip? Well, I'm not doing anything else…

I go to his booth and slide in across from him. "Hey Connor."

His eyes widen slightly, but his voice is calm when he replies. "Mr. White. Good afternoon."

"I haven't seen you in here recently. Did something happen?"

He smiles ruefully. "As I'm sure your lawyers told you, the ATF had nothing to do with your arrest. But it didn't seem… polite to come back right away."

I give him a no-hard-feelings smile. "So you still think you'll find the answers you want by listening to the local gossip? Good luck with that. People assume you know more about what happened than they do."

"I just follow the investigation wherever it leads me."

"Then you don't have any suspects, I take it."

"Like I said, my job is to investigate. I leave it up to the prosecutors to decide who the evidence says is guilty."

"Ah, very impartial. I guess your preconceptions and biases never guide an investigation to focus on any particular suspect, then," I say with obvious sarcasm.

"You surprise me, Mr. White. Most people who've just been arrested either avoid talking to law enforcement or are extremely angry with them," Connor comments wryly.

"Well, we know I'm not the guy you're looking for. And, like you, I wouldn't want to be rude." I flash him another smile.

"Especially by forcing me to speak to you through your attorney." He grins.

"Exactly. I'm actually waiting for him to stop by. My shift ended a while ago. I already had lunch, and now I'm just killing time. I figured I'd say hi."

The bell over the door jingles and I glance behind me to see Nick walk in.

"And here he is now. Excuse me."

Connor nods as I stand and catch Nick's attention with a wave.

"Good to see you again, Tre," he greets when I meet him near the register.

"You too, Nick. Let's head back to my office, such as it is."

"Is there anything happening here I need to get involved with?" he asks, inclining his head toward Connor's table.

"No, he just hangs out here to eavesdrop while he works. I was waiting anyway, so I figured I'd clear the air," I say as I lead him to the back.

"I did tell you not to talk to any law enforcement without your lawyer present."

I shrug. "Thanks for bringing my stuff from the jail."

"Not a problem. I already had a few things to take care of for the Henley and Montank lawsuits, so it was easy enough to finish the paperwork and grab your belongings. I don't know how you managed for a week without your cell phone."

I close the door behind us. "Eh, I don't really use it that often. I'm not big on texting, and I work a lot. Plus, most of my friends come to the diner, so I just see whoever I need to talk to. There's always the restaurant's landline if I have to make a call."

Nick shakes his head as he sets the plastic bag containing my clothes, wallet, keys, and phone on the desk.

"Any news about my case, or fresh charges or anything?" I inquire.

"Nope, nothing. Here, no news is good news. I think you can breathe easy."

"Excellent. What about the lawsuits against Henley and Montank? Some of the guys have mentioned that construction work is on pause, but nobody's telling them why or for how long."

"Yeah, we do have some good news there. One of the reasons I'm in Kalomish was for a hearing this morning. The judge issued a new, stricter injunction against construction on the gondola system until another environmental impact study can be conducted to the court's satisfaction. That's only as strong as its enforcement—and we know how the sheriff's department has handled things to this point—but every bit helps. Plus, the more rules they violate, the more ammo we have."

"Hey, I'll take any win we can get," I respond with a smile. Then, I lean closer and lower my voice, even though we're the only ones in here. "People have been saying that this property destruction was actually orchestrated by Henley and Montank. Some kind of insurance fraud scheme. Do you know anything about that?"

Nick raises his eyebrows. "This is the first I've heard of it. I don't suppose 'people' have any proof, do they?"

"It's just talk so far. It makes sense, though. It might explain why nobody has been caught, too." I sit back. "Is there any way you can use that in your court cases?"

"I wish, but speculation without evidence doesn't help me. Although… Yeah, I might have an idea after all. I can't do anything officially, but I'll mention the rumor to some journalists I know in Portland. They can talk to Henley and Montank, their insurers, and various police and federal agencies. They'll rattle a lot of cages simply by poking around and asking questions." He nods, and his gaze fades into the middle distance as he considers the possibilities.

"Alright, well, thanks again for all of your help with my case. And for bringing my stuff." I stand and offer my hand.

He shakes it and opens the office door. "Certainly. And thank you for the illuminating conversation. I'll see you around, Tre."

Chapter 35
Blinded by the
Sight and Sound

FIONA

It's a bit before noon on Saturday when I park on the street in front of a small, single-story brick house. There's already a car parked in the driveway with a man who's probably fifteen or twenty years older than me leaning against it. He looks up from his phone when I get out of my truck and slam the door.

"Hi. Chris?" I've never met Chris Walker. I only spoke to him on the phone earlier this week when we arranged the time for me to come see the house, but I'm pretty sure it's him, and not just because he's here waiting at the appointed time. He looks like his mom. Same dark skin and light eyes.

"Yes. Fiona?" he asks as he walks toward me, extending his hand.

"Yup. Thanks for coming out here to meet me," I say as I take it.

"No problem. Let me show you the place."

Straight to business. I like it.

He leads me up a short staircase and unlocks the front door, gesturing for me to enter first. I step into a small living room with an arched doorway that leads to a kitchen. The floors are wood, and what I can see of the kitchen looks like something straight out of the fifties.

"The house was built in forty-nine. My grandparents owned it before my mom. It's been in the family since it was built, otherwise I'd have sold it after my mom died."

"I was sorry to hear about that."

"Thanks. Anyway, all the appliances are old, but everything works. You could move in as soon as you like. Rent is sixteen-hundred, due on the first, and you'd be responsible for the utilities. Take a look around and let me know what you think. I'll wait here."

I nod, not bothering to waste words since he doesn't seem like the sort to require unnecessary small talk.

The kitchen is small but bright, and there's enough countertop space to fit a microwave and a toaster oven, which are pretty much all I ever use. The fridge is one of those retro ones with the lever handles that sells for several thousand dollars these days. There's no dishwasher, which sucks, but it's not a deal-breaker.

There's a small yard with a firepit visible through the window above the sink, a dining room with built-in cabinets to the right, and a hallway to the left. I wander down the hallway, having already seen all there is to see of the dining room.

There are two bedrooms, both just large enough to fit a queen-sized bed, a single bathroom with a pedestal sink and a clawfoot tub that likely weighs several hundred pounds, and a small utility room containing the washer and dryer.

Quaint. That's what people would call this place if they were generous. Tiny is what they'd call it otherwise, I muse as I spin in a circle in the second bedroom.

It's big enough though, and it gets me out of my dad's place, which has the added benefit of making it easier to spend time with Tre. Plus, it's only a ten-minute drive from here to my office. I could bike it if I wanted.

Finally, I walk back to the living room. "How would you feel about a month-to-month lease—breakable with thirty days' notice—if I paid an extra hundred dollars each month?"

Chris's gaze goes unfocused as he mulls it over. "Sixty days," he counters.

I take a few seconds to consider it. "If I can move in two weeks from now and you prorate my rent, you've got a deal," I reply. This weekend is already halfway gone, and next is Labor Day weekend, so neither will be great for moving.

"Deal. I've got the paperwork in my car. We can modify the terms, and you can sign it now if you want."

"Works for me."

"WHAT DO YOU THINK IS GOING TO HAPPEN?" EWAN ASKS as more people file in and find seats.

My eyes flick to Special Agent Connor Smith, who's against the wall near the dais. I haven't spoken to him since that day he showed up to talk to my dad. Somehow though, it seems like he's always around, and I'm not sure if he's actually watching me, or if it just feels like it. I let my eyes move over the rest of the room before he notices my interest.

There's still ten minutes until the town hall starts, but the room is filling fast. Everyone wants to know what's going on with Henley and Montank. Construction at their sites has been paused for over two weeks now, but no one seems to know what's happening.

"No clue. Any chance you could help me move this weekend?"

"No can do, sis. I've got tours to guide both days."

I fold my arms across my chest and sigh. Kelly and Tess both agreed to help. Cath is out of town though, and it'd be nice to have another couple of people.

"I can check whether anyone else is free," Ewan volunteers.

"*Not* Cade."

"Not Cade," he agrees.

"Okay. Thanks. I'll text you the address. Tell whoever I'll supply beer and pizza."

Ewan nods, and I scan the room.

"Relax," Ewan says. "He'll be here."

"I know. I just…"

"You just like everything to happen on an imaginary schedule that no one else but you knows about."

I wish I could disagree with him, but I can't, so I settle on huffing instead, and Ewan laughs.

Another few minutes pass, and then the council members are walking onto the dais and taking their seats. I glance to the back of the room once more, and this time Tre is leaning against the wall, near the door. He gives me the barest nod when our eyes meet, and I remember our conversation late last night.

We were in his bed, and I was sprawled across his body. We were both still damp with sweat. *'Don't fuck it up,'* I said.

'Fuck what up?'

'Tomorrow. Don't get kicked out of the town hall before you get them to agree to the festival.'

'I wouldn't… Shit,' he muttered. *'I would do that.'*

He nods again, and I turn back to the front.

"Thank you all for coming," Jacob says to the room. "We have a lot to cover tonight and—"

"What's going on with Henley and Montank?" someone-not-Tre shouts.

"We'll get to that sh—"

"No, let's talk about it now!" someone else yells. "First you arrest one of us, then you let him go, but only after trying to violate his civil rights, and now people are saying that Henley and Montank were behind everything the entire time!"

Jacob glares at the latest speaker, his nostrils flaring and frown lines appearing between his eyebrows.

Goddamnit, I fume. *If they don't shut the fuck up, Jacob might take the city council and walk out of the room before we can even get to the festival idea.*

I raise my hand, and Jacob's entire expression softens when his eyes land on me like I'm a port in a storm.

"Yes, Dr. Carson, please go ahead," he says, and it's clear he's hoping I'll play my usual part of shoring up the council's position.

"Thank you, Councilman Nammier." I stand and face the room prior to continuing. "I think we can all agree the arrest was a mistake. I don't believe anyone would argue that." I pause long enough to look back at Jacob, and the expression on his face is obviously pained, but he's smart enough to grab onto the life preserver I threw in his direction and nods in agreement. "I'm sure everyone involved wishes they hadn't jumped to conclusions. And I would like answers just as much as anyone else. However, if we all keep shouting at the council members, we're not going to get those answers." I stare at the crowd for another second before turning to sit down.

"Yes. That's exactly right, Dr. Carson. Thank you. As I was saying. The situation with Henley and Montank is in flux, and all projects with which they are involved are paused for the foreseeable future. At present, the courts have ordered an additional environmental impact assessment for each site, and until that's completed, there will be no further construction.

"The council understands the anger over the arrest, but decisions like that are not within our purview," he states, apparently deciding to throw the sheriff under the bus.

Color me not surprised.

"Having said that, we would like to issue an official apology to Mr. White for the accusations he experienced."

My jaw doesn't fall open at those words, but it's a close thing, and I don't like it at all. Jacob must be planning something. A run against the sheriff, maybe? Or possibly a run for mayor. Fuck. I don't know which would be worse.

Jacob continues making placating apologies that mean nothing but appear to satisfy more people than I'd like, and Tre remains mercifully silent throughout.

Eventually, Jacob runs out of hot air and opens the floor for questions.

"Thank you for the apology," Tre says before Jacob can take a breath, not giving him the opportunity to call on anyone else. "And in the spirit of restoring some normalcy to Kalomish, I'd like to propose a Harvest Festival to take place the second weekend in October. I've already begun the permitting process and have talked to potential sponsors."

"We can't—" Jacob starts, but I raise my hand, and he says, "Yes, Dr. Carson?"

"*I* think it sounds like a great idea. It'll go a long way in rebuilding a sense of community."

"But the planning and organization—"

"I believe Dr. Carson just volunteered to help me with the planning and organization," Tre asserts, and I can feel every eye in the room weighing and measuring me.

I don't have to fake the uncertainty or the hitch in my breath as I say, "I… guess I could spare some time to help with the planning."

In my periphery, I can see Connor's eyes lingering on me as Jacob turns to look at the rest of the council, who mostly give some variation of a 'sure, why not?' shrug.

"Very well," he says. "I'll make some time to help, too."

It'll have to do. I force myself to give a polite nod when he looks at me, instead of screaming at him to sit down and shut the hell up like I want to. If Jacob wants to unknowingly have a front-row seat to the Tre and Fiona Show, well. That's his business, and he can suffer the consequences.

"Is that the last of it?" my dad asks as we slide the dresser into my truck.

"Yeah. I think so." I push the gate up and lock it in place.

"You need any help unloading it?"

"No. Tess and Kelly and a couple of Ewan's friends are already there helping unload the truck full of stuff I had in my storage unit in Seattle," I tell him. If I'm lucky, Tess will have unpacked my kitchen by the time I return. She was putting away my glasses when I left. "One of them will be able to help."

"Alright. Well, let me know if you need anything," he says, wiping the sweat from his forehead with the back of his hand.

"Will do. Thanks, dad." I give him a quick hug, then hop in my truck to take the last of the stuff to my new place.

Tre and Kelly are carrying in the coffee table when I park at the curb. The entire driveway is occupied by the moving truck full of my life from Seattle. I could've gotten rid of more than I did before moving back to Kalomish, but... even though I bought Dr. Restin's practice, I guess I wasn't certain I'd be staying long term.

I'm not sure when that changed, but it did.

"Hey Fiona," Kelly calls, seeing me first since she's walking backward toward the front door.

"Hey Kell. Hey Tre," I say as I rush to get the door for Kelly, holding it open as they pass and I follow them through. "Where's Lucas? I could use some help with the dresser in my truck."

"Pretty sure he's busy flirting with Tess," Tre grumbles as they set the coffee table down, and Kelly laughs.

"Ah. I saw him casting glances in her direction before I left, but he'd been doing that for most of the morning."

"I'll give you a hand," Tre says, moving back toward the door.

"Thanks."

"So... How long until we let our friends know we're dating?" Tre asks when we reach my truck. "Because your ass looks amazing in those shorts, and that shirt—"

"Really highlights my eyes?" I smirk, and he steps closer.

"Yes. Your eyes," he agrees as his gaze lingers on my boobs. "And I'd really like to kiss you."

"I don't know. Another few weeks? If you can hold out that long," I tease. I'm still worried about the ATF. They don't show any signs of leaving, and they can still come after both of us. It's not like our friends would say anything, but I'd also rather not put them in the position of having to lie for us.

He groans as the tailgate thunks down. "Fine. But only because I can see the finish line."

"Tell me about it. Want to spend the night? Christen the new place?"

"Absolutely."

"Good." I smile as I jump into my truck and push the dresser toward Tre. "Damn," I mutter.

"What?"

"I forgot my bike. I was going to ride it to work on Monday. I guess I can grab it tomorrow."

"Don't you and Kelly have plans to go climbing tomorrow?"

"Shit," I groan. "We do."

"So we'll get it now," Tre suggests. "Put the dresser in the bedroom and then go grab your bike. We'll be back in half an hour. They won't even notice we're gone."

"You just want a chance to be alone with me, don't you?"

"Yes."

I laugh. "Alright." Tre extends his hand. I take it and then jump to the ground. We grab the dresser and haul it inside.

Five minutes later, we're in the icy air conditioning of my truck, and Tre's fingertips are trailing up and down my thigh.

"You know that's incredibly distracting, right?"

"Want me to stop?" he asks, and there's a bit of a dare underlying his words.

"No."

After a few more minutes pass, he says, "We could christen your truck too. My car. Your office…"

"Yeah? Anywhere else you have in mind?"

"I can probably come up with something," he tells me as I pull into my dad's driveway.

"C'mon. You can take a look at the garage. See if you want to christen that too."

Tre gets out when I do. "I'm pretty sure the answer is yes."

As soon as we're out of view from the street, he wraps an arm around my waist and I lean into him.

"In fact, if you want to do that now…" he murmurs, kissing the side of my neck.

"No, sorry. There are spiders everywhere in here."

"You're afraid of spiders?" Tre asks, sounding surprised.

"Not *afraid*. I just don't like them."

"So, afraid. Got it."

I roll my eyes but say nothing, opting to grab my bike and get away from the spiders instead.

"Hold on a sec," I say, leaning my bike against the house as we near the front. "I have to pee. You can come in. Say hi to my dad."

"Or I could wait out here."

"Are you afraid of my dad?" I ask, grinning.

"Yes. Definitely. Your father is terrifying, Fiona. And he hates me."

"Yeah, well, he's gonna have to get over it sometime. Come on." I grab Tre's hand and pull him toward the front door, unlocking it and stepping inside.

And then…

And then my brain breaks, and I stand there blinking, unable to move.

"Fiona," Tre whispers, tugging on my hand, and my dad bolts upright. Off the topless woman he was making out with on our couch.

"Is that," Tre continues, voice low, "your *nurse?*" at the same time I blurt, "Natalie?"

"Fiona? Shit!" Natalie shrieks as she sits up, her hands covering her boobs.

SOS. Come over when you're done, I text Ewan. Bring more beer

"So your nurse's name is Natalie?" Tre asks. He's behind the wheel of my truck, driving us back to my new place.

"Tre."

"I never knew that."

"Not really the time, Tre," I grumble.

"Yeah. Sorry."

We fall into silence, and my brain immediately fills with the image of my dad's face turning a deep crimson as he picked up Natalie's shirt from the floor and shouted at me to '*Get OUT, Fiona! Get out right now!*' Then Tre was pulling me backward and shutting the door without another word.

"So the festival," I say, then fall silent again.

"What about the festival?" Tre finally asks.

"I don't know. I was hoping you'd start talking. I could use the distraction."

"Oh. Okay. Well. Jacob's going to be a huge pain in the ass, obviously. I don't know if he actually wants to be involved, or if he wants to swoop in at the last minute to claim credit if things go well."

"Mmm."

"What do you think about holding a raffle? And then donating the proceeds to the food bank?"

"Sounds like a good idea," I reply noncommittally. "You'll need prizes."

"I know. I can donate some gift certificates for Betty's, and I should be able to convince a lot of the other businesses to do the same."

"That would work," I agree.

Tre does his best to distract me with talk of the festival, but my brain is only partially paying attention. I keep turning over the scene at my dad's house. Whatever that was, it definitely wasn't a *new* thing.

How long have they been dating? I wonder. Has it been since I got back and hired Natalie? Why hide it? How did they even meet? Was it one of the times he came by my office to fix something? Did no one know about this? All those nights he was gone… was that where he was? What do I say on Monday? I should probably just pretend it never happened…

"What's your take on pie eating contests?"

"Hmm. What?"

"Pie eating contests. Should we have one?" Tre asks.

"Sure, why not? How about a three-legged race and a sack hop too?" I say, and I'm not sure if I'm joking. "Maybe the thing with the egg on the spoon."

Tre snorts.

"A petting zoo," I throw out.

"Apparently, you should be traumatized by the sight of your half-naked dad more often. It makes you surprisingly helpful."

"Not funny," I reply, lightly jabbing an elbow into his side.

"You're right. Too soon." He grins. "You think that'll help or hurt my standing with him?"

"Honestly? I have *no* idea."

By the time we make it back to my place, the last of the stuff from the moving truck has been brought inside, and Lucas is in the living room setting up my TV.

"Hey. I was going to ask you where you wanted this, but I didn't know where you guys went, so I decided this seemed like a good spot. I can move it if you don't like it, though," he says, his voice a deep rumble.

"No. That's good. Thanks for the help today. I'm going to order some pizzas. What do you want?"

"Whatever's fine," he says unhelpfully.

"Kelly, Tess!" I shout. "What do you guys want on the pizzas?"

"Tomatoes and mushrooms," Tess yells.

"Sausage and onion," Kelly calls, her voice echoing. She must be in the bathroom.

"DID YOU SERIOUSLY SEND ME AN SOS TEXT BECAUSE YOU ran out of beer?" Ewan asks when he appears from the side of the house an hour and a half later. We're all seated around the firepit, and the pizza boxes are mostly empty.

"What?"

"You sent me an SOS text and said to bring beer," he reminds me.

"Oh. That."

"Yeah. That." He sets a case of beer next to the pizza boxes before searching through them for what's left. "So what's up?"

I glance at Tre, and he shrugs.

"I sort of walked in on dad this afternoon."

"Ooh," Tess murmurs as Kelly snickers.

"Walked in on dad...?"

"On top of a half-naked woman on the living room couch."

Ewan bursts out laughing.

"It gets worse," I say.

"How?" Lucas asks.

"It... was the nurse from my office. The half-naked woman was Natalie," I explain, knowing none of them know her, and none of them will run their mouths about it.

"Oh damn," Kelly says. "That's awkward."

"Yeah. Just a bit."

"Not as awkward as the time I walked in on him and mom on the kitchen table," Ewan says around a mouthful of pizza.

"You *what*? When the fuck did that happen?"

"The summer after eighth grade. Mid-act. And I had to sit across that table from them and eat dinner for almost two years. On a scale of one to awkward, I'd say this is a three at best."

"I walked in on my parents when I was ten. Got the 'when a man loves a woman talk' real early," Kelly chimes in, and we all burst out laughing.

Chapter 36
Planning on Coming Soon

TRE

"YOU ALREADY HAVE THAT MANY VOLUNTEERS?" JACOB asks.

"Of course. There's no time to waste, and people are pretty excited we're doing this," I answer.

It's Monday evening, and the first meeting of the Kalomish Harvest Festival planning committee has been underway for nearly half an hour. I tried not to be a dick at the beginning, but best laid plans and all that.

"You can add Jean and Carol from my office to the list. They wouldn't stop talking about the festival all day," Fiona says.

I don't know if that's true or if she's antagonizing Jacob, but I nod and write their names on the whiteboard.

"Alright, at tomorrow afternoon's planning meeting, we'll match up volunteers with the list of events we'd like to run and figure out how many we can include," I propose.

"Wait, you want to meet on Tuesday too?" Jacob complains. "I can't spend every day on this."

"We're on an extremely tight timeline, which I believe you pointed out *before* you volunteered to help. I never asked you to join, so feel free to quit."

"That's not what I said! You want to—" Jacob raises his voice before Fiona interrupts.

"Knock it off. If you keep up your pissing contest, *I'll* quit and you can both fail. Enjoy explaining that to the entire town."

I let out a deep breath and relax my shoulders while Jacob sits back in his chair.

"Good. Tre is right. We don't have time to spare. But," she continues hurriedly when Jacob straightens up again, "that doesn't mean we *all* need to meet every day. We can assign tasks and each work on those, then meet here every few days. Sound good?"

"You are the voice of reason, as always, Dr. Carson," Jacob answers in a grateful tone with an overly considerate look on his face. I wish I could punch him.

"That's fine," I agree. "I've been working on this for the past week, which is why we have so much done. I'm happy to share.

"Jacob, why don't you take over the sponsorships and business donations? You can stop by Betty's in the morning, and I'll give you my notes of who we have and haven't contacted. You're welcome to add anyone you'd like." I stare at him, daring him to object.

His jaw muscles tense for a moment before he replies, "Sounds great. I'd love to."

"Anything in particular that you think I should handle?" Fiona asks, challenge clear in her voice. I wonder how much of her attitude is a show for Jacob's sake and how much is her daring me to try telling her what to do.

"Well, we've got this preliminary list of events, and we know we want to host as many local vendors as possible. I thought you could take on the location planning. I've filed the permits to make sure it can happen in town, but we still need to know where everything will be situated."

"Alright. I can do that."

I glance past her through the window to find the head librarian tapping her wrist at us.

"Okay, time's up. Meet on Thursday at six-thirty, then?" I ask, looking at Fiona. Our meeting time is dictated by the clinic's hours.

They both murmur agreement as I open the door.

"Hi Ms. K. Thank you so much for letting us use this space as the Harvest Festival headquarters. Even when City Hall is closed, we can count on the library. Isn't that right, Councilman Nammier?"

Jacob steps out of the room with his plastic smile in place and agrees. "It certainly is. The library is a vital hub for our community, and we appreciate your support."

Ms. K. nods, her stern face softening. "I hope you'll remember that at next year's budget meetings, Councilman."

"Such candor. Whatever would we do without you, Ms. K?" Jacob says, neatly sidestepping any promises.

Why can't I punch him?

"We'll get out of your hair and let you close up," he finishes.

On the way out, I say, "Dr. Carson, since we're here already, how about I show you some of my thoughts on the layout?"

Fiona glares daggers at me, then makes a show of looking at the sky. "There's about half an hour until sunset. Why not?"

"Jacob, I'll see you in the morning about that list."

He nods curtly, then looks at Fiona. "And I will see you on Thursday. Good evening."

As I wait for him to leave, I notice the familiar pale face of the Henley and Montank suit watching me from a car across the street. When Jacob walks away, I lead Fiona in the opposite direction. We cross at the corner and meander toward Humboldt Park, with me pointing randomly at things along the way.

"If you ever 'Dr. Carson' me again, I'll kick you in the balls," Fiona hisses once we're out of earshot.

I laugh. "Just putting on a show for our idiotic audience."

Her only response is to continue glaring.

"Okay, fine. Never again. You have to admit, though. Giving you the location assignments was pretty smart."

"Was it?" Fiona asks, and I'm not sure if she's still annoyed or back to being laconic.

"Sure. Not only can you work out most of it on your own, meaning you don't have to socialize constantly, but we can also walk around downtown together any time we want. Look. We can put the petting zoo you asked for right here." I sweep my arm toward the eastern edge of the park.

"And you think *that* constitutes a clever plan?"

"We get to walk through the park and enjoy a beautiful sunset together. We couldn't do that yesterday."

"Yeah. I guess you did alright," she admits, bumping her shoulder into mine. "Why did you give Jacob the donations?"

"Well, I had to task him with something. Anything I assigned him would shift the power dynamic between us, however temporary. You could see he hated it, but he put himself in this situation," I say with a shrug. "Schmoozing is what he does anyway, so it's a natural fit. And this way, he has to talk to people who are going to tell him exactly how they feel about the developments face to face. Plus, I couldn't resist rubbing a little salt in the wound and making him come to me to get the info."

"The banner looks great, Mr. Greyson. We'll get it set up on Main Street tomorrow. When you have the others printed, tell Jordan and he'll hang them around town," I state. "That's the last update on advertising. Fiona, do you have any topics for the team?"

I step away from the lectern so she can replace me. She, Jacob, and I are seated near the circulation desk with a lectern facing the main room. About two dozen volunteers are occupying every spare chair.

"Yes, thank you. My main update is that thanks to the donation from White Construction," Fiona nods an acknowledgment at Jacob, "we'll be able to build a single stage on the north end of Humboldt Park to handle the larger events. This will free up the space we planned for the second stage. Unless anyone objects, we'll use that space for more vendors and an additional walkway to help the traffic flow."

Nobody says anything, and she continues, "Jacob, there will be four new VIP booth spots. You can reach out to any vendors who want to upgrade." To the room, she adds, "I'll send out an updated draft of the map. That's all I have."

I return to the lectern when she takes a seat.

"Okay. That's everything on tonight's agenda. Everyone has their assignments. If questions or issues come up before our Thursday meeting, you know your points of contact. Thank you all for coming, and thank you again for helping."

It's ten to seven. We've been meeting here for the past two weeks, and despite the number of volunteers involved, this is the earliest we've finished.

I help stack chairs against the wall and say my goodbyes. When I walk outside, the familiar grey sedan with the Henley and Montank suit is parked several spaces down the street. Our eyes briefly lock before I turn away.

Fiona meets me outside for what has become our new routine. Ostensibly, we're reviewing locations and planning the festival, so I occasionally point at nothing as we walk through the streets to the park to watch the sunset.

Twilight quickly settles into dusk, and we go our separate ways. Instead of heading home, though, I go to the diner's parking lot and get in my car. I wait several minutes to make sure there's enough separation between us, then drive to Fiona's house, taking the long way to make sure there's no grey sedan following me.

Her truck is in the driveway, and the lights are on inside when I drive past her house and park two blocks away around the corner. I walk back to her place and lock the front door behind me.

Fiona is clattering pots in the kitchen over the sound of The Clash.

"Hey. I figured I'd make some food," she says from the stove when I step through the arched doorway.

I move behind her, wrapping my arms around her waist. "Hmm. You cooking for me. I like the sound of that."

As the pot of water in front of her heats, she reaches into a cabinet overhead and pulls down a box of mac and cheese.

"What are you doing?" I question.

"I already told you. Making food. Surely you're familiar with the concept."

I release her and grab the box before she opens it. "Yes, which is why I know we can do better than this. It was fine the day after you moved, but you've been here long enough to go grocery shopping."

"Whatever. You're lucky I was going to feed you at all."

"Getting lucky? I like the sound of that too," I reply as I search her cabinets.

"Not if you keep insulting my cooking skills. What are you looking for?"

"I need to see what you have so I can figure out what we can make."

"You're going to have to clean whatever you think *you're* making. This place doesn't have a dishwasher, and I don't feel like doing a thousand dishes after every meal," she asserts.

"Well, it'll be a lot easier to figure out dinner when we're living together." My brain takes a second to catch up with my mouth, and I freeze, one hand holding the fridge door open. My eyes go wide, and I turn to look at Fiona, who's focused solely on me.

"Uh, I mean… Shit. This isn't how I meant to bring it up. But I've been thinking about it a lot. Last month I went to jail. A month before that, we couldn't even talk to each other. Weeks from now we'll be done with the festival and openly dating. I know it's too soon to move in together, but I'm open to it whenever you feel ready."

Fiona pushes away from the stove, closing the distance between us, and I shut the fridge to face her.

"You've been thinking about living together?" she clarifies. "You've never said anything."

"Like I said, it seemed like it might be too soon. I don't want to come on too strong or scare you away."

She takes the last step, pressing against my hips, her eyes piercing through me. "You think you can scare me away with that, Tre? I committed multiple felonies to get you out of jail, and you think it's too soon to *talk* about what's next?"

"When you put it that way…" I murmur and wrap my arms around her, pulling her body against mine. I slowly run my hands down her back to grab her ass. "We do have some very important questions to answer first."

"Like what we're having for dinner?" she asks wryly.

"More like, whose furniture will we keep? We've compared both beds, but I have no idea if I like your couch."

I lean in and kiss her, my hands still firmly gripping her ass. Her lips part, and when her tongue glides across mine, my dick swells. I pull my hips back slightly to give it a little room, but Fiona shifts forward to close the gap. The friction makes it ache so much I want to rip our clothes off right here, in the middle of the kitchen.

With our lips locked together, I walk backward into the living room. As we stumble our way between rooms, she lifts my shirt off. The contrasting sensations as she runs her palms over my chest and then rakes her nails down my body are overwhelming.

When the back of my knees hit the couch, I slip my hands under her shirt and guide it over her head. Fiona drops her bra at her feet before I spin us around and lay her across the cushions, one leg dangling to the floor.

I trail my lips in a line down her body, starting at her throat. She arches her back when I graze her boobs. Eventually, I reach her waist and unbutton her pants. I lift her with my left hand so I can use my other to slide them over her ass, pulling them off and tossing them behind me. Then I slowly run my hands up both thighs and use my thumbs to rub her lips while I hook my fingers around her underwear and remove them as well.

I settle onto my knees on the floor, massaging one leg from her ankle to her thigh, following my hands with my mouth. Since we've been together more often over the past few weeks, I've been enjoying finding her erogenous zones and discovering everything that gets her off. I'm exploring a few new areas each time, and I love every moan and shiver.

Finally, my thumbs are caressing the soft skin around her opening. I pause my hands, move my face to within an inch, and breathe deeply onto her clit. She gasps as her stomach quivers. "God, will you please just fuck me already?"

"Oh, so you don't like this?" I ask and flick my tongue across her. She moans, and her legs press against me. Given how wet and relaxed she is, she must be as desperate for release as I am. I smile before beginning to stroke her with my tongue. I slide my left hand under her to squeeze her ass while my right hand softly traces circles around her opening.

She's not asking me to stop what I'm doing and fuck her now, I think.

Her moans grow louder until she's squirming so much it's challenging to keep my mouth on her. I release her ass and pin her hips to the cushion. Within another minute, she screams, "Yes! Yes! Oh!" and her hips rock uncontrollably.

When she stills, I slowly sit up, raking my gaze over every inch of her. She opens her eyes with a lopsided grin while I'm wiping her juices off my chin.

I reposition myself with a knee on the couch, straddling her, and I press my mouth to hers. She must be tasting herself on my tongue, but her response is to wrap one hand around my neck, deepening our kiss. After a minute, she strokes me through my pants, and I groan.

Eventually, Fiona pushes my chest until I break off the kiss. "Stand up," she orders, and I comply.

She sits facing me and pulls my pants down, letting them fall at my feet. I sigh in relief when she frees my dick, which is now inches from her face. She reaches up and fondles my balls with one hand while her other squeezes my shaft. I close my eyes, groaning with pleasure, but Fiona is only getting started.

Her tongue circles my head. The soft wetness teasing the sensitive area contrasts with the sensation of her hands. The confusion of sensory input overwhelms any rational thought. All I know is desire.

When I look down, Fiona is staring at my face. The jade color of her eyes is nearly crowded out by her pupils. Making eye contact with her while my dick is on her lips is too much. I need her now.

I grasp her shoulders and push her back onto the cushions again, this time with her head pressing into the arm of the couch. I quickly grab a condom from my pants pocket and roll it over my throbbing cock.

Once I'm straddling her, Fiona reaches up and grips my ribs with both hands, and I slam into her. I hold myself inside her as deeply as possible while she quivers around me.

"More," she moans, and I begin thrusting steadily. She's so wet that I glide easily in and out, her walls rubbing me with a soft, smooth pressure.

"I need you so much," I tell her, my voice sounding breathy and strained. Her hands release my ribs and try to find purchase on the couch behind her head, but she's pressed into the corner and there's almost nothing to use. I move my hands to her chest, grabbing her boobs and pinning her down.

A small cry escapes her when I shift my angle and her eyes close. I continue rhythmically stroking until she eventually says, "I'm getting close, Tre. Harder!"

I need a better position, though, so I pull out. "Get up. Get on your knees," I order, moving off the couch and standing in front of it.

She moves onto her hands and knees. I grab her shoulder and hip, turning her to face the back of the couch. As soon as her arms are resting on the frame, I sink into her with a series of short thrusts, going a little further each time. When I find the right angle, I grab her hips with both hands and use her for leverage to bury my cock into her cunt, deep and hard.

"Oh god, yes!" Fiona screams.

I maintain this rhythm, fully enveloped in her warmth and wetness as she makes small moans. Eventually, she gasps and rocks her hips wildly. Her legs almost buckle beneath her, but I pull her ass up and toward me. Her coming excites me even more than the amazing pressure of her cunt, and tingling builds at the base of my dick.

Now that she's done, I trade power for speed, ramming myself in and out as fast as my hips will move. Fiona's chest and shoulders are shoved into the cushions, and her head is hanging over the back. The tingle turns into a wave flowing down my legs and up my spine. The condom fills around me while my hips buck erratically.

We remain in place, panting. Occasionally, I flex my cock inside her, and she shivers. When I'm recovered enough to walk, I go into the kitchen and throw away the condom.

Fiona's slumped in a seated position when I return, and I collapse beside her. We lean against each other in silence for a while.

"Your couch is pretty good. I can't wait to see what you think of mine," I eventually say with a grin.

"I like your method of answering questions."

"Speaking of questions that need answering, I assume you don't have a waffle iron. How do you feel about pancakes for dinner?"

Chapter 37
People Are Going to Talk of the Town

FIONA

"Dr. Carson! Good morning!" Jean greets excitedly when I walk into the office.

It's too early for anyone to be that *chipper,* I think.

"Hi Jean," I mumble, gulping down more coffee as I walk past. I rode my bike to work this morning and stopped by Betty's on the way —partly for the coffee, but mostly so I could say hi to Tre.

As has been the case so often recently, Connor Smith was parked in a booth toward the back of the diner, tapping away on his laptop. His gaze lingered on me while I was waiting for my coffee, but there's nothing I can do about that. I don't even really know if he suspects me at all, or if it's just nerves making me think he *might*. But I know he doesn't *have* anything on me. And the waters around Tre are so murky that I doubt he has anything usable there either.

Tre and I have been able to spend a lot more time together planning the festival over the past few weeks, but it'll be nice when we're finally able to stop hiding the fact that we're together. I'd be lying if I said I wasn't nervous about what'll happen once we do, but we've got to roll the dice at some point.

Soon, soon, soon, my brain chants, and the thought sends butterflies racing through me.

There are probably half the number of boxes in my office now, and it's distinctly less claustrophobic. I'll have to find something else for Jean to do when she eventually finishes digitizing the files. *Maybe I could send her to get her medical billing certification. She'd probably be good at arguing with the insurance companies…*

"I had a great idea for the festival, and I wanted to run it by you! I know it's a bit last minute, but it's a really great idea!"

The festival. I want to sigh, but I can't. Tre was right insofar as his assertion that he'd get a bunch of people involved went, but he totally undersold the amount of work we'd have to do. It has absolutely been a second job. It's almost done, though. Nine more days.

"It's *really* last minute, Jean," I begin, but she interjects before I can tell her that we've finally got all the installation and booth locations set in stone, and we can't go changing it again. For what feels like the *hundredth* time. *Nine days* before the festival.

"I know! But I was talking to Carol. She's been volunteering at the cat rescue since—"

"Pussycats Galore?" I ask. It's the best business name I've ever heard.

"Yes, she's been volunteering there, and she said that the rescue is nearly full and won't be able to take in more cats."

"Okay," I say, unsure where she's going with this.

"But there will be so many people at the Harvest Festival, Dr. Carson! We could set up a spot where people could meet the cats and adopt them."

I close my eyes. *Damn. It's a great idea.*

"I'm sorry," Jean blurts, and I open my eyes to see worry lining her face.

"No. It's a great idea. I was just…" *Regretting ever agreeing to Tre's idea to plan a fucking festival,* I think. But out loud, I say, "Trying to picture where we could fit it. I'll need to talk to the owners about the setup, but I'll figure out something."

"Oh, that's great! I have to tell Carol! She'll be so relieved!" Jean says, rushing out of the room and nearly bumping into Natalie in the hallway.

Natalie comes to a sudden stop to avoid a collision. Our eyes meet when she glances into the office, and there's a question written on her face, though she doesn't ask it.

Neither of us has mentioned me walking in on her and my dad, but that hasn't made things less awkward. I'm beginning to wonder if I should say something, but I'm her employer, and I don't want to make the situation worse. It's really none of my business if she and my dad are together, but clearly she didn't want me to know about it.

Finally, she says, "We're running low on gloves and surgical masks. Are you okay with me putting in a new order?"

"Yeah, that's fine," I agree.

"LOOKS LIKE IT ALL CAME TOGETHER," EWAN SAYS.

"'Came together' nothing," I grumble as I watch Tre. He's behind the booth for Betty's, talking to the person at the front of the line.

He must feel my eyes on him, because his gaze lands on Ewan and me. He flashes me a quick smile, and then his attention is back on the customers at his booth.

"I thought Tre was going to strangle Jacob at least half a dozen times in the past month."

Ewan shrugs. "They don't like each other."

"Tell me something I *don't* know."

"Tre doesn't like that Jacob thinks he has a chance with you."

"What?" I ask, swiveling my gaze to stare at my twin, whose green eyes look so much like mine.

"Tre doesn't like that Jacob thinks he has a chance with you."

"Yeah, I heard you the first time."

"It's pretty obvious that Jacob still has a thing for you, sis. Well. To anyone who's paying attention, which I guess excludes you," Ewan snarks, and I roll my eyes.

"Tre hasn't said anything about it."

"Well, he wouldn't, would he? You're with him, and he knows you don't give a fuck about Jacob. He just doesn't like that Jacob doesn't know that. It's not a big deal."

"Did he say something to you?"

"No. But I have eyes. Ah. Speak of the devil," Ewan mutters, and I look away from him to find Jacob approaching.

I paste a bland smile on my face. "Hi Jacob."

"Hi Fiona. Hi Ewan," Jacob says before focusing on me. "You were right about this being a good idea."

"Yeah, it seems like people are really enjoying it. It was Tre's idea though."

Jacob's mouth turns down slightly, and his eyes flick toward Tre. "Yes. That's right. Well, still. I know how much work you put into making this successful. It wouldn't have been half as well organized without your efforts."

I simply nod politely as Jacob continues talking, and Ewan, standing beside me, says nothing. Eventually, Jacob spots someone important and rushes off to speak with them.

I breathe a sigh of relief as I resume my conversation with Ewan. "He asked me to move in with him."

"Jacob?" Ewan asks, clearly confused.

"What? No. Tre."

"Oh. When?"

"A couple of weeks ago."

"You said yes?"

I nod, looking at Tre in the distance and remembering the discussion. The discussion that began with me standing in my kitchen holding a box of macaroni and cheese, and ended a few hours later on my kitchen floor with pancakes forgotten on a plate next to the stove.

Me, pouring maple syrup onto Tre's dick and licking it off slowly. So slowly. Until he was so hard I could feel the blood pounding in his cock beneath my tongue.

Him, gently wrapping his hands in my hair. The whimpering sounds of desperation he made that set my body on fire when I finally wrapped my lips all the way around him.

The taste of semen flooding my mouth as cum hit the back of my throat and I swallowed it down.

His tongue sliding across mine seconds later.

Him, whispering, 'I love you, Fiona. Please move in with me.'

"When's that happening?" Ewan asks, and I jerk my eyes away from Tre, my body having gone hot.

"Um. May. We need enough time to pass to make things at least somewhat believable."

"Cool. You can thank me anytime, you know," Ewan comments, dancing out of the way before my elbow can make contact with his ribs.

"I'M SURPRISED YOU'RE STILL IN TOWN," I SAY AS I SIDLE UP next to Special Agent Connor Smith.

He startles and his head jerks toward me. He tries to cover the motion with a shrug. "Job's not done yet," he supplies before returning his focus to my dad, who's standing in the middle of the cat adoption area. Connor's been watching him from a distance for at least a few minutes now.

"Any leads?"

His lips twitch upward. "You're smart enough to know I can't answer that question."

"Had to try," I say lightly.

"Good turnout for the festival."

"Yeah." I pause a beat and then ask, "Is it normal for you to stick around an investigation for so long? It doesn't really seem like there's much happening."

"No."

I wait a moment, but he doesn't elaborate, and we stand in silence, both obviously watching my dad.

"The cat adoption area," he says after several minutes have passed. "Was that your idea?"

"No," I reply, hoping I don't look as unsettled as I feel. "Someone pitched it to me." He opens his mouth, but I cut him off before he can ask the next logical question. "Sorry. I've gotta run. The raffle's about to start."

Two hours later, I'm back in front of the cat adoption area, and neither my dad nor Special Agent Connor Smith are anywhere to be seen. Half of the wire enclosures now have *'I've been adopted!'* signs hanging from them, and Jean is helping a couple with a little girl fill out forms to adopt a long-haired grey cat.

"Hey," a voice whispers in my ear, and I jump, my reaction mirroring Connor's earlier. "Sorry," Tre says. "I didn't mean to scare you. I thought you saw me."

"Hi. No. Sorry, I was distracted."

"By the cats?"

"Yes." I slip my hand into his, having already decided not to let my worries about the ATF disrupt what remains of our plan. His eyes go wide, and I smirk, enjoying having surprised him. "Did you forget we weren't hiding anymore?"

"No. But I didn't want to... assume."

My smirk changes to a grin as I turn to face him. "You know, I was watching you earlier."

"I know. I saw."

"Do you know what I was thinking about?"

"No. What?"

"Maple syrup," I say conversationally, and the sharp inhale as his lips part is audible. I drop my voice. "And the way you moaned when I ran my tongue around the head of your dick. The way you begged me for more when I had just the first inch of you in my mouth."

"Fiona," he murmurs, and there's a low warning note in his voice.

"I was remembering the way your hips jerked against my face, and the taste as you—"

His lips crash into mine as he tugs me into him, one hand on the small of my back and the other in my hair. I wrap my hands around him and press my body into his. He's already hard, and I slip my tongue into his mouth, enjoying how easy it is to make him all hot and bothered.

I pull away after another handful of seconds has passed, not wanting to make *too* big a spectacle.

"What are you doing?" Tre asks, staring into my eyes. "People are going to talk."

"People were going to talk anyway, Tre." I swear I can feel them watching us already. "We may as well give them something worth talking about."

"In that case…" he says, and then his lips are back on mine.

This kiss lasts longer, and blood is pounding in my head by the time he breaks it off.

"Later," he promises softly.

"Later," I agree. "What would you think about getting a cat?" I ask, moving to step away.

Tre's hands stop me, and he says, "Yes, we can adopt one when you move in, but give me a sec." He closes his eyes, and a dark blush stains his cheeks.

We've been standing there for a minute with Tre using me for cover when I whisper, "Incoming."

A look of panic washes across his face as he spots Nick Trowbridge walking toward us. Tre twists, stepping slightly behind me.

"Hi Nick, enjoying the festival?" I ask as I take half a step forward, hoping to distract him and buy Tre a bit of time. Nick and I met during one of the many planning meetings for the festival when he was helping Tre get a permit for something.

"Hi Fiona! Yeah, it's been great. I was over at the stage checking out the pumpkins when I spotted you and Tre."

Heat is creeping up my cheeks now, but Nick continues before I can say anything. "I wanted to congratulate you both on pulling this together so quickly. And Tre, I thought you might be interested to hear the latest about Henley and Montank."

"That's right, you had a hearing yesterday?" Tre asks, finally stepping forward.

"Yeah, Henley and Montank were appealing the injunction. Their appeal was denied, so they're going to be forced to perform new assessments. It doesn't mean the construction won't start back up, but the next hearing won't be until mid-January. All their work will be paused until then at the earliest."

"What are the chances that the courts will actually stop them from moving forward on their projects long-term?" I ask.

"Mixed," Nick says. "Truthfully, we'll probably have better luck with their insurers refusing to continue underwriting them, but thanks to what's happened over the past several months, that's a very real possibility. Plus, reporters are taking a much closer look at Henley and Montank's financials, and who knows what they'll find. Anyway, I just wanted to update you on where things stand at the moment."

"Sure thing. Thanks, Nick," Tre says, and then Nick is walking away.

"What do you think?" I ask as Tre's hand slips back into mine.

Tre shrugs. "I don't know. I guess we wait and see. In the meantime, I've got you, and that's good enough for me."

Afterword

Hello, dear reader! Yes, you. You made it to the end, and you're reading the afterword. Only the coolest, bestest people do that. This is where I'm going to tell you a couple of interesting things. Maybe you already know them. (Are you stalking me?) But maybe you don't. (Why aren't you stalking me?)

First, this book was cowritten. (You got that from the cover, right? You're so smart.) I (Sam Evans) wrote the chapters that are from Fiona's point of view (POV), and my real-life romantic partner (Travis Walter) wrote the chapters that are from Tre's POV. The book was then jointly edited to provide a coherent reading experience. We did it this way because I thought it would be fun to read a dual-POV romance where the male main character (MMC) chapters were written by a guy. Hopefully you liked it!

Second, this book was inspired by real-life events. Specifically, the acts of sabotage on the Sea to Sky Gondola. It was first sabotaged in 2019, and then again in 2020, despite increased security. Both times, the gondola's cables were cut after operations had ceased for the day, sending its cars crashing to the ground and causing millions of dollars in damage. At the time of this book's publication, no perpetrator has been arrested, and no suspects have been publicly named. (Please do note that I was not involved in either act of sabotage, and I have no idea who was. Tre and Fiona are fictional characters, after all.)

I just wanted to add that bit of detail because I don't know about you all, but I have a torrid love affair with unsolved mysteries (I hold Robert Stack responsible), and this case fascinates me.

Also, I know some of you are going to be like, "Be so for real, Sam.

That couldn't happen! They'd have had so much more security. Tre and Fiona never would've gotten away with it!" And I'm here to tell you that it *did* happen. And they did have more security. And it didn't matter. Because they did it again anyway. And they freaking got away with it! Twice!

Life is stranger than fiction, my friends.

Alright, moving on. Can you do me a favor? A big one? Can you pull out your phone and text at least one friend (or enemy, if you hated the book) and tell them to read it? That would be awesome. If you've done that, can you do me one more teensy-weensy favor? Can you please, please, please go to goodreads, Amazon, StoryGraph, or whatever your review-place-of-choice is and leave a review? Love it or loathe it. Reviews are the lifeblood of indie authors.

If you're interested in my goings-on, and for more details about what's in the works, make sure you're subscribed to my newsletter (sign up at www.sam-evans.me)! Plus, you get a free prequel chapter for one of my other books when you do—and other freebies as they become available. But wait! There's more! Every newsletter includes a dog tax. All the coolest people are subscribed. You should be too! (I'd plug Travis's stuff, but he doesn't really have any because he's, like, too cool for social media, or something. Probably I won't even be able to get him to write anything in the back of the book for you. Ho. Hum.)

Bye!

P.S. Did you catch that every chapter title is a *Jeopardy!*-style before-and-after? Chapter titles are the best! All books should have titled chapters.

Acknowledgments

Thank you to Krys M for doing your best to talk me off ledges. It's an impossible job, but I appreciate that you try.

Thank you to M Kevin H for basically adopting me and making sure I'm not selling myself short, and for generally being excited about this project.

Thank you to Mark P for the idea. It changed so much about the book. All for the better.

Thank you to Lissa L for calling me on my bullshit. I never enjoy it, but I do appreciate it.

Thank you to Laura CW for always helping to make my books stronger overall.

Thank you to Travis for agreeing to go along with the idea! I had fun!

And last but not least, thanks to everyone who reads this book! I love you so much!

- Sam

Thank you to Sam for suggesting this wild idea and rolling with every new idea along the way. Also thanks for being so much better at editing than I could ever be.

Thank you to Laura CW for the repeated reviews. Additional

thanks for having such a vastly different editing approach because we could never.

Thank you to Mark P for the reality check. The changes you drove not only made things more realistic but also unintentionally solved a structural issue we were worried about. It's a double whammy.

Thank you to Lissa L for the stylistic feedback. It made things much cleaner.

Thank you to all the friends on social media who offered encouragement and enthusiasm, even when they had no idea what this was about.

Thank you to everyone who cares enough to fight for what's important. If what you're doing is approved by the powers-that-be, you're not changing anything.

- Travis

About the Author
Sam Evans

Sam Evans has lived all over the US but currently resides in the upper midwest. She's a software engineer by day, but letting her imagination run wild is her full-time occupation. She lives with her partner (Travis Walter), a high-strung border collie, and an insane kelpie. She routinely drinks too much coffee and gets too little sleep.

instagram.com/sam_evans_writer
threads.com/@sam_evans_writer
tiktok.com/@sam.evans.writer
bsky.app/profile/sam-evans-writer.bsky.social
amazon.com/author/sam-evans

About the Author
Travis Walter

Travis Walter is a capital-I Introvert. He didn't even want to share enough to fill out this section. What's he like? Where does he live? Your guess is as good as any. Unless you follow him on social media, where you'll find tantalizing tidbits.

instagram.com/travis_walter_writer
threads.com/@travis_walter_writer